Carla Cassidy is a *New York Times* bestselling author who has written more than 125 novels for Mills & Boon. She is listed on the Romance Writers of America Honour Roll and has won numerous awards. Carla believes the only thing better than curling up with a good book to read is sitting down at the computer with a good story to write.

Jennifer Lewis has always been drawn to fairy tales, and stories of passion and enchantment. Writing allows her to bring the characters crowding her imagination to life. She lives in sunny South Florida and enjoys the lush tropical environment and spending time on the beach all year long. Please visit her website at http://www.jenlewis.com

Candace Shaw writes romance novels because she believes that happily-ever-after isn't found only in fairy tales. When she's not writing or researching information for a book, you can find Candace in her gardens, shopping, reading or learning how to cook a new dish. She lives in Atlanta, Georgia with her loving husband and is currently working on her next fun, flirty and sexy romance. You can contact Candace on her website at www.CandaceShaw.net

After Hours

After Hours: Power and Passion

CARLA CASSIDY

JENNIFER LEWIS

CANDACE SHAW

MILLS & BOON

First Published in Great Britain 2021
By Mills & Boon, an imprint of HarperCollins*Publishers* Ltd
1 London Bridge Street, London, SE1 9GF

www.harpercollins.co.uk

HarperCollins*Publishers*
1st Floor, Watermarque Building,
Ringsend Road, Dublin 4, Ireland

AFTER HOURS: POWER AND PASSION © 2021
Harlequin Books S.A.

Her Secret, His Duty © 2014 Harlequin Books S.A.
Affairs of State © 2013 Harlequin Books S.A.
Her Perfect Candidate © 2014 Carmen S. Jones

Special thanks and acknowledgement to Carla Cassidy for her contribution to *The Adair Legacy* series and Jennifer Lewis for her contribution to the *Daughters of Power: The Capital* series.

ISBN: 978-0-263-29938-0

MIX
Paper from
responsible sources
FSC™ C007454

Printed and bound in Spain
by CPI, Barcelona

HER SECRET, HIS DUTY

CARLA CASSIDY

Chapter 1

"Impossible." The single word escaped Debra Prentice's lips in disbelieving horror as she stared at the three separate pregnancy tests lined up like little soldiers on her bathroom vanity.

Not one, not two, but three tests and each showing a positive sign. Undeniable results that her brain tried to absorb.

Pregnant. There was no question now that she was pregnant. She'd wondered about it when she was late with her period, but had written it off as stress. She'd been late in the past.

Pregnant. How was it possible? Even as the question formed in her mind, memories of a single night six weeks ago gave her the answer.

An unexpected encounter, too many drinks and a mad dash to a nearby hotel room where she'd found complete abandon with a man she had no business being with at all.

Her cheeks burned as she remembered the awkward morning after. Gazes not meeting as they both hurriedly dressed and then the humiliating ride in a cab from the hotel to her front door. And now this, the icing on a cake that should have never been baked in the first place. Pregnant.

A glance at the small clock in the bathroom forced a gasp from her. If she didn't hurry she'd be late to work, and in all the years that Debra had worked as personal secretary and assistant to Kate Adair Winston, she had never been late to work.

She got up and tossed the tests into the trash, then gave herself a quick glance in the bathroom mirror. The slim black pencil skirt she wore didn't display a hint of her current condition but the red tailored button-up blouse only emphasized the paleness of her face, a paleness that the results of the tests had surely created.

Her light brown hair was already attempting to escape the twisted bun she'd trapped it in earlier, but she didn't have time to fix it now.

She left the bathroom, deciding that she couldn't, she wouldn't think about her pregnancy right now. She had a little time to figure things out, but right now she had to get her brain in work mode.

She pulled on a black winter coat and grabbed her purse, then left her two-story townhouse and headed for her car parked at the curb. There was parking behind the townhouse, but she rarely used it, preferring the convenience of curbside parking instead.

The January air was bracing, hovering right around

the freezing mark. Thankfully the sky was bright blue and she didn't have to worry about snow or sleet.

The townhouse was located just off Glenwood Avenue in the uptown district of Raleigh, North Carolina. It was Debra's pride and joy, bought two years ago after years of renting. She loved the area, loved the fact that she could paint walls and hang pictures without getting a landlord's approval. It was cozy and filled with all the colors and textiles she loved.

Once inside the car she checked the clock. It was just after seven, but she still had to maneuver morning traffic to get to North Raleigh where the Winston Estate was located.

Every morning in the capital city of North Carolina the morning rush traffic was bad, but on this Wednesday morning it seemed particularly heavy.

Or, maybe it was the racing of her thoughts that made the ride feel longer and more difficult than usual. Even though it was unplanned and unexpected there was no doubt in her mind that she would keep the baby. For her, that decision was a no-brainer.

She would just need to keep the father's identity to herself for the rest of her life. She would let the people close to her assume that the baby was Barry's, the snake-in-the-grass boyfriend who had broken up with her on the night she'd been in that restaurant bar, the same night she'd done something completely out of character.

But, there was no question in her mind who the father was because she hadn't been pregnant when she and Barry had broken up and she was pregnant now. There had only been that single night of utter madness to account for her current condition.

She steered her thoughts away from the pregnancy as she approached her workplace. The impressive Winston Estate was located on two acres of lush, meticulously manicured grounds.

Built in 1975, the six-bedroom, nine-bath white-and-red brick house also boasted a beautiful swimming pool, a backyard area around the pool big enough for entertaining and a small guest house where Kate's security, a Secret Service detail, worked from.

The front entrance boasted a large black iron gate that was opened only when security and Kate allowed. The entire estate was fenced in except for a side entrance through which staff and service vehicles came and went.

Debra turned into the access entrance and waved to Jeff Benton, part of the security team that kept Kate and her family safe when the former vice president was in the house.

Debra pulled into a parking spot specifically for staff and hurriedly got out of the car. She entered the house through a side door that led into a large, empty mudroom and then into the huge kitchen where at the moment fresh coffee and cinnamon were the predominant scents.

None of the help was in the large, airy room that had the latest cooking equipment, but Sam Winston, Kate's thirty-three-year-old middle son, sat at a small table next to a window with a cup of coffee before him.

"Good morning, Sam," she said tentatively. Since Sam's return from overseas where he'd served in Army Special Forces, he'd been distant, at times downright unpleasant, and she never knew exactly what to expect from him when they happened to run into each other.

He looked up from his coffee, his blue eyes dark and unreadable. "Morning," he replied and then shifted his gaze back into the depths of his cup, obviously not encouraging any further conversation.

Debra passed through the kitchen and entered the main foyer. As always, her breath was half stolen from her by the beauty of the black-and-white marble floors and the exquisite winding wooden staircase that led up to the second level.

Beyond the foyer were Kate's official office and a doorway right next to it that led to Debra's much smaller office. She knew that Kate didn't usually go into her office to begin her day until sometime after eight, but that didn't mean Debra didn't have things to do before Kate made her official appearance.

Debra's office was small but efficient with a desk that held a computer, a multifunctional printer and memo pads. A wooden five-drawer file cabinet sat nearby on the right wall. The other wall was a white dry-erase area that took up the left side of the room, where she kept track of Kate's ever-busy, ever-changing social calendar with dry-erase markers in a variety of colors.

She closed the door, took off her coat and hung it in the tiny closet that stored extra paper and printer supplies and then sat at the desk and powered up her computer.

There was only one personal item in the whole room. It was a framed picture that hung on the wall, a photo of Debra with a Parisian street vendor who sold hot croissants and coffee from a colorful cart just down the block from the U.S. Embassy in Paris.

Debra had lived in Paris for the two years that Kate had served as U.S. ambassador to France. It had been an amazing experience for Debra. She'd learned some of the language, wandered the streets on her time off and breathed in the local ambiance.

When Kate's time in that position had ended and it was time to return to the states, Debra hadn't wanted the usual souvenirs of a picture or a miniature statue of the famous Eiffel Tower.

She'd wanted a photo of herself and Pierre, the charming Frenchman who had begun her mornings with a bright smile, a hot croissant and a cup of steaming café au lait. A fellow staffer had taken the photo and Debra had brought it into a local craft store to have it enlarged and framed.

The time in France had been wonderful, but that was then and this was now. Pregnant. She was pregnant. She couldn't quite wrap her mind around it yet, but she knew one thing for sure, once the baby was born her life would be irrevocably changed.

She shoved the thought away and instead focused on her morning work. It took twenty minutes to go through her emails, deleting spam that had managed to get through the filter, marking messages to forward to Kate and answering those that didn't require her boss's attention.

Once the email was finished, she moved to the file folder on her desk that held a stack of invitations for Kate. As a former U.S. ambassador and vice president, Kate was invited to hundreds of events each week.

As Debra looked at each one, she made a list of who, what and where for each event that required a response in the next week or so. The social calendar Debra kept on the wall was an ever-morphing, color-coded animal that required constant attention.

There were rumors that Kate was being groomed to run for president in the next election and she was already being courted by special-interest groups and powerful party movers and shakers.

So far she hadn't mentioned her plans to anyone, but Debra suspected the idea of becoming the first female president of the United States was definitely appealing. Kate had a reputation as a loving mother, a family-oriented person, but Debra knew she was also a woman of great convictions about how the country should move forward in the coming years.

It was just after eight when a familiar soft knock sounded on Debra's door. She grabbed her memo pad and left her desk. It was their routine; Kate knocked to let Debra know she was now in her office and it was time for a morning update.

At fifty-eight years old, Kathleen Adair Winston was an attractive woman with short, stylish light brown hair and blue eyes that radiated honesty, kindness and intelligence. Debra had worked for her long enough to know that she also possessed a will of steel, a slight streak of stubbornness and a love of her family that was enviable.

This morning she was dressed in a pair of tailored navy slacks and a pale blue blouse that emphasized the bright hue of her eyes. Her jewelry was tasteful, a wedding ring despite the fact that she was a widow and a silver necklace with matching earrings.

"Good morning, Debra." Her smile was warm, and adoration for the woman who had been her boss since she'd been a college graduate swelled up inside Debra.

"Good morning to you, Kate," she replied and took the chair opposite the large ornate desk where Kate sat. "Did you sleep well?"

"I always sleep well," Kate replied. "It seems the days are too long and the nights are far too short for my taste."

Debra nodded and smiled and then got down to business. "I have several pressing things we need to discuss this morning," she said.

It took nearly forty-five minutes for Debra to update Kate and get confirmation or regrets on the invitations that required answers.

When they had finished that particular task, Kate leaned back in her chair and sipped the coffee she must have carried with her into the office. "You look tired," she said. "Did you not sleep well last night?"

Debra stared at her in surprise. Did it already show somehow on her face? Did newly discovered pregnancy make a woman look tired the day she realized she was pregnant?

"Nothing to worry about," Debra said, pleased that her voice sounded normal. "I did do a lot of tossing and turning last night. I think it was indigestion, but I'm sure I'll sleep fine tonight."

"Anything in particular on your mind?"

Debra smiled with a forced brightness. "Yes, I'm wondering along with the rest of the world if my boss intends to make a run for the presidency."

Deflect, she thought. She had always been good about making the conversation about other people rather than about herself.

"Your boss still hasn't made up her mind," Kate replied ruefully. She turned in her chair and stared at the wall that held an array of family photos. Most of them were of Kate with her three handsome sons.

"Although I know I need to come to a decision in

the next couple of weeks. It's a long, arduous process to begin a campaign, but the men who have already thrown their hats in the ring are not what the country needs right now. I do believe I'd do a better job than any of them, but I also realize the price I'd be asking my family to pay if I decide to become an official candidate," she said as she turned back to look at Debra.

"You'll make the right decision," Debra said confidently. "You always do. Either way, you'll do what's best for both your family and the country."

Kate flashed her the bright smile that had been her trademark both when she'd served her four years as vice president and as a beloved ambassador to France. "You're the special secret in my pocket, Debra. There are days that your efficiency and loyalty are responsible for my very sanity. Thank goodness you possess the organizational skills that keep me on track."

"I have a feeling you'd be just fine without me, but I love what I do, and now I'd better get back to my office and take care of the RSVPs on these invitations." Debra stood. "You'll let me know if there's anything else I can do for you. You have nothing on your calendar for the day so hopefully you can give yourself a break and just relax a bit."

"Maybe." Kate stood and carried her coffee to the window that looked out on a lovely garden.

Debra left the room aware that Kate didn't know how to relax—until she made up her mind about the next presidential election, she would worry and stew, weigh pros and cons, until she made a final decision about what her future would hold.

Debra didn't even want to think about her own future. She knew that the first thing she needed to do was see a doctor. She'd try to schedule an appointment with her gynecologist for the weekend to confirm what she already knew.

In the meantime, day by day—that's how she would have to take things right now. She'd scarcely had time to process the reality of her condition.

Eventually her pregnancy would show and she'd have some explaining to do, but until that day came she had to focus on her work.

She remained at her desk until just after eleven when Kate used the intercom to call her back into her office. Debra grabbed her notepad and reentered Kate's office, only to stop short at the sight of the ridiculously handsome man seated in the chair she had vacated earlier.

Trey Winston was not only incredibly handsome with his rich dark brown hair and striking blue eyes, he was also the CEO of Adair Enterprises, the family business, a rich and powerful man who was well liked by his employees and friends. He was also the father of the baby Debra carried.

"Here we are," Kate said as Debra entered the room. She gestured her assistant to the chair next to Trey's. Trey offered Debra a faint, rather uncomfortable smile.

Uncomfortable. That's the way things had been for him whenever he saw Debra after the crazy one night they'd spent together—a night that should never have happened.

He'd been at the popular bar/restaurant celebrating the close of a big business deal and she'd been there commiserating a breakup with her boyfriend. The two of them had somehow hooked up, shared too many drinks and then had continued to make the mistake of heading to a nearby hotel and having hot, passionate sex.

He hadn't been too drunk to know what he was doing and neither had she, but he should never have allowed it to happen at all.

He'd spent the past six weeks putting it out of his mind, trying to pretend that it had never happened. Unfortunately, trying to forget had been difficult.

His mother would kill him if she found out. Kate would give him a motherly smackdown to end all smackdowns if she believed he had taken advantage of her assistant, a young woman he knew his mother loved and trusted.

"Trey has just informed me that I'm not the only political beast in the family," Kate said once Debra was seated next to Trey. "He's thinking about running for the Senate."

Debra looked at him in surprise and then quickly averted her gaze back to Kate. "I'm sure he'd make a fine senator."

"You know that and I know that, but what we need to do is see how much support he would be able to get behind him," Kate replied.

Trey could see the wheels turning in his mother's head. Of all the people in his life, Trey trusted his mother more than anyone. He'd been flirting with the idea of entering politics for some time and finally felt the time was right now.

"What do you have in mind?" Debra asked.

Her voice was sweet and soft, but Trey had memories of husky moans and sighs of pleasure. He also couldn't help but notice and remember the fresh, clean scent of her, so unlike the cloying perfumes most of the women in his social circle wore.

"A fund-raiser dinner party." Kate's words snapped Trey back to the matter at hand. "And we'd need to get it scheduled and on the calendar in the next two weeks."

"Two weeks?" Debra sounded horrified as she stared at Kate. "But that's impossible."

"Nonsense. Nothing is impossible," Kate replied confidently, "especially if you're in charge. You've set up these kinds of things a thousand times for me in the past, Debra."

"But not in less than a month," she protested.

Trey watched the interplay between Debra and his mother, knowing no matter how the conversation went the dinner would get done in two weeks' time. Kate usually got her way and Debra was one of the most efficient women Trey had ever known.

"I'll have Haley step in and do most of the work you normally do for me," Kate said, mentioning one of her senior interns. "That will free you up to work closely with Trey to get this done. I recommend you both go into the sitting room right now and figure out a specific date and a venue. Let's get this thing rolling."

Trey could tell that this was probably the last thing on earth that Debra wanted to do. He could see her reluctance as she slowly stood from her chair, in the small crease that darted across her forehead.

He wasn't exactly thrilled by the idea of working closely with his one-night stand, either. But, he also knew that if anyone could pull this event off on time and with flair, it was Debra Prentice.

They could work together, he told himself as he followed her slender frame into the informal sitting area

at the back of the house. All they had to do was continue doing what they had been doing for the past six
weeks: pretend that crazy night they had shared hadn't
happened.

"I didn't realize she was going to pull you into this,"
he said as she sat in one of the plush, comfortable beige
chairs and he sank down on the sofa opposite her.

The family sitting room was large, with floor to ceiling windows on one side and comfortable, yet attractive
furnishings. A bar was located at the back of the room
and doors led out to the patio and pool area.

It was in this room that the family had often come
together to discuss problems or simply to enjoy each
other's company and catch up on busy lives.

"My job is to do whatever Kate needs done and
since this is important to you, it's important to her."
She stared down at her notepad. "The first thing we
need to do is find a venue. With less than a month lead
time that might be a problem. Do you have any place
specific in mind?" Her vivid green eyes finally made
contact with him.

"I was thinking maybe the Raleigh Regent or the
Capital Hotel," he suggested. "Both places are popular
for such events."

"That's the problem." That tiny crease deepened
again across her forehead. "I'm fairly sure that the Capital Hotel ballroom will be impossible to get at this late
date. I'll check with the Regent and see what's available.
Last I heard the ballroom was undergoing some renovations and I'm not certain if they are complete or not.
I'm still not sure I'm going to be able to make this happen so soon. I'm assuming you want a Saturday night?"

"Or a Friday night would be fine," he replied. He

watched as she made several notes on the pad. Debra Prentice wasn't a knockout kind of woman, but she also didn't play up her pretty features. She wore little makeup and her hair always looked as if it had been tortured into a position at the back of her head that it couldn't possibly hold.

Still, he knew that her light brown hair was incredibly silky and that she had a cute, perfectly proportioned figure that had fit perfectly in his arms. He knew how her eyes sparkled while in the throes of passion and exactly how her lips tasted.

"Trey?" Her eyes held a touch of impatience, making him realize she must have tried to get his attention while he'd been lost in thought.

"Sorry. What was the question?"

"How many people are you expecting to invite?"

"Two hundred or maybe two hundred and fifty," he replied.

"Pick a number," she said with a light edge to her voice. "I need a specific number to tell the event planner when we settle where this is going take place."

"Two hundred and fifty," he said firmly.

She nodded. "I'll need the guest list from you as soon as possible. Invitations will have to go out in the next couple of days or so. Thank goodness it's January and there isn't much else going on around town." She wrote a couple more notes on her pad and then met his gaze again. "I think that's all I need from you to get started. By the end of the day I'll have a list of dates and places for you to consider."

She stood as if dismissing him, her body instantly poised to run back to her little office.

"Then tomorrow let's make arrangements to see

some of the venues together," he said as he also stood. "And I'll want to be with you when you speak to the event planner. We'll need to pick the menu and make decisions on a number of other things."

It was obvious he'd surprised her. She'd probably just assumed everything would be left up to her. But Trey freely admitted that he was something of a control freak. He couldn't run Adair Enterprises and be as successful as he'd been without being detail oriented and on top of every element in his life.

"I just assumed..." Her voice trailed off.

"This is important to me, Debra. Assume that I'll be at your side every step of the way until this dinner party is over."

Her eyes widened slightly and then she gave him a curt, professional nod. "Then I'll call you later this evening and we'll make arrangements for tomorrow."

She left the sitting room and Trey sank back into the chair, his thoughts a riot inside his head. He'd taken over the running of the family business when his grandfather had died. Walt Winston had mentored Trey and instilled in him the need to be the best that he could be.

It was Walt who'd wanted to see Trey in politics. The old man had even made a list of women he thought would be an asset in his quest for public office. At thirty-five years old, Trey knew it was time for him to marry. He also knew he'd make a more attractive candidate if he had a wife by his side.

With that thought in mind he'd dated dozens of women over the past year and finally eight months ago he'd begun to see Cecily McKenna exclusively.

Although he wasn't madly in love with Cecily, he knew she'd make the perfect wife for him. She was a thirty-three-year-old heiress. Articulate, charming and beautiful, Cecily also possessed a fierce ambition not just for herself, but for him, as well.

He knew there were rumors swirling of an imminent engagement between him and Cecily, rumors he suspected Cecily had started herself. He smiled inwardly. He wouldn't put it past her.

He looked up as Sam came into the room. "So, word has it that you're joining the ranks of the sex-scandal-ridden, fake and crooked politicians of the world." Sam threw himself into the chair that Debra had vacated.

It was obvious his brother was in one of his foul moods. "Actually, I'm hoping to do something good for the people of North Carolina."

"That's my big brother, the overachieving perfect son."

Trey drew a steadying breath. He knew the man seated before him with the scowl on his handsome face wasn't the brother, wasn't the man who had left here to serve his country.

"Sam, why don't you talk to me?" he asked softly. Sam had spent three months imprisoned overseas and months in a hospital recovering from the severe torture he'd endured while a prisoner. He had since been deemed unfit to return to duty and had been mad at the world ever since.

"I don't need to talk to anyone," Sam growled and got up from the chair. "I'm fine just the way I am."

Trey watched helplessly, troubled for his brother as Sam left the room. Sam was a powder keg, but he refused to speak about his time in prison or what had been done to him. The scars he carried were deep and dark and Trey wished he'd share some of the horror with somebody…anybody who could help him heal.

Unfortunately, Sam wouldn't be fixed until Sam wanted to be fixed and at the moment he appeared to be perfectly satisfied being angry.

Trey checked his watch and stood. It was time for him to get back to his own office. Now that he'd pretty much made up his mind to run for Senator, he didn't want to just run, he wanted to win.

He also needed to call Cecily. He hadn't even told her yet that he'd made up his mind to begin the process of gaining support and throwing his hat in the ring. She would be beyond thrilled. She'd been telling him for months that he was what the state needed, that he could do great things.

As he left the house he found himself wondering what Debra thought of his decision to run. Did she believe he was capable of doing great things?

Who cares what she thinks? he asked himself. All he needed from her was her skills at pulling together an event that would provide him a solid foundation on which to begin to build his campaign.

Chapter 2

Debra had suffered a crush on Trey Winston from the very first time she'd met him years ago. She'd always known he was out of her league, but her crush had never really diminished over the years.

She couldn't help the fact that her heart always leapt a bit at the sight of him, that she often grew tongue-tied and clumsy in his presence. Even sharing the single night that they'd had together hadn't changed her attraction to him; instead it had only deepened her feelings for Trey.

But, it didn't matter what she felt about him because she knew that she was the last woman on earth he would ever want to have a public relationship with. He had his future neatly planned out with Cecily McKenna by his side.

As she drove to the Regent Hotel to meet both him

and the hotel manager to discuss the event, she couldn't halt the tingling nerves that fluttered through her veins at the thought of working with him so closely.

She knew he'd probably marry Cecily, a gorgeous heiress who had the social savvy and political chops to be an asset to him.

Debra also knew that she would be a definite liability to Trey. She'd been born out of wedlock. Her father, who had been a married CEO of a Fortune 500 company at the time, had never acknowledged her existence personally. In fact, Debra had been raised by her mother to never mention her father's name, to never expect anything but a monthly support check in the mail from him.

When her mother died right after Debra's graduation from college, she had met with her father for the first and the last time. She had requested one thing from him—she wanted him to use his influence to get her a job in the political arena, specifically with Kathleen Adair Winston. As one of Kate's top contributors to her political campaign when she'd run for vice president, he had been instrumental in her attaining her position with Kate.

That's the only thing Debra had ever asked from the man who had never been anything but a name on a check, but he hadn't even managed to follow through on that. In recent years, there had been whispers of scandals within his company and talk of her father having some shady dealings.

Debra could crush on Trey all she wanted, but she knew she would only be an embarrassing one-night stand and right now a valuable tool to use to achieve his dreams. She would work her butt off to help him in his bid for a seat in the Senate. She wanted him to have his dream and she'd also do the best she could because Kate had asked her to.

She parked in front of the prestigious thirty-story hotel and looked at her watch. She was twenty minutes early for their ten-o'clock appointment so she remained in the car with the engine running and warm air blowing from the heater vents.

She'd been surprised when she'd called the hotel and discovered that the ballroom was available on a Friday night two weeks from now. Two weeks. Jeez, Kate must think she was some kind of magician.

But there had to be some magic at work for the ballroom not to already be booked, Debra thought.

Her hand fell to her stomach, caressing the place where she knew eventually there would be a baby bump, a bump that could potentially destroy Trey's future plans.

Politics thrived on scandals and any of Trey's adversaries would turn a simple night between two consenting adults into something ugly to use against him. Everyone knew he'd been seeing Cecily so that one-night stand would be a testimony to a lack of morals on both their parts. He would be painted with the same brush that had darkened his father's Senate term.

Debra knew that neither of them lacked a moral compass. The night had simply gotten away from them, both of them making mistakes in judgment.

He would never know about the baby, although it broke her heart that she felt like she was somehow repeating a history she'd never wanted for any child of her own.

She loved the baby, despite the circumstances of the conception. She would be the best mother she could and maybe eventually she'd meet a man who wanted her and her child enough to form a family unit.

She checked her watch once again and then cut the car engine. She grabbed her purse with her electronic notepad inside and then got out of the car. She'd power dressed today in a stylish dark brown skirt and suit jacket with a beige blouse. Brown pumps adorned her feet and tiny gold hoop earrings were her only jewelry.

Drawing in several deep breaths as she walked to the hotel entrance, she shoved all thoughts from her mind except what needed to be here to do her job well.

She still couldn't believe how lucky they had been that the Regent's ballroom was available on a Friday night two weeks from now. Two weeks was the mere blink of an eye in planning the kind of event they intended to have.

Whenever possible, Debra used the hotel's event planner, but the Regent had a new woman working in that position, somebody Debra had never worked with before. It wouldn't take long for Debra to discern if the woman was adequately prepared to do the job they needed and if she wasn't then Debra would bring in an event planner of her own.

Debra knew she had a reputation as being sweet and accommodating, but she could be a vicious shark when it was necessary to get what was best for the Winston family.

She went to the reservation desk and asked for Donald Rasworth, the hotel manager. She smelled Trey before she saw him, the expensive scent of a slightly spicy cologne that had clung intimately to her skin the morning after their wild, impetuous encounter.

She turned and nearly bumped into him. "Oh. You're here," she said.

He smiled. "Aren't I supposed to be here?"

"Yes, but I just didn't know that you were here... That you'd actually arrived..."

Thankfully she was rescued from her inane ramble by a tall slender man who approached them with a hand extended and a wide smile of welcome on his face.

"Mr. Winston," he said as he grabbed Trey's hand in a shake. "It's a pleasure to meet you, sir. We're hoping here at the Raleigh Regent that we can meet all your needs for whatever event you want to plan."

Trey turned to Debra and introduced her. "This is the person you need to please," Trey said. "She's our special weapon when it comes to planning these things."

"I understand you have a new event planner. Will she be joining us?" Debra asked.

"Stacy Boone and yes, she should be joining us at any moment." He looked around the lobby, as if expecting the woman to be hiding behind a potted plant or an elegant column. "While we wait for her why don't I go ahead and take you to our main ballroom and let you have a look around."

One demerit for the late Stacy Boone, Debra thought as she followed behind the two men. Trey was clad in a navy suit with a matching shirt, and she couldn't help but notice that he looked as good from the back as he did from the front.

Broad shoulders, slim waist and long legs, the man was definitely eye candy even without his confident stride and the aura of power that radiated from him.

A vision of his naked body flashed in her brain, causing her to stumble over a bump in the carpet that didn't exist. Trey turned in time to put a hand on her shoulder to steady her. "Okay?" he asked with concern.

"I'm fine," she assured him quickly. It was a relief when he dropped his hand from her. He was a warm and friendly man, a toucher by nature, but she didn't want him touching her in any way. It evoked too many memories she definitely needed to forget.

They had just reached the ballroom's double doors when a young blonde in a pink dress and high heels to heaven came rushing in. She carried a messy pile of paperwork and a smile of apology. "Sorry I'm late." Her gaze landed on Trey and admiration filled her eyes. "I'm so sorry I'm late."

Donald introduced the woman as Stacy, not only his new event planner but his favorite niece, as well. *Uh-oh,* Debra thought. She didn't have any real problem with the nepotism, but Stacy looked very young and definitely had the aura of an airhead about her.

Even Trey looked slightly troubled as he said hello and then exchanged a quick glance with Debra. Debra returned a reassuring smile to him. She'd know within an hour if Stacy was up to the job or not and if she wasn't then she'd be out and Debra would be working with somebody she knew could help her get this job done right.

Stacy led them into the ballroom and set her papers on a nearby table. "You're lucky you called when you did. Most people don't know yet that we just recently finished the renovation of the ballroom. New lighting, carpeting and wall covering. We also have the ability to remove the carpeting, which is actually big squares, in order to lay down a fantastic dance floor."

"I like that," Trey said with enthusiasm. "Dinner and dancing."

"That means we'll have to hire a small orchestra," Debra said as she stifled an inward groan. She'd been so flustered yesterday when she'd initially met with Trey they hadn't talked about the budget for this affair.

"Then we'll hire an orchestra," he replied breezily. "I want people leaving that night feeling good about their evening and me. Dancing after dinner definitely has to happen," he replied.

"Then we'll make it happen." Debra pulled her tablet out of her purse and made notes to add to the computer file she'd started for Trey's dinner party.

Stacy pulled a paper form from her stack and gestured for the three of them to sit at the single table just inside the room. Debra took off her coat and flung it across the back of her chair while Trey took off his overcoat and did the same.

As they began talking about the basic logistics, the date and time and how many would be attending, Stacy took notes and Trey leaned back in his chair and looked around the room, making Debra wonder what thoughts were tumbling around in his head.

Was he thinking about the dinner and maybe writing, in his head, the speech he'd give that night? Or perhaps he was mulling over how difficult the Senate race would be. The incumbent Senator William DeCrow was seeking another term and he was known to be a down and dirty fighter.

Thankfully, Trey had no dirt from his past or present that could be thrown on him, as long as nobody ever knew about their night together, as long as nobody ever knew about the baby she carried he should be fine.

Stacy might have flown in like an airhead, but when it got right down to business, she appeared to be savvy and eager to please, a perfect combination for getting things done properly.

"I can email you a variety of menus first thing tomorrow," she said to Debra after they'd both signed a contract to rent the ballroom for the date. "And are we doing a cash or an open bar?"

"We'll serve wine with dinner, but set up a cash bar," Debra replied. Trey leaned forward and opened his mouth as if to protest, but Debra didn't allow him.

"Cash bar," she said firmly. "This night is supposed to be about you beginning to build a support base, not about a bunch of drunks who won't remember what you said in your speech the next morning."

"And people never drink as much when they have to pay for it out of their own pockets," Stacy added.

"Okay, then I guess I'm outvoted on this topic," he replied and once again leaned back in the chair.

"Let's talk about room setup," Stacy said.

Debra and Stacy began to discuss placement of tables and the dance floor that Trey wanted. As the two women spoke, Debra was acutely aware of the scent of Trey's cologne, the warmth of his body far too close to hers.

Somehow, someway, she needed to get over the silly, schoolgirl crush or whatever it was she had where he was concerned.

Even though the night they'd shared was burned indelibly into her brain, she doubted that it had crossed his mind after he'd put her in the cab to take her home the next morning.

Trey Winston was off-limits, always had been and always would be. He had no interest in her other than using her as an effective weapon to achieve his ambitious desire of becoming the next senator of North Carolina.

She'd told herself she would do whatever she could to help him because of her devotion to Kate, but the truth of the matter was she'd do it because she cared about him enough to want to see him get everything he wanted in life.

Trey tried to keep his gaze off Debra and Stacy as they went over the initial planning stages. The two women were polar opposites. Stacy looked like a fashion doll with her bleached blond hair and black-fringed blue eyes. Her pink dress hugged her body in all the right places and she would instantly draw the gaze of any man who was breathing.

Debra, on the other hand, flew just under the radar in her brown suit and with her hair pulled back into a messy knot at the back of her head.

And yet it was Debra who kept drawing his gaze. She had the loveliest eyes he'd ever seen, so big and so green. Her slightly heart-shaped face expressed each and every emotion she felt.

As the two women talked, Debra displayed both earnestness and an underlying will of steel. She listened to Stacy's ideas, tossing some while accepting others.

He knew Debra was his mother's go-to woman, practically Kate's right hand, moving behind the scenes to keep his mother's life in order and running as smoothly as possible six days a week.

He also knew that the night they had met up in the bar, Debra had been upset about a breakup with some guy named Gary or Larry, or something like that.

Initially, he'd just wanted to console her, but he was in such good spirits about his own business deal, it wasn't long before he had Debra laughing and the surprising sparks had flown between them.

Debra was a constant at the Winston Estate, but he suddenly realized he knew virtually nothing about her personal life or who she was when she wasn't Kate Winston's assistant.

Did she like to dance? What was her favorite kind of music? Did she have any hobbies? How did she spend her evenings and Sundays?

He frowned and stared up at an elaborate crystal chandelier. He shouldn't be wondering about Debra's personal life. It... *She* was none of his business. Just because they'd hooked up for one night didn't mean anything at all.

He knew without doubt that it was a secret neither of them would speak of to anyone else. He trusted Debra. Her loyalty and love had always been with the family.

Still, she had stunned him with her passion, delighted him with her abandon that night. Granted, they'd both been buzzed on champagne, but neither of them could claim inebriation to the point of a lack of consent.

He knew he shouldn't even be thinking about that night. It had been a foolish misstep on both their parts. Instead he should be thinking about Cecily and her excitement when he'd called her the night before and told her about the dinner party and his decision to enter the race.

"Then I guess we're done here for now." Stacy's perky voice brought him back to the present. "I'll email you the various menus and a couple of tentative table and floor plans first thing in the morning."

Debra nodded and stood. "And I'll get back to you on exactly what we want for a speaker's podium and maybe a head table."

"Sounds like a plan," Stacy replied and also got to her feet. Trey followed suit, rising and taking Debra's coat from the back of her chair to help her into it.

Even her coat smelled of that fresh scent that had dizzied his senses when he'd held her in his arms. She quickly slid her arms in and stepped away from him with a murmured thanks.

Trey pulled his coat on and at the ballroom doorway they both said goodbye to Stacy, who scurried off in one direction while Trey and Debra headed back to the lobby and the front door.

They stepped outside into the bracing air. "It's after eleven. Do you want to go someplace for a quick lunch before you head back to the office?" he asked.

He could tell that he'd surprised her by the look on her face. "Oh, no, thanks. I really need to get back to work. All I need from you is a guest list as quickly as possible so that we can get the invitations out."

"I'll work on it this afternoon and how about I drop it by your place this evening? That way you'll have it first thing in the morning to start working on. I've got business meetings tomorrow that will keep me at Adair Enterprises for most of the day. You'll be home this evening?"

"Yes, I'll be home by six-thirty or so."

He shoved his hands into his coat pockets, noting how the brisk breeze whipped a pretty pink into her cheeks. "How are things with Larry?" It was the first time either of them had made any mention of what had transpired six weeks ago.

"It's Barry, and things are fine. He's gone and I'm happy. He was nothing but a creep."

"You seemed pretty upset about the breakup," Trey replied.

The pink in her cheeks was definitely brighter now and he had a feeling it had nothing to do with the weather. "I was mostly upset because I intended to break up with him that night and he beat me to the punch and broke up with me first." She looked toward her car and shifted from one foot to the other, as if wishing for an immediate escape route.

"Okay then, I guess I'll see you later this evening. Shall we say around seven?" he asked.

She nodded. "That would be fine." With a murmured goodbye she made her escape, hurrying away from him as if unable to get out of his presence fast enough.

He frowned as he headed for his own car. He found it impossible to discern what Debra thought of him. In all the years he'd known her, he'd never been able to figure out if she actually liked him or not. The night of sharing a bed and hot sex hadn't changed the fact that he didn't know what to think about her or what she might think about him.

And it irritated him that he cared. He got into his car and tried to push thoughts of Debra Prentice away. He had so many other things to focus on, like how he intended to continue to run the successful Adair Enterprises at the same time he launched a campaign.

Grandfather Walt would be proud of him. The old man was probably dancing with the angels at Trey's decision to enter the world of politics. Running the family business and politics had been what the old man had wanted for him.

Trey knew he had a good chance of winning. He didn't lean too far left or too far to the right. His politics were middle-of-the-road. He'd already proven his business acumen in the success of Adair Enterprises and he knew he'd made a reputation for himself as a hard worker and decent man who was willing to compromise when it was necessary.

In the course of doing business, he'd made enemies, but he knew that his opponents would have a hard time slinging mud at him.

He'd always been the good son, the firstborn who had excelled in college, had taken the family business into a new level of success and had never done drugs or slept with married women. He'd never taken pictures of his body parts and put them online.

In fact, he'd worked hard to keep his nose clean for just this time. Walt had wanted this for him since Trey was old enough to understand the world of politics and now Trey wanted it for himself.

He knew Cecily would put more pressure on him now for the announcement of their engagement. She would reason that an engaged or newly married candidate only made a man more appealing to the masses. It suggested stability and commitment, considered good character traits by voters.

She was right, but he wasn't ready yet to pop the

question to her. Maybe he'd ask her to marry him once the dinner party was finished. The event would be his first real step in declaring himself ready to be a serious contender and at the moment he needed all his energy and attention focused on that.

The main office of Adair Enterprises was located in downtown Raleigh, but they also had offices in Seattle and factories in Durham and Iowa.

The company had been started by his mother's grandfather in the 1930s as a shipping company for tobacco and local farmers to get their products across the country.

When Walt had taken over, the business had evolved into shipping containers and then to plastics and Trey had transformed it once again into a company also known for computer systems.

One of the strengths of the business was in its ability to be ever-changing with the times, and Trey prided himself on not only being a visionary, but also smart enough to hire equally driven and bright people to work with him.

As he walked through the glass doors of the building he was instantly greeted by security guard Jason Ridgeway. "Good morning, Mr. Winston."

"Morning, Jason. How are Stella and the kids doing?"

"Great, everyone is great."

"Billy's broken arm healing all right?"

Jason nodded. "The cast is due to come off sometime next week. I swear that kid is going to age me before my time."

Trey laughed. "Just keep him out of trees," he said and then with a wave headed to the bank of elevators that would take him to the top floor of the building and his personal office.

The elevator opened into a spacious airy reception area and Rhonda Wilson sat behind the large, modern reception desk. Rhonda was part beauty, part bulldog, the perfect final gatekeeper to Trey.

In her mid-fifties, Rhonda was tall and broad shouldered. She could be exceedingly pleasant and was fiercely devoted to Trey, but she also could tear a new one in any reporter or the like who tried to breach Trey's privacy.

"Good morning, boss," she greeted him with a pleasant smile.

"It's almost twelve," he replied. "Hopefully you're going to tell me I have nothing on my calendar for the rest of the afternoon?"

"You have nothing on your calendar for the rest of the afternoon," she repeated dutifully. "Although you do have a ton of phone messages on your desk."

"As usual," he replied as he took off his coat. "Could you order a roast-beef sub for me and keep everyone out of my hair for the next couple of hours?"

"No problem." She picked up the phone to call the nearby restaurant Trey often ordered his lunch from as Trey went into the inner sanctum that often felt more like home than his huge new mansion just outside the Raleigh beltline.

His personal office was the size of a large apartment. Not only did it boast a desk the size of a small boat, but also a sitting area complete with sofa and chairs, a minibar and a bathroom that had both a shower and sauna, and a large walk-in closet.

There had been many nights when working on an

intricate deal that Trey had slept on the sofa and then awakened the next morning to shower and dress for another day of mergers or hiccups that needed to be solved.

He tossed his coat on the back of the sleek leather sofa and then took his place at his desk and powered up the state-of-the-art computer system that allowed him to monitor every area of the business, video chat with managers in other parts of the country and stay on top of each and every problem that might arise.

Today he did a cursory check of emails to make sure there were no major issues at any of the plants or offices. He quickly flew through the phone messages, setting aside the ones he intended to return later and then pulled up his list of contacts and began to work on an invitation list for the dinner.

He wanted his friends and business associates there, but he knew it was even more important that invitations went to labor-union leaders, local and state government officials, and political backers who could bring both clout and campaign contributions.

He started his list but found himself distracted by the anticipation of going to Debra's place later that evening. He'd never been to the townhouse she'd bought, but he remembered her excitement over no longer having to rent and being a real homeowner.

He knew the silkiness of her skin, the smooth slide of her body against his own. He knew the contours of her body intimately, but he couldn't imagine how her home would be decorated.

What definitely confounded him was the fact that even though it wasn't quite noon yet, he couldn't wait for seven o'clock to come.

* * *

Kate Winston stood at her office window. It was just after six and Debra had left to go home. Business was officially ended for the day, but it would still be twenty minutes or so before dinner was served.

A softness filled her as she thought of Debra. In many ways Debra had taken the place of the daughter nobody knew she'd had, the baby girl who had died at birth. Kate had only been seventeen when she'd given birth and after learning the baby did not survive, she had fallen into a deep depression that she'd believed would last forever.

She'd been sent away to school, where she pretended that she was just like all the other debutantes with nothing to trouble her except which dress to wear to what event, but she'd never quite gotten over the heartache of the loss of the baby girl.

It was only when Buchanan Winston had entered her life that Kate discovered a new reason for living. She had fallen head over heels in love with Buck. She'd not only given him three healthy sons, but had also supported him in his political aspirations that began on a local level and eventually ended in the Senate.

It was during the Senate election that she'd found out that Buck had been having affairs for most of their marriage. Her heart had been broken and she'd threatened to leave him, but he'd told her if she left he'd declare her an unfit mother and seek to gain full custody of their children.

Afraid of his power and influence, Kate had stayed and played the role of supportive wife, and then, like a bad cliché, Buck had died in one of his mistress's arms.

He'd had one year left in his term as senator and Kate had stepped in to fill his shoes.

She'd discovered she loved politics and had run for a term of her own the next year. After that had come a four-year stint as the first female vice president of the United States. Her party had lost the next election and now she had people whispering in her ear about running for president when election time rolled around again.

She wanted it. But her decision about running for the most prestigious and powerful position in the world was tempered by other elements besides her own desire.

She'd made many friends in her years of public service, but she'd also made enemies and she didn't have just herself to worry about when the election got dirty, and elections always got dirty.

Moving away from the window, she thought of her sons and how the decision to run for president might affect each of them. Trey would be all right. He was a strong man and already preparing himself for the battle arena of politics.

She worried about Sam. He'd come home so damaged and unwilling to seek help from either family members or professionals. He was a loose cannon at the moment and she was concerned how the bright spotlight of a national campaign might affect him.

Then there was Thad. Her youngest, Thaddeus had turned his back on the family business and had made a modest life for himself in Garner, North Carolina. He worked for the Raleigh Police Department as a crime-scene investigator.

He led a quiet life alone and would hate having any role in the world she loved. Maybe she should just flip a coin to come to a final decision, she thought ruefully.

She only knew two things for sure. She believed with all her heart that she was the right person for the job, that she would be far better for the country than the front-runners who had already begun the political dance of becoming elected.

The second thing she knew with certainty was that some of the enemies she'd made over the years were utterly ruthless and would do everything in their power to destroy her and anyone she loved, not only politically, but personally, as well.

Chapter 3

Debra arrived home, hung her coat in the hall closet and then raced around like a mad woman to make sure her living room/dining area and the kitchen were spotlessly clean.

She was by nature a neat and tidy woman, so there was little to do, but with the thought that Trey would be seeing her home for the very first time she wanted everything perfect.

She fluffed the red-and-yellow throw pillows on the black sofa twice and dithered over lighting several of the scented candles she normally lit in the evenings. She finally decided against it, not wanting him to believe that she was in any way attempting to create an intimate, romantic setting.

At six forty-five she sat down on the edge of the sofa and told herself she was acting completely ridiculous.

Trey probably wouldn't even take a step into the small, gleaming hardwood-floor foyer. He'd meet her at the door, hand her the list of names he'd prepared and then leave with his mission accomplished.

The last thing Trey Winston cared about was sitting around and chatting with his mother's assistant. Debra had eaten on the way home from the estate and had put on coffee, which now filled the air with its freshly brewed scent.

The coffee wasn't for him. She always made coffee or hot tea when she got home from work, especially at this time of year when outside the cold knocked on every window and attempted to seep into every crack.

She was thankful that the townhouse seemed well insulated and she loved to keep the thermostat low and build a nice fire in the stone see-through fireplace that was between the living room and kitchen.

There were no flames in the fireplace now. Again, she didn't want Trey to get any ideas that she had any thought about another encounter with him. The last thing she wanted was to come off as some pathetic one-night stand who didn't understand exactly what she'd been.

She'd changed out of her suit and into a pair of comfortable jeans and a mint-green fleece sweatshirt. She hadn't even bothered to check herself in a mirror as she'd left her upstairs bedroom to come down here to wait for Trey's appearance.

She jumped when the doorbell rang, nerves jangling discordantly through her as she got up from the sofa and hurried to answer.

Her breath caught slightly in her throat as she opened the door and he smiled at her. Trey Winston definitely had a killer smile, all white straight teeth and warmth. "Hi," he said.

"Hi," she replied.

His smile widened, crinkling the corners of his eyes. "Are you going to invite me in?"

"Oh, of course…if you want to come in… I mean you don't have to if you don't want to."

"Thanks, I'd love to come in." He swept past her, trailing the bold scent of his cologne as she quickly closed the front door and followed him into her living room.

He shrugged out of his coat and slung it across the back of one of the two chairs that faced the sofa as if he'd done it a hundred times before. He'd changed clothes, too. Instead of his usual suit, he was dressed in a pair of casual black slacks and a white polo shirt that hugged his shoulders and chest as if specifically tailored for him.

"Is that fresh coffee I smell?" he asked.

"Yes, it is. Would you like a cup?" To say that she was shocked to have him not only actually in her townhouse, but also asking for a cup of coffee was an understatement.

"I'd love a cup," he replied.

She motioned him to the sofa. "Just make yourself comfortable and I'll bring it in here."

"I don't mind sitting in the kitchen," he said as he followed at her heels. His gaze seemed to take in every nook and corner of the room. "Nice place."

"Thanks, I like it." She was grateful when he sank down at the round wooden table with its centerpiece of a crystal bowl with red and yellow flowers.

The kitchen was her favorite place to spend time.

Located at the back of the townhouse, the windows looked out on a lush flower garden she'd planted last spring, although now there was nothing to see but dormant plants and the redbrick tiers of the flowerbeds.

Above the butcher-block center island hung a rack with gleaming copper-bottomed pots and pans. The counters not only held the coffeepot but a variety of small appliances she used on a regular basis on the weekends.

"You like to cook," he said as he looked around with obvious interest.

"On the weekends," she replied as she reached with slightly nervous fingers to get two of her nicest black mugs down from the cabinet. She swallowed hard as she nearly dropped one. *Get a grip,* she commanded herself.

She poured the coffee and managed to deliver both cups to the table without incident. "Sugar? Cream?"

"Black is fine," he replied.

She sank down onto the chair opposite him, wondering how it was possible that his mere presence diminished the size of her kitchen and sucked up the energy, making her feel slightly lightheaded, as if she was suffering from a lack of oxygen.

"What kind of food do you like to cook?" he asked, his big hands cradling the coffee mug.

"Anything…everything, whatever sounds good. I try to do a new recipe every weekend on Sunday. Last week it was chicken *malai* curry, an Indian dish. The week before that was spicy cherry pork stir fry."

"Sounds delicious and adventurous," he replied, his head cocked slightly to one side and his gaze intent on her as if trying to see inside her head.

She forced a dry laugh. "*Adventurous* isn't exactly

an adjective that is normally used when describing me."
She mentally begged him not to mention the night they'd
spent together, a night that had been out of character
for both of them. She'd definitely been adventurous
and bold then.

"Efficient and driven. Sweet but with a touch of barracuda," he replied. He took a sip of his coffee and then
set the mug back down. "That's how I would describe
you. I was impressed with how you handled the negotiations today with Stacy."

"Thanks. We'll see how well I did when I get the
menus and floor plans from her in the morning," she
replied, beginning to relax. "And we never discussed
what your budget was for the event."

"Whatever it takes to do it right," he replied.

"Everything needs a budget, Trey," she admonished.
"If you can't stick to a budget, then how can the voters
trust you with their tax dollars?"

"Okay." He named an amount that was adequate and
yet not too extravagant. "We'll use that figure as our
budget. What do you think about my decision to run
for senator?"

She looked at him, surprised he would care one way
or the other what she thought about it. She took a sip
of her coffee, unwilling to give him a quick, flippant
answer.

"You've always been successful at whatever en-
deavor you've undertaken," she said thoughtfully. "You
have all the qualities to be a great senator, but have you
considered how you're going to juggle the running of
Adair Enterprises with the responsibilities of being a
state senator? Not only does the job take a lot of hours

and work, but campaigning will be a huge commitment of both time and energy."

"I know, but I'm lucky that I have good people working with me at Adair Enterprises and they will step up to cover whenever I can't be at the business." He took another drink. "Has Mom given you any hint as to whether she's going to take up the challenge and run for president?"

Debra smiled. "Your mother shares a lot with me, but this is one decision she's keeping pretty close to her chest. I know there is pressure on her from a variety of places to run, but I have no idea what she's going to decide."

"She should go for it. She'd be great for the country. Not only is she strong and intelligent, but she's more than paid her dues and she's smarter than any of the other schmucks who are making noise about running."

"You're preaching to the choir," Debra replied with a smile. "She'd have my vote in a minute."

He returned her smile and suddenly the nerves jumped through her veins once again. "This is nice," he said as his gaze swept the room and lingered on the fireplace. "I'll bet it's quite cozy in here when the fire is lit and you have something exotic cooking in the oven or on the stove."

"It is nice," she agreed. "Buying this place was the best decision I've ever made."

He finished his coffee and when he set the mug down on the table and looked at her, something in the depths of his eyes caused her to tense warily.

"Debra, about that night…"

"What night?" she said quickly. "I have no idea what you're talking about." She pled with her eyes for him to take it no further. She didn't want to have a discussion about a night that shouldn't have happened. A hand automatically fell to her lap, as if in an attempt to hide the secret she carried.

"I'm your mother's assistant and I'll do everything I can to help you reach your goal of becoming a North Carolina state senator," she said softly. "And that's really all we have to discuss."

He held her gaze for a long moment and then gave a curt nod of his head and stood. "Thanks for the coffee, Debra, and all your hard work."

"No problem. One more thing, did you bring me the list of names of people you want to invite?" She got up from the table.

He snapped his finger and grinned at her. "I knew there was a reason I stopped by here. The list is in my coat pocket."

Together they left the kitchen and went back into the living room where he grabbed his coat from the back of the chair and put it on. He reached into one of the pockets and pulled out the printed list.

"Thanks," she said as she took it from him. "I'll get the invitations ordered tomorrow and have them addressed and mailed by the end of the next day. Do you want to look at the invitations before they go out? I was thinking something simple and elegant."

"I trust your judgment."

"You can trust me in everything," she said pointedly, hoping her words were enough to put him at ease about that damned night they'd spent together.

He'd probably wanted to mention it to her to assure himself that she had no plans to take it public. She could probably make a little extra money selling the story to the tabloids.

She could only imagine the salacious headlines if the information got out that he'd slept with a member of his mother's staff while practically engaged to a wealthy socialite. But he had nothing to worry about where she was concerned.

"You have absolutely nothing to be worried about," she said to reiterate to him that the secret of their unexpected tryst would remain just that—a secret.

"Then I guess I'll leave you to the rest of your evening," he said, and they walked together toward the front door.

"I'll get in touch with you sometime tomorrow, as soon as I get the things emailed over from Stacy," she replied, grateful that they'd broached the subject of their night together without really talking about it.

"This dinner party is an important first step and together we're going to make it amazing," he said. He gave her one last devastating smile and then stepped out the front door and disappeared into the gloom of a cloudy twilight.

Debra locked the door behind him and leaned against the door. Curse that man. She could still smell the heady scent of his cologne, feel a lingering vibrating energy in the air despite his absence.

She shoved herself off the door with a muttered curse and carried the list of names he'd given her into the small chamber just off the living room that served as her home office.

She placed the list on her desk next to her computer and then left the room and returned to the kitchen. She placed Trey's coffee mug in the dishwasher and silently cursed him for even making her think about that night.

Her body flushed with heat as she thought of how he'd slowly caressed each and every inch of her skin. His kisses had driven her half out of her mind with desire and she knew making love with Trey Winston was an experience she'd never, ever forget.

What bothered her more than anything was the knowledge that even knowing it was wrong, even with the unexpected result that had occurred, she'd do it again in a hot minute.

Trey wasn't sure what he had hoped to accomplish by bringing up the night he'd spent with Debra after all this time. Over six weeks had passed and they'd spoken numerous times since then without ever mentioning what had transpired between them.

So, what had he wanted to say to her tonight? What had he wanted her to say to him? That she'd liked being with him? That he'd been a pleasing lover?

He mentally scoffed at his own thoughts. As terrible as it sounded, he probably just wanted to double-check that she didn't intend to go public with their misdeed, but even thinking that did a disservice to the woman he knew that Debra was. He knew how devoted she was to the family. She would never do anything to hurt any of them in any way.

Instead of heading home to his mansion, he decided to drop in and visit with his grandmother in the nursing home. As he drove his thoughts continued to be filled with Debra.

She'd looked cute as a bug in her jeans and green sweatshirt. He'd never seen her in casual clothes before and the jeans had hugged her long legs, shapely legs that he remembered wrapped around him.

He tightened his grip on the steering wheel, realizing the skies were spitting a bit of ice. January in Raleigh could be surprisingly unpredictable. It might be cold with a bit of snow or ice, or it could be surprisingly mild. Occasionally they got a killer ice storm, but thankfully nothing like that so far this year.

The weather forecast that morning had mentioned the threat of a little frozen precipitation, but nothing for travelers to worry about. Slowing his speed a bit, his thoughts went back to Debra.

Her townhome had surprised him. He'd expected the furnishings to be utilitarian and rather cold, but stepping into her living room had been like being welcomed into a place where he'd wanted to stay and linger awhile.

The living space had been warm and inviting, as had the kitchen, as well. He thought of the stark formal furnishings in his own mansion and for a moment entertained the idea of hiring Debra to do a bit of decorating transformation.

It was a silly thought. If he worked his plan to achieve his ultimate goal, then Cecily would be moving into the mansion and she'd want to put her own personal stamp in place there, although he doubted that Cecily would have the taste for warm and inviting. She'd want formal and expensive. She'd want to create a showcase rather than a home.

He punched the button on his steering wheel that would connect him to phone services. He gave the command to call Cecily on her cell and then waited for her to answer.

"Darling," her voice chirped through the interior of the car. "I was wondering if I was going to hear from you today."

"Between work at the office and planning this dinner party, I've been swamped." He could hear from the background noise on her phone that she wasn't at home. "Where are you now?"

"At a Women's League meeting. I'm already not-so-subtly campaigning for you, Trey."

He smiled, certain that she was doing just that. "You know I appreciate it."

"You'd better," she replied with a laugh. "Rumor has it your mother is seriously considering running for president. We'll let her have that position for two terms and then *we'll* be ready to move into the White House."

Trey laughed. "One step at a time, Cecily. This dinner party will let me know if I can get some of the big hitters in town behind me in order to achieve the first step in the process."

"You can take it one step at a time, but I'm already envisioning what the White House Christmas tree will look like," she replied with a laugh. "Oh, gotta go. I'll talk to you tomorrow."

She ended the call and Trey shook his head. Cecily McKenna was like a force of nature, unstoppable and powerful and completely in his corner. She would make a perfect ally and support as a wife.

He pulled into the parking lot of the Brookside Nursing Home, an upscale establishment where his grandmother, Eunice, had resided since Walt's death.

When she'd lost her husband she had spiraled into a depression so deep nobody seemed to be able to pull

her out. Trey knew one of the most difficult decisions
his mother had made was to move her own mother here
instead of keeping her living at the estate. But Eunice
needed more than what Kate and the family could provide.

After several months of residency Eunice had appeared to rally from her depression. She seemed quite
content where she was, in a small apartmentlike set
of rooms with an aid who stayed with her twenty-four
hours a day.

He nodded to the security guard on duty outside the
front door and entered into a small lobby with a couple
of elegant chairs and a front desk.

"Good evening, Mr. Winston," Amy Fedder, a middle-
aged woman behind the reception desk greeted him. He
was a frequent visitor and knew most of the people on
staff.

"Hi, Amy." He walked to the desk where there was a
sign-in sheet and quickly signed his name and the time
he'd arrived. "Have you heard how she's doing today?"

"I know she had dinner in the dining room and earlier in the day she joined a group of women playing
bingo."

"Then it sounds like it's been a good day for her," he
replied, a happiness filling him. He adored his grandmother. "Thanks Amy, I'll see you on my way out." He
left the front desk and headed for the elevator, which
would take him to the second floor where his grandmother's little apartment was located. It amused him
that her place was in what the nursing home called the
west wing.

There were only forty residents at any given time
in Brookside and almost as many staff members. The

nursing home catered to the wealthy and powerful who wanted their loved ones in an upscale environment with exceptional care and security. Every member of the staff had undergone intense background and security checks before being hired and there was a front door and a back door, both with an armed security guard on duty at all times.

He got off the elevator and walked down a long hallway, passing several closed doors before he arrived at apartment 211.

He knocked and the door was answered by Serena Sue Sana, a tall beautiful African-American woman who went by the nickname of Sassy. She was of an indeterminable age, but Trey guessed her to be somewhere in her mid-sixties.

"Mr. Trey," she greeted him, her white teeth flashing in a bright smile. "Come in." She opened the door wider. "Ms. Eunice will be so happy to see you." She leaned closer to him. "She's had a good day but seems a bit agitated this evening," she whispered.

He nodded and walked into the nice-size living room with a small kitchenette area and doors that led to the bathroom and two bedrooms, one large and one smaller.

His eighty-six-year-old grandmother was where she usually was at this time of the evening, her small frame nearly swallowed up by the comfortable light blue chair surrounding her.

Her silvery-white hair was pulled up neatly into a bun atop her head and her blue eyes lit up and a smile curved her lips at the sight of him. "I know you," she said, her affection for him thick in her voice.

"And I know you," Trey replied as he walked over to her and planted a kiss on her forehead.

"I'll just go on into my room so you two can have a nice private chat," Sassy said.

"Before you go, would you make this television be quiet?" Eunice held out the remote control to Sassy.

"I'll take care of it," Trey replied. He sat in the chair next to Eunice and took the remote control and hit the mute button as Sassy disappeared into the small bedroom and closed the door behind her.

"I love Sassy to death, but she likes to watch the silliest television shows," Eunice said. "And sometimes I just like to sit and visit with my favorite grandson."

"I'll bet you say that to all your grandsons," Trey said teasingly.

She giggled like a young girl. "You might be right about that." Her blue eyes, so like Trey's mother's, sparkled merrily.

"I heard you played bingo this afternoon," Trey said.

Her smile instantly transformed into a frown. "Did I…? Yes, yes I did, although I didn't win. I never win." She leaned closer to him. "That woman from downstairs in 108 always wins. I think the fix is in."

Trey laughed and leaned over and covered her frail hand with his. "You don't have to win all the time."

Her eyes flashed and her chin jutted forward with a show of stubbornness. "Adairs always win," she said, her voice strident as she pulled her hand back from his and instead worried the edge of the fringed shawl that was around her shoulders.

"That's what we do," she muttered more to herself than to him. "We win."

"Speaking of winning, have you talked to Mom lately?"

She frowned again in thought. "She called yesterday…or maybe it was the day before." She shook her head with obvious agitation. "I can't remember. Sometimes I can't remember what happened when, except I have lots of memories of when you boys were young. You three were such a handful. But sometimes my brain just gets a bit scrambled."

"It's okay," Trey said gently. "I was just wondering if she told you that I'm considering a run for the Senate."

Eunice's eyes widened. "No, she didn't tell me." Her fingers threaded through the shawl fringe at a quicker pace. "She never mentioned that to me before."

"Then I guess she didn't tell you that we think she's also considering a run for the White House," Trey said.

Eunice appeared to freeze in place, the only movement being her gaze darting frantically around the room as if seeking something she'd misplaced and desperately needed to find.

"Grandma, what is it?" Trey asked.

She stood from her chair and began to pace in front of him, her back slightly bent from the osteoporosis that plagued her. "No. No. No." The word snapped out of her louder and more frantic with each shuffled step of her feet.

Trey stood in an attempt to reach out and draw her back into her chair, but she slapped his hands away and continued to pace.

"This is bad news…. It's terrible, terrible news." She stopped her movement and stared at him, her eyes wide with fear. "You shouldn't do this. She shouldn't do this. Pandora's box, that's all it will be."

"What are you talking about? Grandma, what are you afraid of?"

Her eyes filled with tears as she looked at him in horror. "Secrets and lies," she said in a bare whisper.

Chapter 4

It has to be here, Debra thought frantically as she searched the area on top of her desk. The early morning sun drifted through the office window, letting her know it was getting later and later.

She moved file folders and papers helter-skelter, her heart pounding in her ears as she looked for the missing paperwork. It had to be here, it just had to be.

She distinctly remembered putting the guest list that Trey had given her next to her computer the night before, but it wasn't there now.

She was already dressed to go to work and had come into the office to grab the list before leaving her place. In a panic she now fell to her hands and knees in the plush carpeting, searching on the floor, hoping that it had somehow drifted off the desk, but it wasn't there, either.

She checked the wastebasket to make sure it hadn't fallen into it somehow during the night. Nothing. No list magically appeared.

Half-breathless from her anxious search, she sank down at her desk chair. *Think,* she commanded herself. After she'd placed it on the desk the night before had she come back in here for any reason and mindlessly placed it elsewhere?

No, she was certain she hadn't reentered the office again last night. After Trey had left she'd watched a little television and then had gone upstairs to bed. She had not come back into the office.

Was it possible she had sleepwalked and moved the list?

She couldn't imagine such a thing. As far as she knew she'd never sleepwalked in her life. Besides, she would have had to maneuver herself not just out of her bed, but also down the stairs and into the office all the while being unconscious in sleep.

Impossible. Utterly ridiculous to even entertain such an idea, but the darned list didn't get up and walk away on its own.

Granted, she'd been unsettled after Trey had left. Maybe she had wandered in here and taken the list someplace else in the house before she'd gone to bed.

With this thought in mind, she jumped out of the chair and raced through the lower level of the house. Her heart pounded in an unsteady rhythm as she checked the kitchen counters, the living-room coffee table and any reasonable place she might have put the list, but it was nowhere to be found.

The thought of calling Trey and asking him for another copy horrified her. She was organized and effi-

cient. She didn't lose things. So how had she lost such
an important piece of paper?

After a run-through of the entire house yielded no
results, she finally returned to the kitchen, defeated and
knowing she needed to get on the road or she'd definitely be late to work.

She hurried to the refrigerator and opened the freezer
to take out a small package of chicken breasts to thaw
for dinner and stared at the piece of paper that was slid
between them and a frozen pizza.

She grabbed the paper, saw that it was the missing
list and hugged it tight to her chest in relief. Hurriedly
yanking out the chicken breasts, she set them in the
fridge and then raced for the front door, grabbing her
purse and coat on the way out.

As she waited for her car to warm up, she folded
the guest list and tucked it into her purse, then pulled
her coat around her shoulders. She tried to ignore the
rapid beating of her heart that still continued, the frantic beat that had begun the moment she'd realized the
list was missing.

Heading toward the Winston Estate, she wondered if
somehow between last night and this morning her brain
had slipped a cog. Had she been so flustered by Trey's
visit that she'd mindlessly placed the list in the freezer?

It was crazy. It was insane, but she couldn't ignore
the fact that she was the only person in the house who
could have put the list in the freezer.

Maybe it had something to do with hormones. She
had called her doctor to make an appointment for the
weekend. Was it possible that pregnancy hormones
made you lose your mind? She'd be sure and ask her
doctor.

As if to make the day worse, Jerry Cahill was on guard duty as she pulled into the side entrance. The tall, sandy-haired Secret Service man gave her the creeps. He seemed to have some sort of a weird crush on her and had asked her out twice. Both times she'd politely declined but one time last month she'd thought she'd seen him standing on the sidewalk in front of her place and staring at her townhouse.

He stopped her car before she could pull into her usual parking space and motioned for her to roll down her window. "Hey, doll, running a little late this morning, aren't you?" He leaned too far into her window, invading her personal space.

"Maybe just a few minutes," she replied.

Jerry had hazel eyes that should have been warm in hue, but instead reminded her of an untamed jungle animal that could spring at a vulnerable throat at any moment.

His breath smelled of peppermint and the fact that he was close enough to smell his breath freaked her out just a little bit.

He held her gaze for a long moment and then stepped back and tapped the top of her car. "Well, I just wanted to tell you to have a good day."

She rolled up her window and parked her car, feeling revulsion just from the brief encounter. Jerry Cahill might be a Secret Service agent, but that didn't make him any less of a creep.

She hurried into the house to find Maddie Fitzgerald, head housekeeper, and Myra Henry, head cook, seated at the small table enjoying a cup of coffee together.

"Good morning, Ms. Debra," Maddie said. Her plump cheeks danced upward with her smile. With red hair cut in a no-nonsense style and her perpetual optimism, Maddie had been around long before Debra. She'd not only been the first person Kate had hired, but she'd helped Kate raise the boys and was intensely devoted to the Winston family, as they all were to her.

"Good morning, ladies," Debra said. She smiled at Myra and drew in a deep breath. "Is that your famous cinnamon rolls I smell?"

"It is. If you want to get settled into your office I'll bring you a couple with a nice cup of coffee," Myra said.

"That sounds heavenly," Debra replied. "Thanks, Myra."

She kept her smile pasted on her lips until she reached her office where she hung up her coat and then sank down at her desk. She opened her purse and retrieved the list that Trey had given her.

She'd just set it next to her computer when Myra arrived with a steaming cup of coffee and two large iced cinnamon rolls on an oversize saucer.

"Those look too sinful to eat," Debra exclaimed as she eyed the goodies.

Myra grinned at her. "I make them special, no calories so there's no guilt."

"Yeah, right," Debra replied with a laugh.

"Enjoy," Myra said and left the office.

Debra took a sip of the coffee and then got to work typing up the list of names Trey had given her so she'd have a hard copy on her computer. Once it was in the computer she wouldn't have to worry about losing it again.

She was still troubled twenty minutes later when she had the copy made and leaned back in her chair and drew a deep breath.

"Crisis averted," she muttered aloud to herself. She picked up one of the cinnamon rolls and took a bite, but her stomach was still in knots because of the morning trauma.

Or was it morning sickness?

She couldn't think about being pregnant now. She'd think about it after she saw her doctor. Right now she had work to do, not only did she have to pick invitations to be printed and addressed and mailed, there was also the matter of finding a good orchestra to hire for the night of the dinner. Once she got information from Stacy she'd need to meet with Trey to make some final decisions.

It would be easy for her to feel overwhelmed, but Debra knew the way to get things done was focus on one item at a time and not look too far ahead.

Kate's morning knock came at eight-thirty and Debra instantly got up to join her boss in her office.

"Good morning, Kate," Debra said as she sat in the chair opposite the desk.

"And a good morning to you," Kate said with a fond smile. "I've already given Haley the things that needed to be taken care of for me this morning. One thing I love about interns is that they're so eager to please. What I want from you is an update on you and Trey's visit to the Regent yesterday."

For the next half an hour Debra filled Kate in on what had transpired at the hotel and where they were in the planning stages.

"I know you're pulling everything together quickly," Kate said. "If you need more help, let me know and I'll assign an assistant for you."

"Actually, I think Stacy, the hotel event planner is

going to be all I need. She seemed to understand exactly what we want, what we need for a successful evening for Trey. I'm expecting her to get me a floor plan and some menu options sometime this morning. That will tell me how good she is at her job."

"Do you think he's ready for this?" Kate asked.

"I think he's more ready than anyone could be," Debra replied. "I know he's saying that this dinner party is just to dip his toes in the water to see what kind of support he might have if he decides to run, but I believe he's already made up his mind. His head is definitely already in the game."

Kate nodded. "That's what I believe, too, and Trey never does anything halfway."

"He'll make a wonderful senator," Debra said, unable to keep the passion of her belief out of her voice. "He'll bring new life and new hope to the people of North Carolina."

Kate nodded. "I know my son. Even if he decided to be a garbage man he'd be the best in the business. He always does everything well."

"He's a chip off the old block," Debra replied with a smile.

Kate laughed. "Get out of here and get to work on helping my son. I won't need anything from you today. I know the time constraints you have to get the details of this dinner party under control are incredibly tight, so get to it."

By the time she got back to her office she'd received a number of emails from Stacy. The young event planner had sent several different seating plans and three menus with prices. Even though she'd had to pull teeth in order for Trey to come up with a budget, Debra intended to negotiate hard to keep costs low and quality high.

She was an old pro at this, having set up dozens of such events in the past for Kate. Despite what Trey had said, budgets always mattered, and it would reflect poorly on his business acumen to not bring the dinner party in as reasonably as possible.

If you wanted the taxpayers to back you, then you had to show a willingness to work within budgets, she thought.

Gathering the emails all together, she knew what she needed now was for she and Trey to have another meeting and make more decisions. She picked up the phone to call him at Adair Enterprises.

The receptionist connected her to him immediately.

"Good morning, Debra." His deep smooth voice was like a physical caress through the line.

She returned the greeting, although what she wanted to do was tell him about her frantic search for his list that morning, the ridiculousness of finally finding it in the freezer and that Myra's cinnamon rolls had made her slightly queasy.

Trey told her he intended to come to the house around two and they would meet then to hammer out any decisions that needed to be made. Then they disconnected.

Debra leaned back in her chair and for the first time in years wished she had a best friend. Her entire adult life had been built surrounded by the Winston family. There hadn't been time for friends outside of the intimacy of the family members.

Certainly her childhood hadn't been conducive to making friends. She'd never invited anyone to her home, afraid that her classmates might see her mother drunk or hungover. Once she started working for Kate, the work and the family had taken precedence over anything and everyone else.

That had been part of her problem with dating Barry. There had been little time to really grow any meaningful relationship. Although ultimately he'd broken up with her because he told her he wasn't getting what he needed from her, she'd already intended to break up with him because she'd figured out he was getting what he needed from his married secretary. The jerk.

Maybe it was best that she didn't have a best friend, she thought as her hand fell to her lap and she caressed her lower belly.

Perhaps she would be tempted to share too much with a best friend, and a secret wasn't a secret if two people knew about it. And Debra knew better than anyone that she had a secret that had the potential to destroy a career before it began.

Trey had been disturbed since he'd left the nursing home the night before. His grandmother had become quite agitated before he'd left, frantic as she continued to whisper about secrets and lies.

Sassy had finally come out of her room to deal with the older woman. She'd given Eunice a mild sedative and by the time Trey had left, Eunice had fallen asleep in her chair.

Sassy had assured him that she'd be fine, but as Trey drove to the Winston Estate, he couldn't help the worry that had been with him since the visit the night before.

He'd always been close to his Adair grandparents and had mourned deeply when Walt had died. Now he was both concerned and confused about his grandmother and after meeting with Debra he intended to speak to his mother about the issue.

The front door of the estate was opened by house-keeper Maddie, who always greeted him as if it had been months since she'd seen him. "And aren't you look-ing just fine today," she said as she took his coat from him. "You know I've always liked you in a nice blue suit, it makes those eyes of yours downright beautiful."

Trey laughed. "You've been charming me since I was a baby, Maddie, and the years haven't changed anything a bit. I'm assuming Debra is in?"

"Holed up in that little office of hers as usual."

"Would you tell her that I'm here and that I'll meet her in the sitting room?"

"I'd be happy to. Tea or coffee? Maybe a plate of cookies?" she asked, knowing his weakness for sweets.

"Coffee and what kind of cookies?" he asked.

She smiled at him slyly. "Does it really matter?"

He laughed. "No, it doesn't, not as long as Myra baked them. Okay, a couple of cookies would be good." He was still smiling as he entered the informal sitting room where the afternoon sun flooded through the floor to ceiling windows at one end.

The weather system that had brought the little bit of icing the night before had moved on, leaving behind blue skies and sunshine.

Trey sank into one of two beige easy chairs in front of the windows, enjoying the warmth of the sun on his back. Within seconds Myra entered the room, carrying with her a tray that held a small coffeepot, two cups and a plate of oatmeal-raisin cookies he knew would be soft and gooey, just the way he liked them.

"Thanks, Myra," he told the cook, who nodded and then left him alone in the room.

He poured the coffee into the two cups and thought about having coffee in Debra's townhome the night before. She was bright and sweet and easy to be around. Last night as he'd sat in her kitchen he'd felt more relaxed than he had in months and he thought it had not been just the cozy surroundings, but also her company.

She didn't seem to have one high-maintenance bone in her body. He found her blushes charming and the fact that she cooked something special and new just to please herself each Sunday intriguing.

He had nearly destroyed the nice interaction between them by attempting to bring up the night they had spent together, but she'd made it clear that she didn't want to discuss it and was more than a bit embarrassed by the whole affair.

He should feel embarrassed about it, too. Still, he couldn't help but admit that he was looking forward to seeing her again. He tried to tell himself that it had nothing to do with any feelings he might have for her. Granted, he'd more than enjoyed his one night with her, but he knew where his duty, where his future lay and it definitely wasn't with Debra.

The subject of his thoughts entered the room. Clad in a pair of tailored black slacks and a white blouse, she looked all business as she offered him a curt smile.

"I had Myra bring in some cookies and coffee," he said as she sat in the chair next to him. "It's been my experience that every important decision should be made over a good cookie."

She smiled and set a handful of papers on the coffee table next to the silver tray of refreshments. "No cookies for me, and no coffee. I've been trying to cut down on my caffeine."

As always whenever she was around he was aware of the scent of her, that fresh, clean fragrance that stirred something deep inside him. What kind of perfume did Cecily wear? For the life of him he couldn't seem to bring it to his mind whenever Debra was close to him.

"So, what have we got?" he asked, slightly irritated with himself and the crazy tug of attraction he felt for a woman who had no place in his future plans.

She leaned forward and grabbed the small stack of papers. "Stacy sent me these this morning. The first three are various floor plans, including an area for an orchestra and dance floor and the table arrangements." She handed them to him.

He tried to focus on the papers in his hands and not on how the brilliant sunshine streaming through the window made her light brown hair sparkle as if lit by a thousand fireflies.

She got up from her chair and moved to the back of his where she could lean over to see which plan he was looking at. "Do you want to hear my thoughts about each one?" she asked hesitantly.

"Absolutely. You're the expert at these kinds of things."

She leaned closer, so close that if he turned his head he'd be able to place his lips on the long length of her graceful neck. He narrowed his eyes and stared at the piece of paper on top.

"I don't like this one because she's got the orchestra and dance floor both on the same side, which makes the room look uneven and off-balance," she explained.

He cast her a quick sideways glance and noted the

long length of her sable eyelashes, the skin that looked bare and beautiful and like smooth porcelain. His fingers tingled as he remembered stroking that skin.

"This is the plan I think works much better," she said, leaning farther over him to take the papers from his hand and shuffle them around.

He stared back down again, wondering what in the hell was wrong with him. Tonight he had a date with Cecily, the woman who was the front-runner to be by his side for the rest of his life and yet all he could think about at the moment was the soft press of Debra's breasts against his back as she leaned over him, the sweet fresh scent that eddied in the air whenever she was near.

"See how the orchestra is on the left side, but the dance floor is in the center, right in front of the head table? The tables all seat eight and that means with a head table of eight and two hundred and fifty guests we'll need thirty-one tables."

"This looks fine to me," he replied and released a small sigh of relief as she straightened up, returned to her chair and gave him a little breathing room from her.

"I figured you, Cecily, your mother, your brother Sam, the governor and his wife, Thad and his guest would comprise the people at the head table," she said.

"Thad won't come." Trey thought of his youngest brother. "There's no point in even inviting him. He has his own life and has no interest in this." He fought back a touch of hurt as he thought of the distance between himself and Thad that had grown bigger and deeper with each year that passed.

"Then we'll put the mayor and his wife at the head

table," Debra replied. "They probably should be there anyway."

Trey nodded, still attempting to regain control of the swift desire that had momentarily taken ahold of him with her nearness.

"This is the invitation I thought would be nice." She handed him a black-and-white invitation, bold and slightly masculine. "If you approve it I've got the printers standing by and I can have them in the mail by tomorrow morning."

He looked at her in surprise. "Hand addressed?"

"Absolutely." The brilliant green of her eyes was filled with quiet confidence.

"But won't that take you half the night?"

She shrugged. "It takes however long it takes. They should have gone out a month ago. They definitely have to go out tomorrow."

He handed her back the invitation. "It's perfect. You can start the printers."

"And now we move on to the menu issue."

It took them almost an hour to go through the variety of menus Stacy had presented, along with the suggested price per plate.

"Don't pay any attention to the prices," Debra said. "There's no way we'll pay what the hotel is asking." This time there was a gleam of challenge in her eyes that he found very hot.

They spoke for another half an hour about food, finally settling on what he'd like to see served. He was almost disappointed when she told him that was all she had to discuss with him today and that she'd be back in touch with him the first of next week to talk about decor and silverware and dish choice.

They left the sitting room and as she disappeared into her office and closed the door, he poked his head into his mother's office, but she wasn't there.

Instead, her head intern, Haley, was filing folders in the file cabinet. "Hi, Trey," she said, a bright smile on her youthful face.

"Hey, where's the boss?" he asked.

"She mentioned a bit of a headache and went up to her room a little while ago. Is there something I can help you with?" Haley asked with the overeagerness of a young woman wanting to prove her worth.

"No, thanks, I think I'll just head up to check on her." With a wave of his hand he headed for the wooden spiral staircase in the entry that would take him to the bedrooms located on the second floor. He could have used the small elevator located just beneath the stairs, but he preferred the exercise of walking up.

When he reached the top of the stairs he continued down the long hallway, passing bedrooms and baths on either side and finally reaching his mother's doorway at the end of the hall. He knocked and heard her say, "Come in."

When he opened the door she was seated in one of the two plush white chairs that formed a sitting area complete with fireplace and French doors that led to an upper-deck patio. At the far end of the room her white-canopied bed was visible through double doors that could be closed at night.

She smiled in surprise. "I didn't expect it to be you. I thought it might be Myra—she's bringing me up some hot tea. Would you like me to ring her to bring you a cup, too?"

"No, thanks, I just had coffee with Debra." He sank

into the chair next to hers. "Are you doing okay? Haley said you had a headache."

She waved a hand as if to dismiss the idea. "Just a little one. I decided to escape the office and come up here to do a little thinking away from everyone else and any distractions."

"Have you come to a decision?"

She shook her head. "No, and I think that's what's giving me my headache. How did things go with you and Debra? Weren't you two getting together to talk about menus and such?"

"I just finished up with her. She'd definitely on top of things. We've now settled on the floor plan and a tentative menu for the evening." He paused a moment and then continued. "She's going to get the invitations out tomorrow and find an orchestra, but I really didn't come up here to talk about all that. I stopped last night and had a visit with Grandma."

Kate sat up a little taller in her chair. "How was she doing? I'm planning on visiting her this Sunday."

Trey frowned. "To be honest, I'm a little worried about her."

"Worried how?" Kate leaned forward and rubbed the center of her forehead as if he'd definitely made her head ache a little more.

"Maybe now isn't a good time to talk about it," Trey said sympathetically.

At that moment a knock sounded at the door and Myra entered with a tray holding a cup of tea and sugar and lemon wedges. She placed it on the dainty table between the two chairs. "Is there anything else you need?" she asked Kate first and then looked at Trey who shook his head.

"We're fine, Myra, thank you." She waited until Myra had left the room and then stirred a spoonful of sugar into the cup of green tea. She squeezed a lemon slice and placed the wedge on the side of the saucer. "Now, where were we?"

"I was saying that if you have a headache, then maybe we should have this conversation another time."

"We'll have it now," Kate replied and lifted her cup to her lips.

"Okay, she seemed fine when I first arrived. She'd eaten dinner in the dining room and had played bingo during the day, but Sassy told me when I arrived that she'd been a bit anxious throughout the evening. Initially the visit went fine, but when I mentioned to her my plans for the Senate and your possible plans to run for president, she went crazy."

Kate lowered her cup with a frown. "What do you mean by that? Went crazy how?"

"She starting pacing and screaming no and muttering about secrets and lies. I mean, she was so upset Sassy had to give her a sedative. I'm not even sure she knew who I was when she was having her tirade." Trey paused to draw a breath, to get the strength to tell his mother what really worried him. "I think maybe she's getting dementia."

Kate's forehead creased with pain, but Trey had a feeling the pain was less physical and more emotional. "She is eighty-six years old, Trey. Maybe her mind is starting to slip a bit."

"Yeah, but all that stuff about secrets and lies? What could she possibly be talking about?"

Kate took another sip of her tea and when she placed the cup back on the saucer she released a deep sigh.

"Trey, I know how fond you were of my father, but to be honest, he wasn't a very good husband and he definitely wasn't the greatest of fathers."

"What do you mean?" Trey couldn't imagine the man who had mentored him as being anything but a wonderful man. Walt had shown Trey infinite patience, had spent hours talking to him, leading him in learning the family business and encouraging Trey's natural competitiveness and ambition.

"You probably don't know that my mother miscarried three sons before she finally had me. My father never let her forget that she had been unable to give him what he wanted most—a son. He was verbally abusive both to my mother and to me. The one thing that seemed to transform him was your birth. He saw you as the son he'd never had. I imagine some details of my mother's tumultuous relationship with my father are coming to play in her mind."

Trey studied his mother, thinking about what she'd just said. Was it possible that Eunice's breakdown had merely been her replaying portions of her own past in her mind? She'd told him she remembered the days of old but had trouble remembering what had happened the day before.

"And you're sure there's nothing more to it?" he asked.

Kate averted her gaze from his and rubbed her forehead once again, as if attempting to ease a much bigger headache than she'd professed to have suffered earlier. "I'm sure I don't want to talk about it anymore. My mother is old and who knows what goes on in her mind anymore."

"Then I'll leave you to drink your tea in peace and

quiet," he replied. He got up from his chair and left her room.

If he'd been troubled before about how his grandmother had reacted to the news that he was running for senator and his mother might be seeking the presidency, the conversation with his mother certainly hadn't eased his concerns.

Was Eunice really suffering from the onset of dementia or working through issues she'd had with her husband? Or were there secrets and lies someplace in the family history that might be dangerous to both his own and his mother's political future?

Chapter 5

The ring of the phone awakened Debra. She jerked up, scattering envelopes not just across the kitchen table but also to the floor.

A quick glance at the kitchen clock let her know it was after eleven. The phone rang again and she jumped up from the table and frowned as she saw that the caller ID indicated a private number.

She grabbed the cordless phone from its base. "Hello?"

Nobody spoke, but Debra was certain somebody was on the line. "Hello?" she repeated. "Are you there?"

Silence, although the line remained open and the faint sound of somebody breathing sent a chill up her spine. "Is this some sort of juvenile prank phone call?" Debra asked and was rewarded by a click.

She hung up the phone, unsettled by the call but

grateful that the ring had awakened her. She still had envelopes to finish up addressing and apparently had accidentally fallen asleep in the middle of the process.

The hot cocoa she'd fixed earlier was now cold in the pot. She poured herself a cup and set it in the microwave to warm and then returned to the kitchen table where she'd been working.

As she sat back down at the table she remembered the dream she'd been having while she slept. It was more than a dream, it had been a memory of a conversation she'd had with her mother when Debra had been about ten years old.

Debra had wanted to know why she didn't have a daddy who lived with them. Why she was never, ever allowed to talk to her father or see him.

Debra's mother, Glenda, had tried to explain to Debra that her father was an important man and that he had another family he lived with and Debra would be a bad girl if she ever tried to contact her father because she would destroy his life.

As she grew older Debra had recognized that the truth of the matter was that her mother had been far more enchanted with the generous support checks that came every month than she had probably ever been with the wealthy married man she'd slept with that had resulted in Debra.

The support checks had allowed Glenda to not have to work, to continue to have a party-girl lifestyle that had ultimately killed her in a drunk driving accident the summer after Debra had graduated from college. Those support checks had stolen Debra's childhood as she'd tried to take care of a mother who was drunk most of the time.

The dream had created ancient memories of rejection, the wistful hopes of a little girl who had just wanted her daddy to want her back. The pang of wistfulness the dream had evoked still lingered in the depths of her heart.

And she was about to place a child of her own in the very same position.

No, it won't be the same at all, she told herself as she dropped down to her knees to retrieve the envelopes that had fallen to the floor when she'd jumped up to answer the phone.

She gathered the envelopes and then sat back down at the table and took a drink of her cocoa. Glenda hadn't been much of a mother, preferring her booze and men to spending much time with her lonely daughter.

Debra would be better than that. She would make sure her child knew the depth of her love. She'd love her son or daughter so madly, so deeply, that he or she wouldn't feel the absence of a father figure.

Besides, there was a chance that eventually Debra would meet a man and marry and then the baby would have a stepfather. She could still create a family unit.

The phone rang again. Debra frowned and once again got up from the table. And again the caller ID displayed a private number. "Hello," she snapped into the receiver.

Silence. Just like the call before.

"Stop calling, you jerk," Debra said and slammed down the phone. She unplugged it from the wall. If anyone important needed to get ahold of her, they'd use her cell phone. Her landline seldom rang and usually it was only sales calls. Anyone who knew her always called her on her cell.

Once again she sat at the table and rubbed her eyes wearily and then took another drink of her cocoa. She hadn't meant to fall asleep. She needed to get the last of the invitations stuffed and addressed before morning.

She knew that most people in Kate and Trey's positions hired professional calligraphers to do the hand writing, but early in her employment with Kate, Debra had taken classes so that she could develop the skills so that nobody would have to be hired. It was just one effort a young new employee had done to try to make herself as indispensable as possible.

It was well after midnight when she finally finished. Exhaustion weighed heavily upon her as she climbed the stairs to her bedroom.

The townhouse had a guest bedroom and bath and a master suite upstairs with its own large bathroom. Debra stumbled into the bathroom and quickly shucked her clothes.

It had been a ridiculously long day. After her meeting with Trey she'd contacted the printers who were standing by to get the invitations done. They'd been delivered to her at the estate right before she'd left to go home for the day.

She'd also made a doctor's appointment for the next day, deciding to get that off her mind instead of putting it off.

Too tired to think about a shower or bath, she pulled on her nightgown and headed for her king-size bed.

The last thing she did before tumbling into bed was unplug the cordless beside her, not wanting her sleep disrupted by any further obvious prank phone calls.

Despite the late night her alarm went off at six and although her desire was to linger beneath the sheets and the navy-and-peach-colored spread, she got up without hitting the snooze button.

After a long hot shower and getting dressed, she plodded down the stairs, feeling almost as exhausted as she'd been when she'd finally gone to bed.

She plugged her phone back in, rechecked the caller ID and was surprised to see that the blocked calls she'd received the night before didn't show up there. Neither did any other calls show up in the history.

Odd, she thought as she leaned against the counter and waited for her teakettle of water to boil. Maybe her machine was on its way to answering machine heaven. It was certainly old enough to die a natural death.

She'd decided to skip the coffee this morning, knowing that she should have as little caffeine as possible in her condition, and instead stick to a nice hot cup of tea and maybe a couple of crackers. Although she didn't feel nauseous yet, she remembered the uneasy roll of her stomach the day before when she'd thought about food first thing in the morning.

The neatly addressed invitations were ready to go in a large tote bag on the table. They would be picked up by a special mail carrier at ten that morning from Debra's office.

She went to the cabinet that held her favorite mug, a pink Support the Cause mug that was her go-to vessel for either hot tea or cocoa.

The mug wasn't in its usual place. She frowned at the conspicuous empty spot in the cabinet. Where was her mug? She felt a déjà vu from the morning before when she'd had the frantic hunt for Trey's guest list.

Although she hadn't used the mug for a couple of days, she walked over to the dishwasher that was full of clean dishes and checked for it there. There was no sign of it.

As the teakettle whistled, she moved it off the burner and then grabbed a teabag and another mug to make her tea.

Still, the mystery of the missing mug bothered her. On impulse before sitting down, she walked over to the refrigerator and checked the freezer, grateful that she didn't see the familiar pink cup nestled uncomfortably next to the frozen pizza.

She sat at the table and drank the hot tea and nibbled on a couple of saltines, wondering if she was slowly losing her mind. First the list yesterday and now the mug today. Maybe she hadn't even really gotten those phone calls last night. Maybe she'd only imagined them and that's why they didn't register on the telephone caller identification.

Despite the fact that it was Saturday, she had a doctor's appointment that afternoon at two. Maybe she'd ask her doctor if pregnancy could make a woman go stark raving mad.

She left her house by seven, deciding to go in a little early since her plans were to leave early for her appointment. She still felt tired. Thankfully tomorrow was Sunday and if she felt like it she could sleep until noon.

When she'd initially taken the job with Kate, she'd known it was a six-day-a-week job, that the hours were often unpredictable and could include evenings, but she hadn't cared. As far as she was concerned, working for Kate wasn't just a job, it was her passion.

As she pulled up to the side entrance of the gate she was relieved to see Secret Service Agent Jeff Benton on duty. He waved her on through with a cheerful smile.

At least this morning she didn't have to start her day with another creepy encounter with Jerry Cahill. She got out of her car and noticed that several of the agents stood in front of the carriage house. Even from the distance she recognized Robert D'Angelis, Daniel Henderson and Jerry Cahill. She figured it was a morning meeting of assignments and knew that on most Saturdays the senior Secret Service man, Robert, gave Kate a security update.

Myra was pulling a tray of golden biscuits out of the oven as Debra came into the house. "Mmm, those look yummy," she said as she greeted the cook.

"Ms. Cecily is joining Ms. Kate for brunch this morning," Myra explained.

"Oh, that's nice." Debra was surprised by the tiny flair of jealousy that winged through her. Of course Cecily and Kate would be growing close, fostering the beginning of a relationship that would probably be a lifelong one. By the time the election happened, Cecily would be Kate's daughter-in-law. Trey was smart enough to know that being married would make him a more enticing candidate.

"I've got biscuits done and I'm about to make that cheesy egg casserole that Ms. Kate loves. I've also prepared little fruit cups."

"Sounds delicious, I'm sure they'll enjoy it."

"Would you like a little plate of your own?" Myra asked.

"Thanks for the offer, but no, thank you. I already had some breakfast this morning," Debra replied.

As Myra busied herself cracking eggs into a large bowl, Debra carried her purse and the large tote of envelopes to her office. Once there she took off her coat and then sat at her desk, fighting against the unexpected jealousy that had momentarily filled her as she thought of Cecily McKenna.

She had no right to feel jealous. She had no right to wish things could be different, because it was just a waste of energy.

Instead of examining the unusual emotion, she shoved it aside and turned her computer on, knowing that she needed to get all her work done early this morning in order to head out around one for the doctor's appointment. She was lucky that her doctor saw patients on Saturday.

What she needed to get together for the morning were table dressings that were available for the dinner party that would now take place in just a little under two weeks' time. She wanted to have a list of tablecloth colors and dinnerware options for Trey on Monday. They also needed to discuss how the head table would be dressed and what kind of centerpieces he wanted for each of the tables.

Details, details. A successful event was always in the minutia of the details and Debra wanted this particular dinner party to be perfect, not just because she was in charge of it, but because it was for Trey.

The special mail courier arrived and Debra was grateful to hand him the tote of invitations, knowing that they would go out today and probably be received by invited guests by Monday or Tuesday at the latest. The RSVPs were due the following week. Debra was expecting very few regrets.

She and Stacy had exchanged half a dozen emails when a knock fell on her door and Cecily poked her head in. Cecily McKenna was a beautiful woman. Her hair was raven-black, cut short and chic, and her eyes were doe-brown. Her features were classically elegant, and when she smiled it gave her face a warmth that was instantly inviting.

"Hi, Debra. I just wanted to stop in before meeting with Kate and let you know how much I appreciate everything you're doing to help Trey."

"No problem, we're all working toward a common goal," Debra replied, hoping her smile hid her unease at the unusual visit.

"I wanted to give you my personal thank-you," Cecily replied. "This isn't just important to the family and staff and me, but I think it's important for all of the people of North Carolina. Trey is the right man for this job and the dinner party is the first step in assuring that he's considered a legitimate contender."

Cecily released a tinkling burst of laughter. "Listen to me babbling on. You know that about Trey already."

"He's definitely got my vote," Debra replied. As she saw the stylish black slacks, gold blouse and tasteful necklace and earrings that Cecily wore Debra felt downright dowdy with her hair in a messy knot at the back of her head and the olive-green skirt and blouse she'd bought two seasons before off a clearance rack.

At that moment Kate called to Cecily. "Oh, gotta go. It was nice seeing you again, Debra. I'm sure we'll be seeing a lot of each other in the future." With another one of her warm smiles, Cecily stepped back and closed Debra's door.

Debra released a deep sigh. Everything would be so much easier for her if she hated Cecily, if Cecily was snarky and egotistical instead of nice. Things would be so much easier if Debra truly believed that the beautiful woman was all wrong for Trey.

But Debra knew Cecily was the right woman to be at Trey's side. She was bright and articulate, she came from a stable wealthy family and had influential friends and she appeared to genuinely love people, just like Trey.

Yes, they would make a perfect power couple. It would only be so much easier if in the past three minutes Debra hadn't realized that she wasn't just crushing on Trey Winston...but that she was in love with him.

Trey got a phone call from Debra at noon. "We need to get together on Monday to finalize the rest of the details for the dinner party," she said. "Is that doable for you?"

"Actually, Monday isn't good for me," he replied. "I'm going to be tied up in meetings all day long. What about tomorrow? What's on your Sunday menu?"

He knew he'd surprised her by the long silence that followed the question. Hell, he'd surprised himself with the question. What was he thinking?

"Actually I was going to try a recipe for bourbon barbecue pork chops," she said tentatively.

"Sounds delicious. Could I maybe wrangle an invite from you and we could talk about the business end of things over dinner?" Somewhere in the back of his mind he wondered what in the hell he was doing. It was obvious he wasn't thinking rationally at all.

He already had dinner plans with Cecily for this evening, there was no reason for him to eat dinner with Debra tomorrow night to discuss work issues. And yet he didn't take back his words. He was surprised to realize he didn't want to.

"Around six?" she asked hesitantly.

"Works for me," he agreed.

When he hung up his phone he didn't want to consider what he looked forward to more: an elegant fine dining experience with the beautiful Cecily or a smoky bourbon barbeque dinner with his mother's personal secretary/assistant?

Maybe the pressure of having made up his mind to run for senator already had him cracking up. Maybe he was already seeking some form of escape from the crazy world he was about to enter, and somehow, someway, Debra felt like an escape.

The minute he hung up the phone Rhonda buzzed him to let him know that Chad Brothers, an experienced campaign manager, had arrived.

Dismissing thoughts of Debra, he rose as Chad walked into the office, extending his hand to the man who looked more like a professional wrestler than a savvy political expert.

"I hope you called this meeting for the reason I want it to be," Chad said after he shook Trey's hand and took a seat in the chair in front of his desk. He leaned forward, his bald head gleaming in the sunshine flowing in through the windows.

"You know I've been kicking around the idea of running for the Senate—" Trey began.

"I'd be happy to," Chad replied before Trey had gotten his entire sentence out of his mouth. "And you know I'm the man who can help get you where you want to go, but if we agree to work together, then we need to get busy right away."

"I've already set up a dinner party that's taking place a week from next Friday night." Trey shared the details of the dinner and dance event with the man he trusted to run a fair and honest campaign.

Chad was not only fair and honest, he was also tenacious and brilliant when it came to putting in place a political machine. He was also an old friend that had shown his loyalty to the Winston family for years.

The two men chatted for a little over two hours, talking about plans and tossing out ideas back and forth. Trey found the meeting invigorating and he was in a great mood when he left the office at six for dinner with Cecily at La Palace, a French restaurant where the food was excellent, but equally important was that most of the mover and shakers of Raleigh could be found there on a Friday or Saturday night.

He was meeting Cecily at the restaurant as she was coming from a charity event she'd attended that afternoon for an anti-domestic abuse initiative.

He was eager to tell her about his meeting with Chad. She'd be ecstatic to hear that he'd be working with a man who had the reputation of running an election both effortlessly and with winning results.

Trey had only been inside the restaurant a few minutes when Cecily arrived. As always when she entered a room, men's heads turned in her direction. Tonight she looked particularly beautiful in a red dress that was just tight enough to showcase her dynamite figure, but not so tight as to be tasteless.

"Darling," she said as she air-kissed near his cheek. "I hope you haven't been waiting for me long."

"Not long at all," he replied. "And our table is ready," he said as the host nodded at him.

Trey placed a hand in the small of her back as they were led to a table by the front windows of the restaurant. They were coveted tables in the world of power, places to sit and eat where you could see and be seen.

The host took their coats and the minute he departed a waitress appeared with menus and the wine listing. Trey ordered them each a glass of white wine and ordered their meals. As they waited for their food to arrive Trey told her about his meeting with Chad.

"So, it's really going to happen," she said, her brown eyes sparkling with not just excitement but that shine of an ambition that resonated deep inside him.

"It's really going to happen," he agreed. "The dinner-dance party will be the official kickoff of my campaign. I've got to write a rousing speech and then I'll officially declare my bid for Senate and hope that the money and the support follow."

"You know it will." Cecily clapped her hands together and then reached across the table and grasped one of his hands with hers. "I'm so excited for you, so excited for us." She released his hand and picked up her wineglass.

"You know it's going to be a crazy ride," he warned her. "It isn't just about parties and fun. It's going to be long days and longer nights, nasty rumors and traveling from city to city, never knowing when or where we'll see each other again."

He saw the flash of disappointment in her eyes, there only a moment and then gone. He knew she'd probably expected a proposal, but he just wasn't ready to take that step right now. He intended to marry only once in his life and he wanted to be absolutely certain when he proposed.

"You know I'm in this for the long run, Trey," she said softly.

"I know," he replied somberly. "I just need to get things moving, get plans together in my head. Once we get beyond the dinner party and a press conference to announce my official declaration, we'll see where things shake out."

"Of course. I understand," Cecily replied smoothly as if that quick look of disappointment that he'd seen in her eyes had only been a figment of his imagination. "And whenever you're not with me, I'll be working to help achieve our goals."

Their food was served and for the remainder of the meal Cecily talked about the charity auction she'd attended that afternoon and her plans to immediately begin to form a Women for Winston coalition.

As she talked and they ate, Trey's mind drifted, first to all the things that would need to be done to achieve his ultimate goals, and secondly to the dinner he would be having the next night at Debra's.

A business dinner, he reminded himself, a dinner that he'd invited himself to. He should be focused on the beautiful woman across from him, a woman who would add her ambition to his own to see that he reached his goals, followed his duties as his grandfather had wanted for him in public service.

Trey had always been so clear on where he was going and who would be at his side when he arrived there... until that night almost seven weeks ago. That night had somehow thrown him off his personal game, awakened yearnings inside him he hadn't known he possessed.

He mentally shook himself and focused on Cecily,

the woman who was right for him, a woman his grandfather and his mother would have handpicked to be at his side as he traversed through the murky waters of politics.

Chapter 6

That morning the pink mug had been front and center in the cabinet where Debra would have sworn it hadn't been the morning before. The mystery of the mug's reappearance had set a discordant tone for the beginning of the day.

Yesterday afternoon Dr. Gina Finnegan had confirmed what Debra already knew, that she was about six and a half weeks pregnant. After Dr. Finnegan had done the blood work and physical, discussed vitamins and handed Debra a pamphlet about pregnancy, Debra had asked about forgetfulness being a part of the condition.

"We've coined a term for it here in the clinic," Dr. Finnegan had said with a laugh. "Pregnesia…the condition of absentmindedness that comes with all the hormonal changes due to pregnancy. Don't worry, most of my patients tell me it goes away by the second trimester along with any morning sickness you might be suffering."

Dr. Finnegan had set her due date around the third week of August. A summer baby, Debra had thought. It would probably be a long, uncomfortable July but it would be worth it. By summer's end she'd have a precious bundle of joy to love.

As she sliced potatoes for a cheesy scalloped dish to go with the pork chops, she tried not to think about the evening ahead, an evening where she'd be sharing dinner, sharing private time and conversation with Trey.

It was a cold gray blustery day and she'd built a fire in the fireplace despite her concern that it might look too romantic. There was nothing she liked better than a roaring fire on a wintry day while she worked in the kitchen and she'd decided she didn't care what he thought, it was just a good day for a fire.

It was just before five and both the potatoes and the pork chops would take about an hour to cook. The table was already set for two with her good black-and-red dinnerware and she had a salad made and in the refrigerator.

The smoky bourbon barbecue sauce smelled like heaven and half of it was in a saucepan ready to be reheated and poured over the chops when they were finished cooking. The other half of the sauce was marinating the meat.

All she had to do was put the two baking dishes into the oven and then take a shower and dress for Trey's arrival at six. She had all the paperwork ready for him to look at to make the final decisions on the setup of the ballroom and that's what the meeting was all about.

It had been *his* idea to do it over dinner. *It was strictly a business dinner,* she reminded herself over and over again throughout the day.

Once they went over those last final details there would be no reason for her to meet with him again until possibly the night before the event.

She would be there the night of the dinner, not as a guest, but she'd arrive at the hotel at least an hour or so before things got started to make certain that everything had been handled properly, that the evening was set perfectly for Trey's special night.

Fifteen minutes later she stood beneath a warm spray of water, far too eager for the night to come. It was wrong of her to want to see Trey, to see him seated at her table across from her. It was wrong of her to want to hear his deep, smooth voice talking just to her. More than anything it was wrong on every level for her to want him again.

He belonged to Cecily. They were so right together. Debra might carry his baby, but nobody would ever know that. She would never screw up his dreams by telling him about her condition because she knew he was the kind of man who would have to do something about it and that something would destroy all of the goals he had for himself.

He was a Winston, bred for business and politics. He deserved to have winners surrounding him. He deserved to have a winner as a wife and that woman was Cecily. He definitely didn't need a mousy, efficient woman like Debra in his life.

By the time she dressed in a pair of jeans and a long-sleeved navy fleece shirt, she felt as if she had all of her emotions under control. They would enjoy a good meal, discuss business and then he would leave.

Once the dinner party at the Regent was finished, she would see him only rarely when he came to visit his mother. Even then it was possible they wouldn't run into each other often at all.

Her emotions remained cool and calm until six o'clock when her doorbell rang. She answered and with a slightly nervous smile invited him in. She took his coat and hung it in her foyer closet, noting that he had dressed casual, as well.

Trey Winston wore a suit like he'd been born in one, but he looked equally as hot in a pair of slightly worn, tight blue jeans and a navy-and-white-striped sweater that emphasized the broadness of his shoulders.

"Something smells delicious," he said as he followed her into the kitchen where she gestured him to a chair at the table.

"Let's hope it tastes as good as it smells," she replied. As with the last time he'd been sitting in her kitchen, she felt as if the walls closed in and got smaller with his very presence in the room. He emanated such energy, commanded all the space around him.

She was grateful she'd done most of the work ahead of time because she suddenly felt clumsy.

"Let me help," he said, and jumped out of his chair as she opened the oven door to take the baking dishes out of the oven.

"Okay, knock yourself out," she replied and handed him two pot holders. She'd nearly tripped just carrying the salad from the refrigerator to the table. "You can just set the pork and potatoes on top of the hot pads here." She pointed to the two awaiting pads on the counter.

She stepped back and watched as he maneuvered the two large dishes onto the counter next to the oven. He smelled so good and as he moved his sweater pulled tightly across his broad shoulders. She averted her gaze, not wanting to care about the way he looked or remember that scent that he'd worn when they'd hooked up on that fateful night.

He pulled the tin foil off the dishes and sighed in obvious delight. "This all looks amazing."

"Wait for it," she said as she pulled the saucepan of bubbling sauce from the stovetop and poured the last of it over the pork chops. "There's enough bourbon in here I'm not sure we'll need before-dinner drinks," she said jokingly. "We'll be half-snookered by the time we finish eating the sauce." She flushed as she remembered that half-snookered was what had put her in the condition she was in.

"Why don't we just bring our plates over here and dig in straight from the baking pans?" he suggested. "No need to be formal on my account."

"Okay," she agreed, grateful that she didn't have to attempt to take the two hot dishes to the center of the table. That was just a disaster waiting to happen.

"Other than cooking, did you have a busy day or were you able to rest up a little on your day off?" he asked as he grabbed the two red-and-black-patterned plates from the table and rejoined her by the stove.

"Actually, I managed to sleep a little later than usual and then I cleaned a bit. I even managed to work in a little reading so it was a fairly restful day."

She waited for him to snag one of the thick pork chops along with a large serving of the cheesy potatoes. "What about you? Busy day?" she asked.

"Not too bad at all. I feel like today was the calm

before the storm. Chad is already busy working to fill every minute of my schedule."

She smiled. "But everyone in town knows he turns out winners." Chad was a household name in the city of Raleigh among the political crowd.

Trey carried his plate back to the table while she served herself, eternally grateful that she didn't drop a chop on the floor or dribble cheese potatoes down the front of her.

Once they were both seated and Debra took out the salad and dinner rolls, they both dug in. "These pork chops are to die for," he exclaimed after his first bite.

She smiled with pleasure. "Thanks, I was hoping they would come out tasty."

"Do you generally invite people over to share in your Sunday culinary delights?"

"Barry used to occasionally join me but since we broke up, never. I cook for myself because I enjoy it and it's the one hobby I have time for one day a week."

"Between your work for my mom and now for me, we've been keeping you too busy."

"Not at all," she protested. "I love my work. I adore your mother and I can't imagine doing anything else. I'm doing what I always wanted to do." *Except for being a mom,* she thought. That would soon be added to the things she loved.

With the thought of motherhood, the sight of Trey so masculine and handsome across from her and with a flash of sudden visions of their hot and wild night to-gether all swirling around in her mind, she attempted to grab a roll from the center of the table and bring it to her plate, but nearly dropped it to the floor.

"That was a close one," he said with a grin.

She flushed. "Lately I seem to be suffering episodes of extreme clumsiness. So if I happen to flip a chunk of lettuce or a cherry tomato across the table at you or drop a roll in your lap, please don't take it personally."

"Will do," he said with a cheerful smile.

"So, are you all geared up to work with Chad? I've heard he's a rough taskmaster."

He laughed and shook his head ruefully. "I'm ready for whatever Chad brings. He has some great ideas and I'm excited to have him on my team."

All that was important to Debra was that she keep her secret. What was important was that Trey maintain his pristine reputation because for him the sky was the limit.

She had to keep her pregnancy as far away from Trey and his campaign as possible. She knew what his adversaries would do to him if they knew he'd slept with his mother's assistant and now that assistant was pregnant.

They would massacre him.

Dinner conversation remained light and pleasant and the meal was better than any Trey had ever enjoyed in a five-star restaurant.

Afterward he helped her clear the table and she suggested they drink her special mint hot cocoa in the living room where she had all the paperwork ready for him to make some final decisions about the ballroom decor.

As they sat side by side on the sofa with the paperwork on the coffee table in front of them, he realized he wasn't ready yet to talk business. What he wanted to talk about was her.

"You know, you've worked for my mother for years and yet I realized the other day that I know so little about you and about how you came to work for Mom. Did you grow up here? Are your parents still alive? I've never heard you mention anything about family."

She leaned back against the black sofa, the dark background making her hair look lighter and her large eyes more green than ever. "Yes, I was born and raised right here in Raleigh. My father is alive, although I've only spoken to him once in my entire life." Her eyes darkened slightly.

He leaned toward her, sensing pain trapped someplace deep inside her. "And why is that?"

Her beautiful eyes darkened even more and a crease danced across her brow. "My father is a highly successful businessman who is married and has two children who are just a couple of years older than me. My mother was his mistress for about six months before she got pregnant. He tried to pay her off to have an abortion, but I think my mother thought that I'd be worth more if I was alive, so she had me and she and my father came to an understanding."

"An understanding?" Trey fought his desire to move closer to her, to take one of her hands in his and offer her some sort of support. While her story was not completely uncommon, especially in the world of politics and successful, egomaniacal businessmen, that didn't make it any less ugly.

She gave a curt nod. "My father would financially support us as long as my mother and I never mentioned his name, never went public and ruined not only his image, but also his happy marriage. For me, my father was a once-a-month check in the mail that kept a roof over our heads and food on the table."

"That stinks," he said softly.

Her lush lips curved up slightly in a wry smile. "Yeah, it did. But what's equally as bad is that the support money allowed my mother the freedom to continue her party-girl lifestyle."

She paused to take a drink of her cocoa and eyed him somberly over the rim of the cup. "Having an alcoholic mother made me grow up pretty fast. She died the year I graduated from college in a drunk-driving accident. She was the drunk driver." She set her cup back down and Trey couldn't stand it any longer, he reached out and took one of her hands in his.

Cold and small, he thought as he held tight in an attempt to warm it. "I'm sorry, Debra. I'm sorry that's the life you were dealt."

She squeezed his hand and then pulled hers away. "They say what doesn't kill you makes you stronger, and in this case maybe it was true. I realized early on that I would not be following in my mother's footsteps. I studied hard and during my free time I watched on television whenever Congress was in session. That's when I first saw your mother, when she was serving out the last of your father's term. I fell in love with her politics, with her style and strength. I researched everything I could about her and when I was ready I went to my father and told him all I'd ever ask of him was for him to somehow arrange for an interview for me to intern for your mother."

She paused and drew a deep breath. It was the longest monologue Trey had ever heard from her. "And so he got you an interview with Mom," he said.

"No, he said he'd do what he could do, but I knew by his dismissive attitude that he wasn't going to do anything. So, I began a writing campaign to Kate. I wrote to her once a week, telling her why I'd be perfect working for her, what I would bring to the table as a valuable employee. I quoted bits and pieces of her speeches and told her why they had resonated with me." She smiled. "I think she finally decided to interview me to cut down on her mail. Anyway, she took me on and I've never looked back since then. I don't have any family but I feel like after all these years your mother has become my family."

Trey had a feeling there was a lot of ugliness in her early life that she'd left out of her story. Having an absent father and being raised by an alcoholic mother had to have been more than just a little difficult.

"So, the truth of my past is that I'm just the illegitimate daughter of an immoral businessman, who, rumor has it, is doing some shady business, and an alcoholic mother who wound up killing herself in an accident of her own doing," she finished. There was no bitterness in her voice. It was just a simple statement of facts.

"Those are just the circumstances of your birth and early life, but that doesn't begin to describe who you are now," Trey said, unable to hide his admiration for her. "I was lucky, I had a great role model in my mother, but my dad certainly tarnished the family name with his many affairs."

"The pitfalls of public service," she replied. "Sometimes I think most of the men in Washington have women on the side. A lot of them eventually get caught with their pants down, but a lot of them never get caught."

"I won't," he said firmly. "I mean I shouldn't have with you. I'm a one-woman man and when it comes time for me to marry, I won't cheat. I saw what my mother went through when the scandal about my father broke. I saw how his lies and cheating broke her heart. Besides, despite what happened between us, I believe in monogamy—one man, one woman and a family."

"Your mother rode out that scandal like the strong lady she is and went on to become vice president," Debra replied. She eyed him soberly. "And I believe you're cut from the same moral cloth as she is and that's why you'll be a great senator, a man who others will admire."

For several long seconds their gazes remained locked. Trey had never wanted a woman as badly as he did Debra at this moment and he was certain he saw a spark of desire in the depths of her eyes, as well.

She was the one who broke the gaze with an uncomfortable laugh. "We'd better get focused on the work. After all, that's why you're here, to pin down all the final details on your dinner event."

"Of course," he replied, still fighting the intense desire she had stirred inside him without even trying. Why didn't he feel this mind-numbing desire to touch, to taste, to make love to Cecily whenever he was with her? What was it about Debra that shot such heat through his veins and made his mouth hunger for hers?

He focused on the papers Debra shoved at him, papers showing tablecloths and dishes, silverware and glassware, but they were all a blur as he heard the snap and crackle of the fire in the fireplace, smelled that dizzying scent of Debra and imagined making love to her on the bright red throw rug in front of the warmth of the fire.

"Trey?"

He turned and stared at her and snapped out of his

momentary vision of her naked and gasping beneath him. "Yeah, I think we definitely want classic white tablecloths." He placed the paper with tablecloth colors to the side and stared at the dishware.

She leaned toward him, only making his concentration more difficult. The plates all seemed to blur together on the page, making it impossible for him to form a coherent decision.

"I think maybe the white plates with the black rims might be nice," she offered after a moment of silence from him. "They look bold and masculine. It wouldn't be a choice I'd usually make, but since this night is all about you, I think they'd be perfect."

"Done," he replied and moved on to the silverware page. What should have been easy decisions had become difficult with her seated so close and muddying his thoughts.

"These," he pointed to a set of plain silverware with tapered ends and moved on to the last page. "And these glasses." He set the paperwork down and reached for his cup, hoping a jolt of cocoa would wash all the inappropriate thoughts of her out of his mind.

"Good," she said with a wide smile as she gathered the paperwork together and set it on the end table next to her side of the sofa. "Now all we have left to talk about are the centerpieces and whether you want an official podium or not."

"Not," he replied immediately. "I figure my speech is only going to be about fifteen minutes long and I'll deliver it from my place at the head table."

"Okay, then I'll make sure we have a cordless microphone ready for you to use," she replied. "And the centerpieces?"

"I'll leave that to you, maybe something in black and white and crystal, but I don't want anything big and ornate. It's irritating to sit at a table and try to talk to somebody across some big plant or fancy centerpiece that is three feet high."

She laughed and again a burst of desire washed over him. She had a beautiful laugh, rich and full-bodied. He picked up his cup again, needing to keep his hands busy so they wouldn't reach out for her.

Other than that single moment when he thought he'd seen a spark of want in her eyes, she'd given him absolutely no indication that she'd be open to having anything to do with him other than on a business level.

He knew that he was here now only because he'd invited himself. Knowing her history with her mother, he was sure the last thing she'd want for herself was to become another quick hit for him on his way to his future.

And he didn't want that, either. She deserved better than that and it was completely out of character for him to even think of such a thing. It didn't fit with his vision for his future, it didn't speak to the kind of man he thought himself to be, the man he wanted to be.

It was bad enough that they'd already made a mistake, sleeping with her again would only compound the error. He turned his attention to the dancing flames in the fireplace.

"I've got five fireplaces in my house and have never burned a fire in any of them," he said.

"It's one of my guilty pleasures," she replied. "I order a cord of wood in the fall so that I can enjoy a fire whenever I want to through the winter, although I rarely burn one during the week. How's Cecily doing?" she asked, as if reading his thoughts and needing to mention the name of the woman he was certain to marry.

He turned his attention from the fire to her. "Cecily is fine. She's excited about what she jokingly calls my coming-out party. She knows I'm going to declare my intentions to run for the Senate on the night of the dinner and then hold a press conference to follow up. Which reminds me, I have one more guest to add to the list for that night."

Debra frowned. "It better be somebody important because I've almost finished a draft of the seating arrangements."

"It is somebody important. It's you. I want you to be there."

"Oh, don't worry, I'll be there well ahead of time to make sure that everything is in place for a successful night for everyone," she replied.

"That's not what I meant," he protested. "I mean I want you there as an invited guest."

"Oh, Trey, I don't think—"

"It's what I think that is important here," he interrupted her. "I want you there as my guest, Debra. It's important to me. You've done all the work, it's only right that you enjoy the fruits of your labor."

"I've enjoyed working on this project," she said, as if that was enough.

"That's nice, but it doesn't change the fact that I want you there in attendance through the entire thing. If you don't have anyone to bring as a guest, then we'll seat you next to Chad Brothers at one of the tables. He's already told me he's coming alone and you'll find him an entertaining companion who will regale you with stories of titillating political scandals and missteps that will make for fun entertainment."

He saw the hesitance in her eyes but pressed on. "Please, Debra. For me. Put on a fancy dress and your dancing shoes. I'll feel better giving my speech if I can look out and see your friendly face in the crowd."

"Okay, fine. I'll come." She said the words as if he'd placed a great burden on her, but her eyes glittered as if secretly pleased.

"Great. It's going to be a terrific night thanks to all your help. I know you got roped into this because of Mom, but I want to let you know how much I appreciate everything you've done to assure the success of the evening."

"It's been my pleasure," she replied, her cheeks dusting with a faint blush.

"And I imagine that once this night is done you'll just have time to barely catch your breath and Mom will announce."

One of Debra's light eyebrows shot upward. "Has she told you she's definitely going to run?"

"Not specifically, but she did mention that she's been invited to speak at a chamber of commerce Valentine's Day ball and I have a feeling that's when she'll make her big announcement."

"It's all so exciting," Debra said.

He nodded. "Exciting days for the Winston family. And now I should probably get out of your hair and let you enjoy what's left of your night off." He stood, oddly reluctant to go, and picked up his cup.

"Just leave that," she replied. "I'll take care of it."

He put his cup down and walked with her to the foyer where she pulled his coat from the closet. He shrugged it on. "Just think, in about two weeks' time you'll be the belle of the ball."

She laughed, that low and husky sound that stirred every sense he owned and surged desire through his veins. "I certainly doubt that, but I will enjoy being there."

"I think you underestimate yourself, Debra," he replied. She opened the door and he took one step out and then turned back to her, unable to halt the impulse he knew he'd later regret.

She gasped in surprise as he drew her into his arms and took possession of her mouth. She stiffened for just an instant and then melted against him, her mouth opening wider to invite him in.

She tasted just as he remembered, sweet and hot as their tongues met, moving together in an erotic dance of pleasure.

He wanted more from her, much more. He wasn't sure where his desire came from, but it burned through him like a white-hot fire. It was she who broke the kiss, stumbling back from him with wide eyes. She raised a hand and touched her lips and then dropped her hand to her side.

"You shouldn't have done that, Trey," she said, her voice trembling slightly and holding a faint touch of censure.

"Yeah, I know." Without saying another word, he pulled his coat collar up more tightly around his neck and stepped out into the cold night.

Chapter 7

It had been a bad week.

Actually, it had been one of the worst weeks of Debra's life.

She felt as if for the past seven days she'd existed in the Twilight Zone. Not only had she had problems forgetting the unexpected kiss that Trey had planted on her the week before, but for the past week she'd felt as if some mysterious imp had entered her life to create utter havoc.

And the worst part about it was that she knew that she was the imp and felt as if she were slowly losing her mind.

As she pulled up Monday morning at the Winston Estate and saw that Jerry Cahill was on duty, she didn't see how things could get any worse.

She stifled a deep sigh as he stopped her car and gestured for her to roll down her window and as usual he leaned into the car and smiled. "Hey, Debra. Did you have a good day off yesterday?" He smelled of a cloying cologne and the ever-present peppermint. The mixed scents twisted a faint nausea in the pit of her stomach.

"It was nice and quiet, just the way I like it." In truth she had slept most of the day away and hadn't even bothered with cooking anything except the frozen pizza that had been in her freezer for months.

"I have just one question to ask you on this fine morning," he said.

"And what's that?" Dread added to the slight nausea rolling around in her stomach. She wondered what he would do if she just hit the button to raise her window while his head was still stuck inside her car.

She nearly giggled as a vision of her driving around town with him hanging off her car like an additional rearview mirror filled her head.

"Why won't you go out with me?" he asked, a twinge of impatience in his tone.

"It's nothing personal, Jerry," she fibbed. "I'm just too busy to date."

He frowned. "You were dating that other guy a few months ago."

"His name is Barry and he's gone because I didn't have time to date." There was no way Debra wanted to tell him that she'd never go out with him because something about him set her teeth on edge and made her feel icky inside.

"You know I could show you a good time," Jerry said.

"I'm sure you could," she agreed. "But I'm not dating right now. I'm completely focused on my professional life. And now I've got work to do, so if you'd excuse me..."

He jerked away from the car as she pulled forward. She wondered if she should say something to Kate about his forwardness, but then dismissed the idea. Kate was already busy working on her speech for the Valentine's Day night celebration and she had enough on her mind without handling a Secret Service man who was more than a little annoying, but certainly hadn't been particularly out of line.

He just wanted to date her and she didn't want to date him. End of story and no need to make a big drama out of it.

She parked her car and took a moment before getting out. She'd only been up for an hour and a half and already she was exhausted.

Of course, it didn't help that three nights in the past week her sleep had been interrupted by hang-up phone calls in the middle of the night. It didn't help that items kept disappearing and reappearing in her home, making her not able to trust her own sanity.

She'd read everything available on the internet about pregnancy. She understood her exhaustion and the bouts of nausea when food was the last thing she wanted in the morning. She understood a little bit of absentmindedness was normal, but surely nothing to the extent of what she had been experiencing.

Pregnesia, indeed. What scared her more than anything was the possibility that for some reason she was having a nervous breakdown.

Maybe she was working too hard. Maybe she'd reached her limits in trying to pull off the party for Trey and process her pregnancy, and now her mind was playing tricks on her because of exhaustion and stress.

She hoped that wasn't the case because if Kate followed through on deciding to run for president, Debra's workload would triple. Hard work had never stressed her before. She loved what she did, so what was the problem?

She grabbed her purse from the seat next to her and shot a glance out of her rearview mirror to see Jerry still staring at her with a frown. Ignoring him, she left the car, grateful that nobody was in the kitchen when she stepped inside.

She didn't feel like interacting with anyone at the moment. She just wanted to get to her office and close the door. Once she was behind her desk she leaned back in her chair and closed her eyes, playing over the disturbing events of the past week.

Absentmindedness was forgetting to return a phone call or that you'd put a load of clothing in the washing machine. It was not remembering to pull something out of the freezer to defrost for dinner.

It wasn't a crystal paperweight that disappeared from the top of your desk and then reappeared where it belonged two days later. It wasn't the dry cleaner's calling to tell you that the suit you'd brought in for cleaning was ready for pickup when you had no memory of taking anything to the dry cleaner's.

She was beginning to wonder if she was not only growing a baby in her belly, but maybe some sort of terrible brain tumor in her head, as well. She was starting to question her own sanity and the timing couldn't be worse for her to be going crazy.

Unexpected tears burned at her eyes and she swiped

at them, feeling foolish and overemotional. Darned hormones. Maybe she needed to start some sort of a diary or journal detailing the things that were happening to her, the things that made her feel as if she were slowly losing her mind.

She could take the journal in to her doctor when she had her next appointment in three weeks and maybe Dr. Finnegan could make sense of the things that Debra seemed incapable of figuring out at the moment.

At least she had something to look forward to tonight. After work she was going shopping for a gown to wear to Trey's party. Because her place was normally behind the scenes, she didn't have an adequate gown to wear as a guest and she was actually looking forward to shopping, which she rarely did.

She checked in with Kate and then worked until just after noon when she heard a knock on her door. The door opened and Trey filled the space. "Can I come in for a minute?" he asked.

"Sure," she replied and fought the sudden rapid beat of her heart. She hadn't seen him since the night he'd had dinner at her place, the night he'd kissed her like he meant it. That darned kiss, this darned man, had haunted her for the entire week.

He plopped down in the chair across from her small desk. "I just thought I'd check in and make sure everything was on schedule for Friday night."

"Everything is in place. Stacy has been like a bulldog getting things done." Debra shuffled several papers on top of her desk and pulled out one that displayed the centerpieces she and Stacy had agreed upon.

Short crystal vases that would hold an array of white and red flowers with silver and black sticks of onyx and crystal poking upward, the centerpieces were sophisticated, chic and short enough not to impede conversation across the table.

"Looks good," he replied and handed her back the paper. He frowned. "But you don't look so well."

"Gee, thanks, you sure know how to flatter a girl," Debra replied dryly. Self-consciously she tucked an errant strand of hair, that had escaped the knot at the nape of her neck, behind her ear.

"No, I'm serious. You look tired. You have dark circles under your eyes and your features looked strained with exhaustion." The worry in his eyes made the threat of tears rise up the back of her throat and burn at her eyes.

She swallowed hard to staunch her emotion. *Darned hormones anyway,* she thought. "I'm fine. I just haven't been sleeping very well, that's all. I'll catch up this weekend, once the dinner party is over and done."

"This has been too much on you, dealing with both my party and mom's work," he said with a guilty tone. "I should have taken a bigger role in putting together the dinner party or I should have seen that I was overworking you and gotten you an assistant."

"Don't be silly," she replied. "Haley has been a big help with Kate's work. I'll be fine and you did take on a big role in this process. I just need to grab a couple of hours of extra sleep this week."

His obvious concern touched her and she told herself that she'd better either get more rest or start wearing more makeup. She suspected it was the pregnancy and the worry about her mental state that was draining her energy, not the work she'd put in on the party.

"Is there anything else I can do to help?" he asked,

his tone gentle and filled with a caring that wasn't appropriate between them.

"I promise I'm fine," she said firmly. "You need to focus on your own health. You're about to enter months of a marathon race to get yourself elected. You'll be traveling all over the state and beyond, getting out your vision of what you want to see for the state of North Carolina in the future."

She wanted to tell him to go worry about the woman he was going to marry, not about a woman who had spent one night with him when they'd both been a little bit drunk and a lot stupid.

"I'm not your concern, Trey. You have bigger and more important things to focus on," she said.

His eyes turned a deep midnight-blue as he held her gaze.

Suddenly she was afraid he might say something, might do something that both of them would regret. "Go on, get out of here," she said, the words coming out more harshly than she intended. "I have lots of work to do and you are holding me up."

She held his gaze, as if daring him to do anything other than get out of her office. He finally sighed, raked a hand through his thick brown hair and stood. "Then I guess the next time I see you will be on Friday night at the party."

She nodded and stared down at her desk, as if already distracted. "See you then," she replied airily.

When he'd left, she once again leaned back in her chair and drew a deep steadying breath. She knew he felt something for her. Passion definitely, a caring certainly, but they were unacceptable emotions from a man who had far bigger fish to fry.

Her love for him was equally unacceptable and would remain unrequited. She had no illusions. She wasn't a dreamer. Trey would do what was expected of him, as he always had done in the past.

He'd choose a wife that would help him accomplish his ambitions and once his campaign kicked into full gear it would be Cecily at his side.

He wouldn't be around the Winston Estate much after that, and that was fine with Debra. Even though she carried his baby, she had to forget him. She had to emotionally separate herself from him.

Somehow, someway, she had to figure out how to stop loving Trey Winston.

Trey felt ridiculously nervous as he pulled up in front of Cecily's house to pick her up for the night's event. His tuxedo felt too tight, although he knew that it fit him exactly right. The evening air seemed too hot as he got out of his car, but in truth it was in the low forties.

Tonight was what he'd waited for. Tonight was his night to shine. Out of the two hundred and fifty invitations they'd sent out they'd only received eight regrets. It would be a full house and he was nervous as hell now that his moment had finally arrived.

Cecily's butler, John, met him at the door. "Good evening, Mr. Winston. Ms. Cecily will be down momentarily," he said.

In all the months that Trey had been seeing Cecily, she'd never been ready when he arrived to pick her up for any occasion. He stood patiently, knowing they had plenty of time as he'd made sure to build in waiting-on-Cecily time when he'd made the arrangements to pick her up.

At that moment Cecily appeared at the top of the staircase. She stood for just a moment, as if allowing him to appreciate how beautiful she looked in her silver formfitting gown and with her short dark hair coiffed to perfection.

"You look nervous," she said as she started down the stairs.

He grinned at her. "Does it show that badly?"

"Only to somebody who knows you as well as I do." Her ruby lips smiled as she reached him.

Up close she was utter perfection. Diamond earrings adorned her ears, sparkling as brightly as her brown eyes, and her makeup appeared effortless and yet enhanced her elegant beauty. She reached up and straightened his black bow tie. "Don't be nervous. You're going to be dynamite."

John held out her wrap for the evening, a silver cape that matched her dress. Yes, Cecily was perfection in heels. She would spend the evening at his side saying all the right things to all the right people.

It would be a good night for a proposal, he thought as he ushered her out to his car in the driveway. Yes, he knew Cecily was ready for the ring, but he hadn't bought a ring yet, and he had a feeling she'd much rather have a proposal be all about her instead of at the tail end of a party that had been all about him.

On second thought, it was a bad night for a proposal. Cecily would expect roses and him on bended knee, at least a five-carat ring and a band playing their song. Did they have a song? He frowned and tried to think of what it might be.

Proposing to her was going to be a lot of work, but he couldn't think about that now. He had a party to throw, people to persuade and a speech to give that would hopefully make campaign donations fall into his hands.

Tonight was the beginning of a long process and he knew with certainty that he was up for the battle. His nerves calmed the minute they were in the car and headed to the Raleigh Regent Hotel.

He knew his speech by heart, he knew that Debra and Stacy would have everything on point. The night was going to be a huge success, in large part due to Debra.

He didn't want to think about her right now, either. Thoughts of Debra confused the hell out of him and he needed to be clearheaded. Besides, the woman he intended to marry sat just beside him.

"You're very quiet," Cecily said.

"Just going over everything in my head," he replied.

"It's all going to be fine. Debra and Stacy have done a great job putting things all together and you always perform well. You'll charm everyone in the room."

"From your lips…"

She laughed. "Trey, honestly, for a man who has accomplished everything that you've done, you manage to have a humble streak in you that is quite charming." She paused a moment. "Is Sam planning on attending?"

"No. He told me he'd rather eat dirt than go anywhere tonight." Trey frowned. "I just wish we could get him to talk to somebody, to help him process everything he's been through."

"What about Thaddeus?" she asked.

"He sent his regrets also, as I figured he would."

She was silent for another long moment. "Will either of them become a liability to you as you move forward?"

"Not as far as I'm concerned. Sam is a war hero and

Thad is a respected crime-scene investigator. The fact that neither of them are particularly enthralled with politics shouldn't be an issue for anyone to use against me."

He frowned as he thought of his grandmother. Secrets and lies. What had she meant? Did she know something that could destroy them all?

Each time in the past week he'd tried to talk about his concerns with his mother, she'd insisted he needed to forget about his conversation with his grandmother and get on with his business of winning an election.

"I can't believe I haven't heard your speech yet," Cecily said.

He flashed her a quick smile. "Nobody has heard it. I wanted it to be all mine, with no input from anyone. If I can't write a fifteen-minute speech without help to excite people to get behind me, then I have no business being in politics at all."

"You're definitely bullheaded enough to be in politics," she replied teasingly. "Is your mother giving any kind of a speech?"

"No, just me. She's showing her support by being at my side, but we don't want to confuse what tonight is about, and it's about the state Senate race, not the next presidential race."

"You're a wise man not to let her steal any of your thunder," Cecily said.

For some reason her words irritated him. The last thing his mother would ever do was attempt to overshadow him or "steal his thunder," and the fact that Cecily's brain worked that way showed the cold, calculating streak he knew she possessed, but didn't show often.

Of course, it was that calculating, unemotional streak that would make her such a good wife. He would be able to depend on her to remove any emotion from any issue he might have to address if he became the next senator.

The Raleigh Regent Hotel was at the top of a fairly steep hill and Trey was thankful the weather was co-operating, not making it difficult for people to attend this special night.

By the time they reached the entrance of the hotel, any irritation he felt toward his beautiful passenger had passed and he couldn't wait to get inside and see the final results of all of his and Debra's preparations.

They were half an hour early, as Debra had requested them to be and as he handed his keys to the valet, his heart thrummed with restrained excitement.

As they walked into the lobby, there was an air of anticipation that he breathed in eagerly as he led Cecily toward the ballroom.

The doors were closed and an attendant stood at attention, obviously there to keep people out before the appropriate time for the festivities to begin.

He greeted Trey with a respectful nod of his head. "Mr. Winston, Ms. Prentice said to let you in as soon as you arrived." He opened the door and Trey and Cecily stepped inside.

"Oh, Trey," Cecily said and grabbed his hand. "It's all so perfect."

Members of the orchestra were already there, pulling instruments from bags and setting up on a raised stage on one side of the room. Black-and-white-uniformed waitresses and waiters scurried around the room, checking tables that already looked beautiful.

The dance floor gleamed with polish and the centerpieces with their pop of red were perfect foils against the white tablecloths and with the black-and-white dishes.

The head table was also on a dais and Debra had made the decision for it to be a table of nine, placing him in the center with four people on his left and four on his right. His mother and Cecily would sit directly on either side of him. The two most important women in his life, he thought.

Stacy came up to greet them. Clad in a plain black dress, with little makeup on her face, it was obvious she was here to keep things running smoothly with the staff and work behind the scenes.

"Everything looks great," Trey said after he'd made the introductions between the event planner and Cecily.

"It does look nice, doesn't it?" Stacy replied with obvious pride. "Of course, you can thank your assistant, Debra, for bringing things together. She's a tough taskmaster and a killer at negotiations."

"Is she here yet?" Trey asked.

"She's been here for about a half an hour. She checked everything out and then went to the office to sign off on some paperwork. She should be back here any moment now."

Trey nodded, hating himself for wanting to see her when he had the beautiful Cecily right by his side.

Stacy checked her watch. "We have about twenty minutes before people will begin to arrive. Debra wanted the two of you to stand at the doors and personally receive each guest as they arrive. We'll have hosts that will then see people to their assigned tables and on the tables are nameplates to indicate where they are to sit."

She flashed them a bright smile. "It should go relatively smoothly as long as you keep the initial greetings at the door to just a handshake and a welcome."

"Got it," Trey replied, his heart once again thundering in anticipation for the evening to come.

In just a little while he would take the place that his grandfather had groomed him for, he would begin to fulfill dreams long ago destined for him.

This was just the beginning and the excitement, the energy that flowed through him was one of challenge and there was nothing Trey loved more than a good challenge.

At five minutes before the doors were to open, the orchestra began playing soft dinner music and Cecily grabbed him by the arm, her eyes lit with a calm determination. She would perform brilliantly tonight, charming friends and adversaries alike.

His mother entered through the doors. Clad in a blue gown that emphasized the bright color of her eyes, she looked beautiful.

"Good luck tonight," she said as she pulled him to her for a hug. "And Cecily, you look wonderful on my son's arm."

"Thank you, Kate. We're all here for the same reason and it's going to be a wonderfully successful night for Trey."

At that moment the door opened once again and Debra walked in. Trey felt as if he'd been sucker punched in the gut as he took in her dazzling appearance.

The emerald-green dress she wore skimmed her body in silk from her shoulders to the tips of her silver high-heeled shoes. The neckline dipped just low enough to show a flirty hint of the tops of her breasts.

It was the first time since that crazy night they'd shared that he'd seen her with her hair down, rather than in one of her usual messy buns. It fell in soft waves to her shoulders, looking shiny and touchable.

Mascara darkened her eyelashes and a coppery pink lipstick colored her lips. Her cheeks grew pink and he realized he was staring at her as if she were the only woman in the entire room.

He also realized that this had been part of the anticipation he'd felt upon arriving at the hotel, the desire to see her all dressed up. He knew she'd look great, but he hadn't expected such beauty.

Everyone said hello to everyone else and then it was time for Trey and Cecily to stand at the door and greet the guests who had begun to arrive.

As Debra faded back near a large potted plant in the corner of the room, Trey swore that before the night was over he'd hold her in his arms. It was only right that he dance with all the women who had arrived without male companions. He told himself it was the gentlemanly thing to do, but deep in his soul he knew it was a simple decision of desire that he didn't want to try to justify or analyze.

He just wanted to hold Debra.

Chapter 8

The night was going magnificently well. Trey had begun the festive evening with a short but rousing speech about his desire to make a difference in the state of North Carolina. He'd spoken with passion and enthusiasm that had resulted in the crowd being on their feet clapping and cheering when he'd finished.

Cecily and his mother had beamed and Debra felt the same pride and joy that she knew they must be feeling for him. Once the speech was given, dinner was served.

The servers moved like silent, efficient ghosts, filling glasses, placing plates with filet mignon and salmon without interrupting conversations.

Debra found Chad Brothers to be exactly the way Trey had described him, an entertaining dinner companion who had a big, bold laugh that escaped him often.

By the second course he'd declared himself madly

in love with her and wanted to hire her away from Kate to work for him. "Sorry, Chad," she said with a laugh. "No matter how many times you declare your undying love for me, my loyalty is with the Winston family."

"You cut me to my very soul," he declared with a mock look of dismay. "But I suppose I'll forgive you if you cut the rug with me when the dancing begins."

"I would be most delighted," Debra replied. "Though I have to warn you that I don't dance very well at all."

"Not a problem, I've got two left feet so we should be just fine together," he assured her with a charming smile.

Tonight she wasn't thinking about the fact that within another few weeks or so her pregnancy might be impossible to hide. She refused to dwell on the troubling events that had her believing herself half-crazy.

Tonight she wasn't anyone's assistant, she was simply a guest at a dinner party in a waterfall of green silk that made her feel sexy and carefree.

She'd refused wine at dinner, but felt intoxicated by the surroundings, the soft music and the fact that each time she glanced in Trey's direction she caught his gaze on her and her heart would beat a little bit faster.

He probably found it hard to believe that she could actually clean up so nicely, she thought. Still, she felt heady with knowing she had actually managed to turn a few male heads, that the event she'd worked so hard to put into place was going off without a single hiccup.

When the last dish had been removed from all the tables the band began to play a little louder and Trey and Cecily took to the dance floor.

"They make a nice couple, don't they?" Chad said.

Debra watched the couple gliding smoothly as if born

to dance together and couldn't help the wistful yearning that filled her. "Yes, they do," she replied.

"She'll make a perfect political wife," Chad continued. "She's bright and beautiful, but more importantly, she probably wants this more than Trey does. She knows the ins and outs of the game and she plays well with others when she needs to."

Cecily plays well with others and I run with scissors, Debra thought dryly. Chad couldn't know that with each compliment he gave Cecily, every time he mentioned what a perfect couple she and Trey made, he broke Debra's heart just a little bit.

Even though she knew that everything Chad said was right, that didn't mean that Debra couldn't wish that things could somehow be different.

But she knew her future, and there was no Trey in it anywhere. She would be a single parent raising a child alone unless she eventually met a good man she wanted to invite into her life, into her child's life.

Even without a man she would be fine and at the moment her love for Trey made it impossible for her to think of having any other man in her life.

There were moments when she ached with her love for Trey, but it was a love that would destroy him, destroy every plan he had for his future. It was a love she would have to lock deep in her heart forever.

By ten o'clock the cash bar was active and the dance floor was filled with couples enjoying the music. Small groups of people dotted various areas of the room, talking and laughing among themselves.

She saw Trey on the dance floor with his mother while Cecily danced with the mayor. Debra danced once with Chad and then gracefully declined two other men who approached her.

She was growing tired, and by eleven she'd found a spot at the edge of the room where a chair sat beneath a potted tree. She was content to hide out and just watch the rest of the evening unfold.

Another hour and it would all be over. The laughter, the music and the spirit of community that permeated the room would be finished and the tables would be broken down, chairs stored away to await the next big event.

After tonight there would be no more meetings with Trey. She wouldn't be surprised if this evening was followed fairly quickly by a public announcement of his and Cecily's engagement.

"Hiding out?"

The familiar deep voice shot a fire of warmth in the pit of her stomach. She turned to see Trey standing next to her. "Just watching the fun," she replied, and tried to ignore the slight flutter of her heartbeat.

"You look much too lovely tonight to be hiding out beneath a potted plant," he replied and held out a hand to her. "Come dance with me. I think they're playing our song." His eyes twinkled brightly.

"We don't have a song," she replied. The orchestra was playing a slow song and the last thing she wanted was to be held in his arms. The last thing she needed was to dance with him. Even as these thoughts flew through her head, she found her hand in his as he pulled her up from her chair.

She felt extremely self-conscious as he pulled her to the dance floor and into his arms. It was only then that she leaned closer to him. "I have two left feet, I can't dance," she whispered.

He smiled down at her. "You can dance with me." His words held such confidence that he made her believe if she was in his arms she could float across water.

His hand on her back was strong and masterful as they took off across the dance floor. "You look amazing tonight," he said and thankfully didn't mention that at that moment she stepped squarely on his toes.

"Thank you," she replied, hoping he couldn't hear the loud thunder of her heartbeat. She wanted to dip her head into the hollow of his throat, feel his body scandalously close against hers. "Your speech was pretty amazing, too. You had everyone in the room eating right out of the palm of your hand."

He laughed. "We'll see about that by the campaign donations that appear in the next few weeks. If nothing else it seems that everyone has had a wonderful time tonight. My only regret is that I haven't had a chance to dance with you before now."

She raised her head to gaze up at him and in his blue eyes she saw what she felt, desire and want and everything that shouldn't be in those blue depths.

She broke the eye contact and gazed over his shoulder. "I'm just glad it's finally over and I can get back to my regular work."

He stiffened slightly, as if perhaps hurt by her words. "I've enjoyed working with you," he finally said.

"And I've enjoyed working with you, too," she replied with forced lightness. "But now it's over and it's time for us each to get back to our own work, back to our own worlds."

Thankfully the music ended and she immediately dropped her hands from him and stepped away. "I'll just tell you good-night now," she said. "You'll be busy later telling your guests goodbye."

She turned and hurried away, leaving him on the dance floor as she returned to the chair beneath the potted plant. For just a moment as he'd held her in his arms and glided her across the floor, she'd felt as graceful as a ballerina, as beautiful as a fairy-tale princess.

It was a single moment in time that she would cherish for a very long time to come. By the time she was seated once again, Cecily was back at Trey's side, smiling up to him with a possessive confidence that Debra could only envy.

At midnight the orchestra stopped playing, indicating that the festivities were over. As people began to straggle out, Debra went in search of Stacy and found her in a small office just off the industrial kitchen.

The two women remained there, chatting about the evening and what a success it had been until everyone had left. "Come on, I'll walk you out," Stacy said.

As they reentered the ballroom Debra looked around. There was something almost sad about a ballroom with no people, an orchestra pit without music and a silky green dress going home all alone.

"You'll keep me and the hotel in mind for anything that comes up in the future?" Stacy asked as they reached the lobby.

"Absolutely," Debra replied without hesitation. "We worked very well together and I look forward to doing it again."

"Great." The two women said goodbye and Debra walked out into the cold night air.

She got into her car and waited for her heater to begin to blow hot air. Her exhaustion hit her like a ton of bricks. It had been a long night. It had been a long couple of weeks and now the letdown of it all being over made her realize just how tired she was.

Maybe she was crazy because she could have sworn Trey's gaze had been on her far too often throughout the night. And she must be crazy because she thought she'd seen desire in those beautiful blue eyes of his.

But that couldn't be right. She had to be misreading him. His life was mapped out before him by duty and responsibilities. He had a path to follow that didn't include her, but she couldn't get that spark in his eyes when he'd looked at her out of her head.

With the interior of her car finally warmed, she pulled out of the now-quiet parking lot and onto the outer road that would take her to the highway. Thankfully the weather had cooperated tonight, with a big full moon overhead and no clouds. A snow or ice storm would have been a potential disaster.

Eager to get home, she picked up speed as she went downhill, just wanting the comfort of her bed now. It had been a magical evening but she definitely felt as if she'd been turned into a pumpkin.

When she saw the red light gleaming in the night at the intersection coming up, she stepped on her brakes and the pedal slammed right to the floor.

With a sharp spike in her adrenaline that drove all tiredness from her body, she tried to pump the pedal, but there was no pump in it. It remained depressed to the floor as her car continued down the hill, picking up speed as it traveled.

The red light turned green just as she zoomed through

the intersection, now frantic as she realized she had no brakes at all and she was a long way from the bottom of the hill.

If she turned off the engine, then she would lose her ability to steer.

Frantic terror poured through her. She was going almost seventy miles an hour as she continued downward and there was no way to slow down. Several stoplights were between her and the bottom of the hill and although traffic was light, it wasn't nonexistent.

Panic crawled up the back of her throat and in desperation she yanked up the emergency brake, but nothing happened. In that instant, with another red light approaching, she realized the possibility that she might die. She was in a speeding bullet with no way to avoid some sort of impact.

As the red light came closer and her car careened down the hill, she gripped the wheel tightly and fought the impulse to close her eyes.

With the red light and the intersection imminent, she took one of her hands and laid on the horn, hoping to warn anyone else that might be coming that she was out of control. The horn blared, echoing inside her brain.

A hill was just ahead. If she could just make it to the hill then hopefully the car would slow down enough that she could maneuver it off the side of the road safely.

She was halfway through the intersection when she saw a car coming from the left. She turned her head, blinded by its headlights and braced. There was a squeal of brakes and then she felt the slam to the back left side of her car.

Instantly she went into a spin. The car swung around and around, dizzying her as she tried to control it, but the steering wheel careened wildly and with a gasp of resignation, she followed her impulse and squeezed her eyes closed.

The car came to an abrupt halt, crashing into something. As the airbag deployed, everything went black around her.

"The night couldn't have gone any better for us," Cecily said as Trey pulled into her driveway.

"It was a great time," he agreed. He parked his car in front of her door but didn't turn off the engine.

"You aren't coming in?" Cecily arched a perfect dark brow and looked at him with disappointment.

"I'm exhausted, Cecily. I think I'm going to head on home," he replied. It had been weeks since he'd had any intimacy with Cecily. In fact, he hadn't slept with her since he'd been with Debra. How could he make love to Cecily when he couldn't get the feel of Debra in his arms, the scent of her, out of his head?

"It's been weeks," Cecily said softly. "Are we okay?"

He forced a tired smile. "We're fine. I've just been so tied up with business and putting together tonight, I'm afraid my sexual drive has taken a temporary vacation."

She leaned over and placed a hand on his shoulder, her gaze soft with understanding. "Okay, I'll give you a pass for now. I know how hard you've been working to get things lined up between Adair Enterprises and starting the campaign. I just want to remind you that sex is a great stress reliever," she added flirtatiously.

He laughed, but wasn't a bit tempted. "I'll keep that in mind." He sobered as he looked at her. "I think what I need most from you right now is a little patience."

"I can give you that," she replied. "Just don't shut me out, Trey."

"That won't happen." He opened his door to get out and usher her to the front entrance, but she stopped him.

"Don't bother." She opened her car door and then leaned over to give him a kiss on his cheek. "No point in both of us getting out. You'll call me tomorrow?"

"You've got it," he replied.

He watched as she got out of the car and then headed to her front steps. Only when she was safely inside did he pull out of her circular driveway.

What was wrong with him? His sex drive had never taken any kind of a vacation before.

As he thought over the night he could think of two high points—the applause and hoots and hollers that had followed his speech and dancing with Debra.

Debra.

Why couldn't he get her out of his head? He'd hardly been able to take his eyes off her all night long. Surely it was just because it had been the first time he'd seen her in evening wear.

Dancing with Cecily was like dancing with a professional. She moved smoothly and gracefully, accustomed to partnering with him. Dancing with Cecily was effortless.

That hadn't been the case with Debra. She'd been stiff in his arms, difficult to guide in a natural rhythm and had stepped on his toes more than once, and yet he'd enjoyed that dance more than any one he'd had throughout the entire night.

His duty dictated that he chose a wife that would be best suited for his future plans and that woman was Cecily. But there was no question that Debra had somehow managed to crawl into his brain where she didn't belong.

But at the end of the dance they'd shared, she'd reminded him that their work together was over and it was time for both of them to get back to their separate lives.

Of course she was right. She was his mother's personal assistant and he hoped to become the next state senator. It was time to put her firmly out of his mind. He'd probably be far too busy in the next weeks and months to even think about her.

By the time he got home the adrenaline of the night had left him and he couldn't wait to get out of his tux and hit the hay. Tomorrow he would know how well he had been received tonight. Hoots and hollers were great, but donations to his campaign, endorsements from unions and fellow politicians would tell the true tale.

Included in the guest list had been several reporters to ensure that he got a little press time, all of them friends of Cecily's.

He knew Chad would already be busy filling his schedule with speaking engagements and burning up the phone lines to solicit support. Thankfully his right-hand man at Adair Enterprises was ready to step up when Trey wasn't there. He'd done everything humanly possible to prepare for what was ahead.

He'd just gotten his clothes off and was looking longingly at the king-size bed in his massive master suite when his cell phone rang.

Who would possibly be calling him so early in the morning? He grabbed his cell phone and saw his mother's number on the display.

"Are you calling to tell me how terrific I was tonight?" he asked teasingly upon answering.

"Actually, I'm calling to tell you there's been an accident," Kate's voice was brisk and filled with a concern that dropped Trey's stomach.

"Is it Grandma?" he asked.

"No, it's Debra. She had a car accident on the way home from the hotel and has been rushed by ambulance to Duke University Hospital."

Trey's heart hammered. "Is...is she badly hurt?" The words came out tortured by his tightening of the back of his throat.

"I don't have any details. Apparently Debra had me written down as her emergency contact. I got a call from the hospital but that's all they would tell me. I'm on my way there now."

"I'll meet you there," Trey replied. He hung up the phone and grabbed a pair of jeans and a shirt from his closet. His heart threatened to erupt from his chest with its frantic beating.

He was out the door and back in his car within ten minutes. An accident. She'd been in a car accident where an ambulance had carried her away. That meant it hadn't been a simple fender bender. It had been something far worse. How badly was she hurt? *Please, don't let her be hurt badly*, his heart pled.

At just a little after two o'clock in the morning he had little traffic to fight to get to the hospital. Had she fallen asleep at the wheel? He knew she'd appeared more tired than usual lately, but tonight she'd appeared well rested and glowing with good health.

He was relatively certain alcohol wasn't involved. He'd noticed that she'd only had club soda all night long and hadn't even drunk the wine that had been served with dinner.

So what could have happened and how badly was she hurt? By the time he entered the hospital parking area he had whipped himself into a near frenzy.

He followed the bright red signs that pointed him to the emergency area and found his mother already seated in one of the chairs. She rose at the sight of him, her features taut and radiating her own worry.

"I've let them know I'm here, but so far nobody has told me anything about her condition," Kate said. She had changed out of her evening gown and into a pair of black slacks and a blue-and-black-print blouse.

She looked tired and afraid, and seeing his mother's fear only increased Trey's. "How long have you been here?"

"Just a few minutes. They assured me that a doctor would be out as soon as possible to let me know what's going on and how she's doing."

Trey leaned back and released a deep sigh. Patience wasn't one of his strong suits. He wanted to rush through the double doors that separated him from wherever she was and demand immediate answers.

He needed to know that she wasn't clinging to life by a mere thread. But he also understood that he had to be patient and let the doctors perform whatever miracles needed to be accomplished to help Debra.

A police officer appeared just inside the door. He walked over to the receptionist station and then was allowed back through the doors to the emergency rooms.

Was he here about Debra? Had he been at the scene of the accident? Had anyone else been hurt? He felt as if he was going to explode with all the questions and frantic worry whirling around in his head.

It felt as if they'd been sitting there for hours when a

doctor finally came out to greet them. "Kate Winston?" he asked as Kate stood and nodded.

"I'm Dr. Abel Morsi and I've been tending to Debra."

"How is she?" Trey asked, unable to hide the worry in his voice.

"At the moment she's just starting to become conscious. From what I understand from the police who were at the scene, she blew through a red light, got hit on the rear end by another vehicle, spun out and hit a traffic pole head-on going at an excessive speed. Thankfully nobody else was hurt."

"And her injuries?" Kate asked, her voice trembling slightly.

Trey held his breath, his head pounding along with his heart in anxiety.

"She's a very lucky young woman," Dr. Morsi replied. "The worst of her injuries appears to be a concussion. She also has enough bumps and bruises that she isn't going to feel very well for the next few days. We're moving her to a regular room now. We'll keep her overnight for observation but she should be able to be released sometime tomorrow if all goes well and there are no complications."

Trey released the breath he'd been holding. "Can we see her?"

The doctor hesitated a moment and then nodded. "She's going to room two twenty-five. They should be getting her settled in there right now. My suggestion is that you peek in and let her know you're here and that she's in good hands, but don't stay too long."

Trey grabbed his mother's arm and pulled her toward the elevator bank, his mind tumbling inside out as he thought of what he'd just learned.

"She hit a pole at a high speed?" He looked at his mother with disbelief as they stepped into the elevator. "Debra isn't the type to speed or run a red light."

"Maybe she was so tired she didn't notice her speed," Kate replied. "Only she can tell us exactly what happened." They exited the elevator and followed the signs that would take them to her room.

They found it and entered, but stopped just inside as a tall nurse with long dark auburn hair was taking her vitals. She looked up at them, her eyes green like Debra's. She gave them a soft, caring smile. Her nametag identified her as Lucy Sinclair.

Debra lay on the bed with her eyes closed, a bruise already forming on her forehead and another on her cheek. She looked so pale, so lifeless. Trey could only imagine how many other bruises would appear over the next couple of days.

Lucy was just about to move away from her bedside when Debra's eyes snapped open and she gasped in obvious terror. Her hands rose out of the sheet and clawed the air.

Trey took a step forward, but his mother held him back as Lucy grabbed one of Debra's hands and leaned over her. "Debra, you need to relax. You're fine." Lucy's voice was soft and soothing.

"You're in the hospital," Lucy continued. "You've been in a car accident."

Debra's arms dropped and her hands covered her stomach. "A car accident? Oh, God, my baby," she whispered in what sounded like frantic desperation. "Is my baby okay?"

Baby? Trey felt as if all air had suddenly been sucked

out of the room, as if all the sound had completely disappeared. Debra was pregnant?

It was at that moment that Debra turned her head and saw him and his mother standing just inside the door. Her eyes widened and she began to weep.

Chapter 9

Debra sat on the edge of the hospital bed, waiting to sign release forms and for one of Kate's staff members to come and pick her up. The midafternoon sun shone through the nearby window, but there was a chill inside her that had refused to go away since the moment she'd opened her eyes that morning.

A policeman had been her first visitor of the day, needing details from her of what had happened to file a report. She'd told him about her brakes not working, but when he heard where she had been right before the accident, she had a feeling he believed she might have been drunk. The blood work the doctors had arranged would clear her on alcohol being a contributing factor in the accident.

But what had happened? Why had her brakes failed? She got her car maintenance done regularly. In fact, it had only been about two months since she'd brought her car in to have the oil changed and hoses checked. So what had happened?

The chill intensified as she remembered the speeding of her car, the knowledge that she was going to crash and the frantic blare of her horn to warn anyone in her path.

The horn blare still resounded deep inside her brain, along with the terror that had accompanied the sound.

She'd been assured that the baby was fine, but there wasn't a single part of her body that didn't hurt. She felt as if somebody had taken the traffic pole she'd hit and beaten her with it over and over again.

Kate had called at ten that morning to tell her that arrangements had been made for Debra to spend the next couple of days in a guest room at the Winston Estate. There had been no arguing with Kate and Debra had to admit that the idea of being pampered and waited on for a day or two held more than a little appeal.

What she didn't want to think about was that moment the night before when she'd asked the nurse Lucy Sinclair about the welfare of her baby and then had realized that Trey and Kate had also been in the room.

They'd heard what she'd asked. They both now knew she was pregnant. The thought added to the echoing blare of the car horn from the night before, intensifying the headache that had been with her since she'd awakened.

Trey's face had radiated such a stunned expression and then Debra had burst into tears and the nurse had chased both Trey and his mother out of her room.

The cat was definitely out of the bag, Debra thought as she plucked a thread from the sweater that Haley had brought to her an hour before. Kate had sent Haley to Debra's townhouse to gather up not only clothing for her to wear while leaving the hospital, but also items for the next couple of days of recuperation.

Although Debra knew Kate and several of her staff had a spare key to her townhouse, she assumed Haley had used the key that had been in her purse since her purse was now missing and the morning nurse on duty had told her somebody from the Winston family had come to retrieve it.

"Here we are." RN Tracy Ferrell swept into the room with a handful of papers in her hands. "Dismissal papers for your John Hancock, and your driver has arrived to take you home."

She was somehow unsurprised to see Trey step into the room, followed by another nurse with a wheelchair. Debra's hand trembled slightly as she signed the dismissal papers, knowing that she had some lying to do in a very short time.

"How are you feeling?" Trey asked once the papers had been signed.

"Like I've been beaten up by the biggest thug on the streets," she replied. She winced as she transferred herself from the bed into the wheelchair.

They spoke no more as they got on the elevator and then she and the nurse waited at the hospital's front entrance while Trey went outside to bring the car to the curb.

Aside from the aches and pains that seemed to exist in every area of her body, she now had to face Trey and lie to him about the baby she carried.

As she slid into the passenger seat she saw the fatigue that lined his face; she could only guess the stress and concern that had probably kept him tossing and turning all night long.

"I was so worried about you," he said as he waited for her to pull the seat belt around her. "When we got the call that you'd been in an accident, I was scared to death."

"It isn't yours," she said, wanting to put him out of his misery as soon as possible. "I was already pregnant on the night we slept together."

His features showed nothing as he pulled away from the curb. "You're sure about that?"

"Positive," she replied with all the conviction of a woman telling the truth.

"So the baby is Barry's?"

"The baby is mine," she replied firmly.

He shot her a quick glance and then focused back on the road. "I'm assuming it wasn't an immaculate conception," he replied dryly.

"As far as I'm concerned that's exactly what it was," she replied. "Barry definitely isn't father material. I have no intention of telling him or ever talking to him again. The baby is mine and I'll... We'll be just fine."

He was silent for a long moment. "I'd want to know. If a woman was pregnant with my child I'd definitely want to know."

His words were like arrows through her heart, but she couldn't allow her own personal wants and desires to screw up his whole future, and that's exactly what this baby would do to him. She couldn't tell him the truth. She had to maintain her lie because despite what he'd just said to her the consequences to him were just too high.

He'd want to know, but he also wanted to be a senator and there was no way that she could see that the two could fit together.

"Barry wouldn't care," she finally replied. "A woman having his baby wouldn't change the kind of man he is, and he's not a good candidate for fatherhood. I'd rather raise my baby alone."

They drove for a few minutes in silence and she was sure that she'd convinced him the baby wasn't any of his concern. "So what happened last night?" He broke the slightly uncomfortable silence. "The report we got was that you were speeding and blew through a red light."

An arctic breeze blew through her as she thought of the night before and the certainty that she was going to die. "I was speeding and blew through a couple of red lights because my brakes didn't work."

"What do you mean?"

She shrugged and winced as every muscle in her back and shoulders protested the movement. "I braked and the pedal hit the floor, but nothing happened. I even pulled up the emergency brake, but the car still didn't slow."

A shudder went through her. "I was going down that big hill in front of the hotel and I picked up speed, but I couldn't stop. I couldn't even slow down. I kept thinking if I could just make it to the bottom and then start going uphill the car would slow enough that I could maneuver it off the road, but I never got the chance. I think the police officer who spoke to me this morning thought I left the party drunk last night and that's what caused the accident, but I didn't have a drop of alcohol last night."

"We'll get it all sorted out," he said. "Right now I'm just glad you survived. I was scared about your well-being, Debra." His voice was smooth as a caress and she wondered if he charmed all the women he came into contact with. It was possible he wasn't even aware of how deeply he affected her when he spoke to her, when he gazed at her with those beautiful blue eyes of his.

She settled deeper into the seat, exhausted both by her thoughts and the emotions that were far too close to the surface.

Thankfully the rest of the ride was accomplished in silence and by the time he pulled up at the front door of the Winston Estate, she was ready for a pain pill and bed.

Maddie met her at the front door and took her directly to the elevator that would carry her upstairs to the bedrooms. "You poor dear," Maddie said as she wrapped a gentle arm around Debra's shoulder. "We'll just get you into bed and take good care of you until you're feeling better."

Emotion rushed up inside her and tears burned at her eyes. Debra had never had anyone in her life who had taken care of her and right now she was more than grateful to Kate for insisting that she come here for a couple of days.

"Ms. Kate thought you might feel better with a nice new nightgown. It's hanging in the bathroom, if you'd like to change and go back to bed for a nap."

"That sounds perfect," Debra replied wearily. From a small sack she'd been sent home with she took out the bottle of pain pills she'd had filled at the hospital pharmacy and slowly walked to the adjoining bathroom. She'd been assured by the doctor that the pills were a low dosage that could cause no harm to her baby. Besides, she only intended to take one or two and then she'd be fine without them.

The nightgown was long white cotton with green trim and had a matching robe. Debra was grateful it wasn't silk. She was a cotton girl when it came to her favorite sleepwear.

A glance in the mirror showed her what her earlier reflection had shown her in the hospital bathroom. She had no idea how she'd gotten the bruise across her forehead, but since the accident it had turned a violent purple. *Lovely,* she thought and turned away.

The rest of her injuries were bruised knees, a friction burn on her shoulder from the seat belt and just the overall soreness of muscles. With a moan, she got out of the clothes she'd worn home and pulled on the nightgown that Kate had provided for her. The soft cotton fell around her like a comforting cloud.

She used a crystal glass next to the sink to wash down two pain pills and then carried the glass and the pills back into the bedroom where Maddie awaited her.

"You need to rest now," Maddie said as she took both the pill bottle and the glass from her and set them on the nightstand. She then tucked the sheets around Debra like a mother hen securing her chick for the night. "Myra is making her famous chicken soup for you to have later."

"She shouldn't go to any trouble," Debra replied, already feeling a deep drowsiness sweeping through her. The trip home from the hospital and the conversation with Trey had exhausted her.

"Don't you worry about it. Don't you worry about anything. You just relax and if you need anything, Birdie is working up here today and she'll be checking in on you regularly. You call for her and she'll come running." With a final sympathetic smile, Maddie left the room.

"Birdie" was actually Roberta Vitter, a fifty-year-old woman who worked as one of the maids in the house. Her domain was the upstairs, dusting and cleaning the bedrooms and baths so they were always ready for any guest who might arrive.

Debra had been placed in the bedroom they all referred to as the blue room. The walls were a faint blue and the bedspread was a rich royal-blue. The lamp next to the bed had a blue-and-white flower pattern and the furniture was all dark cherry.

It was a beautiful room, but as Debra waited for sleep to take her all she could think about was that the blue of the room reflected the blue of Trey's eyes and the blueness of her emotions.

She'd done it. She'd managed to make Trey believe the baby wasn't his. She should be feeling enormous relief, as if a big weight had been lifted from her heart.

Instead her heart felt as if somehow in the past half an hour it had irrevocably broken.

Trey had left the Winston Estate the moment he'd delivered Debra there, knowing she would be in good hands between his mother and the staff. He'd driven to Adair Enterprises and holed up in his office.

A deep weariness made the sofa look inviting, but he knew a quick power nap wouldn't solve the problems. At the moment he wasn't even sure what the problems were, he only knew he was troubled on a number of levels.

He should be feeling triumphant. The morning paper

had carried a photo of him and Cecily with the headline of North Carolina's New Power Couple, and had gone on to quote part of his speech from the night before and his aspirations to serve as senator for the beautiful state that was his home.

However, the trauma of Debra's accident and then the bombshell news that she was pregnant had kept him awake most of the night. He'd alternated between praying that she would be okay and wondering if the baby she carried was his, and if it was, what he intended to do about it.

He hadn't come to any concrete conclusions other than he would support Debra and be an active participant in his baby's life. He wanted children and while he hadn't thought about a pregnancy being the consequence of the night he'd shared with Debra, he realized he wasn't so upset to believe that he might be the father of her baby.

He'd been oddly disappointed this morning when she'd told him the baby wasn't his and that small twinge of disappointment had only managed to confuse him. He wasn't sure he absolutely believed that the baby was Barry's and not his. Unfortunately there was nothing he could do about it as she'd told him so.

She'd created a confusion in his life since the night they'd spent together. Since that night he had desired her to the point of distraction, but he had to be stronger than his desire for her.

Duty. It had been pounded into his head by Walt and his mother since he was a child, duty to the family business and to a place in politics. As the eldest of the Winston children, his mother had encouraged him to be a good example to his younger brothers and Walt had told Trey his destiny was to do great things both for Adair Enterprises and for the country.

And duty required difficult decisions, personal choices that were smart. And Debra definitely wasn't a smart decision, especially now if she was in fact carrying another man's child.

What concerned him the most at the moment was her telling him that the car accident had been caused because her brakes had failed. It took him a single phone call to find out that her car had been towed to an impound lot.

The next call he made was to his brother Thad. Thad answered his cell phone on the second ring. "Winston."

"Thad, it's Trey."

"Ah, half of the new power couple in town," Thad said dryly. "I saw your photo in the paper. Calling to try to get my vote?"

"Actually, I'm calling you because I need a crime-scene investigator. Would you have some time this afternoon to stop by my office so we can have a discussion about something that has come up?"

"You've definitely captured my attention, brother," Thad replied. "Anything else you can tell me?"

"I'd rather we talk in person," Trey said.

"How about four o'clock?"

"Whatever works for you."

"Then let's make it four o'clock at your office. And if I'm not out of there by five you buy dinner from that bistro or whatever it is where you normally order those killer sandwiches."

Trey smiled. "It's a deal."

The two men hung up and Trey's smile fell. He leaned

back in his chair and steepled his fingers in thoughtful contemplation.

There was no way he believed that the car accident had happened in any way other than what Debra had told him. She had no reason to lie about the brakes not working and it was something that could easily be checked.

He didn't have the resources to fully investigate what had happened in Debra's car, but Thad did. And what good was it to have a law-enforcement official in the family if you didn't occasionally take advantage of the fact?

With the meeting set for four, Trey got to work on Adair Enterprises business. Saturdays were always the time he checked in with their satellite operations and with the end of the month approaching he had the usual financial busywork to do.

The afternoon flew by both with work and thoughts of Debra. He had been so frightened last night when he'd heard she'd been in a car accident and rushed to the hospital. She had appeared so fragile, so vulnerable this morning when he'd arrived to pick her up.

The bruise on her forehead told only part of the story of her injuries. He could tell with each movement of her feet, with every small action of her body that she ached from the near-death ordeal.

It could have ended in such tragedy. She could have been killed. She could have killed other innocent people. It was only by sheer luck she'd survived with only a concussion and various bumps and bruises.

He knew she was in good hands and was grateful that his mother had insisted Debra spend a few days recuperating at the estate. The thought of her all alone and hurting at her townhouse swelled a pain inside him.

He had a feeling from what little she'd shared of her past that she'd been alone for most of her life, that she'd never had anyone to depend on but herself.

Thank goodness she hadn't lost her baby. He could tell by the way she'd talked of her pregnancy that she was already invested in the baby she carried, was probably already making plans for the birth and life after.

It had been a little over two months since they'd slept together and if she already knew she was pregnant on that night, then she had to be approaching or already be in her second trimester.

It hadn't shown. As he thought of the vision she'd been the night before in that amazing spill of emerald green, there had been no hint of a baby bump or maybe he just hadn't noticed.

He kept busy until four when Rhonda announced the arrival of his brother. Thaddeus Winston was thirty-one years old and wore his light brown hair slightly shaggy. He was dressed in a pair of black slacks, a white shirt and a jacket that Trey knew hid his shoulder holster and gun. He was not just a crime-scene investigator, but had all the full capabilities and powers of a member of the Raleigh Police Department.

"How are you doing, brother?" Trey got up from behind his desk and shook Thad's hand. He then motioned him to the sitting area of the room. "On duty or would you like a drink?"

Thad sank down on the sofa. "Off duty and Scotch neat would be perfect," he said.

Trey went to the minibar at the back of the room and poured two glasses of Scotch. He handed one to

Thad and then sat in the chair opposite him. Thad took a sip of the drink, placed it on the coffee table in front of him and then leaned back, his hazel eyes filled with curiosity.

"What am I doing here? We don't exactly hang out on a regular basis."

"That was your choice," Trey replied. Thad had long ago turned his back on the family business and definitely didn't like anything that had to do with politics.

Thad nodded, accepting the fact. "You mentioned something on the phone about needing my skills as a crime-scene investigator. What's happened?"

Trey explained to his brother about the event the night before and Debra's car accident on the way home. As he spoke Thad listened attentively.

Trey knew his brother had a reputation for being an intelligent, valued asset to the police department. If anyone could get to the bottom of Debra's brake issue, it would be Thad and the strings he could pull with his police buddies.

"Alcohol not an issue?" Thad asked.

"Definitely not, and when her toxicology results come back they will prove that she wasn't drinking. She's pregnant, so she didn't even have wine with dinner."

"You know traffic issues and accidents really aren't my field," Thad said.

"But you know the people on the force that could launch an investigation into this. I just want to know if it was some sort of mechanical failure or something else."

Thad raised an eyebrow. "Something else? As in something nefarious?"

Trey shrugged. "It just seems odd that something like

that happened on the night I pretty much told everyone that I intend to run for senator."

Thad's frown deepened. "And what has Mom decided to do? Has she said anything about her own political future?"

"It's my personal opinion that she's going to run," Trey said truthfully. "Although officially she hasn't said anything yet, it's just a feeling I have."

Thad took another drink of his Scotch and then leaned back against the sofa. "To be honest with you, I hope she doesn't run. Politics has never done our family much good."

Trey knew his brother was thinking about their father. "Dad was a cheater first, a senator second," he said softly.

"It's not just that," Thad said, although Buck's cheating had taken a toll on their entire family. "It's also the idea of a national spotlight being on all of us again. It's bad enough that you've gone to the dark side," he said wryly.

"You know that Mom is going to do what she decides to do and she'll make her decision based on many factors, including the price we'll all have to pay if she decides to run for president."

"I know, but I also know that I intend to maintain some distance from all of it. You know I love you all, but I love my job and I don't want everyone else's ambition to screw around with my nice, quiet life."

"I understand that," Trey replied. "But as far as I'm concerned, running for public office isn't just a job for me, it's a calling."

"I get it, but I don't have to particularly like it. You

know you'll win the election. You always get what you go after."

Trey smiled. "I hope to win, but who knows what could happen between now and the day that people actually cast their votes." His smile faded as he thought of another subject. "Have you visited with Grandma Eunice lately?" he asked.

"Not lately enough," Thad admitted. "It's been a couple of weeks. Why? Is she sick?"

"I'm not sure what's going on with her," Trey replied and explained what had happened the last time he'd visited their grandmother. "Secrets and lies, that's all she kept saying before Sassy finally gave her a sedative. Do you know any deep dark secrets about our family that might come to the surface during a campaign?"

Thad shrugged. "Beats me. We all weathered the biggest secret in the family, that our father was a womanizer who didn't give a crap about his wife and kids. When Mom became vice president I'm sure there were people looking for secrets and lies to bring her down, but nothing ever came out."

Trey knew their father's betrayal was responsible for Thad deciding to remain a bachelor. He maintained he had no taste for family life given what they'd seen in their parents' marriage. Thad finished his drink and then stood. "I'll have to call in some markers but I'll get Debra's car from the impound lot to the police-station garage where a mechanic can take a close look at it."

"I really appreciate it, Thad."

His brother flashed him a smile. "You just appreciate the fact that I'm leaving here before five o'clock and you don't have to buy me dinner."

Trey laughed and walked his brother to the door. "If you want to hang around, I'll be glad to buy you dinner."

"Thanks, but I want to get right on this thing with Debra's car. Hopefully I'll have an answer for you by the end of the evening."

"That would be terrific," Trey replied.

Once Thad had left, Trey returned to his desk, his thoughts scattered like the seeds of a dandelion in a breeze. At least he'd set into motion obtaining some answers about what had happened to cause Debra's accident last night.

She might have blown a hose and the brake fluid had all drained out. Or the brakes might have failed for some other mechanical reason.

Trey admitted he knew a lot about business and politics, but he was fairly ignorant of the workings of a car. A trained mechanic at the police garage would know what to look for and in the meantime all Trey could do about that particular issue was wait.

He'd already spoken to Cecily first thing this morning, but he found himself wanting, needing to check in on the woman who was in the forefront of his mind.

He called the house and Maddie answered the phone. "Hi, Maddie. I just thought I'd call and check in on our patient."

"Do you want me to transfer the call to her room?"

"No, that's not necessary. I was just wondering how she's doing." He didn't want to bother her if she was sleeping, nor did he feel like it was a good idea to speak to her until he had something concrete to say. It wasn't enough that he just wanted to hear the sound of her voice.

"She's been sleeping most of the afternoon, poor

thing. Myra is getting ready to take her up some of her chicken soup and she'll probably go back to sleep after she eats. It's the best thing for her. Sleep heals, you know."

"I know," Trey said with a smile. "You've spent most of my early life telling me that."

"And that's because of you three boys you were always the most difficult to get to sleep each night," Maddie replied. "You always had a hard time winding down."

"I still do," he admitted. "Well, I just wanted to do a quick check in to see that Debra was resting comfortably," he replied.

"You know we're all taking good care of her."

Once he was finished with the conversation, he decided to call it a day and head home. Thad would contact him by cell phone and his work in the office was done for now.

It took him only twenty minutes on a Saturday late afternoon to get from the Adair Enterprises offices to his home just outside the Raleigh beltline.

The six-bedroom, eight-bathroom mansion wasn't as impressive as the Winston Estate, but it was more house than Trey had ever imagined for himself.

It had been his mother who had encouraged him to buy it when it had come on the market a year before. It still didn't feel like home and he knew what he was missing were the skills of a decorator and the company of a spouse.

Sooner or later he'd need to rectify that situation. There was no question that he would be a more appealing candidate with a wife by his side, especially given his father's reputation for being a cheating ladies' man.

As a single man, Trey knew the public might be more apt to tar him with the same brush. A wife was as important as a good campaign manager.

He frowned as he walked through the front door and threw his car keys on the nearby marble table in the foyer. When had he become the coldhearted soul who would make a decision as important as marriage simply because it was politically appealing?

The silence of the house thundered around him as he walked through the great room with its high ceilings and modern furnishings. There was just the minimum of furnishings, nothing decorative to add any warmth or personality.

He had a cleaning service who came in once a week, but other than that he had no house staff. Most days he ate all of his meals out so he didn't require a cook and he figured once the time was right his wife would staff the house with the help she thought was important and do the decorating that would make the house feel like a home.

He went into the kitchen and put on a pot of coffee and as he waited for it to percolate, he stood at the windows that overlooked a lush backyard and a large patio surrounding a swimming pool.

His head filled with a vision of a hot summer day, of the large brick barbecue pit spewing the smoky scent of cooking meat, of colorful umbrellas open against the shimmer of the sun and the taste of tart lemonade in his mouth.

He closed his eyes and allowed the vision to play out. There should be children in the pool, laughing and shouting as they splashed and swam from one end to the other... *His* children.

A sense of pride, of joy buoyed up in his chest as he thought of the children he would have, children who would carry on the Adair Winston legacy.

And in his vision he turned his head to smile at the woman who'd given him those children, the woman who was his wife. His eyes jerked open and he realized the woman he'd seen standing beside him in the vision wasn't Cecily at all, instead it was Debra.

Irritated with the capriciousness of his own mind, he poured himself a cup of coffee and went back into the great room where he sank into the accommodating comfort of his favorite chair.

Lust. That's all that it was, a lust that he felt for Debra that refused to go away. But he certainly wasn't willing to throw away all his hard work, all his aspirations, by following through on that particular emotion. That would make him like his father and that was completely unacceptable.

No matter what he felt toward Debra, she was the wrong woman for him. He had to follow his goals, his duty to pick the best woman possible to see him to his dreams, to the dreams his grandfather Walt had encouraged him to pursue.

Besides, it wasn't like he was in love with Debra. He liked her, he admired her, and he definitely desired her, but that wasn't love.

Debra inspired his lust, but Cecily inspired confidence and success and encouraged his ambition. If he used his brain there was really no choice. The lust would die a natural death, but his relationship with Cecily would only strengthen as they worked together for his success. At least that's what he needed to believe.

It was almost eight when his cell phone rang and he saw that it was Thad.

"Hey, bro," he said.

"Trey, Debra was telling the truth," Thad said. His voice held such a serious tone that Trey's heartbeat reacted, racing just a little bit faster.

"A malfunction of the brakes?" he asked.

"I'd say more like a case of attempted murder. The brake line was sliced clean through."

Chapter 10

Debra stared at Trey in stunned disbelief. He and his brother Thad had come into the bedroom just after breakfast to tell her the news that somebody had cut her brake lines. Somebody had obviously tried to kill her.

"But who? And why?" She was seated in a chair next to the bed, clad in her nightgown and robe. She raised a trembling hand to her head, where a pounding had begun. None of this made any sense. How could this be happening to her?

"That's what I want to talk about with you," Thad said. He remained standing with a small pad and pen in his hand as Trey eased down onto the foot of the bed. "We were hoping you might have some ideas for us."

She looked from Thad to Trey and then back again. "Ideas? Ideas about who would want to hurt me? Who might want to kill me? There's nothing for me to tell you. I can't imagine anyone doing something like this to me."

"You were lucky you weren't killed," Thad said, his hazel eyes hard and intent. "At the very least you could have been hurt badly."

"It has to be some sort of a mistake," Debra protested, her heart taking up the pounding rhythm of her head.

She felt as if she'd once again taken a plunge into the sea of insanity, like her items disappearing and then reappearing, like the guest list found in the freezer.

Somehow, someway, this was all part of her craziness because it felt impossible that Trey and Thad were here to tell her that somebody had intentionally tried to kill her by cutting her brake lines.

Maybe she should mention those other things to Thad? Perhaps she should tell him that she felt like somebody was trying to gaslight her, that she couldn't possibly be as absentminded as she'd been over the past couple of weeks.

She immediately dismissed the idea, certain that one thing had nothing to do with the other. Her absentmindedness didn't cut her brake lines and telling him about the other things might only manage to muddle the case.

"Have you had problems with anyone? Old boyfriends you've ticked off?" Thad asked. "People maybe you worked with on the event that you might have rubbed the wrong way?"

"No, nothing like that," she replied.

"There is an old boyfriend," Trey said and Thad looked at him and then gazed back at her expectantly.

"Barry. Barry Chambers. He owns Chambers Realty, but he wouldn't want to hurt me. We broke up weeks

ago. He's old history and in any case he's not the type
of man to do something like this."

"Who broke up with whom?" Thad asked.

"It was a mutual thing, but he broke up with me before I got a chance to kick him to the curb." Once again
she raised a hand to her forehead, where she knew her
bruise had already begun to take on the colors of green
and yellow. "The breakup was quite civilized, done in
a public place over dinner."

She steadfastly kept her gaze away from Trey, who
had ended that night with her in a hotel bed where they'd
had wild, passionate sex. "Trust me, Barry doesn't care
enough about me to try to kill me or hurt me in any
way," she added.

Thad frowned. "That brake line didn't just cut itself.
Somebody had to have intentionally crawled under your
car while you all were inside the hotel dining and dancing. That somebody had something sharp enough to cut
the brake line." He looked at his brother. "Could this
have anything to do with Mom or you?"

"I don't see how," Trey said slowly. "But I have no
clue what to think."

"I'm just a glorified secretary, for God's sake," she
exclaimed as horror washed over her. She dropped her
hand from her forehead to her lap. "Maybe somebody
got the wrong car?"

Trey's frown deepened. "What do you mean?"

"I drive a common type of car, nothing fancy or unusual. Probably half the staff at the hotel drives something similar to my car. This has to be about somebody
else. It can't be about me. I can't imagine anyone wanting to hurt me for any reason." She swallowed hard
against a rising hysteria.

Thad drew a hand through his hair. "If you think of somebody, no matter how crazy it sounds, you need to contact me." He reached into his coat pocket and withdrew a card. "Meanwhile, I'll check out the hotel and see if the answer lies with somebody there. In any case, it's possible somebody saw something that night that might help us find out who is responsible for this."

"Thank you, Thad," Debra said. He nodded and left the room. Trey remained seated at the foot of the bed, his gaze focused intently on her.

"How are you feeling?" he asked.

"A little shaken up, especially now that I've been told that somebody tried to kill me," she replied, her voice trembling slightly. "Honestly, Trey, I can't imagine anyone hating me enough to do something like this. I can't imagine anyone hating me at all."

"I can't either," he admitted with a soft tenderness that soothed every exposed nerve of her emotional chaos.

"Maybe it really was just a case of mistaken car identity and Thad will figure it all out. Maybe it has something to do with somebody who works at the hotel."

She shifted positions in the chair. "You know, there is one person who kind of creeps me out and keeps asking me out on dates. I turn him down all the time, but, I can't imagine him having anything to do with this."

Trey's eyes narrowed to blue slits. "And who is this person?"

She hesitated a moment and then replied. "Jerry Cahill."

One of Trey's eyebrows lifted in obvious surprise. "You mean Secret Service Jerry Cahill?"

She nodded and released an uncomfortable laugh.

"I'm sure it's nothing, that I'm just overreacting. It's just whenever he's on duty at the side entrance he always stops my car and wants to know why I don't want to go out with him."

"And what do you tell him?"

"That I don't have time to date and obviously I'll be having less time for personal relationships in the future." It was a backhanded reference to the fact that it wouldn't be too terribly long before she'd be juggling both her job and single parenthood.

"I'll check it out," Trey said, his voice filled with a simmering anger. "His job is to guard the house and my mother, not to make any of the staff feel uncomfortable."

"I don't want to get him into any trouble," Debra replied hurriedly. "He's never done anything to me except flirt, and one day I thought I saw him just standing outside my townhouse."

"Why didn't you mention this before?" Trey asked.

"Because I thought he was harmless. I mean, he's a Secret Service man. They go through all kinds of security and background tests to get their jobs. They can't be the bad guys."

Trey's jaw clenched. "Anyone can be a bad guy, Debra. Men have been known to do terrible things to women they feel have rejected them."

Wearied both physically and mentally, Debra sagged back in the chair. It all felt like too much… The accident that wasn't an accident, the crazy incidents of forgetfulness or whatever they were. She felt as if her brain was stuffed with too many strange things and she had somehow entered an alternate universe like the Twilight Zone.

Trey stood up and walked over to her. He held out his hand. "Come on, I think it's time for you to be back in bed. It's not even noon yet and you look exhausted."

"Attempted murder does that to a woman," she replied. She eyed his hand and hesitated a moment, almost afraid to touch him, afraid that a simple touch would force out all her emotions that she'd tried to keep in check.

She finally slipped her hand into his and he pulled her not just out of her chair, but into his arms. A sob caught in her throat as he held her against him, his hands lightly caressing up and down her back.

"It's going to be okay," he murmured, his breath a warm promise against her hair. "We aren't going to let anything happen to you."

She couldn't help it, she began to cry. All of the uncertainty of the past few weeks coupled with the accident and now the knowledge that somebody had deliberately tampered with her car mingled together in a roar of emotions she could no longer contain.

She hadn't realized until this moment how badly she'd needed to be held, how much she'd wanted strong arms wrapped around her, assuring her that she was okay.

She leaned into him, drawing in the comforting heat of his body, breathing in the familiar scent of his cologne. His heart beat against her own, a steady rhythm that slowly calmed the racing of her own heartbeat.

Her tears finally ebbed, leaving her spent and clinging with her arms around his neck, her face turned into the hollow of his throat. She wanted to kiss him, to tip her head up and feel his lips pressed against hers.

She felt loved. In his arms she felt loved as she'd

never felt in her entire life. She wanted to stay in this room, in this moment forever.

And for just a crazy instant she wanted to tell him that she was madly in love with him, she wanted to confess that the baby she carried was his.

Thankfully at that moment he released her and she got back into bed, her love for him shoved down and buried deep inside her as she pulled the sheet up to cover herself.

It was unusually warm for the last few days of January as Trey drove to his mother's mansion to take Debra home to her townhouse Wednesday morning.

He didn't want her to leave the safety of his mother's place, but Debra had insisted that she'd overstayed her time at the estate and needed to go home and get settled back into her usual routine.

She'd told him she was also ready to get back to work. Haley had stepped in to take her place while she'd been recuperating, but now it was time for Haley to step aside and let Debra resume her position.

So far nothing had come out of the investigation Thad was conducting in regard to the cut brake line. Nobody at the hotel had seen anything unusual the night of the dinner and Barry had an alibi for the evening.

Thad and Trey had spoken to Jerry Cahill together the day before. Trey had found the Secret Service man slightly arrogant and completely indignant that anyone would believe he would do anything to harm a member of the family or the staff.

He confessed that he liked to tease Debra, but Trey told him in no uncertain terms that his "teasing" wasn't welcomed and he should not bother Debra or anyone else on staff again. It was not only unbecoming, but it was unprofessional, as well.

Jerry had agreed, but Trey had seen a flash of anger in the man's eyes that he didn't like. Jerry didn't know it, but he was under investigation by his bosses to make sure he wasn't some loon who had managed to slide into the system where he didn't belong.

Trey pulled up to the front door of the mansion and got out, enjoying the fact that no coat was needed and the forecast for the next week mentioned highs in the upper sixties.

Thankfully the long-term forecast was for Raleigh to enjoy an unusually mild week or two. That was fine with Trey, he'd prefer not to battle the cold and ice or snow, although he doubted that winter was finished with them yet.

Spring was his favorite season, the time for rebirth and green grass and lush flower gardens. He reminded himself that he needed to hire a gardener so that he would have some flower beds when spring arrived.

Maddie let him into the house and told him that Debra was waiting for him in the sitting room. He walked in and couldn't help the way his heart lifted at the sight of her.

Her forehead bruise was still visible, although fading with each day that passed. She was seated on the sofa, clad in a pair of jeans and a pink sweater.

A medium-size pink duffel bag and her purse sat on the floor next to her. Her eyes lit up as she saw him and he didn't know if she was happy to see him or just happy to see her ride home.

"I still think you going home right now is a bad idea,"

he said as he sank down in the chair next to the sofa. "I'd prefer you stay here for a while longer."

"I'm feeling fine and I need to go home."

"If I were your boss, I'd insist that you stay here," he countered.

"Thankfully you aren't the boss of me," she replied, "and I've taken advantage of your mother and the staff's kindness long enough. It's time for me to get back to my own home and my own routine. Tomorrow I intend to be back at my desk here as usual."

She lifted her chin in a show of defiance, as if she expected Trey to give her more of a hard time. He knew that look of steely strength that arrowed from her eyes. He'd seen it when she'd been negotiating with the hotel. Sweet little Debra had a will of iron when necessary.

"Besides," she continued, "if I don't get back to work, Kate will hire Haley to take over my position permanently."

Trey laughed at the very idea. "Yeah, like that's ever going to happen. You know my mother is totally devoted to you. You don't have to worry about your job."

"All the more reason that I need to get back to work for her. I'm feeling much better, my bruises are going away and it's time to get back to my own life."

"That's what scares me," he replied. "We still don't know who was responsible for your accident."

"And we may never know, but that doesn't mean I have to suddenly stop my life." She stood and grabbed both the duffel and her purse. "My car was targeted, not me, and I still believe that somehow it was a crazy mistake and some creep cut the lines on the wrong car. Besides, why not target my house, smother me in my sleep or shoot me when I'm driving to work?"

She shook her head. "This was done in a public place. For all we know it was done by a couple of whacked-out teenagers looking to cause trouble."

Trey stood and took the duffel bag from her. He knew she was right in that she couldn't just stop living because of what had happened, but he still didn't like the idea of her being all alone in her townhouse when they couldn't be sure that she wasn't the target of the brake failure. He definitely didn't believe that it was the work of teenagers looking for a thrill.

"Do you really think Haley wants your job?" Trey asked when they were in his car and headed to her townhouse.

"Of course she would," Debra replied without hesitation. "She's bright and ambitious, but there's no way I think her desire to have my job led to her trying to kill me, if that's where you're going with this conversation. I still refuse to believe that anyone tried to kill me."

Trey hoped she was right, but just to be on the safe side he made a mental note to tell Thad to check out Haley and any of the other interns that worked for his mother.

"What are you going to do about a car?" Trey asked as he pulled up to the curb in front of her home. He knew her vehicle would be in police impound for quite some time.

"The insurance company has totaled mine out, so I'll be getting a check in a week or two. I'm going to call for a rental later this afternoon and then maybe when the insurance pays out I'll go car hunting. It was time for a new car anyway."

They got out of the car and as he grabbed the luggage, she dug her keys out of her purse. When they reached the front door she unlocked it and pushed it open, then turned to him and took the duffel bag from him.

"Thanks for the ride home, Trey. I really appreciate it."

"Not so fast," he said and slid inside the foyer. "I want to do a check of the locks on your doors to make sure you're secure when you're home."

While he did want to check her doors and windows, the honest truth was he wasn't ready to leave her company yet. He walked through her living room and into the kitchen where he knew she had a back door.

He was intensely aware of her trailing behind him, having dropped the duffel bag and her purse in the living room. "I'm sure my locks on my doors are more than adequate and, besides, nobody has ever tried to break into my house," she said.

He checked the dead bolt and lock on her back door and then turned to look at her. "While I'm here I wouldn't mind a cup of tea or maybe some of that special mint hot cocoa of yours."

Her beautiful eyes narrowed. "Why didn't you just ask me to invite you in for something to drink instead of making up some stupid pretense of looking at my locks?"

"I did want to look at your locks," he protested and then laughed as she gazed at him in disbelief. "Okay, you busted me. I just wanted to sit with you for a little while."

"Why?"

He looked at her in surprise. The simple question wasn't easily answered, at least not completely honestly. He wanted to tell her that he loved watching her, that she was charmingly uncomplicated and he found her lack of artifice refreshing. He wanted to tell her that he'd much rather spend time with her than the woman he intended to marry, but he didn't.

"I enjoy your company," he finally replied. "And I'm formally declaring my intentions to run at a press conference next week and I have a feeling the next couple of days are the last I'm going to see of any real peace and quiet."

She pointed to a chair at the table. "I'll make the hot cocoa."

She worked with a graceful efficiency that hadn't been present on the night he'd danced with her. He smiled to himself as he thought of how often her feet had knocked into his in the short period he'd held her in his arms. Okay, so she wasn't going to win a dance contest anytime soon, but he didn't intend to enter one anytime soon, either.

To be as far along in her pregnancy as she claimed she was, she didn't show at all. "Are you eating enough?" he asked.

She turned from the counter to look at him in surprise. "I'm eating fine…. Why?"

His gaze drifted down to her abdomen. "You don't have any baby bump."

A blush colored her cheeks and one hand fell to her stomach. "The baby is just fine. I'm eating fine and if you saw me without my clothes you'd be able to see the baby bump." She turned back to the cabinets to get some cups.

It was the worst thing she could have said to him, because a vision of her naked took hold of his brain and refused to shake loose. Even with a huge pregnant belly, she'd still be beautiful naked. He clenched his fists, his short nails digging into his palms. He couldn't think about her like that. He had no right to entertain such thoughts.

By the time she carried two cups of cocoa to the table and sat down across from him, he'd managed to banish the evocative vision from his brain.

"How are you going to manage it all?" he asked. "I mean being a single working mother?"

She took a sip of her drink and then lowered her cup. "The way hundreds of other women do it every day of their lives. I'm blessed that I make enough money that I'll be able to hire a good nanny to take care of the baby while I'm at work. I'm equally blessed that I work for your mother, who for all intents and purposes was a single mother herself while your father was a senator."

Trey had a difficult time arguing with her about that. When he was young, weeks would go by when his father wasn't in the house. Of course none of them knew about the mistresses that were a part of his life.

"Do you know whether you're having a boy or a girl? Isn't this about the time they can tell the sex of the baby?" It was ridiculous, the little rivulet of jealousy that tingled through him as he thought of her carrying another man's child.

"I don't want to know the sex ahead of time," she replied. She took another sip and then stared down into her cup, as if the topic of conversation was making her uncomfortable. But, when she looked back at him it was with a soft smile. "All I care about is having a healthy baby."

"If you don't know the sex of the baby then how will you know what color to paint a nursery?"

"There are more colors than pink and blue," she replied. "I'm planning to paint the guest bedroom a bright yellow with lots of bold primary color accents. I've heard using bright colors stimulates a baby and helps them learn."

Emotions rose up inside him as he gazed into her eyes, where the love for her unborn child radiated. "You're going to make a fantastic mother."

"I know I will," she replied with an easy confidence. "I know what it's like to grow up feeling unloved and unwanted. I know all the things I didn't have as a child and this baby is going to be the most important, beloved thing in my world. I intend to spend each and every moment of the day and night letting him or her know that."

He remembered the vision he'd had of children laughing in a swimming pool, the joy that had filled him as he'd experienced the love of his imaginary family.

He wanted to be part of Debra's family. He wanted to be as important to her as the child she carried. It was the very last thing in the world he should want. He took another drink, finding it suddenly bitter.

Pushing back from the table, he stood, needing to get out of there, needing to get away from her. "I should go and let you get settled back in here," he said.

An oppressive force pushed against his chest and he knew it was the ever-present desire he felt whenever she was near him. It wasn't just a desire to hold her in his arms. He wanted to hear the ring of her laughter, watch her as she cooked. He wanted to know her opinions about everything from the weather to religion, from baby diapers to politics.

She was dangerous to him. He knew it in his heart,

in his very soul. She was dangerous to everything he'd dreamed about, everything he wanted in his future.

He left the kitchen and didn't realize she'd followed him to the front door until she called his name. He turned back to face her.

"Did I say something wrong?" she asked, obviously confused by his abruptness.

"No...nothing like that."

"Then what? I can tell something is wrong," she said, her green eyes so soft, so inviting.

Something snapped inside him. He pushed her up against the foyer wall as his mouth captured hers. He'd lost his mind, given in to the raw driving need inside him. There was no right or wrong, just his desire for her.

She gasped in surprise and he plunged his tongue into her mouth as she wrapped her arms around his neck and pulled him close...closer.

His hands slid up under the back of her sweater, reveling in the feel of her silky bare skin. She moaned in pleasure as his fingers worked to unclasp her bra.

Wild. He was wild with the taste, the scent of her. Reason had left his mind as he moved his hands around to cup her bare breasts.

Trapped between the wall and him, Debra made no attempt to escape, but rather turned her face to break their kiss and then pulled her sweater over her head. It dropped to the floor, along with her bra and once again their lips met in a fiery kiss that filled the void in his soul, that stoked the flames of his passion for her even higher.

He wanted her naked and gasping beneath him. He wanted a repeat of the night they'd shared. He'd wanted it since he'd put her in the cab the morning after.

"I want you, Debra," he finally managed to gasp. "I've wanted you again ever since we spent that night together."

It was as if the sound of his voice shattered her, splintered the moment and harsh reality intruded. She shoved against his chest and quickly leaned down to grab her sweater to cover her nakedness.

"This is madness," she whispered, her eyes glowing an overbright green. "I won't lie, Trey. I want you, too. But we both know we can't do this. It would be a mistake for both of us."

He suddenly felt small and selfish. He backed away from her. "Of course you're right." He released a deep sigh, but he wasn't sure if it was a sigh of regret because she'd stopped him or one of relief because she had.

"I know your hopes and dreams and I want those for you, Trey. I also know that I'm a complication you don't need in your life." She remained leaning against the wall. "You will do great things, Trey, and you need the right woman by your side. We both know I'm not that woman."

She straightened and took a step back from him. "This…energy or chemistry or whatever you want to call it between us can't be allowed to flourish. I think it would be best if we see as little of each other as possible in the future. I understand that we'll run into each other at the estate, but there's no reason for you to come here anymore."

"You're right," he said. "Of course you're right. And now I'll just say goodbye."

He turned and lunged through the door. He didn't look back as he strode to his car. Once inside he stared at the front door, which was now closed.

Closed. Debra had to be a closed book in his life. Making love to Debra wasn't fair to her and it certainly wouldn't be fair to Cecily.

Duty versus passion, he thought as he drove away from her townhouse. Passion waned, but duty and dreams lived on and ultimately Trey knew that Debra was right. He would do the right thing and choose his duty over any crazy desire that was probably fleeting.

Chapter 11

It had been two days since Debra had almost lost her mind in Trey's arms, two days ago that they'd nearly made a terrible mistake.

She was back at her desk, although her thoughts weren't on her work and she forcefully kept them off Trey. Instead she wondered how much longer she could keep up the pretense that everything was just peachy in her personal life.

This morning when she'd driven through the side entrance to come to work, Jerry Cahill had been on duty. He'd motioned her on through and it was only when she parked and glanced in her rearview mirror that she'd seen him glaring at her.

Obviously he'd been questioned about her car accident and wasn't too happy about being called on the carpet. Still, he wasn't uppermost in her mind as she contemplated the past two days.

Things had begun disappearing again. Her favorite pink mug had been missing this morning when she'd gone to the cabinet to retrieve it for a morning cup of tea. Yesterday she'd been half-crazed when a throw pillow she normally placed in the center of her bed was found in the bottom of the clothes hamper.

She was obviously suffering some sort of a mental breakdown and it not only frightened her for herself, but also for her baby. Her hand fell to her lap and she rubbed her belly in a circular motion. Her slacks had felt tighter this morning. The baby was growing and she was losing her mind.

What if she cracked up altogether? What if she wound up in some mental institute? Then what would happen to her baby? If she gave birth would somebody hand the baby to Barry to raise because everyone thought the baby was his?

She shuddered at the very thought.

Despite her desire to keep Trey out of her thoughts, he kept intruding. She wasn't sure what caused her more stress: the thoughts of losing her mind or her overwhelming feelings for Trey.

He'd held an unexpected press conference the day before and had officially announced his decision to run for the office of state senator. Cecily had been at his side, as she should have been, as it was supposed to be. They had looked perfect together, poised and at ease in front of the cameras.

But, for the first time in her life, Debra understood why some women chose to be mistresses. It wasn't always about money or the thrill of forbidden fruit, sometimes it was just about love.

She loved Trey enough to want any piece of himself

that he could give to her. Fortunately she loved herself enough not to compromise her true wants and needs, her very soul, by becoming his mistress. And in any case, she knew the core of him, she knew who he was as a man and knew he would never take a mistress. It wasn't in his moral fiber to do such a thing.

Debra was an all-or-nothing kind of woman when it came to love and commitment. Besides, Trey hadn't spoken to her about love, he'd told her he wanted her, that he desired her, and that would never be enough for her.

The Friday morning flew by as she focused on the usual work that kept Kate's schedule running smoothly. At noon she stopped and went into the kitchen where Myra fixed her a sandwich and some coleslaw. She ate quickly, grateful that she didn't encounter any other members of the family, and then returned to her office.

She wasn't in the right frame of mind to put up with Sam's moodiness and although she'd spoken to Thad a couple of times over the past few days, he'd had no new information to give her as to who might have been responsible for her car accident, an accident she still refused to believe was a specific attack on her personally.

She'd just settled back at her desk when a knock fell on her door. Kate poked her head in. "How about we have a chat in my office?" she asked.

"Sure," Debra agreed. She picked up a memo pad.

"You don't need to bother with that. We won't be talking about anything that requires note-taking."

"Okay." Debra got up from her desk and followed Kate into her office. As Kate sat behind her desk Debra sank down into one of the chairs in front of her.

"I just wanted to check in with you and see how

you're doing. How you're feeling." Kate leaned back in her chair, obviously relaxed.

"To be honest, I think my pregnancy hormones are making me a little crazy," Debra replied. "I've been misplacing things and finding them in strange places. I'm having a little trouble concentrating, although it isn't affecting any of my work for you," she hurriedly added.

Kate smiled. "I wasn't concerned about that. I remember when I was pregnant with Sam I had the same kind of issues."

"Really?" Debra asked.

"Really. Of course, Trey was two at the time and he didn't help my sanity any. I remember one day I took him to the park to play and then an hour or so later I got into my car and realized I was about to drive off without him." She laughed and shook her head. "Thank goodness I had Maddie here to keep me at least partially sane."

Debra's relief was enormous. Maybe all of the strange things that had been happening to her really were due to hormones gone wild.

"One of the things I wanted to talk to you about was next Sunday I'd like to have a family continental breakfast on the patio. The weather has been so unusually lovely I thought it would be nice to get everyone together and discuss the ramifications of my running for president."

"Is there something you need me to do? Pastries to be ordered or anything like that?"

"No, Myra will take care of everything. I'm just telling you because Sunday is your day off and I'd really like for you to be there."

"I'd love to come," Debra replied, pleased to be included.

"My decision will affect you as well as the family," Kate continued, "so I want you to have a voice in the process. Are you planning on taking off time when the baby is born?"

"Maybe just a couple of weeks," Debra replied, although the idea of leaving the baby at all with anyone for anything was painful.

"You know, there's no reason for you to leave the baby while you work here. We can set up one of the bedrooms as a nursery and Maddie would love to take care of a little one again."

"Really? So I could bring the baby to work with me?" Debra's heart expanded with happiness.

"I don't see a problem at all." Kate grinned. "My goodness, we've been together so long, Debra, I feel like you're giving birth to my grandbaby. It will be nice to have a little one in the house once again."

Debra prayed the expression on her face didn't change, although the weight of her lies about the father of her baby slammed into the bottom of her heart. "Your family has always been like my own. You know I think of you as a surrogate mother."

A wash of pain flickered across Kate's face, gone so quickly Debra wondered if she'd imagined it. She stared at a family photo on her desk. "I always did want a little girl." She looked back at Debra. "But fate gave me three strapping boys who have been the joys of my life."

"And this baby will be the joy of my life," Debra replied, feeling terrible that Kate would never know that the child she carried *was* her first grandbaby. "But, you can count on me to juggle motherhood and work with no problem."

Kate gave her an affectionate smile. "It never occurred to me otherwise."

Minutes later back at her desk, Debra thought of the Sunday morning breakfast. She would have to see Trey again. It would be the first time she'd seen him since they'd practically attacked each other in her foyer.

He'd started it, but she'd desperately wanted him to finish it. She'd wanted him to drag her up the stairs to her bedroom and make love to her. It had only been a surprising flash of sanity that had saved them both from making another mistake. Whatever it was between them was strong and just a little bit frightening in that Debra had almost no control in her desire for him.

At least Kate had managed to put her at ease a bit as far as her forgetfulness was concerned. She smiled as she envisioned Kate getting into her car to leave a park and suddenly realizing the car seat where Trey should be was empty. Now that was the height of absentmindedness.

By the time six o'clock came she was ready to call it a day. She knew the unusual fatigue she suffered was from her pregnancy, a fatigue that hopefully would pass when she went into her second trimester in the next few weeks.

On her way home she thought about stopping in at some department store to pick up a few pairs of maternity pants and skirts. It wasn't going to be long before the clothes she owned would no longer fit her belly bump.

It was a fleeting thought. She was too tired to shop. She'd make plans tomorrow to take off an hour early and shop then. It would be nice to have something comfortable to wear to the breakfast on Sunday.

At the moment she just wanted to get home, eat some dinner and curl up on the sofa in front of the television where hopefully a good sitcom or crime drama would chase away thoughts of the man she loved, the man she was certain would be the next North Carolina senator… as long as she stayed out of his life.

Trey felt as if he were living some sort of weird double life. During the days he worked at Adair Enterprises and then in the past three evenings he'd had two business dinners to attend and had dined with Cecily the other night.

He hadn't slept with Cecily since the night he'd slept with Debra. He'd made a million excuses to Cecily about their lack of intimacy. Too busy, too tired, not good for his public image to be seen coming and going from her house before they were married, the excuses had fallen from his lips with a surprising ease.

He knew that Cecily was frustrated with him, but she took each of his excuses in stride, telling him coyly that they'd catch up on lost time once they were married.

The truth of the matter was that Trey couldn't imagine making love to Cecily when his passion and his emotions were still tied to Debra.

And it was emotion and fear for her that had him doing something crazy each night. When darkness fell he found himself parked across the street from Debra's townhouse where he'd remain until the wee hours of the morning.

He knew it was crazy, but he couldn't help himself. Even though there was no concrete evidence that somebody specific had targeted Debra by cutting her brake line, Trey believed danger had touched her and wasn't finished with her yet.

He was afraid for her, and so he had taken it upon himself to be her secret nighttime bodyguard. Anyone who got too close to her house while she slept peacefully inside would have him to deal with.

He had a conceal-and-carry permit and a 9 mm with him on these nightly surveillance details. He was dead serious about seeing that no harm came to Debra or the baby she carried.

The only downfall of these nightly visits was that each morning when he got to his office he directed Rhonda to hold all his calls for a couple of hours so he could catch up on his sleep.

Tonight was like the past two nights. It was just after midnight and although it was Saturday the neighborhood was quiet. Debra had turned off the light in the house around nine or so, letting him know she was having an early night.

He yawned and slumped down a bit in the seat, trying to find a more comfortable position to sustain for the next couple of hours.

Was he being foolish? Maybe, he conceded. But he'd rather be foolish than take a chance and have any harm come to Debra. Did he intend to do this nightly vigil every night for the rest of his life?

Definitely not, but he would be here until something or someone managed to make him believe that the cut brake lines had been as Debra had believed, an accident of the wrong car being targeted and not something personal against her. Only then would he stop this madness and get on with his life.

His life.

He stared unseeingly at the center of his steering wheel. He should be thrilled with the direction his life was traveling. Since the dinner party and the press conference the donation dollars had begun to pour in, Chad had put together a machine made of devoted people to work campaign headquarters, which was being set up in a downtown storefront.

Banners and signs had been made to hang on the outside of the building and it always jarred him just a bit to pull up and see his own face smiling from one of those signs.

Cecily was more than ready to step in as a supportive wife and partner and there was no question that she would be an asset to his career. She had money, connections and the personality that would serve him well.

Yes, everything was falling nicely into place. So, where was his happiness? He'd assumed he'd be euphoric at this point in the process, but his happiness seemed to be sadly absent.

He glanced back at Debra's house and frowned as he saw a faint red glow coming from someplace inside, a glow that hadn't been there minutes before.

Was Debra awake? Had she turned on some kind of light? If so, it was a strange red light. A lick of flame danced before the front window.

Fire! It was fire.

His mind screamed the word as he fumbled with his cell phone and called 911. As he gave Debra's address to the dispatcher he got out of the car and raced for the front door.

With the call made, he tossed his cell phone in the

grass and pounded on the door with his fists, calling her name at the top of his lungs.

The odor of smoke drifted through the door, making his blood freeze. Was she unconscious? Already overcome by smoke that had risen to her upstairs bedroom?

Panic seared through him as he rang the doorbell and then pounded once again, screaming her name as the flames at the window grew bigger and more intense.

Vaguely aware of lights going on in the houses around hers, conscious of the distant sound of sirens, he picked up a flowerpot that was on her stoop and raced around to the back of the townhouse.

His heart thumped painfully fast with every step. He finally made it to the kitchen windows where just inside he'd sat at the table and had coffee with her. He raised the heavy pot and threw it through one of the windows, shattering the glass and allowing him entry.

The air in the kitchen wasn't bad, but when he entered the living room the smoke tickled the back of his throat and obscured his vision.

The curtains at the windows blazed and dropped malicious imps of flames onto the carpet below. Although his first impulse was to race up the stairs to Debra's room, instead he ran to the front door, unlocked it and pulled it open so that the arriving firemen could easily access the house.

Swirling cherry-red lights announced the arrival of the emergency vehicles as Trey raced up the stairs, the smoke thicker now, causing him to pause as he was overcome with a spasm of coughing.

He clung to the banister until the spasm had passed and then continued upward. There were three doors upstairs and thankfully all of them were closed, hopefully keeping most of the smoke in the narrow hallway.

A night-light shone in a wall socket, guiding him forward despite the thickening smoke. The first door proved to be the guest room.

Across the hall was a bathroom where he quickly wet a hand towel with cold water. He entered the door at the end of the hallway and saw Debra unmoving in the bed.

His heart stopped beating for a second. Was she dead? Overcome by smoke? But the smoke was only now just drifting faintly into the room.

"Debra?" He ran to the side of her bed, but she didn't move at the sound of her name. "Debra!" He shook her and gasped in relief as she roused.

"Trey?" She sat up in obvious confusion and shoved a tangle of hair off her face. "Trey, what's happening? Why are you in my bedroom?"

"Fire. There's a fire downstairs. We've got to get you out of here." He didn't wait for her to get out of the bed. He handed her the wet cloth. "Put this over your nose and mouth," he said and then he scooped her up in his arms and rushed down the hallway toward the stairs.

On the lower level he could hear the sound of firemen at work and when he reached the living room the fire was out and only the smoke and soot remained.

Trey carried Debra directly out the front door, where emergency vehicles had been joined by news vans. It wasn't until he tried to lay her down in the grass that he realized she was crying.

"It's okay," he said, shouting to be heard above the din. He was aware of a familiar reporter standing nearby, but his focus was solely on Debra. "You're safe now," he said in an effort to comfort her.

She shook her head and clung to him, her sobs of fear breaking his heart. "You saved my life," she said, the words coming out in deep gasps. "You saved our baby's life."

In the glow of the headlights around them he saw the horror on her face as the words left her lips. Everything else faded away...the lights, the people and the sound. The entire world shrunk to just him and her and the words that had just fallen from her lips.

She released her hold on him and instead wrapped her arms around herself as she shivered, refusing to meet his gaze.

"*Our* baby?"

She looked up at him. Her tear-filled gaze held his as she slowly nodded her head and then began to weep once again. He stood, his head reeling with the information that the baby she carried was his. Not Barry's, but *his* baby.

He helped her to her bare feet as the fire chief approached them. "There's not a lot of damage," he said. "It looks worse than it is, mostly smoke. We didn't even have to use our hoses. We got it out with fire extinguishers. It was intentionally set, an accelerant used. I'm guessing gasoline by the smell of things," he said to Trey and then turned his attention to Debra. "We'll do a full investigation but I'm afraid you'll need to find someplace else to sleep tonight."

"I'll take you to Mom's," Trey said. He took Debra's arm and looked at the fire chief. "You'll see to it that a guard is posted for the duration? I broke a window in the back to get inside."

"A police officer is already standing by. We'll make sure everything is secure before we leave here."

"And you'll let us know what your investigation discovers?"

"Absolutely, Mr. Winston." He smiled sympathetically at Debra. "We should be finished with our documenting the crime scene by midday tomorrow. If you get a good cleaning crew in here you should be able to return home either tomorrow night or by Monday."

"Thank you," she replied, her voice barely audible among the other noise.

"Let's get out of here," Trey said. He found his cell phone where he'd tossed it in the grass and then they started for his car.

Before they could get there a bright beam of a camera light flashed in Trey's face and a microphone was thrust in his direction.

The reporter he'd seen earlier smiled like the cat that had swallowed the canary. "Mr. Winston, would you like to make a statement about Ms. Prentice's pregnancy?"

"No comment," Trey growled and grabbing Debra closer to his side, he hurried her to his car.

Once she was in the passenger seat, he slid behind the wheel and started the engine with a roar. He pulled away from the curb, a myriad of emotions racing through him and he was afraid to say anything to her until he'd sorted them all out.

She shivered and he didn't know if it was because she was clad only in a copper-colored short nightgown or if it was because she didn't know what to expect next.

Hell, he didn't know what to expect next. There was a part of him that was filled with great joy at the idea of her carrying his child and there was also a part of him that battled anger that she'd intended to keep the baby a secret from him, to pretend that the baby belonged to her old boyfriend.

He couldn't begin to think about the fact that somebody had gotten into her house without him seeing them. That person or persons had set her living room on fire. He hoped the initial assessment was wrong and that it had been faulty wiring or something other than a man-made flame.

For several long minutes they rode in silence and it was finally he who broke it. "You were never going to tell me the truth about the baby?"

"The last thing I wanted to do was screw things up for you," she replied. "I figured it would just be easier to pretend the baby was Barry's and then you get to have your shining future with Cecily and everyone would be happy."

The fact that she'd lied for him to keep his dream alive stole away any anger he might harbor against her. She was willing to sacrifice the Winston power and influence for his happiness, to assure that he reached his dreams.

She'd been willing to go through all the struggles and sacrifices as a single mother to allow him to reach his own goals.

Once again silence fell between them. His brain felt half-contused from bouncing around in his skull. Too many things had occurred in too short a time.

"I'll arrange a cleaning crew to come to your place as soon as the fire department releases it," he said. "I'll also see to it that a security system is installed." He didn't even want to acknowledge at this point that somebody had apparently entered her house and set fire to the curtains.

He pulled up to the side entrance of the estate but didn't turn off the car, nor did she make a move to leave. "That reporter, he heard what I said." Her voice was a whisper. "It will be all over the news tomorrow." She stared straight ahead, her face pale in the illumination from the dashboard. She finally turned to him, her eyes wide and holding a soft vulnerability. "What do you want me to do?"

"What do you mean?" He eyed her curiously.

"I could lie. I could say that the reporter misunderstood what I said, that I was confused by the fire and everything that was going on."

"That's definitely not going to happen," he replied. And it was at that moment he knew he wasn't going to marry Cecily. Even if he got to be where he wanted to be in the political arena, he didn't want the cool, absolutely perfect Cecily next to him.

"Marry me," he said.

Her eyes widened. "Don't talk crazy."

"It's not crazy," he responded. "You're the mother of my child. We'd make a family and you'd never have to worry about anything."

"That's a ridiculous idea and I won't marry you." She opened the car door and in the dome light she looked ghostly pale and exhausted. "Right now I'm going inside to sleep and in the morning I have to figure out who got into my house and tried to burn it down with me still inside. You deal with the press however you want to. I'll follow your lead. I just can't deal with anything else tonight."

She got out of the car and slammed the door. He remained sitting in the car long after she'd disappeared inside the house.

A baby…a fire… His head ached with the night's events. Cecily was going to be angry when he broke it off with her, but that was the least of his problems at the moment.

What concerned him more than anything was the fact that he believed twice now somebody had tried to kill not just Debra, but the child she carried, as well… His child.

Tomorrow he'd deal with Cecily. Tomorrow he'd also discuss his intention to be a huge part of the baby's life. He'd have to deal with whatever the news reports contained and he needed to speak to Thad about this newest threat against Debra.

The one thing he didn't care about at the moment was any ramifications this might have on his career. And the odd thing was that he wasn't sure he cared.

Chapter 12

"Marry me."

Debra awoke with the ring of Trey's words echoing in her head. She was in the same bedroom where she'd stayed following her car accident and as she thought of everything that had happened the night before she wanted to pull the blankets up over her head and never get up again.

A glance at the clock on the nightstand let her know it was after ten. Obscenely late for her to still be in bed. She should be at her desk, she thought and then realized it was Sunday. She should at least be at her house finding out what the fire marshal had learned. She should be anywhere but under the covers thinking about how often she'd fantasized Trey saying those two words to her.

"Marry me."

In her fantasies he'd spoken the words because he

loved her, because he couldn't imagine a life without her. In her dreams he'd held her in his arms and kissed her with love and commitment as they planned a future together.

In reality she knew he'd said the words in an effort to begin damage control and perhaps because he wanted to be a part of his baby's life. He'd proposed to the baby inside of her, but not to her.

There had been no love offered from him. If she'd agreed it would have been like a business deal to him, a merger to get accomplished for the best results possible.

She was worth more than that. The off-the-cuff proposal had stabbed through her loving heart like an arrow. She wouldn't be his lover and she refused to be an inconvenient wife to him.

Hopefully, despite her pregnancy, he could make things right with Cecily and continue on his way. Surely he could figure out a way to make Cecily forgive him for a single night's indiscretion. Of course eventually there would be custody issues to deal with, weekends and holidays when the child would be with him... With them, instead of with her.

She turned over on her back and stared up at the ceiling, reluctant to face any part of the day. Somebody had tried to kill her last night. Somebody had come into her home and started a fire in the wee hours of the morning. If Trey hadn't been there she probably would have died of smoke inhalation long before the flames reached her bedroom.

She frowned thoughtfully. What had Trey been doing at her house at that time of night? How had he managed to be at exactly the right place at exactly the right time when it should have been the last place he'd be? It didn't make sense, but then nothing about her life lately had made any sense at all.

Somebody had gotten into her house. Who? Who had crept in and started a fire that would have certainly been the death of her if Trey hadn't rescued her?

A knock fell on her door and Kate came in carrying a cup of hot tea. Debra wanted to hide her face in shame. Instead she pulled herself up to a sitting position and took the cup of tea that Kate offered her.

Kate sat on a tufted chair next to the bed. "Well, my dear, you've created quite a stir."

"Kate, I'm so sorry," she said miserably.

"Sorry about what?" Kate smiled at her kindly. "I should be angry with you for not telling me that you're carrying my first grandbaby, but I'm not. I understand why you lied about the father of the baby."

"I didn't want to mess things up for Trey and now I've ruined everything," she said, fighting back a wave of tears that threatened with every word. She set the tea on the nightstand, afraid of spilling it and making even more of a mess of everything.

"Nonsense," Kate said briskly. "Oh, there's no denying that some adjustments will need to be made, but Trey is intelligent and flexible. This won't stop him from getting where he wants to go."

She pursed her lips and held Debra's gaze. "You know, somehow I'm not surprised by the news. There is an energy between you and my son that I've noticed every time the two of you are in the same room."

"It was just one night. One crazy, stupid night," Debra replied. "Only I would be stupid enough not to think about birth control."

"Debra, darling, you aren't the first woman in the world to make a mistake where that's concerned."

"But…the press," Debra protested.

Kate gave her a look of distaste. "The news is out everywhere with such salacious headlines that one would think the two of you committed some heinous murder rather than slept together. Trey has a press conference this afternoon at four to address the issue."

Kate motioned to the cup on the nightstand. "Drink that before it gets cold." Debra grabbed the cup and raised it to her lips as Kate continued. "Trey spoke to Cecily this morning. He told her that under the circumstances he was breaking off their relationship for the time being. He told her he needed some time to figure out all the ways this will impact him."

Debra swallowed hard. "How did she take it?"

Kate leaned back in the chair. "According to Trey she was a bit upset, but in the end quite gracious about the whole thing. She said she still intended on being involved in his campaign and wished him well in his personal life if they didn't manage to reconnect. Cecily is a survivor, Kate. She's a barracuda who will find a mate based on criteria that will make her the most successful in the endgame."

"But surely she's terribly hurt and Trey has to make her understand that I don't mean anything to him, that it was all just a terrible mistake. Surely they can work through it. She is in love with him," Debra replied.

Kate smiled. "I seriously doubt that Cecily is in love with Trey. She is in love with who he will become and where that would take her. If they don't get back together she'll move on and will be quite fine, I'm sure."

She stood. "I'm not sure how you and Trey intend to

work things out between you, but I'll have you know that I intend to embrace that baby with all the love I have to give. And now, speaking of Trey, he and Thad are in the sitting room and want to talk to you."

She moved toward the doorway. "Haley happened to have a pair of sweats and a T-shirt that you can put on. Anything I own would be too short on you. The clothes are laid out in the bathroom. Once you're showered and dressed, we'll see you downstairs."

The minute she left the room Debra set her cup down and flopped her head back on the pillow. She didn't want to face Trey. She didn't want to talk to Thad. She just wanted to hide for the rest of her life.

But she couldn't hide. Reluctantly she got out of bed and carried her teacup with her into the bathroom and set it on the counter while she got into the shower.

She hadn't noticed the odor of smoke that had clung to her until it was washing away down the drain. She'd spent her morning thinking about Trey and all the ramifications of her secret unexpectedly being spilled. Now it was time to think about who had been in her house and who wanted her dead.

Haley's gray sweatpants fit comfortably and the navy T-shirt hid the fact that Debra didn't have on a bra. Trey had carried her out the night before in her nightgown and so she hadn't been wearing one. Kate had even provided a pair of flip-flops for her to wear.

She slid on the shoes and then walked down the stairs with dread weighing down each footstep. She dreaded seeing Trey again and she knew that Thad was here to talk about the fact that somebody had tried to kill her. The fire made the cut brake lines very personal and this thought chilled her to the bone. Two attempts on her life… Who could be behind them? And why would anyone go to such trouble to kill her?

Trey was seated on the sofa and Thad in a chair opposite him. Both of them stood as she entered the room. She motioned them back down and then sat on the opposite end of the sofa from Trey, carefully keeping her gaze away from him.

He probably hated her for spilling her secret at a place and a time where a reporter would overhear. He probably hated her for making him scramble to deflect any negativity that might come in his direction at this important time in his life. She was also the reason he'd had to break it off with Cecily. Such a mess she'd made of everything.

"How are you feeling?" he asked.

"I'm okay," she replied and finally forced herself to look at him. There was no anger shining from his eyes, there was nothing but a gentle caring. *For the baby,* she thought. He would put aside any anger he might feel toward her for the sake of the baby she carried.

"We need to talk about what happened last night," Thad said.

She nodded and then looked at Trey again. "Why were you there last night? How did you happen to be there at just the right time?"

She was surprised to see a faint color creep up his neck. "I'd been parked outside your house every night since you quit staying here. I just had a bad feeling after the car accident and so I was spending my nights parked outside your place, watching to make sure nobody bothered you."

She stared at him in stunned surprise. He'd been doing that for her and he hadn't even known yet that the baby was his. He'd been there each night, keeping vigil over her. Maybe he did care about her just a little bit.

"Thank goodness he was there," Thad said. "I touched base with the fire marshal this morning and the fire was definitely set at the foot of the curtains in the living room, probably with a pile of papers and gasoline."

"I just don't understand this," she replied. "I mean, if somebody wanted to kill me, then why set the fire? Why not just creep up the stairs and stab me while I slept? Why not shoot me with a gun and be done with it?"

"I'm guessing that whoever is behind all of this wants your death to look like an accident. The point of ignition in the living room was just beneath an outlet. If the fire department hadn't gotten there as quickly as they did because of Trey's phone call, then the fire chief might not have smelled the gasoline and it might have been written up as a tragic electrical fire."

Debra rubbed her hand across her forehead, where a small headache was forming. "I don't understand any of this."

"My team checked the house. Other than the window Trey broke to get inside and him unlocking the front door to enable the firemen to enter, there appeared to be no point of entry that wasn't a normal one, which leads me to believe somebody got in using a key. So, my question to you now is who has keys to your house?"

She stared at Thad. A key? Somebody had used a key to get into her home? The misplaced items, the guest list in the freezer... Was it possible somebody had been accessing her house all along? Was it possible she wasn't losing her mind after all, but rather was being made to believe she was going mad?

"Strange things have been happening for the last several weeks," she said. "Cups disappear and reappear in the cabinets, a paperweight on my desk vanished and then two days later was back where it belonged. I thought I was losing my mind. I believed I was going insane."

"Why didn't you say anything before now?" Trey asked in surprise.

"Because I thought it was me. I thought I was doing those things to myself." She slumped back on the sofa, horrified and yet relieved. "Keys, your mom has a key and Haley has one. I imagine several people on staff have a key to my house because occasionally they're sent to pick something up from there."

"What about Barry?" Trey asked.

She looked at him and slowly nodded. "Yes, Barry has a key. He never gave it back to me after we broke up." Her head reeled. Was it possible Barry had known she intended to break up with him and had pulled an end run by breaking up with her before she got a chance? Was it possible he was so angry with her that he could be behind these deadly assaults on her?

At this point she didn't know what to think. "Can I get into the house?"

"You won't want to stay there until some cleanup work is done," Trey replied. "I've got a crew in there now. They should be finished by sometime late this afternoon. I suggest you stay here for tonight and tomorrow you should be able to go back home."

"You'll have a new security system that Trey is having installed. It will alert you if anyone tries to get into a door or window in the house. He's also made sure that all the locks on the doors are being changed. Whoever has a key now will find that it doesn't work if they try to get in again." Thad looked down at the notes he'd taken and then back at her.

"Right now I'm going to see how many house keys I can retrieve from the people you've said have one and each person better hope they have good alibis for the night of the dinner and last night." He rose from the chair. "And on that note I'm out of here and will check in with both of you later."

Debra turned to look at Trey, unsure what to say to make anything better. "I'm sorry about you and Cecily. Hopefully you two can work things out despite everything that's happened. I never meant for any of this to get between the two of you. I hope you told her that I don't expect anything from you."

Trey held up a hand to halt her ramble. "Cecily is fine," he replied. "I told her I needed a break to figure things out, but right now I'm more worried about you than any other relationship. I think you need to take the day and rest. Later tonight if everything is ready and I know that the security is up and working, then, if you want, I can take you home."

"How bad is the damage?"

"Actually less than what I initially thought. The only area that was damaged was around the front windows. Your living room will need a new paint job, but the firemen got enough windows open quickly after putting out the flames that the smoke damage was minimal."

She nodded and stared at the coffee table. "I'm sure we'll have lots of things to discuss and work out in the future, but right now everything just seems too overwhelming."

"Which is why I would encourage you to eat a good

breakfast and then maybe go back to bed for some extra sleep." His voice was tender and filled with a caring that both soothed and somehow hurt at the same time.

He cared about her because of the baby, she reminded herself. As she thought about the car accident and the fire, she only hoped she managed to stay alive long enough to give birth to a healthy full-term baby.

Trey stood in Debra's living room, checking to make sure everything had been done that could be done to clean up the mess and secure her safety. The doorknobs had already been changed out and the security company was finishing up its work.

He'd even had a painting crew come in to Sheetrock and paint the wall that had been damaged. At least the house now smelled of new paint instead of smoke.

His press conference had gone as smoothly as he'd expected it to go. He'd made an announcement that Debra Prentice was carrying his child and while the two had no plans to marry he intended to be a loving, supportive father to his baby and a friend and support to Debra.

Surprisingly, in the world of political news it had made only a small splash. Both he and Debra were single, consenting adults and that fact took any salacious elements out of the situation.

Cecily had even made a statement of support for him, showing her to be a classy lady as she lauded the many good qualities he possessed and the fact that she and Trey had agreed to take their personal relationship one day at a time.

Trey knew she was giving a signal that she would stand by her man. But as much as Trey appreciated her loyalty, after speaking with her and telling her they needed to take a break from each other, he'd felt more relief than he'd expected.

He hadn't realized how much pressure everyone had been subtly putting on him to pop the question, make a formal announcement of an engagement. Now with that pressure off him, he realized whether good or bad for his campaign he wasn't ready to marry Cecily.

All in all, politically he'd weathered the storm, but that didn't mean all was well. There was no question he was frightened for Debra and he'd spent much of the day working names of people around in his mind, as if the guilty person would suddenly appear in his head like a magical vision.

At the moment his suspicions were on Haley, who had jokingly told Debra time and time again that she was after Debra's job.

As he thought of the sequence of events as he knew them it made a strange kind of sick sense. How better to undermine Debra's confidence in her ability to do her job than by gas-lighting her into thinking she was losing her mind?

Maybe the results of that hadn't worked as quickly as she'd hoped. Haley had known that Debra would be at the dinner party and Haley also knew Debra's car.

He didn't believe that Haley had actually crawled under the car herself, but she was young and pretty and probably had a male friend who could do it.

What he'd like to do was grab Haley by the scruff of her neck and force her to tell the truth one way or the other. But Thad had made it clear to Trey that he was to stay away from the investigation because it was now in the hands of the Raleigh Police Department.

Just when Trey had convinced himself that Haley was responsible, he'd change his mind and think about Jerry Cahill. The Secret Service agent had made it clear that he wanted to date Debra, and Debra had made it equally clear to him that she wasn't interested. Cahill would know how to cut brake lines. He probably even had the ability to break into a house and leave no trace behind.

And then there was the possibility of it being somebody not even on Trey's radar. The only thing he knew for certain was that Debra was in danger and he was doing everything he could to assure that her home was secure.

Although as a crime-scene investigator Thad wouldn't specifically be driving any investigation, Trey also knew his brother would make sure that things were being done right and that the people who needed to be interviewed and checked out would be.

Thad might not spend a lot of time with the family, but when anyone was threatened, he was definitely a Winston at heart, ready to jump in and protect them at any moment.

"Hey, thought you might be here."

Trey looked at Sam in surprise as he walked through Debra's front door where a technician from the security company was at work. "What are you doing here?"

Sam shrugged. "I got bored at home, so I figured I'd take a ride and I wound up here. I brought you a present."

He tossed a plastic bag to Trey, who looked inside and laughed as he saw a package of tiny diapers. "Thanks, I think we're going to need a lot of these."

Sam and Trey walked outside into the front yard

and away from the men working in the house. "Do you have any ideas about who was responsible for this?" Sam asked.

"Lots of ideas, but not a real clue," Trey replied.

"What about that guy Debra was dating before?"

"Barry Chambers. Debra insists he wouldn't be involved in anything like this."

"What about Cecily?"

Trey laughed. "Definitely not her style, besides what would be her motive?"

Sam raised an eyebrow. "Uh…you're having a baby with another woman?"

"The things happening to Debra started long before anyone knew that Debra was pregnant. In any case, Thad and the police are involved, so hopefully they'll figure things out."

Sam pointed to the cameras located on each corner of the house and above the front door. "It's going to be easier to break into Fort Knox than this house when you get finished with it."

"That's the idea," Trey told him.

"Why don't you just marry her and put her in that secured mansion you bought?" Sam asked.

"I asked her and she said no."

Sam's eyebrows rose. "That's a surprise. I didn't think anyone had ever told you no," Sam said with a touch of dry humor.

Trey smiled with affection at his brother. Sam's calm moods came so rarely and when they did he remembered how much he loved Sam, how much he wished for better things for the brother who had served his country with honor and come home damaged. "I can't believe I'm going to be a father."

"You'll be good at it," Sam assured him. "I'll tell you one thing, I like Debra a hell of a lot better than I ever liked Cecily."

Trey looked at Sam in surprise. "Why don't you like Cecily?" He'd thought the entire family was happy when he'd started dating the beautiful, wealthy socialite.

Sam scowled. "Cecily has eyes like a shark… Cold and dead. She smiles prettily, but the smiles never quite reach her eyes. She reminds me of…" His voice trailed off and he shook his head. "Never mind," he said, tension in his voice.

"What, Sam? She reminds you of what?"

"Nothing. I've got to get out of here. I just wanted to deliver the baby's first gift to you."

"Sam?" Trey called after his brother as he turned on his heels and headed for his car. Sam didn't look back or acknowledge Trey again. He got into his car and drove off.

Trey couldn't begin to imagine what demons chased his brother since his imprisonment and torture at enemy hands. Apparently he saw something in Cecily's dark eyes that brought back those terrible demons to his head.

He wondered if Sam would feel the same way about Cecily if she had blue or green eyes. He just wished that somehow, someway, his little brother could find some help and ultimately peace in his heart.

He checked his watch. He had a seven-o'clock meeting with Chad to discuss any further ramifications of Debra's pregnancy and Trey's impending fatherhood and how it might affect the campaign going forward.

As far as Trey was concerned, his press conference had addressed the issue and now it would be a nonissue.

He still wanted his dreams of becoming a state senator, but he also wanted to be the best father in the world.

When he'd asked Debra to marry him and she'd turned him down, there was no question that he'd been hurt and that had made him realize he cared about her more than he wanted to admit to himself.

But it was obvious she didn't feel the same way about him. There had been no hesitation when she'd told him no. Her firm reply had left no room to even discuss the matter.

She didn't love him. It was as simple as that. They'd had a night of passion and it was a passion that still simmered inside him, still boiled between them, but ultimately she didn't love him.

And he wasn't sure why that fact ached in his heart. While he cared about Debra deeply, surely he wasn't in love with her?

He thought of how she'd looked the night of the dinner dance, with that spill of emerald-green silk clinging to her curves. Despite her lack of dancing skills, she'd felt so right in his arms.

He remembered how much he enjoyed sitting in her cozy kitchen, talking about anything and everything except politics. He'd felt relaxed and at home. Was it the surroundings or was it the woman herself?

Cecily had seen him as a candidate, as a means to an end—her end. And he'd accepted that as being enough because he knew that ultimately they would make a good team.

But was being a good team enough for him? Why had he so easily accepted a relationship without love? He was fairly certain the answer was in his own childhood, where it was clear his mother and father didn't love one another but had stayed together because of an understanding between them.

He stared back at Debra's house and remembered that hot, sexy moment when they'd almost made love in her foyer. She'd said they couldn't do that anymore, that they couldn't allow themselves to lose control, but that was before he and Cecily had called it quits.

Debra might not love him, but she definitely felt passion for him. Why couldn't they follow through on that again? Every muscle in his body tensed and his blood flowed hot through his veins as he thought of making love to her once more.

He'd like that. He'd like the pleasure of stroking her smooth skin once again, hearing her soft moans of pleasure as he took possession of her.

Now all he had to do was somehow convince her that she wanted him again, too.

Chapter 13

It was Sunday night and Trey was on his way to the estate to take Debra back home. It was almost nine o'clock and while she knew she should be growing tired, she'd already spent most of the day in bed resting.

From what Trey had told her on the phone, he'd spent most of his day making sure her townhouse was ready for her return. She didn't know how she would ever repay him for everything he'd accomplished in such a short amount of time.

She knew he'd probably pulled all kinds of strings to get the place clean and secure in a single day so that she could get back where she belonged.

Maybe she should be afraid to go home since it had only been the night before that somebody had crept into her house and tried to kill her. But Thad was hunting down anyone who might have had a key to her place, new doorknobs and locks had been installed and according to Trey if a squirrel managed to so much as brush against a door or window the police would arrive within minutes.

Besides, she knew that Trey would never allow her to return to a place that wasn't safe, not as long as she carried his baby.

She absently caressed her stomach as she sat in the family sitting room waiting for Trey's arrival. Kate had left earlier for a charity event and Sam had gone to his room. Maddie had retired for the night and the house held an uncharacteristic silence.

It wouldn't be quiet for long. She had a feeling in the weeks and months to come the estate would be a buzz of activity as both Trey and Kate began campaigning in earnest.

Although Kate had yet to make an announcement that she intended to run for president, Debra had a feeling next Sunday's morning breakfast would be her time to hear any concerns that the family might have to say and then she'd let them know that she'd decided to run.

Kate was as much a political animal as her husband before her and now her son. Debra knew she had a steely will and was not just ambitious but truly believed she would be the best choice for the country. Ultimately, Kate would be driven by a sense of duty.

She jumped as Trey suddenly appeared in the doorway.

"You startled me. I didn't hear you come in." She tried not to notice how handsome, how sexy he looked in his jeans and a blue button-up shirt.

"Sorry, I didn't mean to startle you." His gaze was dark and unreadable. "Are you ready to go?"

"I'm definitely ready." She rose from the sofa, feeling strange not to have a suitcase or a purse. But she'd arrived here with nothing but the nightgown she'd been wearing when Trey had pulled her out of the townhouse. She'd thrown the nightgown away, not wanting any memories of the night somebody had gotten inside her home and set a fire in an attempt to kill her.

"I can't believe everything you got accomplished today," she said when they were in her car.

He flashed a smile. "It helps to be a Winston when you want to get things done. People tend to jump through hoops in an effort to please."

"Even on a Sunday?"

"Even on a Sunday," he replied.

She imagined he'd paid extra dollars to get the work done on a Sunday. She wasn't sure she would ever be able to pay him back, but she was determined to do so even if it took years.

"Sam got me a present for the baby," she said. "It's a cute bib that says I Love Mommy." Her heart expanded as she thought of the unexpectedness of the gift.

"He brought me a present for the baby, too. Diapers." Trey laughed. "I guess he figures you get feeding duty and I'm going to get diaper duty."

"It works for me," Debra joked. But of course she knew that separation of baby duties would never work. They'd be living in different homes, leading separate lives. He would be a busy state senator while the child was growing up, but no matter how busy his life would become, Debra knew he'd be a fabulous father.

She knew that if you stripped away the political aspirations, the trappings of the shrewd businessman, what would be left was a caring, giving man. He was a loving grandson to his grandmother, a role model for his younger brothers, and a help and support to his mother.

He had a good sense of humor and a large streak of kindness. That was who Trey Winston was at his very core. And those qualities were what would make him a loving, caring father and what made her love him.

"You know I'd never let you return home if I didn't think it was safe," he said, interrupting her contemplations.

"I know that," she affirmed. "Have you spoken to Thad today about the investigation?"

"Officially the investigation is being headed by Lieutenant Al Chase, but unofficially Thad is working on it as much as he can. He called me about an hour ago and said they had interviewed Barry, who indicated that on the nights of both incidents he was working late with his secretary. Apparently his secretary confirmed his alibis."

Debra released a dry, humorless laugh. "Well, of course she would. They've been sleeping together for years. That's why I wanted out of the relationship with him. He's had a relationship with his secretary, who is married and has kids, since he opened the real estate office."

"From what Thad said, Lieutenant Chase wasn't impressed with the alibi so Barry isn't home free."

Debra frowned thoughtfully. "Barry is a slimeball, but I just can't see him being behind any of this. He has no motive to hurt me."

"He has no motive that you know about," Trey countered. "If there's one thing I've learned in big business and politics, it's that there are some crazy-ass people out there."

"And it's so comforting to think that one of them is after me," she replied.

Trey reached out and placed his palm on her thigh. It wasn't a sexual touch, but rather meant to soothe her. "We're not going to let anyone hurt you, Debra. Thad and the police will be able to figure this out and put the guilty party behind bars." He removed his hand from her leg and returned it to the steering wheel in time to park by the curb in front of her house.

She knew he'd be coming inside. He needed to show her the new security system and how to work it. She gasped in surprise as she walked into the living room. It smelled of new paint and carpet cleaning, of washed walls, and showed no sign of the life-threatening event of the fire.

She shuddered to think of what might have happened if Trey hadn't been parked outside, if he hadn't seen the first flames and jumped into action. Consciously she shoved those thoughts away and continued to look around. The curtains that had hung in the window were gone, but wood-slatted blinds were in their place.

"I didn't want to buy new curtains for you. My mother has always told me all my decorating taste is in my mouth, but I thought the blinds would be fine until you can shop for something else," he said.

"They're perfect," she replied. "Everything looks perfect. I don't know how to thank you. We'll set up some sort of payment plan so that I can pay you back for everything this has cost you."

He waved a hand to dismiss her offer. "I'm not worried about that now. Let me show you how to work the new security system."

As he showed her the monitor next to the front door

and how to switch it to views of different areas from the cameras mounted outside, she tried not to smell his cologne, not to revel in the warmth of his nearness.

"If the alarm goes off, you'll immediately be contacted by the security company. If there is no danger, then you're to answer that everything is fine. If there's somebody with you and you're in danger, then you're supposed to say that everything is okay. Fine is safe. Okay is danger."

Debra nodded, taking in the information that might save her life. "When you enter the house you'll have two minutes to punch in a code that will reset the security behind you. I set up the code and I've got it right here." His gaze held hers intently as he handed her a small piece of paper he pulled from his pocket. "You and I are the only ones who know the code. Don't share it with anyone on staff at the estate or friends or neighbors," he said.

"Trust me, I intend to memorize the number and then I should probably eat this piece of paper to assure nobody finds it," she kidded.

He grinned. "I'm not sure that's necessary."

"After everything I've been through I think it is." She wrapped her arms around herself, suddenly chilled as she thought of everything she'd endured. "Would you like something to drink?" she asked, not sure if she wanted to be alone just yet. "I think I might have some orange juice in the fridge."

"I'll tell you what, why don't you get the juice and I'll build you a nice fire."

"That sounds perfect." He started work on the fire and she went into the kitchen. By the time he had the fire crackling in the fireplace, she had two tall glasses of juice waiting.

"We can take it into the living room," she said.

"Sounds perfect," he agreed. Together they went back into the living room with their glasses and sank down on the sofa.

"What a difference a day makes," she said, and released a pent-up sigh. "I feel like I've ruined things for you."

"You haven't ruined anything, Debra. You've given me a great gift. Your pregnancy will be old news within a couple of days, but for me it's the beginning of a wonderful event that will last the rest of my life."

Debra took a sip of her drink. "I was so afraid, I mean it wasn't exactly like we planned this. I was so worried that if you found out, if anyone found out that the baby was yours, then it would ruin all of the dreams you had for yourself and I didn't want to do that to you."

"As far as I'm concerned nothing has changed my dreams. The only thing you have done is added to the dreams I have for myself."

"But, I totally messed things up between you and Cecily," she replied.

He shrugged. "Cecily and I made a great political team. But I wasn't in love with her and I'm sure she wasn't in love with me. You probably did me a favor, because had we gotten married based on mutual ambition alone, we may have ended up two bitter, unhappy people and in the end that's what I experienced with my own parents. I don't want that for myself."

Debra shook her head in amazement. "You Winstons have always managed to turn any negative into a positive."

"That's because we don't see negatives, we only see opportunities. You're giving me the opportunity to be a dad." His eyes darkened with emotion. "And I didn't realize how badly I wanted that until you told me you were pregnant with my baby."

He turned his head and stared at the fire. "I don't know what the future holds, but I can tell you what I want at this very minute." He turned back to look at her. "I want you to know that I haven't had sex with Cecily since the night you and I spent together and what I want right now is to make love to the mother of my child on that red rug in front of the fire."

Debra paused with her glass halfway to her mouth, stunned by his words and by the heat of desire that pulsed in his eyes, desire that instantly pulsed through her.

Part of the reason she'd stopped their near lovemaking in her foyer was because she knew he was going to marry Cecily, because she didn't want to be that woman who cheated with a man who was already taken.

She'd made that mistake on the night they'd been together, and had refused to make it yet again when they'd almost lost it in her entryway.

She set her glass down, her hand trembling slightly. "I won't be your mistress, Trey. I won't be your baby mama who you occasionally stop by to have sex with. I want better than that. I deserve more than that." She drew a tremulous breath. "But I won't lie. I want you again. I want you tonight and then we're never going to be together intimately again."

One last night with him to remember, she told herself. One final time to be held in his arms, to feel his body against hers. A final chance to love him without inhibition, without restraint, surely after all she'd been through she deserved that.

"Are you sure? I don't want to talk you into doing something you aren't comfortable with."

"The only thing that is making me uncomfortable is how long it's taking you to kiss me," she replied.

He shot across the small space between them on the sofa and wrapped her in his arms as his mouth covered hers in a fiery kiss that stole her breath away. Her heartbeat responded by rapidly fluttering in her chest.

It was almost frightening how easily he could take her from zero to a hundred on the desire scale. Although she would never speak of her love for him aloud, she could show him in her kiss, in the intimacy that was about to follow.

The last time they'd had sex, it had been hot and wild and completely spontaneous. Now she wasn't having sex with him, she was making love with him…for the first and the very last time.

They kissed for some time before he broke the contact and stood. He held out his hand and she took it as he led her to the soft throw rug in front of the fireplace.

He lowered her to the floor as if she were a fine piece of china and then he stretched out next to her and took her in his arms once again.

As their lips met, Debra fought against the wild emotion that rose up in her heart. Love. She felt as if she'd loved Trey Winston forever.

Despite the fact that she knew he loved her because she carried his baby, at the moment it didn't matter what he felt for her. She just wanted to give to him everything her heart had to give. It didn't matter if he couldn't give her back what she wanted from him.

The fire warmed her, but not as much as Trey's mouth plying hers with heat, not as much as the love that burned hot in her soul.

As they continued to kiss, she began to unfasten the buttons of his shirt, wanting, needing to feel his bare, muscled chest, the strength of his naked shoulders.

Once she had his shirt unbuttoned, he threw it off and reached for the bottom of her T-shirt. He pulled it over her head and tossed it across the room and then he drew her against him, their nakedness melded together as her breasts rubbed his naked chest.

His lips once again captured hers and she tried not to think about the fact that after tonight they would both be going cold turkey in their addiction to each other.

It didn't take long before kissing and hugging wasn't enough. He kicked off his shoes and tore off his socks, then shucked his jeans and navy briefs in a hot minute. At the same time she shimmied out of the sweatpants and her panties.

For several sweet moments he hovered just above her, his gaze sweeping the length of her. "You are so beautiful," he whispered.

He was beautiful as well, with the light of the fire illuminating his muscles and emphasizing his handsome features. "Don't talk…. Kiss," she said breathlessly.

He complied, once again slanting his mouth down to hers where their tongues swirled as their bodies fell together like two pieces of a puzzle.

His hands were everywhere, cupping her sensitive breasts, sliding down her stomach, running across her back. It was as if his fingers, his palms hungered for the feel of her skin and she couldn't halt the small moan of pleasure that escaped her.

She, too, loved the feel of his skin and ran her fingers down the length his back and then up to grip his shoulders and then the biceps that were like rocks.

He tore his mouth from hers and trailed kisses down her jawline, into the soft hollow of her throat and then licked one of her nipples, creating an electric current that raced through her from head to toe.

He toyed with first one nipple and then the other and she could feel his turgid manhood against her thigh, letting her know he was fully aroused.

His mouth left her breasts and dragged down to her lower stomach, lingering there as if he were kissing the baby she carried inside. She squeezed her eyes tightly closed as once again emotion welled up from deep inside her.

Love my baby, love me, a little voice whispered in the back of her head. The voice was silenced as his hands slid down her stomach, lightly touched her inner thigh and then caressed the center of her that throbbed with need.

Rational thought left her as she raised her hips to meet the intimate touch, as the build-up of sexual tension climbed higher and higher.

He moved his fingers faster and then slowed as he teased and tormented her. She dug her fingers into the rug on either side of her as his fingers once again worked faster and she gave in to the waves of pleasure that washed over her, leaving her gasping, crying and laughing all at the same time.

"Again," he whispered, his eyes filled with the joy of her pleasure. Once again his fingers found the same spot and began to move…slowly, sensually rubbing and caressing as she struggled to catch her breath.

He seemed to know exactly what she needed, what she wanted and then she was there again, crying out his name as her body shuddered with a second release.

She grabbed his hand to stop him from touching her again. She needed to catch her breath, she wanted to give back to him a little of the sheer pleasure that he'd just given to her.

She sat up and pushed him onto his back, determined that if this was the last time they were going to be together, she would make sure he had as much trouble forgetting it as she would.

He lay perfectly still as she leaned over him and kissed him on the lips. Her kiss was soft and light, just a promise and then she began to trail kisses down the length of his chest and stomach.

Light and teasing, she kissed and licked his skin, loving the taste of him on her tongue, loving the way he groaned her name as she made her way down his lower abdomen.

His body held a tension that she reveled in as his hands tangled in her hair and he once again moaned her name. She licked first one inner thigh and then the other as she took him in her hand. Hard and throbbing, his arousal was magnificent and she loved the fact that it was her he wanted.

"Debra." Her name escaped him in a husky, strangled protest. "I need to be in you now. If you touch me anymore I'll lose it."

"We wouldn't want that," she replied, surprised by the husky want in her own voice.

He sat up and laid her down and she opened herself to receive him as he moved into position on top of her. As he eased into her, his mouth sought hers. The kiss was achingly tender and brought tears to her eyes once again.

Love my baby. Love me.

The words reverberated around in her head as he moved his hips against her in a slow, long stroke and she gasped at the sheer pleasure that soared through her. He broke the kiss and cradled her against his chest as his hips moved faster against her, into her.

She was vaguely aware of the crackling fire nearby, but the real fire was inside her, burning a forever impression onto her heart and into her soul as he took her to the heights of pleasure once again.

He tensed and whispered her name as he found his own release and then collapsed, holding the bulk of his weight off her and onto his elbows on either side of her.

He stared down at her, his features relaxed, yet his eyes dark and fathomless. She had no idea what he was thinking. She wasn't even sure he was thinking.

She only knew that this was a kind of goodbye for her, that she would never compromise herself again with him, no matter how much she loved him, because she loved him.

He finally rolled over to his back beside her. "It was even more amazing than I'd remembered."

She sat up, feeling too naked, too vulnerable as he gazed at her. "It's just sex, Trey, and it's never going to happen between us again."

She got up and pulled a red-and-yellow-striped blanket from the back of her sofa and wrapped it around herself. He sat up and reached for his briefs, as if he, too, suddenly felt too naked.

"We'll be great at co-parenting," she continued.

He finished dressing without saying a word. Had she

made him mad? Had he really thought he could maybe convince her to continue a sexual relationship with him?

She'd be an easy sex fix throughout the stresses of a campaign, a quick drive-by physical relief whenever he stopped by to see the baby.

No way, no how, she thought firmly. She'd compromised herself enough tonight. She'd sworn she'd never settle for a piece of a man's heart instead of the entire thing. She'd determined long ago that when it came to love, for her it was all or nothing.

When he was fully dressed he stepped over to her and pulled her into his arms. She allowed the embrace, even leaned into him, knowing that if nothing else she could always trust him to have her safety and her welfare in his heart.

"I won't let you down, Debra," he said, his voice a whisper against her ear. "Anything you need, at any time, I'm just a phone call away. We're tied for life now through our baby and all I want for you is happiness." He released her and stepped back.

She followed him to the front door, emotion a tight knot in the center of her chest. "I'll see you next Sunday at your mother's place," she said as he reached the door.

He turned back to face her. "I can't say that I'm not sorry we aren't going to be intimate again. I love making love to you, but I have to respect your wishes. Everything is going to work out fine. If nothing else, we'll parent our child and be good friends."

"I'd like that," she replied, but of course it was a lie. At the moment she couldn't imagine loving Trey the way she did and settling for a friendship. Hopefully, eventually she would be able to do just that.

"Then I'll see you Sunday morning."

Her tears began the minute she punched in the code to reset the security after he'd left. Hot and burning, they trekked down her cheeks as her chest grew more and more tight.

She should just go to bed and forget about tonight, forget about Trey Winston. Instead she curled up back on the hearth and wrapped the blanket more firmly around her, chilled despite the warmth of the fire.

She stared into the flickering flames and remembered the gentleness of his kiss on her belly, a kiss she'd believed was meant for the baby growing inside her.

Her child would always have a place in the Winston family. Trey would make sure that his son or daughter was loved and accepted without question.

A sob escaped her, followed by another and another. She curled up on her side on the rug where she could still smell the scent of his cologne and she wept.

She cried because somebody was trying to kill her and she had no idea who or why. Finally she cried because despite what Trey had just said to her, she'd never felt so alone. Everything had changed and she no longer knew where she belonged.

Chapter 14

Trey slept little the night after making love with Debra again. He'd tossed and turned with thoughts rioting in his head, creating a chaos of visions that had made sleep next to impossible.

The week had flown by since then. He'd kept himself busy at work and had given a couple of speeches to local businessmen and at a lunch for the fire department. He'd spoken to Debra on the phone each day, but hadn't gone by the townhouse to see her.

The investigation into both the cutting of her brake lines and the fire in her house had stalled out despite Thad's working hard to find the guilty party in any spare time he had. But there was always another crime scene for him to investigate, always a new mystery to be solved.

Trey had also stayed away from the estate for the

past week. He had no reason to go by there and didn't want to make Debra feel uncomfortable.

It had been a long week for him. He felt as if he was in withdrawal... Debra withdrawal. The idea of never making love with her again was downright depressing. But, he knew it was time to think of her only as the mother of his child, a woman who intended to go on living her life without him in it other than as the father of her firstborn child.

She would probably eventually marry somebody and perhaps have other children. Trey would make sure that whatever man she chose would be a stellar stepfather to his child. This thought also depressed him.

He was ridiculously glad when Sunday morning came and he knew at least he'd see Debra at the breakfast his mother had arranged.

It was a perfect Sunday morning as he left his home to head to the estate. The sun shone brightly and although it was only just before ten the temperature had risen to the mid-sixties as the area enjoyed an unusual streak of mild temperatures that, unfortunately, wasn't going to last. Still, right now it was perfect for breakfast outside by the pool.

He'd chosen a lightweight black-and-gray-patterned sweater with a pair of black jeans for the casual family breakfast that morning.

Hopefully the weather would stay decent through the next weekend, when his mother was the keynote speaker for the chamber of commerce Valentine's Day celebration.

During the past week he'd spoken to his mother several times and knew how she was looking forward to the Valentine Ball, but more importantly to the speech she would be giving at the event.

He had a list of things he wanted to accomplish in the next week that had nothing to do with either Adair Enterprises or his campaign. He wanted to visit his grandmother again. It had already been too long since his last troubling visit with her.

Secrets and lies. He hadn't been able to forget how upset his grandmother had become during his last visit, and he hadn't been completely satisfied by his mother's explanation. Secrets and lies. Hopefully it was just the meaningless ramblings of an old woman whose mind was starting to slip.

He knew things were going to start to go crazy with his schedule in the next weeks and it was important that he get out to the nursing home to see how she was doing. His last visit had been so unsettling, but he hoped his next one would be better, that she'd be better.

He also wanted to find a contractor who could paint one of his bedrooms in yellow with primary colors as trim to sort of match what Debra would be doing in her guest room for a nursery.

He'd use the guest room closest to his master suite and turn it into a baby wonderland. He planned on being a hands-on father in a way his own dad had never been. He loved that baby already and, like Debra, he intended to let the child know that he or she was both wanted and loved.

Buck had been too busy being an important senator and sleeping with other women to be much of a parent to his three sons. Trey wanted to be a better kind of father even though he and Debra wouldn't be together.

And it had been that which had kept him tossing and

turning all night. He was so confused about his feelings toward Debra. He'd somehow hoped that in making love with her one last time his constant, overwhelming desire for her would wane or disappear altogether.

But that hadn't happened. Even now, driving to his mother's home for breakfast as he thought of Debra a fresh wave of physical desire punched him in the gut.

His feelings for her didn't stop with the simple, uncomplicated emotion of physical lust. He wanted her safe from harm, he wanted to say things that caused her eyes to twinkle and laughter to spill from her lips.

He not only wanted to talk to her about his campaign, but he also wanted to share with her his worry about his grandmother. He wanted to confess the fact that he loved to watch old John Wayne movies and he liked his popcorn with extra butter, that some country songs could bring tears to his eyes.

He wanted to tell her that he and his brothers had once played cowboys and he and Sam had tied Thad to a tree so tightly they hadn't been able to untie him. Thankfully a gardener had been working nearby and had used a pair of gardening shears to cut the ropes.

For an hour afterward, Thad had chased them with a big stick, threatening to whip them if he managed to catch them. He tightened his hands on the steering wheel as the happy memory played out in his head.

He had so many memories of home and his brothers. Growing up they had been almost inseparable. But adulthood had brought so many changes. Sam had closed himself off mentally after coming home from overseas and Thad had removed himself both emotionally and physically from the core of the family.

For the first time in his life Trey realized he was

lonely. He was thirty-five years old and had nobody in his life who saw the essence of the man he was at his very core. Everyone only saw the top layer, the successful businessman, the new candidate for senator.

He could be something different with Debra. He thought of the peace of just sitting with her in her kitchen, of how relaxed he felt when it was just the two of them together and he didn't have to put on any kind of a public facade.

Was it possible he was in love with Debra? The thought shot through his head so forcefully, it momentarily took his breath away.

Was this what love felt like? This need to see her face, to make her happy? This desire to keep her safe and see no harm ever came to her? This passion to hold her in his arms, not just while making love but through the night while she slept?

Even if he did love her, it didn't matter. He'd asked her to marry him and she'd told him no. It was obvious she wanted him in a physical sense, but she wasn't in love with him.

Funny that the first thing he would fail at in his life was love. Although he wasn't laughing. He pulled through the side entrance of the estate and as he parked his car it was with an aching heart that felt somehow bruised.

He glanced at his watch as he got out of his car. He was early and from the lack of cars in the side parking area none of his siblings had arrived yet.

He knew that Debra had been invited to attend his mother's breakfast also. With the realization of the depths of his feelings for her, he felt unusually vulnerable.

Somehow, someway, he had to get over it. They had a lifetime of working together as partners to raise their child. He couldn't let unwanted emotions get in the way.

He walked into the kitchen where it was obvious Myra had been busy since early this morning as the fragrances of a variety of foods mingled together to make a heavenly scent.

"Don't you go touching anything in here, Trey Winston," Myra said sternly as she hurried into the kitchen from another area of the house. At her heels was Tiffany Burgess, one of the kitchen helpers.

Trey held his hands up in innocence. "I was just thinking about maybe pouring myself a cup of coffee, that's all."

"Everything is already set up out back by the pool. We just have a few more things to finish up to get the food out there. Now go on with you, coffee is there and your mother should be downstairs anytime now."

He left the kitchen, walking past Debra's and then his mother's office. Just off the foyer was a large ballroom that his mother used when giving charity balls or other such events. It had been a while since she'd used it.

He passed it, as well, and went on to the family sitting room where double doors led out to the pool area. The staff had been busy.

A long glass-top table had been set up with bright turquoise placemats and white plates. Turquoise-and-white-patterned cloth napkins were neatly folded by each place and the silverware gleamed in the sunshine. It looked both inviting and like a signal of the summer to come.

A second table held the beginnings of a buffet. A silver coffeepot and cups took up one end along with a pitcher of orange juice and a tiered serving platter that held a variety of sweet rolls and plump muffins. On the other side of the table hot electric servers awaited food to be placed into their bins.

Trey served himself a cup of coffee and then carried it to a chair away from the table and closer to the pool. In the springtime the beauty of his mother's backyard was breathtaking, with flowerbeds splashing color and a waterfall that spilled over rocks and then disappeared into a large decorative urn.

In the distance a tree line stood outside the black wrought-iron fence. The trees were far enough away that they couldn't be used to help anyone scale the fence, but in the springtime when in full leaf, provided a beautiful green backdrop to the large yard.

Looking around the yard and pool area, Trey made a mental note that it was past time for him to do something about his own property. He'd talk to his mother about her landscaping services and see if he could borrow somebody to tell him what would be best to plant.

It was impossible to miss the men who were stationed at the four corners of the yard. The Secret Service would never allow Kate to sit in her own backyard without them present. He doubted that his mother even thought about their presence anymore. They had been a constant in her life since she'd served as vice president.

He sat up straighter in his chair as Thad walked outside. Clad in a pair of black slacks and a white shirt and jacket, he looked more like a businessman than a cop. But Trey knew the slight bulge beneath his sport coat indicated a shoulder holster and gun.

The two brothers had been on the phone to each other several times a day throughout the week as Trey checked in to see if there had been any new information about the attacks on Debra.

He raised a hand in greeting to Trey and then poured himself a cup of coffee and walked over to where Trey sat. "Don't ask," he said in greeting. "Because if you ask I'll have to tell you we have nothing new."

"You still haven't been able to identify any real person of interest?" Trey asked.

"We have a couple persons of interest, but no evidence to tie them to any of the crimes. Everyone we've spoken to has an alibi that so far we've been unable to break."

"What about Haley?" Trey asked in a low voice, even though he knew the intern wasn't at the house on Sundays.

"We spoke to her. Her alibi for the nights in question was that she was at her place alone." Thad shrugged. "We haven't been able to absolutely place her at home, but we also haven't been able to disprove that she was there. The motive that you've come up with, that somehow she wants to get rid of Debra so that she can have Debra's job is a bit weak."

"It's the only motive I could come up with given that Debra isn't the type of woman who makes enemies."

"I know you've got her all locked down in that townhouse of hers, but she still needs to watch her back when she's out of the house," Thad said. "Since we have no real motive and no real suspects, we can't warn her in advance should something else happen."

Trey nodded, a new little hole ripping in his heart as he thought of something bad happening to Debra. "I'm thinking about talking to Mom about maybe getting her some full-time security. Maybe one of the Secret Service men knows somebody who wants to moonlight and shadow Debra to make sure she stays safe when she's away from home."

"Might not be a bad idea," Thad agreed. "At least until we can get a break on the case." He took a sip of his coffee and eyed Trey with open speculation. "Why do you want to run for the Senate?" he asked.

Trey looked at him in surprise. "Because I think I can make a real difference for the state of North Carolina, because I see problems and issues that I believe I can help to fix. Why?"

Thad raked a hand through his hair and released a deep sigh. "I just feel like politics is what screwed up our whole family life and I can't imagine why you'd want to put yourself out there like that."

"Thad, I know you love what you do. I know you feel a true calling in your work. That's the way I feel about politics. That's the way mom feels about politics. It's not just a job—it's a true calling, a real passion and a need and desire to make things better in the world."

At that moment Debra stepped outside. Clad in a pair of leg-hugging jeans and a blue-and-green-patterned sweater, she looked more beautiful than ever.

She paused just outside the door and offered a smile to the two brothers. It was at that moment, with her hair gleaming in the sunshine and her smile warming him from head to toe that Trey knew without a doubt that he was madly in love with Debra Prentice.

That crazy anxious jangle of nerves accompanied an acceleration of her heartbeat at the sight of Trey. She turned and poured herself a glass of orange juice, grateful that at least her hands remained steady.

She had to get used to seeing him and not loving him. She had to transform her love to a friendship for the sake of their baby. She had to figure out how to stop being in love with him and just love him as the father of her child.

"Good morning," she said as she carried her cup to where the two men were located near the pool.

"Back at you," Thad said with a smile.

At least he was here to serve as buffer, she thought as Trey murmured a greeting, his blue eyes far too intense as his gaze remained on her.

Was he thinking about their last moments together, a flickering fire, a red throw rug and desire spiraled out of control? Certainly she'd been thinking about it since then, every single day for the last week.

But, she refused to think about it now. It was done. They were finished, and this morning's breakfast was all about Kate. "Where is the lady of the hour?" she asked.

"She hasn't made an appearance yet," Thad replied.

"Neither has Sam," Trey added.

They all turned to look as Myra and Tiffany came back outside, each carrying metal baking pans that they placed in the awaiting electric warmer.

"Your mother and Sam should be out here any minute," Myra said as she and Tiffany disappeared back into the house.

"I have a fairly good idea that I'm not going to like what I hear here this morning," Thad said.

"I'm sure you're probably right," Trey agreed.

Debra sipped her orange juice, wishing Sam and Kate would come outside so things could get underway and she could get back home.

She wasn't even sure why Kate had included her in this family gathering. It wasn't like Debra was really a part of the family.

Sam was the next one outside and once he'd joined them with a cup of coffee in hand, he pointed to the glass of juice Debra held.

"I'm glad my niece or nephew is getting a dose of vitamin C this morning instead of a cup of caffeine," he said.

The shadows that always darkened his blue eyes were gone for now and Debra was grateful that he appeared to be in a fairly good mood. Hopefully nothing that occurred during the breakfast would bring the terrible darkness back into his eyes.

"What are you all doing over there when I have this lovely table set beautifully for everyone?" Kate's voice pulled everyone's attention toward her as she stepped out of the back doors and onto the patio.

"We were making plans to overthrow the monarchy," Thad said with a wicked grin.

Kate laughed. "I know Debra isn't a part of such a plan and it would take far more than three big men to get the job done right."

She looked stunning in a pair of tailored black slacks and a red blouse with a black cardigan sweater flung over her shoulders. "Come on, come on. Let's fill our plates and get this party started."

It took some time for all of them to serve themselves and then get seated. Debra was grateful to find herself across the table from Trey rather than seated next to him. Instead she sat next to Thad with Sam across the table next to Trey, and Kate at the head of the table.

The conversation remained light and easy as they ate.

Debra was pleased to discover that it was late enough in the day that the food tasted delicious and she suffered no nausea or belly rolling.

As the conversation turned to the brothers' childhood, stories began to roll out that had Debra both relaxing and laughing. The stories of brotherly antics and love also made her realize how much she'd missed out on by being the only child of an alcoholic mother.

She also realized that she didn't want her baby to be an only child. Siblings weren't just brothers and sisters; they were also friends and support systems for lifetimes.

But she couldn't be sure what the future held. Right now she just wanted to have a healthy pregnancy and baby, deal with the co-parenting issues with Trey and figure out what the next step in her personal life might be.

The breakfast talk went from old memories to the mildness of the weather and finally to Kate's upcoming speech for the chamber of commerce event the following Saturday night on Valentine's Day.

It seemed ironic to Debra that she was pregnant and yet had nobody to send her flowers or chocolates for the special lovers' day. But she'd never gotten flowers or anything from a man on Valentine's Day.

Barry had been one of few men she had dated in her lifetime and they hadn't even known each other last Valentine's Day.

Throughout the meal she was acutely conscious of Trey's gaze lingering on her. Dark and unreadable, something about his unwavering attention made her uncomfortable.

What was he thinking? Was it possible that he might fight her for full custody when the baby was born? Certainly with the Winston power, influence and money, it would be a battle she'd lose.

Her hand fell to her stomach, as if to somehow protect her baby from such a confrontation. Surely that couldn't be what he was thinking. They'd spoken about co-parenting. But what might happen when he married? Once he had a wife, might not he want his child to live with them full-time?

Stop borrowing trouble, she reprimanded herself. Without a magical crystal ball there was no way to see what the future might hold, and she'd just have to deal with everything one day at a time from here on out.

She definitely didn't want to think about the fact that the investigations into the attacks on her had yielded nothing. At least with her new security in the townhouse she felt completely safe when she was there.

It wasn't until they had all finished eating, their plates had been removed and their coffee and juice refilled that Kate raised a hand to get everyone's attention.

"I'm sure you're all wondering why I asked you to come here for breakfast this morning," she began.

"Not really," Thad muttered under his breath.

"Before I make my final decision about what my future is going to hold, I wanted to give you all a chance to talk about your concerns," she said.

Debra stared over Trey's shoulder to the distant tree line, knowing that she didn't have a pony in this show. Kate needed to hear from her sons, not from one of her son's baby mama. Besides, Kate already knew that Debra was up for whatever she decided.

"I'm considering announcing formally my decision to run for president of the United States next Saturday night at the chamber of commerce event." She looked at her sons expectantly.

Debra focused her attention back to the table. "You know I'll support that decision," Trey said.

"You're going to do what you want to do anyway," Sam added, his voice holding resignation.

Thad frowned. "I just don't understand why you'd want to do this given what politics has done to our family in the past."

"If you're talking about when you were young and your father was a senator, the only thing I can tell you is that our family fell apart because of your father's bad choices, not because he was in the Senate," Kate replied.

"You should have left the bastard," Sam said, his eyes taking on the darkness that they held far too often.

"I did what I needed to do to keep the family together," Kate replied with a steely note. "Things weren't so terrible for all of you when I served as vice president and as an ambassador."

"That's because nobody ever cares that much about the vice president," Thad said. "But as President of the United States every move you make will be in the spotlight and a lot of that spotlight is going to bleed over onto us." He raked a hand through his shaggy brown hair. "But I guess we can all handle that if this is what you really want."

"Sam?" Kate looked at her middle child with affection.

He shrugged. "I know you want to do this and I'm not going to be the one who stops you from pursuing what you want."

"So I have tentative blessings from everyone?" Kate asked.

"I think you can say that you have complete blessings from everyone," Trey replied.

Kate turned and motioned to Myra, who stood just inside the door and held a silver tray with flutes of champagne. "Then this calls for a celebratory toast."

Thad laughed dryly. "You've already got the champagne poured. You weren't worried a bit about getting our blessings."

Kate beamed a smile around the table as Myra stepped outside. "I knew my boys would only want my happiness and this is something I feel destined to do."

Myra went around the table, handing each of them a glass of champagne. "No bubbly for you," she said when she got to Debra. "You have a flute of nice white grape juice."

"Thank you, Myra," Debra said as she accepted the delicate, thin glass.

Kate stood and held up her glass. "Bear with me, I have a rather long toast to make."

Debra smiled inwardly as she saw all three of her sons roll their eyes, as if they were accustomed to "bearing with" their strong, assertive mother.

The rest of them remained seated, giving Kate her moment to shine even at a family breakfast.

"First of all to Debra, who will forever be a part of this family and hopefully continue to play an important role in my professional life as well as my personal one." Kate smiled at Debra and then looked at Sam.

"To my middle son, Sam. You awe me with your bravery, with your honor and duty you showed by serving your country. I only pray that your heart and soul eventually heal as your body does. I love you, Sam."

Debra felt herself getting a bit teary as Kate honored each of her children.

"Thaddeus," Kate continued. "I'm so proud of the life you've made for yourself as a part of law enforcement. You honor the family name with your work as a public servant. I love you, Thad."

She turned her attention to Trey. "And to my first-born, who has not only driven the family business to new heights, but is also about to discover the insane world of politics and parenthood. I love you, Trey, and wish only good things for my boys in the future."

She raised her glass. "Cheers."

"Gun!" Thad suddenly screamed and pointed to the trees in the distance.

And then the world exploded.

Chapter 15

A thousand things occurred almost simultaneously, creating wild chaos. A shot sounded. The glass table shattered, cups and glasses crashing to the ground. Trey dove across the broken table to reach Debra who sat in her chair stunned.

He scrambled to her, yanked her from the chair and pulled her to the ground. Sam grabbed his mother's hand and pulled her down also as Thad and half a dozen Secret Service men raced in all directions. Thad and a couple of men ran to the side entrance gate and out of the backyard.

Two other agents rushed to stand next to the shattered table, their backs to each other and their weapons drawn as they protected everyone on the ground. Several more agents raced to the back of the yard, their guns pointed up at the tree where the shooter was no longer visible.

"Are you okay?" Trey asked as he covered Debra's body with his on the hard concrete near the pool.

Around them chaos continued to reign as men yelled to each other and another gunshot split the air. Trey could feel the frantic beat of Debra's heart against his own.

Her breath came in gasps of terror against his collarbone and his brain worked to try to make sense of what had just happened, what was still happening. "Yes," she replied, her voice small and scared.

There was no question that somebody had been in those trees, that Thad had spied what apparently had been a man with a gun. The gun had been fired, shattering the table, but had the bullet been meant for his mother or for Debra?

His body shuddered at the thought of either woman being shot. He looked over at Sam, who had their mother down against the concrete, a look of anguish on his face.

Trey knew his brother was probably wishing he had his weapon on him, but Sam had been deemed unfit for duty and all of his weapons had been taken from him by the army brass who had released him.

Trey's body jerked as another gunshot exploded and then Thad's voice rose in the distance. It had a triumphant tone and Trey felt the muscles in his body begin to relax a bit.

One of the Secret Service men standing near them talked into his radio, listened a moment and then turned to face everyone on the ground. "They've got the shooter in custody."

The two agents remained on guard as both Trey and Sam rose and helped Debra and Kate to their feet. It was only as he saw Debra's terror-filled eyes that he recognized the bottomless depth of his love for her.

He pulled her to him and she willingly huddled in the secure embrace of his arms. Love. It flowed through him, unmistakable and undeniable. But he didn't know what to do about it, knew there was nothing to be done about it.

"Well, that's the way to end a toast with a bang," Kate said in a slightly shaky voice as Sam helped her to her feet.

"We'd like all of you to move as quickly as possible into the house," Secret Service Agent Daniel Henderson said as he took Kate by the arm. "It's for your own safety. We don't know who else might be out here somewhere."

As Daniel ushered Kate back into the house, Trey did the same with Debra, still unsure who the ultimate target had been. They all took seats in the sitting room and waited, the silence in the room growing more and more tense with each minute that passed.

Had there been more than one shooter? Had this been some sort of an organized attack? Trey's mind raced to make sense of what had just occurred.

Thad, Jerry Cahill and Robert D'Angelis appeared at the back door. Between Thad and Robert was a thin man in scruffy jeans and a black jacket. His hands were cuffed behind him and Robert held a high-powered rifle with a scope in his hand.

"Ms. Winston, do you know this person?"

Trey stared at the man. He was small and slender and wore a black sweatshirt and jeans. His eyes were dark and a smirk formed on his thin lips as if everyone else was in handcuffs and he was free.

Sam lunged toward him. "Who are you and why were you shooting at my mother?" he yelled. Kate stopped him from advancing by grabbing his arm.

"I don't have to talk to you," the man said with a scowl. "I don't have to talk to any of you. I know my rights. Besides, if I don't talk then I get some time in prison. If I do talk then I get a bullet to the back of my head. It's a no-brainer. I don't have nothing to say to nobody."

"I've never seen him before in my life," Kate finally said.

"Get him out of here," Sam growled. "Get him the hell out of here."

Thad and Cahill took the man back out the door where Trey assumed he'd be handed over to Secret Service agents and other authorities to deal with.

Sam turned his wrath on Daniel Henderson and Robert D'Angelis. "How in the hell did this happen? How did that little creep manage to get up in a tree with a rifle without any of the agents noticing? I want to know who didn't do their job."

"I don't know how this happened, but I promise you by the end of the day we'll have some answers," Robert replied, his gray eyes cold and narrowed. "Now if you'll excuse me, I'll go find out as much information as I can right now."

He headed through the house, toward the kitchen and the side door that would bring him out by the guesthouse where the security operations and agents worked from.

Trey turned to look at Debra, who stood beside him, frozen like a deer in headlights. It was only then that he saw a trickle of blood seeping from her hairline down the side of her face.

His heartbeat spiked as he grabbed her by the arm. Had one of the bullets grazed her? "Debra, you're hurt," he said. Had a piece of shattered glass from the table ricocheted to her?

"What?" She looked at him with blank eyes.

"Your head… You're bleeding." He dropped his hand from her arm.

She raised a hand up and touched the area and then stared at the blood on her hand and then back at him. "It must be glass from the table."

"We need to get you cleaned up," Kate said briskly, back in control despite the horror of what had just happened.

Somewhere in the back of his mind Trey knew it was this very trait, the ability to function with a cool head in a crisis, that would benefit the country if Kate was elected.

"Maddie," Kate turned to the housekeeper who hovered in the doorway. "Take Debra into one of the bathrooms and clean up her face and check to make sure she doesn't have any glass in her hair or on her clothes. I'm going upstairs where Birdie can help me do the same thing. Sam and Trey, you both need to make sure there isn't any glass in your clothing or hair."

"Come on, honey," Maddie said to Debra as she walked across the room and gently took Debra's hand in hers. "Let's go get you all cleaned up."

The two women left the sitting room and Kate turned to Daniel Henderson, the last agent left in the room. "You can go, Daniel. We're good now. Just please keep me informed of anything you hear about the investigation into what just happened."

Daniel gave Kate a stiff half bow. "You know I'll do whatever I can to get to the bottom of this, but I imagine by now all kinds of agencies will be moving in to take over the investigation. Of course the Secret Service will be doing most of the work."

"Just keep me informed." Kate headed out of the sitting room while Daniel left by the back doors.

Sam remained in place, his hands in fists at his sides and angry frustration evident in every muscle in his body. "I should have seen that guy in the tree. I should have been paying more attention. I was trained to watch out for snipers."

"Cut yourself a break, Sam," Trey replied. "You weren't trained to look for snipers in our backyard at a breakfast. But I'd like to know who hired that guy. From what he said he was definitely a hired gun."

Sam's hands relaxed. "Either that or he was just a thug trying to make a name for himself and he just added in that bit about a bullet to the head business to make us believe he was nothing more than a hired gun."

Sam threw himself into one of the nearby chairs. "Hell, she hasn't even formally declared yet and already somebody is trying to kill her."

"At this point we can't be sure exactly who the target was," Trey replied, also sitting down in a chair near Sam.

"Who else would the target be?" Sam asked, looking at Trey as if he'd lost his mind.

"Maybe rumor had gotten out that you've been a real cranky ass to live with and Mom actually hired that man to put you out of your own misery," Trey said with a teasing tone.

"Ha ha, very funny," Sam replied.

"Okay, then Thad could have been the target because of his police work, or me because I've declared my intentions to run for senator." He paused a moment, his chest burning with anxiety. "Or the target could have been Debra. She's already been targeted by somebody twice. Maybe this was a final attempt to get rid of her."

Sam drew a deep breath and fell back into the chair. "What a mess."

"I suggest we both do what Mom said and head into bathrooms to check ourselves for glass," Trey replied.

Definitely a mess, Trey thought as he went in one direction and Sam disappeared in another. Somebody had just missed being shot and even though they had the shooter in custody Trey wasn't feeling optimistic that any agency would be able to get any real information out of the creep.

Was it possible that this would make his mother change her mind about running for president? Somehow Trey believed that if anything this would make her more resolute to follow through on her plans.

Trey knew that beneath Kate's pleasant exterior beat the heart of a warrior and a will of steel. She knew the dangers the office held and he had a feeling she would still be just as determined to make a run for the White House.

What he needed to do was talk to Thad and bring up the fact that it was possible the target wasn't Kate at all, but rather Debra.

Debra.

His heart filled with the newly realized love he felt

for her. Yes, everything was a mess. A man had just shot to kill somebody seated at the table and he was in love with a woman who apparently didn't love him back, a woman who might have been the intended victim of the shooting.

Debra sat on the toilet lid as Maddie used tweezers to pick pieces of glass from her hair and off her sweater. Maddie had already cleaned the blood off her face and Debra had sat like a child being ministered to by a loving mother.

She knew that she was in a little bit of shock because everything felt surreal. Her heart had finally found a normal rhythm after having beat nearly right out of her chest.

Everything that had happened to her—the mad drive in the middle of the night with no brakes, the fire that had occurred in her house—both seemed like mere nuisances when compared to what had just happened.

Somebody had shot a gun with the intent to kill. It was only by chance that Thad had seen the man in the tree and his warning shout had apparently made the gunman lose his aim.

Who had he been aiming at?

Who had been his target?

The logical answer would be Kate, but Debra couldn't stop the idea that kept coming back into her head, the idea that the target had been her. A shiver worked through her.

"Are you cold?" Maddie asked with concern. "Would you like a blanket or something around your shoulders while I finish up?"

"No, I'm fine. I'm just suffering from a little bit of

post-traumatic stress. I don't think I've ever been quite so frightened."

"You just need to relax now. You're safe and at least they caught the man. Besides, it's not good for your baby for you to be so stressed out."

Debra nearly laughed. Her baby wouldn't know how to exist without stress. Debra had been mentally frazzled since the moment she'd taken those three pregnancy tests. God, that felt like years ago. So much had happened in the past four weeks.

The thought that she was losing her mind, the crash of her car, the fire in her house... The only good thing that had happened was that since the new security system had been installed nothing in her home had disappeared only to reappear later.

Still, the idea that somebody had enjoyed free access to her home to try to drive her crazy and then had moved to more deadly means of getting rid of her would haunt her until somebody had been caught and jailed for the offenses.

"There, I think we got them all," Maddie said as she stepped back from Debra. On the vanity counter on a paper towel were about a dozen slivers of glass in various sizes.

Maddie took Debra's chin and raised her face so that she could look into Debra's eyes. "Are you sure you're okay, honey? Maybe a nice hot cup of tea would help calm you down a bit."

"That sounds wonderful," Debra agreed as she got up from her sitting position. "And thank you, Maddie, for taking such good care of me."

Maddie smiled. "That's what I do. I take care of

Winstons." She swept up the paper with the glass in her hands and then left the bathroom.

But I'm not a Winston, Debra thought as she stared at her reflection in the mirror over the sink. She looked shell-shocked, her hair a mess, her eyes too big and still filled with the terror that had momentarily made it impossible to move away from the shattered table.

Trey had virtually thrown himself across what was left of the table to get to her and pulled her to the ground where he'd covered her body with his, protecting her from harm.

No, not her, but their baby. He'd been protecting his baby from harm. She just happened to be carrying that baby. She left the bathroom, unsure if she wanted the cup of tea or not.

What she really wanted was to be at the townhouse, safe within the walls of her highly secured home. What she wanted was to know who was behind the attacks on her, who was responsible for wanting her to believe that she was going crazy.

Trey met her in the hall, his eyes dark and his expression radiating concern. "Are you sure you're okay?" he asked.

She nodded. "It was just a small cut. Maddie got it to stop bleeding and I'm perfectly fine." She raised a hand to tuck her hair behind her ear and knew the tremble of her hand belied her words.

"Okay, so I'm not so fine," she admitted. "I'm definitely shaken up and Maddie is making me a cup of tea to calm my nerves."

"Then let's go to the kitchen and have a cup of tea." He took her by the elbow, his touch gentle and warm.

They entered the huge kitchen and went directly to

the small table where Sam often sat to have his morning coffee.

"Just in time. Maddie told me you would be in for a nice cup of tea," Myra said, and set a cup in front of Debra. "Do you want sugar? Lemon? And do you want a cup, too, Trey?"

"No, thanks, I'm good."

"And this is fine for me. Thanks, Myra." Debra wrapped her hands around the heat of the cup in an attempt to warm the cold places that had found a home inside her during the past thirty minutes.

For a few moments she and Trey sat in silence. Debra sipped her tea and looked out the window where a number of security agents were gathered in front of the guesthouse.

Somebody's head would roll for the breach in security, she thought. "I wouldn't want to be the agent in charge of security for that quadrant of the yard."

Trey followed her gaze and then looked back at her. "Somebody will figure it out. I just thank God that Thad saw the guy before he managed to hurt somebody."

Debra took a sip of her tea and then returned the cup to the saucer. "You know it's possible it wasn't about your mother."

He held her gaze and in the depths of his troubled eyes she realized the thought had already crossed his mind. "We can't jump the gun. We don't know who the target was supposed to be right now."

"But you understand that given everything that has happened to this point in time, it's very possible I was the target." Just saying the words out loud leeched any warmth she might have gained back out of her body.

She shoved the cup of tea aside. "What I'd really like

to do right now is go home." Tears burned at her eyes and blurred her vision as she stared down at the table. "I just want to go home," she repeated softly.

"Then I'll take you home." Trey stood and touched her shoulder.

"But my car is here."

"Debra, I'd feel better under the circumstances if I drive you home. You're still upset and I can always bring you back here for work in the morning and you'll have your car here to drive home tomorrow night."

She nodded and stood. She was grateful that he was taking charge, that she didn't have to drive herself. Sometimes it was better to allow somebody else to take care of things and this was definitely one of those times. She'd been taking care of herself for her entire life and just for a little while she wanted to abdicate control.

They were escorted to Trey's car by two agents with guns drawn and gazes narrowed and focused on their surroundings. Debra felt as if she had entered an action film set. Surreal. How had her life gotten so dramatic, so intense?

She breathed a sigh of relief as Trey pulled out of the driveway and away from the estate. "I have to say, Kate sure knows how to put on an exciting breakfast."

"Let's hope we never have one as exciting as this one again," Trey replied. "The shooter, you didn't recognize him, did you?"

"No, I'm fairly sure I've never seen him before in my life, but that doesn't mean he wasn't hired by somebody to kill me." The words created an almost physical pain inside her. The idea that somebody hated her so much was unbelievable.

"Keep in mind that we don't know that this attack was about you," Trey said.

"I understand that. I get that your mother might have political enemies, but we both know I have an enemy, too, and maybe that person has given up trying to kill me and make it look like an accident."

"Thad will be checking it out along with the Secret Service," he replied. "I intend to talk to Thad about the fact that this might have been an attempt on you and not on Mom."

Debra stared out the side window. "It just all feels so horrible, to know that there's somebody out there who wants me dead. I've never done anything to anyone. I've never harmed anyone. Who could have such hatred for me?"

"I wish I knew, Debra."

They were silent for the remainder of the ride and she was grateful for the quiet. She still was trying to process what had happened, how quickly a lovely family toast could have turned into a complete and utter tragedy.

When Trey pulled up to the curb in front of her townhouse, he shut off the engine and then turned to look at her. "Stay put," he said.

She watched as he got out of the driver side and then came around to her side of the car and opened her door. He instantly pulled her out of the seat and surrounded her with his own body.

Awkwardly they made their way to the front door, him like a shield wrapped around her back. She was tense, expecting a gunshot at any moment or a knife-wielding maniac to jump out of the bushes nearby.

She didn't relax until they were safely inside the house with the security on. She collapsed onto the sofa and Trey sank down next to her. It only took a simple touch from him and she was in his arms, crying out the stress and fear as he held her tight and murmured words of comfort.

Her crying jag lasted only a couple of minutes and then she sat up and wiped the tears from her face. "I'm okay now. I just needed to get that out."

He smiled at her. "My mother always said that a good cry never hurt anyone." He leaned back against the sofa cushion. "So I guess there's no Sunday specialty cooking planned for today."

"I'm thinking dinner is going to be something nice and easy," she replied.

"Maybe you should put something in your stomach now," he suggested. "I noticed you didn't eat much earlier."

It was obvious he was in no hurry to leave and she wasn't sure she wanted him to go just yet. Nerves still jangled through her and the horror of the morning lingered.

"A bowl of soup might be good," she replied. She pulled herself up from the sofa and he followed suit.

"Why don't you just go into the kitchen and sit at the table and I can handle the soup," he said.

She thought about protesting, but instead merely nodded. "Thank you, I appreciate it. I'm still feeling just a little bit shaky."

Together they went into the kitchen where Debra took a seat at the table and Trey moved to the pantry where she stored her canned goods.

"I see chicken noodle, tomato and split pea." He looked back at her and made a face. "You don't really eat that split-pea stuff, do you?"

She laughed, unable to help herself at his look of utter disgust. "Actually I do and I love it. But I think a bowl of chicken noodle will be just fine, and open two cans if you'd like some, too."

"Maybe I'll just do that," he replied as he grabbed a saucepan from the baker's rack.

"Wouldn't you rather be back at the estate checking on the investigation instead of here babysitting me?" she asked, suddenly feeling guilty for taking up his time.

"The Secret Service will take over any investigation so there's really nothing I can do there. Thad will have his nose in things and will let me know of any breaking news."

He paused to use the can opener and poured the contents of the two soup cans into the saucepan. "Besides, I can't think of anyplace else I'd rather be right now than here with you eating canned soup."

He placed the saucepan on a stove burner and turned it on and then dug into her silverware drawer for a big spoon. She stared out the window and wished he wouldn't say things like that to her. He shouldn't be so nice to her. He made her want more than what he'd ever be able to offer to her.

She shouldn't have even let him come inside. This whole scene was a little too domestic for her taste. It brought up the yearning for it to be real, for them to be together as a true couple.

As he stirred the soup, Debra found her gaze wandering around the room, looking everywhere but at him. It was bad enough that she could smell his familiar cologne, a scent she thought she'd never get out of her mind.

She frowned as she spied something under the edge

of one of her lower cabinets. Had she dropped something that had rolled there? She couldn't imagine what it was, but it appeared to hold a touch of sparkle.

"What are you doing?" he asked as she got up from her chair.

"There's something here on the floor under the cabinet." She bent down and grabbed it, then stood and opened her hand. It was an earring. A diamond and ruby earring that she'd never seen before in her life.

"What is it?"

"It's an earring, but it isn't mine." She looked at him in confusion.

Trey stepped away from the stove to see what she held. His face paled and he stumbled backward a step.

"Trey? What's wrong?" Debra's heart began to pound as she saw the odd look on his face as he stared at the piece of jewelry.

"I know that earring. I bought a pair of them for Cecily."

Debra frowned. "How would one of Cecily's earrings get into my kitchen?" She gasped in stunned surprise as the realization of who was behind the attacks on her became apparent by the piece of expensive jewelry she held in her hand.

Chapter 16

Trey stared at Debra for a long moment, trying to make sense of the earring she held in her hand. They were an unusual design and unmistakable. He specifically remembered purchasing them five months before and surprising Cecily with them over dinner at La Palace. Since that time she had worn them often.

Had she worn them when she'd set the fire in this house? Had they adorned her ears when she'd been moving cups and shifting around items to make Debra doubt her own sanity?

Cecily?

His mind boggled with the irrefutable evidence that she'd been inside Debra's home. Cecily had been behind everything. He couldn't seem to wrap his mind around it.

"I understand if she was angry when she found out

I was pregnant with your child, but most of the terrible things that happened occurred before anyone knew I was pregnant by you," Debra said thoughtfully. "Why would she try to hurt me when she didn't know anything about us?"

"I need to call Thad," Trey said as he fumbled his phone out of his pocket. "If she's responsible for everything that's happened to you then she needs to be arrested and charged."

As he punched in the number to connect him with his brother, Debra moved the saucepan and turned off the stove. "Thad." He was surprised that his voice shook with tension as he heard his brother answer the phone. "Can you get over to Debra's townhouse? I think we've found the source of the attacks on her."

With Thad's assurance that he'd be right over, Trey sank down at the table, still stunned by this new development. Debra sat down next to him, the earring on the table between them.

"I'm sorry, Trey," she said softly.

He looked at her incredulously. "Why are you sorry?"

"Because I know you cared about her, that you had intended to make her your wife. I'm sorry because I know that if what we believe is true you have to be hurting."

"Hurting?" He stood and slammed his hands down on the table. "I'm so angry right now she's lucky she isn't here in front of me. I knew she had a cold streak inside her, but I had no idea the evil that she has to possess to do what she's apparently done."

"She must have known about that night we spent together," Debra said.

Trey drew a deep breath and once again sat down

at the table. "I don't see how she could have known. I certainly never said anything about it to anyone and I'm sure you didn't, either. It was spontaneous, neither of us planned for it to happen. How could she have known about it?"

He closed his eyes, trying to recreate that night in his mind. He'd called Cecily and had invited her to join him in his celebration, but she'd been at a charity event and had told him she really couldn't get away.

Was it possible she had decided to show up at the restaurant anyway? Had she seen him and Debra and watched them as they left together to get the room in the nearby hotel?

Why hadn't she confronted him at the time? Why hadn't she told him that she knew about his tryst with Debra?

The doorbell rang and Trey got up, indicating that Debra should stay seated while he let his brother in. "I figured you'd be tied up with the shooting at the house," he said as Thad stepped inside.

"Right now the Secret Service is in charge of the crime scene and investigation, but if they think I'm going to leave it to them, then they don't know me," Thad said grimly. "So what's this about you believing you know who is behind the attacks on Debra?"

"Come on into the kitchen," Trey said. As Thad followed him Trey realized the stunned surprise he'd initially felt had transformed into a cold hard knot of anger in his chest.

Cecily had tried to kill the woman he loved, the woman who carried his baby. He'd sat across the table from her a hundred times at special events and in restaurants. He'd held her in his arms and gazed into her eyes and considered a future with her and yet he'd never seen the evil that had to dwell inside her.

As he and his brother entered the kitchen, the sight of Debra seated at the table made him realize just how superficial his feelings had been for Cecily.

The woman he truly loved sat in the chair with big green eyes and a touch of worry on her face. Debra might not love him, but he knew without a doubt she cared about the man he was, not the man he might someday become.

It took only minutes for Trey to explain about the earring that Debra had found beneath the lower cabinet. Thad immediately called Lieutenant Al Chase, who agreed to meet them at Debra's house and then Thad placed the earring inside a small plastic bag and joined them at the table as they waited for Al to arrive.

"I have no idea how she might have gotten a key to my house," Debra said.

Thad gave her a rueful smile. "I've news for you, Debra. There are key rings all over the estate that somebody could have plucked up and brought to your house, found the appropriate key, had a copy of it made and then returned the original to the key ring."

"And she could have hired some thug to crawl beneath my car on the night of the dinner and cut my brake lines." Debra shook her head as she stared at the earring encased in plastic on her table. "She smiled at me that night, thanked me for everything I'd done for Trey. She was so nice and all the while she'd plotted my death."

Trey reached across and covered one of Debra's hands with his. "It will be over soon," he said. If Thad hadn't been present he would have told Debra what was in his heart, that obviously Cecily had seen her as a threat because somehow Cecily had known Trey was deeply in love with Debra.

"It's definitely possible that sniper in the tree this morning had nothing to do with Mom, but was somebody Cecily hired to kill Debra," he said instead.

Thad frowned thoughtfully. "That would definitely be nice for the Secret Service who are not only investigating but pointing fingers at each other as to who was responsible for that area."

At that moment the doorbell rang again and Lieutenant Chase arrived. Once again Trey told the story of the earring and everything he now suspected Cecily of being responsible for, including the possibility of her being behind the shooting that morning at the estate.

"Sounds to me like we need to speak to Cecily," Al said. "Do you know if she's home?"

Trey pulled his cell phone from his pocket. "I can find out." He punched the number he'd dialed a hundred times before and when she answered he was pleased that his voice betrayed none of the rage that had built up inside him with each moment that passed.

"Cecily, it's me," he said when she answered.

"Trey!" She was obviously surprised.

"I was wondering if you were going to be around for a little while this morning. There's something I'd like to talk to you about."

"Yes, certainly I'll be here. What time do you want to come by?"

"Right now."

"Oh, okay. I'll be waiting for you."

He could tell by the slight purr in her voice that she was expecting a reconciliation.

He was looking for reconciliation, too. He hoped that

by the time they finished talking to her they would finally have the answers as to who had been behind the attacks on Debra.

And once he knew she was safe, despite the intense love he felt for her, it would be time for him to give her the space to go on with her life, a life that would include him only as the father of their child, not as the husband, the lover, the life mate he wished he could be.

Debra knew that neither Al nor Thad were particularly happy that she had insisted she go with them to Cecily's house, but she wanted to be there, she wanted to look into Cecily's eyes as she attempted to deny what Debra knew in her heart she had tried to do.

Trey and Debra were in his car, followed by Thad and Al in a police car behind them. They drove in silence and Debra absently rubbed her lower abdomen as she stared out the passenger window and thought about the coming confrontation.

Even if Cecily lied about having done anything, the evidence of her earring in Debra's kitchen at least indicated that she'd been in Debra's house without an invitation.

She wasn't sure why a little bit of anxiety dwelled within her, but it was there, along with a huge hope that this truly was the end of all the madness for her.

She just wanted to get back to her work, back to a normal life. She wanted to focus on the baby, on transforming her guest room into a nursery and interviewing potential nannies.

She just wanted her life back—a normal, sane life that made sense. Was that too much to ask?

Her anxiety mounted as Trey drove up the long driveway to Cecily's large home.

Cecily had been born wealthy and it showed in the house she lived in. Although not as grand as the Winston Estate or Trey's home, it was a two-story colonial with massive columns and a sweeping veranda.

It was a perfect backdrop for a beautiful Southern socialite who spent most of her time attending charity events and getting her photo in the society pages.

It had already been agreed that Trey would greet Cecily at the front door and then the others would follow him inside. It would be a surprise attack that would hopefully catch the woman off guard and allow her to make a mistake.

When Trey knocked on the front door, Thad, Al and Debra stood out of sight on one side. Debra's heart thudded rapidly in her chest. Was she about to come face-to-face with the woman who had tried more than once to orchestrate her death?

The door opened and Cecily's voice drifted out on the cool air. "Trey, darling. Come in."

Thad and Al stepped up behind Trey. "Oh, I didn't realize you'd brought company with you." Her voice remained pleasant until Debra showed herself. "What's she doing here? Trey, what on earth is going on?"

"We need to talk to you, Cecily. May we all come inside?" Trey asked.

Cecily was dressed in a chocolate-brown dressing gown with jeweled buttons running from her breasts to the floor. Her hair and makeup were perfect and Debra would guess that she'd expected something far more intimate to happen when Trey had called to visit her.

"Of course," she replied with a new coolness in her

voice. She ushered them all into a formal living room that was a mix of white furniture and mirrored coffee tables.

Debra's discomfort level immediately increased. The room was cold, almost sterile, the only color coming from a large painting of a younger Cecily that hung on the wall.

Introductions were made between Al and Cecily, who had never met, and then Debra and Trey sat on the sofa while Cecily sank down in a nearby chair. Al and Thad remained standing. "So what's this all about?" Cecily asked. "I don't believe I've ever had one of Raleigh's finest in my home before, although I contribute heavily to the Wives of Fallen Officers charity."

"And we appreciate that," Al replied. "But I have some questions to ask you that have nothing to do with your charitable contributions," Al said.

"Questions about what?" Cecily's gaze met Trey's, Thad's and then Al's, but she refused to acknowledge Debra by even glancing at her.

"We'd like to know where you were on the night that Debra's living room was set on fire," Thad said.

Cecily released a tinkling laugh. "I have no idea. I'm not even sure what night she had the fire." Al told her the date. "I'd have to check my social calendar," she answered. "I stay so busy, off the top of my head I can't remember that specific night."

"We'll wait for you to get your calendar," Al replied, his deep voice filled with a firm resolve.

The pleasant smile that had curved Cecily's lips fell as she rose from her chair. "My secretary usually takes care of this, but I have a copy of my calendar on my notebook. I'll just go get it."

She left the room and as she did Trey reached over and lightly touched Debra's hand, as if to offer silent support, a hint of protection against the woman everyone had thought he would one day marry.

Cecily returned with her electronic notepad in hand. She sat back down and touched the screen to flip pages until she came to the one that held her calendar. "Ah, that night I was at a birthday party for a girlfriend."

"And what time did this birthday party end?" Al asked.

She frowned. "I think it broke up around ten."

"And then what did you do?" Al asked.

"I came home and went to bed…alone." She shot a quick glance at Trey and her brown eyes darkened to black. "Just tell me what this is all about. I'm an important woman and I have things to do. I have no idea why you're asking me such silly questions." There was a definite edge to her voice. "And I still don't understand what Debra is doing here. She's nothing but Kate's assistant and if you're here on some sort of official police business, then she has no place here."

Debra opened her mouth to respond, but Trey once again placed a hand on hers to halt anything she might be going to say. "Debra wanted to be here because she doesn't understand what you were doing in her home when she didn't know you were there," Trey said.

"I don't know what you're talking about. I've never been in Debra's house before. I don't even know exactly where she lives," Cecily protested.

"Then maybe you could explain how this got beneath her kitchen cabinet." Al pulled the earring in the clear plastic bag out of his pocket.

Cecily stared at it and then looked at Al. "I've never seen that earring before in my life."

"I have," Trey replied and got up from the sofa. "I bought them for you. I still have the sales receipt for them and I distinctly remember you wearing them when we went to the Christmas ball. I'm sure we can dig up a photo from that night."

When Cecily looked at Trey her lips twisted into an ugly sneer. "I came to the restaurant that night. I was late and saw the two of you together... You and that slut leaving the restaurant and going to the hotel. I sat in my car all night at the hotel and then I saw you put her in a taxi the next morning."

Debra gasped. "It was just a stupid mistake, Cecily. It would have never happened again, and you and Trey could have stayed together."

"You're having his baby!" Cecily's voice was a near screech of outrage.

"And I didn't intend for him to ever know about the baby," Debra replied.

"He's in love with you, you stupid cow." Cecily jumped up from her chair, the notepad falling to the floor and she glared at Trey.

"You think I didn't know? You think I didn't see the way you looked at her? The way you look at her now? You were supposed to love me. I was the woman who was going to help you achieve greatness. She's nothing, and yet you even stopped sleeping with me after you had her that night in the hotel room."

"So you tried to kill her," Trey said flatly as he stood to face her.

Cecily appeared to have lost all consciousness of the presence of anyone else in the room except herself and Trey. She took a step closer to him. "I did what was best for you…for us, Trey. At first, I just wanted her to think she was going crazy, believe that she was no longer capable of doing her job with Kate. I thought it would protect you if she decided to go public. Who would believe a crazy woman who couldn't even keep track of things in her own house?"

"But that didn't work." Trey's voice was emotionless.

"I had to do something. I couldn't just let all of your dreams and all of mine slip away." Cecily gazed at him as if she didn't understand why he would be upset with her.

"And so you hired somebody to tamper with her brakes."

Cecily stepped closer to him, her gaze softening as she toyed with one of the jewel buttons on her gown. "Don't you understand, Trey? She had to go." Her eyes took on a pleading look. "You might think you love her, but she isn't right for you. I'm what you need to get you where you want to go. She was nothing more than an obstacle that had to be removed so that we could build your future together, the way it is supposed to be."

She's insane, Debra thought. She's crazy as a loon, first in believing that Trey was in love with Debra and secondly in believing that by killing Debra she was assuring him the bright future Cecily saw herself in with him.

Debra held her breath as Cecily placed a hand over Trey's heart. "Don't you understand?" Cecily said. "The brakes…the fire… Everything I did was for you, for us. We want the same things; we are the same kind of people."

Trey grabbed her hand by the wrist and threw it off

him. "We aren't the same, Cecily. We aren't the same at all. At the very least the difference between us is that I have a conscience."

Cecily stared at him and then threw back her head and laughed. "A conscience? You stupid fool, you'll never make it in the world of politics if you have a conscience."

"Cecily McKenna, you are under arrest for the attempted murder of Debra Prentice," Al said, ending the confrontation.

Cecily gasped as he pulled her hands behind her and cuffed them. "I was only doing what had to be done," she replied and then laughed again. "You have no real proof that I've done anything wrong. I have a reputation as a charitable, law-abiding citizen. I'll hire the best defense attorney in the United States!" She screamed the words as Al led her out of the house.

"You haven't seen the last of me, Trey. We were destined for greatness. We're the power couple and you belong to me."

"Shut up." Al's voice could be heard just before the slam of his squad car silenced Cecily's voice.

"Is that earring enough to build a solid case against her?" Debra asked worriedly as she got up from the sofa.

Thad smiled at her. "Don't worry, Debra. They'll build a rock-solid case against her, and you and Trey will never have to worry about her again. Can I catch a ride back to your place with you guys? It appears Al forgot that I rode with him. He's already gone."

They locked Cecily's front door and minutes later were on the road back to Debra's place. As Thad and Trey talked about the case they would build against Cecily, Debra stared out the window and thought about what Cecily had said about Trey loving her.

How ironic was it that she'd nearly been killed by a woman who was under the mistaken impression that Trey loved her when nothing could be further from the truth. Trey cared about her as the mother of his child and he certainly loved the baby she carried, but Cecily had been twisted by knowing about the night Trey and Debra had shared together, a night that had just been a terrible mistake.

Then how do you explain the second night? The question whirled around in Debra's head, but she dismissed it as they pulled to the curb in front of her house.

It was over now. Cecily was arrested, the threat was finally gone and it was time for her to get back to living a new kind of normal life and planning for a baby and shared custody.

Her momentary worry that Trey would want to fight her for full custody seemed silly now. She knew Trey's heart and she knew there was no way he would do anything like that to hurt her.

They would co-parent well together because despite the fact that he didn't love her, they respected and genuinely liked each other and that's what was important.

Trey parked in front of her house and they all got out of the car. If felt like it had been a lifetime ago that they'd all been seated at the table in the Winston backyard about to celebrate with a toast when the gunfire had erupted.

"She never said anything about hiring somebody to shoot me," Debra said as they all got out of the car.

"We'll figure it all out, Debra," Thad assured her. "As it stands right now we can't be sure if she was responsible for the shooter or if somebody else was, but we won't stop digging until we have all of the answers. We know for sure she was in your house and she admitted to being responsible for the cut brake lines and the fire. That's enough to hold her on attempted murder charges even without what happened this morning at the breakfast. I'm out of here." With a lift of his hand in a wave, he hurried toward his car.

Trey walked with her to her front door. "Can I come in?" he asked. "As I remember, there's soup meant for the two of us waiting."

She smiled at him, her heart filled with both love and relief. "I think I could even rustle up a couple of grilled cheese sandwiches to go with that soup."

"Sounds good to me."

It felt far too comfortable, him following her into the kitchen. "I still can't believe she did everything she did because she thought you loved me," Debra said as she opened the refrigerator door to get out slices of cheese.

"I do love you."

She ignored the slightly faster beat of her heart as she closed the fridge door. "You love me because I'm the mother of your baby."

"No, I'm in love with you, Debra." His blue eyes held her gaze. "I would be in love with you whether you were carrying my baby or not, but I know you don't love me. When I proposed to you, you made it clear you weren't interested in me in that way."

The slices of cheese slipped from Debra's fingers and fell to the floor. "I thought you were proposing to the baby... I mean, I thought you were proposing to me because you thought it was the right thing to do and you always do the right thing."

"Then let me make it perfectly clear to you," he said as he took a step closer to her, his eyes lit up with a warmth, with a promise as he reached out and placed his hands on her shoulders. "I'm in love with you, Debra Prentice, and I can't imagine living the rest of my life without you by my side."

"But I'm not good material to be a politician's wife," she protested, finding it hard to think, to concentrate as she stared up into the bottomless depths of his eyes. "I don't know how to help you make your dreams come true. I don't know how to dance and sometimes I can be quite clumsy…"

His hands squeezed her shoulders with gentle pressure. "Just love me, Debra. I don't need you to work my campaign for me. I have Chad to do that. I don't need you to be the perfect political asset. I just need you to be my wife, to cook me special meals on Sundays and listen to everything that's in my heart. I just need you to love me and no matter what else happens in my future, my dreams will come true."

Debra's heart swelled so big in her chest she couldn't speak. She could only nod like a bobblehead doll. He seemed to understand as he pulled her tight against his chest and captured her lips with his in a kiss that stole her breath and lifted her heart to a place it had never been before.

Love my baby. Love me.

"I love you, Trey," she finally said as his lips left hers. "I've loved you since the moment I first met you. I don't care if you're a senator or you empty the garbage pails at the Senate. I just want to be your wife, to be a soft place for you to fall after a long day. I want to sit in front of a fire snuggled in your arms and watch our baby play."

"Babies," he replied and took her mouth once again in a kiss that banished loneliness, healed wounds and promised a lifetime of passion and love.

Chapter 17

The ballroom at the Capital Hotel was magnificent, with five-story, floor to ceiling windows on three sides, and chandeliers that appeared to be sparkling stars against the deep blue high ceiling; it would have been impressive empty.

But tonight it wasn't empty. White-clothed tables surrounded the large polished dance floor, each table decorated with a red-and-pink floral arrangement in the center. Tiny red glittering hearts had been scattered around the arrangements, an instant reminder that it was Valentine's Day.

Debra felt as if it had been Valentine's Day for the past week, ever since she had accepted Trey's proposal. That morning she'd awakened to him serving her breakfast in bed and along with the bacon and eggs and orange juice had been a blue velvet ring box. As the server took their plates away from one of the front tables where they all sat, she admired the sparkle of the two-carat solitaire.

"Wishing it were bigger?" Trey asked her as he leaned closer to her.

She smiled at him, as always her heart expanding at the very sight of his handsome face. "Not at all. As it is now I have trouble lifting my hand."

He laughed and settled back in his chair and looked around the table with the expression of a contented man. For the past week they'd shared many long talks about their future, deciding on two children but keeping the possibility of a third open.

He'd taken her to his house where she'd declared that she absolutely hated it and that she'd need a big budget to transform the cold, beautiful house into a warm, inviting home. He'd taken her into his arms and assured her that it would be warm and inviting as long as she was there with him.

The plan was for her to put her townhouse on the market and within the coming weeks move into Trey's home. She wanted to be settled and married before the birth of the baby and she knew Trey felt the same way.

Every night of the past week he'd slept at the townhouse, snuggled with her in her bed. They'd made love each night and she wondered if she'd ever tire of the feel of his arms holding her tight, the taste of his lips against her own. He rubbed her belly each night and told the baby a ridiculous made-up bedtime story that always ended in her laughing.

No, she would never tire of Trey Winston. They would be together through good times and bad, through thick and thin, with their mutual love for each other to shelter them from each and every storm.

It had definitely been a magical week. Cecily was still in jail. Surprisingly, the wealthy socialite hadn't been so wealthy after all. She'd been living on credit and had been on the verge of bankruptcy. She had been unable to make the huge bail the judge had set.

It was obvious that Trey had not only been her dream man because he wanted to be a senator, but also because he was wealthy enough to save her from her own financial ruin.

Debra released a sigh of happiness. They shared the table with Kate, Sam, Thad and the president of the chamber of commerce, Bob Duke, and his wife, Sherri.

Dinner had been a pleasant affair, with everyone in the festive mood of the evening. All of the men wore tuxes and the ladies were visions in ball gowns, the prevailing colors red and white and pink.

Debra and Trey had gone shopping for her dress, a bright pink with a fitted bodice with tiers of white and vivid pink that went from her waist to the floor. The tiers effectively hid the baby bump that was now clearly visible.

The guest of honor for the night, Kate, was a vision in white with ruby bling in a gorgeous necklace and matching earrings to add color to the sophisticated, simple white gown.

Dinner had been entertaining, a bit of political chatter at first, but then the conversation had changed to the weather forecasting cold and snow possibilities in the next week. Bob had shared disastrous Valentine's Days he'd spent with his wife, Sherri, in the thirty years they had been married.

"Men just don't always get it right." Sherri had laughed after Bob had tried to justify that a new garden tractor was a perfectly acceptable Valentine's Day gift to his wife.

There had been plenty of laughter, but Debra would have been perfectly happy if it had just been her and Trey alone in front of her fireplace.

Trey leaned closer to her once again. "It won't be long now and I'll have you in my arms on the dance floor."

"Be afraid...be very afraid," she replied in mock soberness.

She got the expected result she'd wanted. He laughed, that low, rich laughter that she desired to hear every day and every night for the rest of her life.

When the last table had been cleared, Bob turned and whispered something to Kate. She nodded and smiled around the table at all of her family as Bob got up from his seat and approached the podium at the front of the room.

He tapped the end of the microphone, testing to make sure it was turned on and then began to speak. "I'd like to welcome you all to the Chamber of Commerce Valentine's Day Charity Ball. I hope you've enjoyed your dinner and I also hope you've all had an opportunity to check out the room next door where we have a silent auction taking place. Pull out your checkbooks, men, there's plenty of jewelry and goodies over there that the ladies will want."

Everyone laughed and Trey's hand found Debra's beneath the table, radiating his love, his happiness through their physical contact.

"And don't forget to stick around for the dancing,"

Bob continued. "We have a terrific band standing by for your dancing pleasure. But now, it's my great pleasure to introduce our speaker for the night, although she scarcely needs an introduction. Kate Adair Winston is one of our own who has served not only the city of Raleigh with her charitable work, but also has served the United States as former vice president and former ambassador to France. Her family business, Adair Enterprises, has brought jobs and revenue to our fair city. Kate, we welcome you."

Applause filled the room as Kate rose from the table and took her place behind the podium. She had no notes. Debra had helped her work on the speech over the past couple of days and she'd heard it a dozen times as Kate had practiced it over and over again so that she would have it fully memorized.

Trey released her hand and relaxed back in his chair as Debra rubbed her lower stomach, caressing the baby who would be born into love, a child who would grow up in an intact family.

The room was utterly silent as Kate reached the podium, an indication of the respect she commanded. She turned to thank Bob and there was a distinctive ping sound.

"No!" Sam erupted and lunged from the table in an attempt to reach his mother.

Everything happened at the same time. The center of Kate's white dress exploded in red as Secret Service agent Dan Henderson reached her before Sam, took her down to the floor and covered her body with his. Two more pings resounded, followed by the crackling of glass at one of the huge windows.

Screaming filled the ballroom, along with the sound

of running feet and Secret Service swarming the area. Thad was on his phone, and then raced for the exit as Trey tugged Debra under the table.

Gunshots, Debra thought in horror. Kate had been shot. She squeezed her eyes tightly closed as she thought of the red stain that had suddenly appeared on Kate's stomach. Was Kate dead? Debra's heart pounded with dreadful intensity.

As Trey huddled next to her, his arm tightly around her shoulders, she was able to pick out familiar voices among the din. Sam sobbing and screaming in agony, somebody else shouting about a lockdown and finally the scream of sirens as emergency vehicles and local law-enforcement officials began to arrive.

Jerry Cahill leaned down beneath the table, his eyes cold and hard. "We need to get the family out of here right now," he said. "We're clearing the ballroom. All the guests are being moved to other areas of the hotel, but we have a car waiting for you two and Sam to head to the hospital where your mother is being taken."

Trey nodded and as he pulled Debra from beneath the table, he motioned to the distraught Sam to come with them. Two ambulance stretchers had already arrived in the room and it looked like both Kate and Dan Henderson were being loaded.

"I should have seen this coming," Sam sobbed as Trey threw an arm around his shaking shoulders and they all followed Jerry out of the ballroom. "I should have been able to save her. There were so many I couldn't save, but I should have saved her." Sam appeared to be shattering, his words indicating some sort of post-traumatic stress in addition to his fear for his mother.

Jerry led them to a back entrance of the hotel, all the while talking and listening on his radio. He stopped them at the door, appeared to get some sort of confirmation, and then with his gun in his hand, opened the door.

Directly ahead of them was a black sedan that Debra knew probably had bulletproof windows. Sam got into the front seat and she and Trey in the back and then Jerry slammed the doors, gave the top a thump and the driver pulled away.

The driver was Secret Service man Jeff Benton and as Sam managed to pull himself together, Jeff told them everything he knew, that from the direction that Kate had been shot, apparently the gunman had been in one of the darkened high-rise buildings on the left side of the street from the hotel ballroom and both local and federal agents were clearing those buildings now.

He couldn't tell them the condition of either Kate or Dan Henderson, who apparently had been shot also. He was driving them to Duke University Hospital where both Kate and Dan would be taken and were already in transport.

It was only then that Debra's brain began to process the horror. She leaned into Trey and began to silently weep, her heart aching for the entire Winston family. What should have been a night of triumph for Kate and her sons had become a night of sheer terror.

The ride to the hospital seemed to take forever. Was Kate still alive? *Please, don't take Kate,* Debra prayed as Trey held her tightly against his side. Sam, Thad and Trey needed their mother and Debra needed Kate, too. Her baby needed a grandmother. *Please, let Kate be okay.* It was a mantra that echoed over and over again in her head.

What about Dan Henderson? Had he sacrificed his life in doing his duty tonight? Four shots. There had been four bullets. One of them had hit Kate, but had the others hit Dan?

And where was Thad? Why wasn't he safely in this car with them? They should all be together right now, praying that Kate wasn't badly hurt, that nobody had been critically injured. They should all be praying that the gunman was captured and somebody could make sense of what had just happened.

She gazed down at the glittering ring on her finger and cuddled closer to the man who would be her husband. She told herself that no matter what happened tonight, she and Trey would get through the future together.

By the time they reached the hospital Trey was frantic and trying hard to hide it not just from Debra but also from Sam, who appeared to be on the very edge of his sanity.

They were led into a private waiting room with Jeff Benton stationed just outside the door. Thad was already there and he stood from the loveseat where he'd been sitting as they all entered the room. Thad looked haggard, as if the past forty-five minutes or so had sucked the very life out of him.

"What do you know?" Trey asked.

Thad gestured for Trey and Debra to sit on the loveseat and then he and Sam sank down into two straight-back chairs. "Nothing, other than the two victims have arrived and are with the doctors or whoever. I just got here a few minutes ago myself." Thad sat only a moment and then jumped up to begin to pace the small confines. Thad was tightly wound, his movements jerky with tension, his jaw taut.

Trey noted the fact that Thad had referred to their mother and Dan Henderson as the victims as if in an effort to completely divorce his emotions from the situation.

Sam had grown silent, his eyes staring unseeingly at the wall in front of him with his hands clasped together tightly in his lap.

As the oldest and the unofficial leader of the family, Trey felt helpless to do anything to help his brothers through this horrifying time. As he thought of that moment when his mother's white dress had turned red and she'd fallen, his heart felt like it stopped beating.

How could he help his brothers when he felt the open hand of utter despair attempting to grab him around the throat? The only thing keeping him partially grounded was the warmth of Debra's body next to his, the feel of her small hand gripping his so tightly and the baby that would make them a family.

Thad stopped pacing and stared at the doorway that they all knew somebody would eventually come through to give them an update. He looked as if he wanted to tear through the door to find some answers right now.

"You know, Cecily never confessed to hiring a gunman to shoot at Debra at the breakfast last week," Trey said, trying to gain Thad's attention.

"And the gunman has continued to refuse to talk about who hired him," Thad replied. "There's no way he wasn't a hired gun. His rap sheet shows him as a low-rent thug with charges of robbery and check fraud. He's not bright enough to mastermind his way out of a paper bag."

"But, after tonight, I believe his target was Mom that

day and not Debra." Trey tightened his arm around the woman he loved, remembering how frightened he'd been for her even before he'd acknowledged the love he had in his heart for her.

Thad turned back to stare at the doorway, as if he could will somebody to show up to give them some kind of a report as to what was happening with their mother.

"I wonder what's going on back at the hotel. I wonder if they've caught the shooter," Sam finally spoke, his hands curled into tight fists in his lap.

Thad looked at his brother. "I'm cut out of the loop for obvious reasons. I guess at some point we'll get an update from the Secret Service when they have something to share with us."

At that moment the door opened and a nurse stepped inside. Trey immediately recognized her as the same pretty nurse who had tended to Debra after her car accident. Lucy, that was her name. Lucy Sinclair.

"I just want to let you all know that your mother and Agent Dan Henderson are being attended to by our trauma team. Unfortunately, that's really all I can tell you at this point," she said sympathetically.

Thad took a step closer to her. "Well, that's not good enough," he said tersely. "Do you have any idea who my mother is?"

Lucy's green eyes widened a bit and then narrowed. "At the moment your mother is nothing more than a patient who needs immediate medical treatment."

"I demand to speak to the doctor in charge," Thad replied. "I'm Officer Thad Winston of the Raleigh Police Department and I want to speak to the doctor right now."

"Right now every trauma doctor we have on staff is desperately working to keep your mother and Agent

Henderson alive. They are both in critical condition." She took a step closer to Thad, her eyes flaming in aggravation. "You need to stand down, Officer Winston."

She stood toe-to-toe with him until Thad stepped back and fell back on the chair, his features crumbled in with defeat and fear.

As Lucy left the room, Trey looked at his family. Shell-shocked, that's what they were and yet despite the trauma that they were now experiencing, Trey's commitment to continue in politics only surged stronger inside him.

The bad guys didn't get to win. No matter what the outcome of tonight was, Trey intended to be on the ballot when it came time to elect the next senator of North Carolina.

One way or the other they would all survive this night. They carried Adair Winston blood inside them—they were strong and would carry on.

Debra took his hand and held tight, as if knowing what he was thinking and silently telling him that she would be right at his side.

* * * * *

AFFAIRS OF STATE

JENNIFER LEWIS

For Charles Griemsman, editor extraordinaire, and the authors in this series who were such a pleasure to work with: Barbara Dunlop, Michelle Celmer, Robyn Grady, Rachel Bailey and Andrea Laurence.

One

"The prince is staring right at you."

"Maybe he needs a refill." Ariella Winthrop sent a text requesting another round of the salmon and caviar. The gala event that Ariella had planned was a fund-raiser for a local hospital and nearly six hundred guests were milling around the ballroom. "I'll send a server his way."

"You haven't even looked at him." Her glamorous friend Francesca Crowe was an invited guest at the party. With her long dark hair in a shiny sheet down her back and her voluptuous body encased in an expensive beaded dress, Francesca fit right in with the crowd of billionaires and their buddies. It was often awkward when friends came to Ariella's events and wanted to chat and hang out while she needed to attend to the details. Luckily, Francesca was the kind of person she could be blunt with.

"I'm busy working." She responded to another text from her staff about a spill near the main entrance. "And I'm sure you're imagining things." She didn't glance up at the prince. Hopefully he wasn't still looking at her. She was starting to feel self-conscious.

"Maybe he's as intrigued as everyone else by the mysterious love child of the United States president."

"I'll pretend I didn't hear that. And I'm going off the idea of meeting President Morrow on your husband's TV network." Francesca would know she was kidding, but her heart clutched as she thought about it. Everyone was talking about her and her famous father and she'd never even met the guy.

"Go on. Look. He's gorgeous." Her friend's conspiratorial tone, and the fact that she'd ignored her comment about the TV special entirely, made Ariella glance up in spite of herself.

Her eyes locked with a tall man halfway across the room. His short-cropped dirty blond hair contrasted with his black tuxedo. A jolt of energy charged through the air as he started walking toward her. "Uh-oh, he's coming this way."

"I told you he was looking at you." Francesca smiled and stared right at him. "And he doesn't need champagne, either. Look, his glass is full."

"I wonder what's wrong." Her pulse quickened and she plastered on her most helpful smile as he approached. It was never easy to know if you should introduce yourself in these situations. She was working at the event, not attending as a guest, so was it a breach of etiquette to greet a prince? She wished her business partner, Scarlet, was here. With her background as a D.C. socialite, she knew just how to handle these dilemmas.

Before she could collect her thoughts he stood right in front of her. He held out his hand, so she shook it. His handshake was predictably firm and authoritative. "Ms. Winthrop, Simon Worth."

He knew her name? Her brain scrambled. He must have read the media stories like everyone else. "Pleased to meet you." His eyes fixed on hers with startling intensity. A dark honey color, they seemed to see right past her studied professional façade to the woman beneath.

"I'm impressed." His voice was deep, with a masculine gruffness that stirred something inside her. Oh dear. There was nothing good about being attracted to a royal guest. Still it was kind of him to compliment her.

"Oh, thank you. That's sweet of you." It wasn't often that guests thanked the party planner personally. Or even noticed that she was alive. "We do enjoy hosting these fund-raisers."

He'd let go of her hand, but his gaze still held her like a deer in a rifle sight. Humor sparkled in his golden eyes. "Not your party planning skills, though I'm sure those are impressive, too. I admire how well you've handled the blazing spotlight of press attention on your personal life."

"Oh." She felt her cheeks heat, which was unusual for her. This man was having an unsettling effect on her sanity. "I suppose it helps that I don't have much of a personal life. I'm all work all the time so they haven't found a lot to write about." Now she was babbling, which made her feel even more hot and bothered. "And it's easy to stay detached when I genuinely have no idea what they're talking about half the time."

"I know how you feel." He smiled. "I've had cameras poked in my face since before I could speak. I finally realized that if there isn't a good story, they'll just make one up and hope you play into their hands by making a fuss over it."

She smiled. "So it is better to put your hands over your ears and hope that they go away?"

"Pretty much." He had a sexy dimple in his left cheek. He was taller than she'd expected. And more strapping, too. His tuxedo stretched across broad shoulders and his elegant white shirt collar framed the sturdy neck of an athlete. "It helps if you travel a lot, then they have trouble keeping up."

"I'll have to plan more parties abroad." He was easy to talk to. Which was weird. Especially with this unsettling attraction clawing at her insides. "I did one in Paris a couple of months ago, and we have one coming up in Russia, so it should prove quite easy once I get the hang of it."

He laughed. "There you go. I travel to Africa a lot now that I'm ex-military. It's quite easy to lose photographers out in the bush."

She chuckled at the image. "What do you do in Africa?" She was genuinely curious. Surely Britain didn't have colonies there anymore?

"I run an organization called World Connect that brings technology and education to remote areas. The staff is all local so we spend a lot of time recruiting in the local villages and helping them get things off the ground."

"That must be very rewarding." Gosh, he was adorable. A prince who actually cared about something other than entertaining himself? There weren't too many of those around.

"I thought I wouldn't know what to do with myself once I left the service, but I'm busier and happier than ever. I'm hoping to drum up some donations while I'm in D.C. That's another challenge that keeps me on my toes. Perhaps you can help me with that?"

"You mean, plan a fund-raiser?" Scarlet would be thrilled if she enticed another royal onto their roster of clients. They attracted other clients the way a sparkling tiara attracted glances.

"Why not?" He'd drawn so close to her that she could almost feel his body heat. "Would you join me for tea tomorrow?"

Her brain screeched to a halt. Something about his body language told her he wanted more than tea. He had a reputation for boyish charm, and although she couldn't remember reading about any romantic scandals in the papers, the last thing she needed was to give the tabloids more fuel for their gossip furnaces. "I'm afraid I have an appointment tomorrow." She stepped backward slightly.

Instead of looking angry or annoyed, he tilted his head and smiled. "Of course. You're busy. How about breakfast? That's got to be the quietest meal for a party planner."

She swallowed. Every cell in her body was telling her to run screaming from the room. He was dangerously good-looking and must have years of experience seducing women in far less vulnerable emotional states than herself. But he was a prince, so in her line of work she couldn't afford to offend him. At least not here, in public. Planning a fund-raiser for his charity would be great for DC Affairs, so Scarlet would kill her if she turned him down. And really, what could happen during breakfast? "That sounds fine."

"My driver will pick you up at your house. It will be discreet, trust me."

"Oh." Somehow that sounded more worrying than ever. If the meeting was to be all business, why would they need discretion? But she managed a shaky smile. "My address is—"

"Don't worry. He'll find you." He gave a slight nod, like an ancient courtier, and backed away a step or two before disappearing into the crowd of well-dressed partygoers.

She wanted to sag against a wall with relief. Unfortunately she wasn't near a wall, and her phone was buzzing.

"Well, well, well." Francesca's voice startled her.

"I'd forgotten you were there."

"I could tell. You forgot to introduce me to your royal friend. Very hot. And I thought his older brother was supposed to be the good-looking one."

"His older brother is the heir to the throne."

"Just think, if the USA was a monarchy like England, you'd be next in line to the throne." Francesca looked at her thoughtfully. "Your dad is the president, and you're his only child."

"Who he didn't even know existed until a few weeks ago." She tried to stay focused on her job. "And I still haven't actually met him in person." That part was beginning to hurt more and more.

"Liam's in negotiations with the White House press office about the date for the reunion special. Ted Morrow's on board with doing it. I'm sure he wants to meet you, too." Francesca squeezed her arm gently.

"Or not. I was an accident, after all." She glanced around the room, packed with wealthy movers and shakers. "It's hardly a reunion when we've never met before. We really shouldn't be talking about this here. Someone could be listening. And I'm supposed to be working. Don't you have bigwigs to schmooze with?"

"That's my husband's department. I wish I could be a fly on the croissants tomorrow morning."

"I wish I could have found an excuse not to go." Her heart rate quickened at the thought of meeting Prince Simon for breakfast. They couldn't talk business for the entire meal. What kind of small talk did you make with a prince?

"Are you crazy? He's utterly delish."

"It would be easier if he wasn't. The last thing I need is to embark on a scandalous affair with a prince." Ariella exhaled as butterflies swirled in her stomach. "Not that he'd be at all interested, of course, but just when I think things can't get any crazier, they do."

"Um, I think someone's throwing up into the gilded lilies." She gestured discretely at a young woman in a strapless gown bending over a waist-high urn of brass blooms.

Ariella lifted her phone. "See what I mean?"

The long black Mercedes sedan parked outside her Georgetown apartment may not have had "By Appointment to His Majesty" stenciled on the outside, but it wasn't much more subtle. The uniformed chauffeur who rang the bell looked like a throwback to another era. Ariella dashed for the backseat hoping there were no photographers lurking about.

She didn't ask where they were going, and the driver didn't say a word, so she watched in surprise, then confusion, then more than a little alarm as the car took her right out of the city and into a leafy suburb. When the suburbs gave way to large horse farms she leaned forward and asked the question she should have posed before she got into the car. "Where are you taking me?"

"Sutter's Way, madam. We're nearly there." She swallowed and sat back. Sutter's Way was a beautiful old mansion, built by the Hearst family at the height of their wealth and influence. She'd seen paintings from its collection in her art history class at Georgetown University but she had no idea who owned it now.

At last the car passed through a tall wrought iron gate, crunched along a gravel driveway and pulled up in front of the elegant brick house. When she got out, her heels sank into the gravel and she brushed wrinkles from the

skirt of the demure and unsexy navy dress she'd chosen
for the occasion.

Simon bounded down the steps and strode toward her.
"Sorry about the long drive but I thought you'd appreciate the privacy." She braced for a hug or kiss, then chastised herself when he gave her a firm handshake. Her head
must be getting very large these days if she expected royalty to kiss her.

He was even better looking in an open-necked shirt and
khakis. His skin was tanned and his hair looked wind-
blown. Not that it made any difference to her. He was just
a potential client, and an influential one, at that. "I am becoming paranoid about the press lately. They seem to pop
out in the strangest places. I don't know what they hope
they'll find me doing." *Kissing a British prince, perhaps.*

She swallowed. Her imagination seemed to be running
away with her. Simon probably just wanted ideas about
how to attract high rollers who would donate money to
his charity.

He gestured for her to go in. "I've learned the hard way
that photographers really do follow you everywhere, so it's
best to try to stick with activities you don't mind seeing
under a splashy headline." His grin was infectious.

"Is that why I'm afraid to even change my hairstyle?"

"Don't let them scare you. That gives them power over
you and you certainly don't want that. From what I've seen,
you handle them like a pro."

"Maybe it's in the blood." Her private thought flew off
her tongue and almost made her halt in her tracks. Lately
she'd been thinking a lot about the man who sired her.
He faced the press every day with good humor and never
seemed ruffled. It was so odd to think that they shared
the same DNA.

"No doubt. I'm sure your father is very impressed."

"My father is…was a nice man called Dale Winthrop. He's the dad who raised me. I still can't get used to people calling President Morrow my father. If it wasn't for sleazy journalists breaking the law in search of a story, he wouldn't even know I existed."

They went into a sunlit room where an elegant and delicious-smelling breakfast was spread out on a creamy tablecloth. He pulled out her chair, which gave her an odd sensation of being…cared for. Very weird.

"Help yourself. The house is ours for now. Even the staff have been sent packing so you don't have to worry about eavesdroppers."

"That's fantastic." She reached for a scone, not sure what else to do.

"So you have the press to thank for learning about your parentage. Maybe they're not so bad after all." His honey-colored eyes shone with warmth.

"Not bad? It's been a nightmare. I was a peaceful person living a quiet life—punctuated by spectacular parties—before this whole thing exploded." She cut her scone and buttered it.

"I'm impressed that you haven't taken a big movie deal or written a tell-all exposé."

"Maybe I would tell all if I knew anything to tell." She laughed. How could a foreign prince be so easy to talk to? She felt more relaxed discussing this whole mess with Simon than with her actual friends. "The situation surprised me as much as anyone. I always knew I was adopted but I never had the slightest interest in finding my biological parents."

"How do your adoptive parents feel about all this?" He leaned forward.

Her chest contracted. "They died four years ago. A plane crash on their way to a friend's anniversary party."

She still couldn't really talk about it without getting emotional.

"I'm so sorry." Concern filled his handsome face. "Do you think they would have wanted you to get to know your birth parents?"

She frowned and stared at him. "You know what? I think they would." She sighed. "If only they were still here I could ask them for advice. My mom was a genius at knowing the right thing to do in a tricky situation. Whenever I run into a snarl at work I always ask myself what she would do."

"It sounds like a great opportunity to welcome two new parents into your life. Not to replace the ones who raised you, of course, no one could ever do that, but to help fill the gap they left behind."

His compassion touched her. And she knew his own mother had died suddenly and tragically, when he was only a boy, so he wasn't just making this stuff up. "You're sweet to think of that, but so far neither of them seems to want a relationship with me."

"You haven't met them?" He looked shocked.

She shook her head quietly. "The president's office hasn't even made an official statement about me, though they've stopped denying that I could be his daughter since the DNA test results became public." She let out a heavy sigh. "And my mother... Can I swear you to secrecy?"

"Of course." His serious expression reassured her.

"My real mother refuses to come out of hiding. She wrote to me privately, which I appreciate, but mostly to say that she wants to keep quiet about the whole situation. Weirdly enough, she lives in Ireland now."

"Does she?" He brightened. "You'll have to come to our side of the Atlantic for a visit."

"She certainly didn't invite me." Her freshly baked

scone was cooling in her fingers. Her appetite seemed to have shriveled. "And I can't say I blame her. Who'd want to be plunged into this whole mess?"

"She can hardly bow out now when she's the one who had the affair with the president in the first place. Though I suppose he wasn't the president, then."

"No, he was just a tall handsome high school senior in a letter jacket. I've seen the photos on the news like everyone else." She smiled sadly. "She told me in her letter that she kept quiet about her pregnancy because he was going off to college and she didn't want to spoil what she knew would be a brilliant career."

"She was right about his prospects, that's for sure." He poured her some fragrant coffee. "And maybe she needs time to get used to the situation. I bet she's secretly dying to meet you."

"I'm quickly learning not to have expectations about people. They're likely to be turned on their head just when I least expect it."

"You can't get paranoid, though. That doesn't help. I try to assume that everyone has the best intentions until they prove otherwise." His expression made her laugh. It suggested they often proved otherwise but he wasn't losing sleep over it.

She didn't know what to think about Simon's intentions. She had a strong feeling that he didn't invite her here to plan a party, but there was no way she could come out and ask him. Maybe he really did just want to give her a pep talk on how to deal with her unwelcome celebrity.

"So I should try to approach everyone as a potential new friend, even if they're trying to take a picture of me buying bagels in the supermarket?"

"If you can. At the very least they won't get a really bad picture of you and you won't get in trouble for smashing their camera." He managed to be mischievous and deeply serious at the same time, which was doing something strange to her insides.

"Ever since your older brother got married the papers keep speculating about your love life, but I haven't seen any stories about it. How do you keep your personal life out of the papers?" Uh-oh, now she was asking him about his love life, in a roundabout way. She regretted the question, but also burned with curiosity to see how he'd answer. Was he involved with anyone?

"I have privacy." He gestured at their elegant surroundings. "I just have to be cunning to get it." His eyes shone. They were the color of neat whiskey, and were starting to have a similarly intoxicating effect on her. He had a light stubble on his cheeks, not dark, but enough to add texture under his cheekbones and she wondered what it would feel like to touch it. This was the private Simon the public didn't see, and he'd invited her into his exclusive world.

Her breathing had quickened and she realized she was still holding her uneaten scone in her hand. She put it down and had a sip of orange juice instead. That had the bracing effect she needed. "I guess I need to get more cunning, too. It must help to have friends with large estates." She smiled. "It looks like it has a beautiful garden."

"Do you want to see it? I can tell you're not exactly ravenous."

"I'd love a walk." Adrenaline and relief surged through her. Anything to dissipate the nervous tension building in her muscles. "Maybe I'll be hungrier after some fresh air."

"I already went for a run this morning. Just me and two Secret Service agents pounding the picturesque streets." He stood and helped pull out her chair as she stood. Again she was touched by his thoughtfulness. She'd expect a prince to be more…supercilious.

"Where are the agents now?"

"Outside, checking the perimeter. They'll keep a discreet distance from us."

"Oh." She glanced around, half expecting to see one lurking in the corner. Simon opened a pair of French doors and they stepped out onto a slate patio with a view over a formal rose garden. The heady scent of rose petals filled the air. "You picked the perfect time to invite me here. They're all in bloom."

"It's June. The magic moment."

He smiled and they walked down some wide steps to the borders of roses. They were the fragrant heirloom roses, with soft white, delicate yellow and big fluffy pale pink heads, so different from the gaudy unscented blooms she sometimes dealt with for parties. She drank in their scent and felt her blood pressure drop. "How gorgeous. It must take an army of gardeners to keep them so perfect."

"No doubt."

She glanced up at him, instantly reminded of how tall he was. Six-two, at least. His broad shoulders strained against the cloth of his shirt as he bent over a spray of double pink blossoms. He pulled something from his pocket and snipped off a stem, then stripped the thorns.

"You carry a knife?"

"Boy Scout training." He offered her the posy. Their fingers brushed and she felt a sizzle of energy pass between them before she accepted it and buried her nose in it. How could she be attracted to a British prince, of all people? Wasn't her life crazy and embarrassing enough already? Surely she could at least develop a crush on a prince from some obscure and far-flung nation that no one had heard of, not one of her nation's closest allies.

"You're very quiet." His soft voice tickled her ear.

"Thinking too much, as usual." She looked up. The

morning sun played on the hard planes of his face and illuminated the golden sparkle of her eyes.

"That's not always a good idea." A smile tugged at the corner of his mouth. "Maybe we'd better keep walking." His hand touched the base of her spine, sending a thick shiver of arousal darting through her. Things just got worse and worse!

She walked quickly, first to lose his hand, and then to outpace her own imagination, which already toyed with the idea of kissing him.

"I think I've been working too hard lately." That must be why the simple touch of a handsome man could send her loopy.

"Then you need to take a break." He made it sound so easy.

"It's not as if I can just step off the carousel and spend a few weeks in the islands."

"Not without the entire press corps following you." His wry glance made her chuckle. "You have to be crafty about it when you're in the public eye. You don't want to be caught topless in Vegas."

She laughed aloud. "I don't think there's much danger of that. Oddly enough, I've never been there."

"No quickie weddings in your past?"

"No, thank goodness. Otherwise my former husband would probably be preparing a tell-all biography about me."

He slowed. "Is that a risk? Do you have people from your past who could reveal things you don't want to be made public?" Was he tactfully inquiring about her romantic history?

"No." She said it fast and loud. "I guess that's something to be grateful for. My past is very plain vanilla. I was a bit embarrassed by how unexciting my life has been up to this point, but now it's a huge relief."

"But a little dull." She glanced at him as he lifted a brow slightly. As if he wanted to tempt her into sin.

"Sometimes dull is good."

"Even in the party planning business?"

"Oh, yes. Believe me, dull and tasteful goes a long way, especially when there are scandals swirling like tornadoes all around you."

"Hmm. Sounds like a waste to me. If you're going to have a party you might as well make it a live one. I suppose I feel the same way about life. Sometimes it drives the family mad that I can't just plod around opening supermarkets and smashing bottles against ships, but I have to climb mountains and trek across deserts. Turning my adventures into fund-raising activities gives them an air of legitimacy, but frankly I'd be doing it anyway, simply because I enjoy it. Maybe you need an adventure." His voice brightened.

"Oh, no." Adrenaline shot through her. "No. Adventure is definitely the last thing I need. Really, I'm a dull and boring person. Happiest with a cup of herbal tea and a glossy magazine." That should stop him in his tracks. And maybe she was trying to convince herself that she wasn't experiencing a surge of excitement just from walking close to this man.

"I don't believe a word of it." He touched the small of her back again—just for a split second—as they descended a short flight of stone stairs. Again her skin prickled as if he'd touched it right through her clothes. An odd sensation was unfurling in the pit of her belly. One she hadn't felt in a very long time.

"Trust me," she pleaded, as her body threatened to succumb to far more excitement than she needed. "All I really want is my ordinary, quiet life back."

"Well." He stopped and took her hands. Her fingers tingled and her breath caught in her lungs. "That is most certainly not going to happen."

Two

It took every ounce of self-control he possessed for Simon not to press his lips to Ariella's soft pink ones. But he managed. Years of royal training, accompanied by thinly veiled threats from older members of the family, had taught him to handle these situations with his brain rather than other more primitive and enthusiastic parts of his body.

He didn't want to blow it. Scare her off. Something deep in his gut told him that Ariella Winthrop was no ordinary woman. He trusted his gut in the line of fire and on the face of a sheer cliff. It rarely steered him wrong.

Something about Ariella sent excitement coursing through him. He couldn't explain it, or even put his finger on the feeling; it was just a hunch that meeting her could change the course of his entire life.

He even managed to let go of her hands, reluctantly, and turn toward the rhododendron border as a distraction. "The reality is that your life has changed forever."

He glanced back, and was relieved to see her following closely. "Whether you like it or not, you're public property now." It made him feel close to her. They shared a bond and his years of hard experience could help her negotiate the minefield of a life lived on the pages of the daily papers.

"But I'm still the same person I've been all along. People can't expect me to suddenly welcome the entire world into my private life."

"You're not the same, though. You didn't know the president was your father, did you?"

"I was as surprised as he was. I'd never have guessed it in a million years. Now people are even saying I look like him. It seems insane to me. I don't feel in the least bit related to him."

Simon surveyed her strikingly pretty face. She had elegant, classical features, highlighted by the sparkle of warmth from her people-oriented personality. "You do look rather like him. You both have striking bone structure, and something about your eyes seems familiar."

She let out an exasperated sigh. "You're just imagining it. Or trying to make me feel better, and it's not working. Yes, I'd like to meet him, since we do share the same genes, but I'm sure I'll never have the same feelings for him as I do for the man who actually raised me."

"Of course not." He frowned. Her moss-green eyes were filled with concern. "No one expects you to do that."

"I feel like they do." she protested. "Journalists keep talking to me as if I must be happy to have President Morrow as my father. He's so popular and successful that I must be dying to claim his revered family tree as my own. I couldn't care less. I'd rather be descended from some nice man whom I could actually meet and get to know, not some almighty, carved-from-stone figure that everyone bows down to. It's exasperating."

He chuckled. "Maybe he isn't as carved in stone as you think. Sometimes people expect members of the royal family to behave like granite statues, but believe me, we have feelings, too. It can be very inconvenient." Like right now, when he longed to take this troubled and lovely woman in his arms and give her a big bear hug.

Once again he restrained himself. He'd learned to do a pretty passable impression of a granite statue when the occasion called for it.

"I don't think the press wants me to be a granite statue. I think they'd like to see me go right to pieces. The way they've been hounding me and peppering me with questions, it feels like they're just waiting for me to say the wrong thing or break down sobbing. They must be exasperated that I'm so dull I couldn't give them a good story even if I wanted to." The morning breeze whipped her dark dress against her body. The soft fabric hugged contours that would bring a weaker man to his knees. If only he wasn't a gentleman.

"You're anything but dull."

"Why are we talking about me? That's a dull topic if there ever was one." Her eyes flashed something that warned him off. "Didn't you invite me here to help you plan a party?"

He frowned. Had he used that as an excuse? He just wanted to get to know her better. It was a good idea, though. He'd like to raise awareness of World Connect in the US and gain some new donors. "Do you think you could help me put together a fund-raiser for World Connect? We've never done one on this side of the Atlantic before."

"Absolutely." Her face lit up and he could almost feel her lungs fill with relief. "We organize gala events all the time. We can pretty much print out a guest list of people who like to support worthy causes. Happily there are a lot of them in D.C."

"They sound ideal. And I wouldn't turn up my nose at people who want to donate for the tax benefits, either."

She grinned. "They're often the most generous ones. What kind of venue did you have in mind?"

He tried to look like he'd put some thought into it. "Somewhere…big." It was hard to think at all with those big green eyes staring so hopefully at him. "I'm sure you could come up with a good place."

"The Smithsonian might work. There are a lot of possibilities. I can make some phone calls once you pick a date."

"A date?" He drew in a breath. "What would you suggest?" A date far off into the future might be good, so he'd have plenty of excuses to get together with her for brainstorming and planning.

"Summers aren't ideal because a lot of people go away to the beach. I'd recommend the fall or winter. Something about the short days makes people want to get dressed up in their sparkliest outfits and stay out late."

"November or December, then. You can choose a date that works for the venue." Perfect. Five or six months of meetings with Ariella should be enough time for…

For what? What exactly did he intend to do with her?

For once he wasn't sure. All he knew is that he wanted to be close to her. To hear her voice. To touch her…

"My partner, Scarlet, keeps a master list of venues and cultivates relationships with the people who run them. We should talk to her. It's important to find out what else is going on that week, too. You don't want two similar events taking place on the same night, or even back to back."

"Of course not." He jerked back his hand, which was heading toward hers. He needed to keep himself in check or she'd send her partner to meet with him. "I'll rely entirely on your expertise. I usually raise money for our endeavors by ringing people up and asking them for money."

"Does that work well?" Humor danced in her eyes.

"Surprisingly, it does."

"That sounds a lot less expensive than throwing parties."

"But think of all the fun I miss out on. And hardly anyone in the US has heard of World Connect, so I need to get the word out."

She stopped walking. "I have an idea."

"Yes?"

"How about an outdoor concert?"

"In the dead of winter?" Was he following the conversation? He might have lost track when he just got lost in the way her navy dress hugged her hips.

"No!" She laughed. "You could do it in September or October. The weather's usually lovely then and we've pulled festivals together quicker than that. You could get a much larger and more diverse crowd and make the same money by selling more tickets."

"I love it. World Connect is about inclusion, so the more people who can come and hear about it, the better."

"If the bands are enthusiastic enough they might even perform for free, so all the profits would go to World Connect." He could see her getting excited, which had a strange effect on his own adrenaline. "A good friend of mine is a music agent so I'm sure she can hook me up with some interesting performers."

"And how about some musicians from Africa? I could talk to some friends over there and see who would be interested. Already the world is coming together. I'm so glad I convinced you to come here today." Again his fingers itched to seize hers. Again he shoved them into his pockets. They'd walked past the rhododendrons and out onto a lawn that circled around the tennis court. "I can't believe I lucked into meeting you."

"You hardly lucked into it." She shot him a teasing smile that sent heat right to his groin. "You came right up to me."

"I like to make things happen, not sit around waiting for them to happen."

"I guess that's the best way to live your life. I'm going to adopt that attitude from now on."

"Just keep on being yourself and don't worry about the press or anyone else. Don't let the bastards grind you down."

A smile tugged at her mouth. "I bet you wouldn't say that in front of the press."

"True. So more accurately, you have to be yourself, but not put every aspect on public display. I won't lie, it's a delicate balance, but I can already see that you're more than capable of doing it."

She shrugged her slim shoulders. "I don't really have any choice."

"In some ways, I think that makes it easier." He slid his arm around her shoulders, which sent a delicious sensation of warmth flooding through his torso.

He instantly regretted the rash move when she sprang forward toward a herb border. He shook his head in frustration at himself. He could see that beneath her calm and controlled demeanor she was nervous and skittish as a startled filly. It hadn't been easy to persuade her to come here and he didn't want to add to her anxiety by being yet another person who wanted a piece of her.

Her scent filled his nostrils, delicate and feminine, like their lush floral surroundings. "A garden is the perfect backdrop for you." The sunlight sparkled in her dark hair and lit up her eyes. Even the bird on a nearby tree branch seemed transfixed by her beauty, still and unblinking, head cocked.

"I don't know why. I haven't spent much time in gardens."

"You grew up in the city?"

"Nope, in a tiny town in Montana, but my parents didn't have a garden like this. It was a smooth clipped lawn with a fence and a doghouse. No camellias to bury your nose in or arbors to stand gracefully under."

"The president's from Montana, isn't he?"

"Yes, that's how the journalists found me. They went there to do a story on his childhood and decided to tap the phone of a former White House maid who lived in his town. She inadvertently revealed that my mother— his high school sweetheart—had become pregnant and never told him."

Anger surged inside him. He knew the story already. Who didn't? It had been setting headlines on fire for months. And since he was here to sign a treaty between the United States and the United Kingdom to punish those who used technology to violate other people's privacy, it was his business to know the more intimate details. "Have you been following the story in the press? Angelica Pierce, the ANS journalist who did the illegal wiretapping is going to prison, last I heard. She's expected to get a two- to five-year sentence."

"I know. Everyone seems to think I should be thrilled about it, but I feel sorry for her. It turned out that Graham Boyle, the former head of ANS, was her biological father and had denied all knowledge of her for years. I'm not sure if she was trying to impress him or ruin him with her illegal antics, but it certainly was a cry for help. I did hear that she and her father have started writing to each other now that they're both behind bars. Hopefully they'll have a better relationship once they've both served their sentences."

"Now that's a family situation that makes almost anything seem normal by comparison, even discovering that your father is president."

"I suppose you're right. And I did have a ridiculously normal childhood." The sun sparkled in her hair. She looked so fresh and pretty out in the sunlight. None of the newspaper images did her justice.

"Did you like growing up in Montana?"

"Sure. I didn't know anything different. I thought everyone could bike to the store with their dog in the handlebar basket, or fish in a river all day long on Sunday. Sometimes I miss the simple life."

"Really?" She was relaxing a little.

"Only for a moment, though." She flashed a slightly mischievous smile. "I do love the hustle and bustle of D.C. I guess when it comes right down to it, I'm a people person rather than a hiking in the wilderness person."

"Why can't you be both?"

"I suppose I could. But in the last three or four years I've been so madly busy I can barely sleep in on the weekends, let alone commune with nature."

"Time management is an important part of life in the spotlight."

"There you go again! I refuse to believe that the rest of my life will be lived in a spotlight." She hadn't tensed. She was teasing him.

He shrugged. "Who knows? Maybe the president will get voted out of office in three years and everyone will forget all about you."

"Hey, that's my dad you're talking about!"

He laughed. "See? You feel attached to him already."

"I admit I have been thinking a lot about meeting him, and my mother. I'm nervous, though."

He shrugged. "What have you got to lose?"

"What if I hate them?"

A smile tugged at his mouth. "Then you hate them. That's hardly worse than not knowing them at all."

"I wonder." She inhaled deeply, and started walking across the lawn. He kept pace with her, trying to tug his eyes from the seductive swishing movement of her slim hips beneath her dress. She swung suddenly to face him. "What if I adore them and they don't like me?"

"That'll never happen."

"How do you know?"

"Because you're the kind of daughter any parent would be thrilled to have. The universe seems to be pushing them toward you. Take a chance, live dangerously."

"That sounds like your kind of motto rather than mine." She touched the delicate red petal of a hibiscus in a tall clay pot. "My life is spent reducing the chances that something can go wrong and trying to be as cautious and well prepared as possible. I suppose that is an occupational hazard."

"Time for a change, then." He said it softly. She was so afraid of stepping outside the boundaries of the life she'd made for herself. Too worried about her reputation and the media and what the future might hold. He'd like to shift her focus to much more interesting things like the feel of their lips touching or their hands on each others' skin.

The urge to kiss her was growing stronger each second. He wasn't quite sure what would have happened if it wasn't for all the discipline he'd developed during his royal upbringing and honed in his army training. Even her thoughtful gaze was driving him half mad.

But the way she'd leaped away from him like he'd stung

her warned him to slow right down. He'd have to go very slowly and carefully with Ariella.

"Maybe you're right." Her words surprised him.

"You're going to meet them?"

"I'm scheduled to have a televised 'reunion' with my father on ANS, but I'm not as sure about my mother. She's in a trickier position than me, really. My mom abandoned me and failed to tell the man who fathered me that I existed. She has good reason to stay hidden in some ways." Her eyes flashed with emotion. "I'm sure a lot of people would criticize her choices, regardless of why she made them."

She inhaled, that mysterious expression in her eyes growing deeper. "And my father didn't even know he was a father. He's been rolling merrily through life with no ties and no responsibilities except to his constituents and his country, and now he's discovered that he had a child all along but he's missed the whole experience. I'd be pretty cheesed off if I was him."

"I wonder if they loved each other." He still wasn't entirely sure his own parents had. There were so many forces rushing them together, only to tear them apart again.

"All the salacious media stories made it sound like they did. Puppy love."

"Perhaps you can bring them back together?"

"You're worse than the *National Enquirer!* Either that or you're a hopeless romantic."

"I suspect it's the latter."

She lifted her chin, watching him. Probably deciding that his professed romanticism was simply a cunning ploy to get up her skirt. His unfortunate reputation as a ladies' man sometimes preceded him. "How come you're not in a relationship? Your brother dated the same woman his entire adult life and now they're married."

He shrugged. "I haven't been as lucky as him."

"Or maybe you've just been too busy scaling mountains." She lifted one of her delicate dark brows.

He chuckled. "That, too. There aren't too many lovely, intelligent women at the top of mountains."

"Obviously you've been scaling the wrong ones." She turned and strode off again, but this time her movement had a teasing air. She wanted him to follow her, and knew that he would.

The level of desire in his blood climbed a few notches. He followed her into a square herb garden, with gravel paths bisecting geometrical beds of fragrant lavender and sage and oregano. She bent over a tall rosemary plant and buried her nose in its needles.

Of course his attention snapped immediately to the way her dress hugged the delicious curve of her behind and the graceful way she stood on one leg and extended the other slightly behind her as she leaned forward.

Alarm bells were ringing in his head. Sexual attraction was usually accompanied by danger of some sort. Every girl he even pecked on the cheek was immediately investigated by the media as a future princess. There was no question of having sex with them unless the utmost secrecy was maintained. His military background helped in matters of subterfuge, but the fact remained that usually when he wanted to kiss—or sleep with—a beautiful and intriguing woman, he had to tell himself no.

On the rare occasions when the stars aligned and he managed to secure total privacy, the moment was loaded and often quite magical. He'd even managed several actual relationships over the years, and had had the good luck to adore women who'd proved utterly discreet.

And here he was again, at the moment where he knew exactly what he wanted to do—climb every mountain in order to kiss Ariella Winthrop.

It was never as easy as that.

"You look more relaxed." Her entire demeanor had softened.

She looked up at him with a flirtatious sparkle in her eye. "I feel much better. I'm not sure why."

"Talking to me, of course. And breathing some fresh air doesn't hurt, either. You should come visit Whist Castle. It's my home in England where I go to get away from it all." And the perfect location for a secluded tryst.

Her eyes widened. "Oh, no. I couldn't." Then she laughed. "Of course. You're just being polite. People do tell me I take everything too seriously."

"I most certainly was not being polite. It would give us plenty of time to plan the fund-raiser for World Connect. In fact I might have to insist."

"And how exactly will you do that?" She crossed her arms over her chest. Which drew attention to the way her nipples pushed against the soft fabric of her dress.

"Perhaps I'll have the palace guards bundle you into a plane. It's primitive and high-tech at the same time."

"That may work in Europe, but you can't just shove American citizens into planes. We've started wars with less provocation than that." A smile danced around the corners of her mouth.

He pressed a finger to his lips. "Hmm. I suppose you're right. And you are the daughter of the president. I'll have to resort to more cunning means. A hand-engraved invitation, perhaps."

"I'm afraid I'm the queen of hand-engraved invitations. I've probably stuffed more than a million of those into envelopes at this point. You'll need a lot more than that to impress me."

He stepped forward, uncrossed her arms and took one

of her hands. Her fingers were cool, but heated inside his. "What exactly would it take?"

Heat pulsed between them for a solid second. He watched her pupils dilate and her lips part slightly. Then she snatched her hand back and hurried down the brick path. "I'm afraid I couldn't possibly come right now. We have a lot of events going on and I'm booked almost solid."

Now she was trying to run away from him. Could she know that only made him more eager and determined? He walked slowly, knowing that to stalk any creature you need calm and patience, so you don't spook it and lose your chance altogether. "My loss. I quite understand, though. I'm sure we can plan the fund-raiser over lunches and dinners here in D.C. Speaking of which, perhaps we can get back to breakfast? I suspect those brioche are holding up well and we can fumble a fresh pot of coffee together."

"That sounds perfect."

"Where have you been? I was trying to reach you all morning." Scarlet's voice exploded out of Ariella's phone as she collapsed onto her living room sofa. She'd only just arrived home from her morning with Simon and felt very topsy-turvy. "We have to make a decision on the courses for the DiVosta dinner by four this afternoon so they can source the lobster and crab."

Ariella drew in a silent breath, glad her friend and business partner couldn't see her right now. She was flushed and her eyes were glassy with overexcitement. "I'm sorry. I got…swept away." That was the truth, at least. "I thought they decided on the stone crab."

"They want you to make the final choice."

"Then I've just made it." She sat up. Gosh, she had so much to do. "Did the tablecloths arrive from Bali yet? I keep phoning DHL and they never seem to know what I'm talking about."

"Yup, they're here. And worth the wait, as they're absolutely stunning. Maybe I'll have one turned into a dress afterward. I ordered the cases of Dom Perignon to be delivered to the venue. Their butler swears he'll lock it all up for me so it won't be drunk before the event. Hey, are you still there?"

"Um, yeah. I'm here." Her thoughts wouldn't seem to cooperate. They kept filling up with visions of Simon's handsome and deliciously determined face. Could she really not tell the person she saw every day about her royal adventure? "I just had breakfast with Simon Worth."

"Breakfast? It's nearly three." Trust Scarlet to breeze right over the part about the prince. Raised in D.C.'s most elite circles, she was hard to impress.

"We had a lot to talk about."

"Francesca told me he approached you at last night's event." She sounded intrigued. "And you do have a lot in common. Both descended from heads of state, both lost their mother tragically young and both lamentably still single. Quick, tell me everything and I'll still have time to call about the stone crabs by four."

She laughed. "There isn't that much to tell. You pretty much summed it up. Except the single part. We didn't talk about that."

"But you did kiss."

"Not even a peck." She was a little disappointed about that. She'd braced herself for a decorous kiss when his driver dropped her off—the prince had accompanied her in the backseat, where they were hidden by tinted windows— but he'd simply held her hands for a moment, looked into her eyes and said goodbye. "He wanted to give me a pep talk. I think he's going back to England later this week. He was in D.C. to sign some international pact to stop journalists from using illegal means to dig into our business."

"He must be madly in love with you."

"Are you nuts?" The idea of Simon even lusting after her did something strange to her stomach. At first she hadn't been sure, but by the time he dropped her home she was feeling some pretty heady chemistry. Unless it was all in her head. "Why would he be interested in me?"

"Because you're brilliant, beautiful and fascinating. And now that your daddy is a head of state you're eligible to be a royal bride. Wow. Just think, DC Affairs' first royal wedding! Can we have it on the White House lawn? I think everything should be silver and ivory, with little royal crests engraved on the glasses."

"Your imagination is really running away with you. Being madly in love must be messing with your mind as none of that is even the slightest bit likely to happen."

"You're right. I'd imagine Simon would need to get married in England. A royal procession in the mall down to Buckingham Palace. You in yards of lace and tulle…"

"Stop! Now. I command you." Part of her wanted to laugh. The rest was horrified by how easily Scarlet's crazy vision came to life in her head. She must be losing her mind from all the stress she was under lately.

"Regally imperious already, I see."

"I think I have enough problems in my life without starting an affair with a prince."

"I don't know." Scarlet sighed. "That's the kind of problem most women would be happy to have."

"I don't think so. Sure, the idea of living in a castle and dressing in designer clothes and eating banquets all day might sound nice…."

"Don't forget the pet unicorn."

"But the reality of being a modern royal is very dif-

ferent. It's all smiling at opening ceremonies and photographers trying to get an unflattering picture of you in
a bikini."

"Sad but true. And the queen is rather forbidding. I'm
not sure I'd want her as my in-law."

"See? Being a royal bride is too much hassle. At the
end of the president's time in office he'll go off to monitor
elections in Turkmenistan and I'll slip quietly back into obscurity and maybe get myself a friendly cat for company."
She realized she was pacing around her small apartment
like a caged lion. She forced herself to sit on the sofa again.

"Only eight years to go." She laughed suddenly. "You're
not going to believe this. Or maybe you are. This headline
just popped up on my screen: *Prince Simon to extend fund-
raising trip in D.C.* I told you he's besotted."

Ariella realized she'd sprung to her feet again. "He totally is not. He wants to plan a fund-raiser for his charity,
World Connect."

"Fabulous! I can't wait to add his name to our client
list."

"I knew you'd say that." She smiled. Then frowned. "I
mentioned doing an outdoor concert, and soon, so it'll be
a lot of work."

"Work? We love work." Scarlet sounded pleased. "Did
you talk about dates?"

"He's flexible, so we can pick a date when the perfect
venue is available. The more publicity, the better." It was
so odd to be courting publicity at work and shrinking from
it at home. "I need to go to the gym."

"Why? You're already perfect."

To work off some adrenaline so I don't burst into flames.
"It helps give me energy. And the way business is boom-
ing I need all the energy I can get."

"Well, congratulations on roping the prince into a party.

Go pump some iron, lady, and I'll see you in the office tomorrow."

In the old days, oh, six months ago, before her life exploded, she would have gone for a quiet jog around leafy Georgetown and maybe down to the Capitol. Now that reporters sniffed around her heels, she had to work up a sweat in the privacy of a high-security gym next to well-toned congresswomen and senators, just to preserve some privacy. Wearing headphones and focused on their fitness goals, they left her in peace. Something she'd had very little of lately.

And now Simon Worth had decided to stay in D.C.

Three

How did a prince ask a girl on a date? The question kept Ariella awake late that night. The days of messengers delivering quill-penned invitations were over. Did His Majesty email it? Or was a discreet phone call possible in this age of rampant wiretapping?

She cursed herself for wondering. If Simon called her again it would be a simple business meeting to plan his party. If he even still intended to do the fund-raiser. He probably wouldn't want to see her again after she'd turned down his invitation to visit him in England. Which would be perfect, since the last thing she needed was more drama in her life.

But her question was answered when he showed up on her doorstep, totally undisguised and unannounced.

"Hi." She managed, after a moment of rather stunned silence. "Would you like to come in?"

"Thank you." His tall and broad form made her eighteenth-century doorway look small.

She glanced nervously around. Thank heaven she was a neat freak and had just put away her laundry. It was Saturday around noon and she'd been trying to decide whether to spend her afternoon looking at paintings in a museum or fondling interesting objects at a flea market. Since she hadn't made up her mind (frigid air conditioning versus sticky D.C. summer humidity) she was dressed in jeans and a spaghetti-strap tank top. Not exactly what you'd don if you expected a prince to stop by.

"Your house is lovely."

"Thanks. I only have the first floor. I rent it from the couple who own the upstairs. They have a separate entrance around the side. I do like it, though." She was babbling. He was only being polite. Her tiny and rather overstuffed space must have seemed quaint and eccentric to him. "Do sit down. How did you know I'd be here?"

"I didn't." He eased himself into her cream loveseat. "Do you live alone?"

"Yes. I keep such crazy hours and really need my sleep when I finally have time for it. I tried living with roommates but it never worked out for long."

"So all of these interesting things are yours?" He picked up a pocket-size nineteenth-century brass telescope she'd scored at an estate sale in Virginia.

"I'm afraid so. You can see I love to collect interesting trinkets."

He expertly opened the piece and trained it out the window, then glanced up and his eyes met hers. Her breath stuck at the bottom of her lungs for a moment. How did he have that effect on her? She dealt with celebrities and big shots all day long and had a strict policy of treating them like the ordinary people that they were, if you ignored all those extra zeros in their bank accounts. She'd worked with royals from Sweden, Monaco and Saudi Arabia, among others, and hadn't given a second thought to their supposedly blue blood. But somehow around Simon Worth she felt lightheaded and tongue tied as a naive schoolgirl.

"I can see you have good taste. I've grown up surrounded by fine things, and never had to exert myself to acquire any. It looks as if you've done the work of three hundred years of collectors." He picked up a hand-painted miniature of a lady and her poodle.

"Isn't she sweet? A client from England gave her to me to thank me for planning her wedding in Maryland. In a way I suppose I've stolen her from among your national treasures."

"Perhaps she's simply traveling for a while." His smile melted a little piece of her. "Objects might get restless, just as people do."

She laughed. "I sometimes wonder how they feel about being bought or sold or traded to a new person. I know that inanimate objects aren't supposed to have feelings, but they must carry some energy from the people and places they've been before."

"I know places can have their own spirit. My home at Whist Castle practically bustles with it." He leaned forward, his eyes sparkling. "If places can have a feeling, why not things as well?"

"I'm glad you don't think I'm a nut. I do enjoy seeking out little treasures. In fact I was thinking of ducking past any photographers and doing that this afternoon at the Eastern Market."

"Perhaps we could go together." He said it quite calmly, as if it wasn't the most outlandish idea she'd every heard.

"But if people see us together…they might talk."

"About what?" He leaned back, face calmly pleasant.

Suddenly she felt like an idiot for suggesting that people might gossip about a romance between them. Obviously that existed only in her own mind. What would a British royal be doing with her? "I'm being paranoid again. I probably think the press cares far more about me than they actually do."

"If anyone asks, we can tell them you're helping me source interesting items for a fund-raiser we're planning." He picked a pair of tiny silver sewing scissors and snipped the air with them.

"The outdoor concert?"

"A mad hatter's tea party, perhaps?" A cute dimple appeared in his left cheek. "People do expect us Brits to be eccentric, after all. You won't actually need a reasonable explanation."

"Well, in that case, let's go."

"Is there another way out of here?" He'd risen to his feet and offered his hand to her.

"You mean, besides the front door?"

He nodded. "I'm afraid I was spotted arriving here."

"The short guy with the ponytail?"

"The very same."

"Ugh. He's freelance and has sold pictures of me to at least three different papers. One was a picture of me carrying two grocery bags, and somehow he managed to bribe the cashier into handing over my receipt so everyone could learn what brand of aspirin I prefer. And there isn't another way out. I guess you'll have to stay here forever."

Her hand heated inside his as he helped her to her feet. He didn't look at all put out by either the photographer or the prospect of spending the rest of his life in Apt. 1A.

"I do hate to assist these lowlifes in their trade. We'll leave separately so there's no picture. I'll leave first in my car, you leave five minutes later and walk around the block. I'll have a blue Mercedes meet you in front of the Mixto restaurant."

"Goodness, I feel like I'm in a James Bond film." He must have planned this. Which sent sparkles of excitement and alarm coursing through her.

"Don't worry. I have years of experience in dodging these leeches. I think of it as an entertaining challenge."

"I'm game. What should I bring?"

"Just yourself."

Simon left via the front door and she rushed to the window, where she saw him get into a waiting silver SUV, which pulled away. She took a couple of minutes to fix her hair and face, and put on a light blouse and some boots, then she headed out in the opposite direction, toward the tiny restaurant as if she was just on her way to the local deli. She didn't cast a glance at the depressing figure in his dull green jacket and faded black baseball hat, though she felt his eyes trained on her.

Simon was right. As long as they weren't seen together, there was no picture to sell. The whole world knew he was in D.C. Everyone was already tired of pictures of her leaving for work and coming back home again. No picture, no story.

A tiny ripple of triumph put a spring in her step as she rounded the corner and spotted a blue Mercedes idling double-parked halfway down the block. The car's rear door opened and she saw Simon's reassuring face. Feeling like a ninja, she climbed in, and they cruised off down the block. Her heart was pounding, and she wasn't sure if it was because of all the subterfuge, or being so close to Simon again.

"He didn't follow you."

"Nope. He rarely does. I think he's too lazy. Just snaps a couple of pictures a day and hopes a story will break so he can sell them. So far his biggest coup is the day I wore my Montana Grizzlies T-shirt. They plastered that picture all over the papers right as the story about my father was breaking, as if it was proof I was his daughter or something."

"Once you're in the public eye people read into your every move. You learn to laugh at it."

Up close like this she could see a slight haze of stubble on his jaw. She wondered what it would feel like against her cheek, and felt her breath quicken. She tugged her gaze out the window, where D.C. scrolled by. "We're going in the opposite direction from the market."

"My driver knows some antique shops in Maryland. We'll enjoy more privacy there." He leaned back against the seat, shirt stretching over his broad chest. "And I very much doubt any photographers will find us."

Was this a date? It certainly felt like one. There hadn't been any real mention of the event they were supposedly planning. And it wasn't exactly professional of him to show up on her doorstep without warning. "Do you whisk women off in cars on a regular basis?"

He shot her a sideways glance. "No, I don't."

Her chest swelled a little. So she was special? She wondered if he'd prolonged his trip to see more of her. Then chastised herself for having such a vain thought. She'd better steer this conversation in a business direction. "I told Scarlet about your plans for the fund-raiser and she's going to start work on finding the venue. How are your other fund-raising efforts going?"

"That's an abrupt change of subject." His tawny eyes glittered with humor. "And I'm forced to confess I haven't made much headway. Every time I try talking about education in Africa, people's eyes glaze over and they ask about my latest climbing expedition. I'm afraid I can never resist talking about climbing."

"You need to make your cause sexier." Uh-oh. Just saying the word caused the temperature in the car to rise a degree or two.

He cocked a brow. "Sexy? How do I do that?"

"You focus on the elements of your organization that make people feel good about themselves. For example, with breast cancer, pink ribbons make people think about triumph and recovery. That makes them want to get out their wallets a lot more than lectures about incredible new discoveries in small cell cancer treatments. For a party I'd have pink pearls and pink roses and pink champagne. They don't have anything at all to do with cancer, but they make people feel happy about embracing the cause."

Forehead furrowed, he looked intrigued. "So you think I need to rebrand my charity?"

"I don't really know enough about it. Do you have a brand or logo or imagery you use often?"

He made a wry expression. "Not at all. We simply print the name in blue on white paper. I'm beginning to see what you mean."

"So what excites you the most about what your organization does?"

He frowned for a moment and looked straight ahead, then turned to her. "Including people in the conversation about our future. Giving them access to technology that makes them part of our world and a way to be heard in it."

"That's sexy. And big technology companies are a nice target market for your fund-raising. You'd certainly be speaking their language. How about 'join the conversation' as your marketing ploy, so you're inviting everyone to be part of the future you imagine."

He stared at her. "I like the way your mind works."

She shrugged. "I brainstorm this kind of stuff all the time."

"I had no idea party planning was so involved. I thought it was all choosing napkins and printing invitations."

"That's the easy part. The hard part is making each event stand out from the thousands of others taking place during the year. In your case, people would expect a prince to have a very exclusive, private dinner, so an outdoor concert rather takes people by surprise. It also creates the sense of inclusion that your charity is all about. In addition to the event's raising money from ticket sales, it'll get people talking and that will generate additional donations and bring in people who want to help."

He still stared right at her, and she could almost hear his brain moving a million miles a minute. "Where have you been all my life?"

A smile crept across her mouth. "Read the papers. You can learn more about my past than I can even remember."

He laughed. "I know that feeling. I think we have a lot in common."

How could she feel so comfortable talking to this man from one of the great royal houses of Europe? Well, she'd never been too impressed by royalty. That probably helped in situations like this.

"That's probably why I've appeared in your life to help you cope with it."

"Destiny at work." She swallowed. Did she really believe that some mysterious workings of fate had brought her and Simon together?

No. They were simply going to spend a pleasant afternoon looking at antiques. They'd put together a fun concert that would get people talking about World Connect. Then he'd go back to England and she'd get on with whatever her life was going to be.

What about the chemistry crackling between them right now in the back of the car? What about the way her skin heated when he leaned toward her, or her stomach swirled with strange sensations when he fixed her with that thoughtful gaze?

She was going to ignore that. So was he. No one was going to do anything they might regret. They were both grownups and far too sensible for that.

What a relief.

The driver took them to a little town called Danes Mills, where he parked behind a quaint restaurant that reminded Ariella of a British pub. The entire main street appeared to be upscale antique shops, with maybe a gift shop or bookstore for variety. Simon helped her from the car while the driver held the door. It was all very formal and majestic and made her feel like a princess. Which she wasn't.

People did turn to look at them. She wasn't sure if she imagined the whispers. While she knew people thought she was pretty, she didn't have the kind of looks that demanded attention. In fact she considered herself a nondescript brunette, so she didn't usually have to worry about standing out from the crowd. People recognized Simon, though. He was tall and broad and attracted admiration without even trying. They'd probably stare at him even if he wasn't a well-known prince. Maybe they were turning to look at him for the same reasons she wanted to—because he was handsome and his smile could melt an iceberg.

In the first store they looked through some old paintings and drawings, all rather in need of restoration, and admired a painted cupboard. In the second, Ariella became entranced by a group of tiny snuff boxes. She loved to open them and find the tobacco smell still there, as if the owner had just finished the last pinch.

"Which is your favorite?"

"I'm not sure." She pressed a finger to her lips. "The silver one has such delicate engraving, and I love the colors on this enameled one. But I think I like this black one best." She picked up a shiny black box. She wasn't even sure what it was made from. Possibly something insubstantial like papier-mâché. It had a delicate painting of a girl standing under a tree that must have been painted with the world's tiniest brush.

He took it from her, which surprised her. She grew even more surprised when he handed it to the shop owner—who had to be roused from some old books he was sorting through—and paid for it. After the shopkeeper had wrapped it in tissue and deposited it in a tiny brown paper shopping bag, Simon handed it back to her. "For you."

She blinked. "I didn't mean for you to buy it."

"I know. I wanted to."

"I don't think a man has ever given me a snuff box before." She kept her voice hushed, not wanting to convey any impression of romance to the store owner.

"You can't accuse me of being clichéd, at least." That infectious smile again. She found her own mouth curving up. Surely there was no harm in the gift. It wasn't terribly expensive, just a sweet gesture. "I notice you like miniature paintings. I saw several at your flat." He opened the shop door and they stepped out into the sunlight.

"I do. A perfect world in microcosm. And just for one person at a time to look at and enjoy. Maybe it's the opposite of my parties where everyone must have a good time all at once."

"You keep giving me a new perspective on things I take for granted." He smiled. "Our driver, David, tells me there's a state park near here. What do you say we take a picnic lunch there?"

"That sounds great."

It was lucky she agreed because David had already been given orders somehow. The car was piled high with white deli bags and a newly bought cooler containing chilled drinks. She was so used to creating fairy-tale meals for other people that it was rather bizarre to have someone else pulling all the strings. All she had to do was enjoy.

David drove them into the park, past several battlefield sites, to the bank of a winding river. He spread a pretty French provincial patterned cloth—which must have been a rather expensive purchase back in Danes Mill—and unpacked the deli bags filled with gourmet salads.

Ariella settled onto the cloth and Simon poured her a sparkling glass of champagne. "I don't think I've ever been this pampered." They helped themselves to a warm tortellini salad and a crisp slaw of carrot and beetroot with a sesame seed dressing.

"You deserve it. You've been under a lot of pressure lately and it's time for you to let off some steam."

She sighed, and they sipped their champagne. Not surprisingly, it was very good. "Is your life like this every day?"

"If only." That intoxicating smile again. "My life is usually far more prosaic."

The driver had tactfully vanished, and they were all alone beside the rushing stream. Tiny yellow flowers bloomed along the banks, and the rich mossy smell of the trees and the soil soothed her frazzled nerves. "I used to wish my life would go back to normal, but if this is the new normal, I'm not complaining." She looked up at him and spoke with sudden conviction. "And I intend to meet both my birth parents." Her confidence had grown since she met Simon. "It's too big an opportunity to waste. Sure, I'm scared, but the potential reward is worth the risk."

"Fantastic. I'm glad you've come to that conclusion. I thought you would. Have you managed to make contact with your mother?"

"I wrote to her but I haven't heard back yet. It's so odd that I don't even know what she looks like. All I've seen is her high school yearbook photo from the year she got pregnant with me."

"What did she look like then?"

"Young, sweet, sort of shy. She had a terrible hairstyle. It was the 1980s after all."

He laughed. "I bet she's a lot more nervous than you are."

"She has good reason to be apprehensive. She's the only one who could be accused of doing anything wrong here. She says she didn't tell my father about me because she didn't want to prevent him from going off to college, but surely he could have made his own decisions about how to handle it. After all, if he can manage to become president of the United States, I think he could probably handle supporting a family while taking his classes."

"You're right. I'd be devastated if I got a girl pregnant and she didn't tell me."

Her eyes widened. Sometimes Simon was shockingly frank. He hadn't even looked up from his plate, and was busy munching on some arugula. "Is that something you have to worry about a lot? I mean, any child you had would be in line to the throne."

"Believe me, I've heard that over and over again since I was old enough to understand. My grandmother, the queen, would prefer that none of us date at all. If she had her own way we'd all be safely tucked away in arranged marriages by age twenty."

"Have they tried to pair you up with anyone?"

"Oh, it never stops." His eyes were smiling. "They're

constantly digging up blushing blue-blood virgins and inviting them to palace tea parties."

"But so far none of them has piqued your interest." She nibbled on a crisp green bean.

"Oh, several of them have piqued my interest." He chuckled. "But not in the way Grandmama was hoping, I'm afraid. And luckily, I haven't gotten any of them pregnant, either."

"You're shocking me."

"Why? You don't think a prince has feelings like any other man?"

"Well…" She bit her lip. "Of course I know you do, it's just…"

"You can't believe I'm talking about it out loud when I should be much more subtle and surreptitious?" He raised a brow. His dimple was showing. "My family hates how blunt I am. I can't stand beating around the bush. Heaven knows I do enough of it when I'm out in public, so in private I prefer to speak my mind. Don't be too shocked."

"I'll try not to be." She smiled. His candor was refreshing. He was so different from what she'd expected. It was disarming and intriguing and she had a hard time maintaining her own cool reserve around him.

"How did we start talking about me? I was asking about your mother. Didn't you say she lives in Ireland?"

"When she wrote to me there was an address on the inside of the letter. A post office box in Kilkenney, Ireland. She must have rented it so no one would find out where she lived. I haven't told anyone she wrote to me, except my closest friends. I told her I'd like to meet her and I'm willing to travel to Ireland if she needs me to."

"How will you do that without taking the international press corps with you?"

"I'm cunning when I need to be." She smiled mysteriously. "And it's always a good idea to do some location scouting for a big wedding, or something."

"Your profession lends itself to international travel. I'm forced by circumstance to do most of my travel in the British Commonwealth."

"The countries that were in the former empire?"

"Exactly. Lucky thing it was big and had so many interesting countries." He grinned, looking disarmingly boyish. "How did your mother end up in Ireland, anyway? I thought she was from Montana."

"I don't entirely know. I think she met an Irish man after she gave me up for adoption. Hopefully I'll find out the details once we meet."

"I'm sure she's missed you far more than you know."

She drew in a shaky breath. "I don't know. She might have other children. She didn't say. She didn't mention anything about wanting to meet me."

"She's probably nervous that you don't want to meet her. She did abandon you, after all."

"I told her in my letter that I have no hard feelings and that I had the best childhood anyone could want. I said it would mean so much to me if I could meet her."

"Has she responded?"

"Not yet." A sudden chill made her shiver. She put down her plate. "What if she doesn't?"

He smiled. "She will. I can feel it."

"Psychic, are you?" She sipped her champagne. The slight buzz it gave her was soothing, given the tense topic of conversation. "I wish I had your confidence."

"You do. You just don't know it yet." He sipped his champagne. "Let's see how cold this water is." He stood and walked to the bank, where the river rushed by only about a foot below. Before she had time to join him, he'd removed his shoes and socks, rolled up the leg of his dark slacks, and slid his feet into the water. "Cold."

"Is it really? It must be from an underground spring." The summer afternoon was downright balmy. Her own toes itched to dip into the sparkling depths. She sat on the bank next to him and slipped off her shoes. Her jeans were tight-fitting so she could barely roll them up at all, but she managed to get them above her ankles. Then she dangled her feet down the bank until the water lapped against her toes. "Ooh, that feels good."

Tentative, she slid her feet beneath the surface. The chill of the water contrasted with the warm throb of intimacy that pulsed between them, helped by the glass of champagne. Her shoulder bumped gently against his, then she felt his arm slide around her waist. It felt as natural as the cool clear water splashing against her ankles.

Now his torso almost touched hers, and they seemed to be growing closer by slow degrees. His rich masculine scent tugged at her senses. She could see the pale stubble on his chin, and the sparkle of light in his eyes—they were hazel up close—and then she couldn't see at all because her eyes shut and she found herself kissing him.

Four

The daylight dazzled unpleasantly as Simon opened his eyes. He'd had to tug himself away from kissing Ariella, and the taste of her lingered on his tongue, forbidden and delicious. She looked unbearably beautiful, sitting there on the bank, her eyes dark with desire and the forgotten cuffs of her jeans darkening in the water.

"We shouldn't have done that." Her voice was barely a whisper.

"I beg to differ." His entire body growled at him to do a lot more with this lovely woman. He let his hand wander into her long, dark hair. "Mostly because I don't think we had any choice."

"You always have a choice." One neat brow lifted slightly. He could feel her shrink back from him.

"Theoretically, I suppose. But some things are just irresistible." Her raspberry-tinted lips were among those things, and he lowered his lips toward them again. But this time she hesitated. "Simon, I really don't think this is sensible."

"Why not?"

"Uh…because your grandmother would be horrified."

"Nonsense." He stroked her hair. She stiffened slightly, as if she wanted to resist, but he saw his own desire reflected in her eyes. "I'm sure she'd adore you." He really didn't want to think about the queen right now. He didn't want to think about anyone but Ariella. He could deal with everyone else later.

Ariella shivered slightly, as anticipation rose in the air. If she didn't want to kiss him she could have leapt to her feet and darted back to the car. But she hadn't.

He waited for her to come to him, and she did. Her mouth rose to meet his and they sank deep into another sensual kiss. He was almost breathless when they finally broke again.

"Uh-oh." Her cheeks were flushed. "I couldn't help that kiss at all." She'd twisted into his embrace, and her nipples peaked against her T-shirt and the bra underneath it.

"See? Sometimes you just don't have a choice."

Desire made his thoughts spin. He certainly hadn't had enough champagne to feel this tipsy. He stroked the silky skin of her arm, wishing he could bare other parts of her. But he could still resist doing that—for now. "Sometimes you have to give in to forces more powerful than a mere human."

"You're not a mere human, you're a prince." She winked.

He loved how she seemed totally natural with him, not affected or intimidated at all. "Even royalty are subject to the whims of passion." He traced her cheekbone with his thumb. "Which can be quite inconvenient at times."

She glanced about nervously. "I hope there aren't any photographers hiding in the bushes."

"I've learned to go to places that would never occur to them. Why would a man with a large rural estate go to a popular state park?"

"Because it has this cool stream with yellow wildflowers growing along its banks." Her slender fingers touched the petals of a flower. How he'd like to feel them running over his skin, or through his hair.

"That is why I come, but they don't think like that. They expect me to go to expensive restaurants and exclusive gatherings. Of course I do that as well, it's my job, but I've become quite skilled at doing the unexpected when I'm off duty. I always have my driver study natural areas near wherever I'm traveling. A man can withstand a lot more dreary meetings around a conference table if he knows there's a bracing kayak trip waiting for him at the end of it."

"Very cunning, and keeps you fit, too."

"And sane. At least as sane as I'm going to be." He grinned. He didn't feel terribly sane right now. He wanted to do all kinds of things that weren't sensible at all, especially not when you did them with a girl who was already in the public eye and who didn't fit the queen's narrow ideas of what constituted a suitable consort.

But no one, including the queen, was going to keep him from bedding the lovely Ariella.

"I'd really better get back to D.C. I have a busy week to plan for."

Again he felt her pulling away from him. He stood and helped her to his feet. Landing a kiss on Ariella's lovely mouth was enough excitement for today. Their time together had only confirmed his intuition that she was no ordinary woman. He could pace himself and wait for the right moment to claim his prize.

"I need to do some planning myself. Now that I'm staying in D.C. a while longer I want to make sure I make the most of the opportunity." They walked back to the pretty clearing where they'd had their picnic. "I'd better think about who I want to wine and dine while I'm here—other than you, of course."

She bit her lip as they packed the remains of lunch back into the bags. He could see she still felt misgivings about their kiss. It was hard not to come on too strong with her when he wanted to throw her over his shoulder and take her back to his hotel.

Instead he helped her into the car and returned her discreetly to a location two blocks away from her apartment. From there she walked home alone, chin lifted in sweet defiance against anyone who wanted to know her business.

He sank back against the back seat of the car and let out a long breath. Ariella Winthrop. Something about her had grabbed him hard. He tried to distract himself by pulling his phone out of his pocket. He'd had it turned off all day. A message from his younger brother Henry seemed like the perfect diversion, so he punched his number.

"Are you really staying over there for another week?" His brother's incredulous voice made him smile.

"At least a week and with good reason."

"Let me guess, the reason has long legs and a toothy American smile."

Simon reached forward and closed the partition between him and the driver. "There's nothing toothy about her smile," he retorted, thinking about her lovely mouth.

"I knew it."

"You knew nothing of the sort. I'm here to raise public awareness of World Connect. I have big plans. We're going to hold an outdoor concert here in D.C."

"Nice. But let me guess—she's involved somehow."

"She might be." Was he really so predictable?

Henry laughed. "Don't let Grandma find out about it."

"Why not?" He bristled.

"She'd have a fit about you dating anyone who isn't marriage material. Remember that last lecture she gave you about it being time to settle down. She's got your wedding all planned and all you have to do is show up."

He growled. "I'm not marrying anyone."

"You'll have to sooner or later. You're next, big brother."

"Why don't you worry about your own love life, instead of mine? I suppose I'm lucky that the scandalous state of your affairs distracts attention from mine."

"That's why I need you to get married and draw the spotlight off me for a while." Henry had been photographed in compromising situations several times over the last year. "Why can't you make them all happy so I can keep on having fun?"

"That might actually be possible." He watched D.C. pass by his window. "I've met someone who could well be the one."

"You're not serious."

"Do I joke around?"

"Yes, often."

"Then you can just assume I'm jesting."

"An American girl?"

"The president's newly discovered daughter, Ariella, no less." He felt a bit sheepish using her media handle to describe her to his own brother. "She's quite something."

"Don't even think about it."

"I'm afraid it's gone well beyond thinking." He smiled as memories of their kiss heated his blood.

"Gran will need sedation. And can you imagine Uncle Derek's reaction?"

"I'll try not to." He shook his head. Their mother's brother took a keen interest in meddling in their affairs and throwing up obstacles at every turn. "If only he'd been born royal he wouldn't have to try so hard to be more royal than the rest of us."

"You do realize you can't marry an American."

"Why not? In the old days we nearly always married into royal families from other countries."

"Exactly. Married into royal families. You need a nice Swedish princess, or one from Monaco or Spain."

He shoved aside an annoying twinge of misgiving. "I'd say that the president's daughter is American royalty."

Henry laughed. "For four years, maybe eight, but I don't think our grandmother will see it that way."

"I'm sure she'll love Ariella once she meets her." Who wouldn't? And in his experience, people usually got over their prejudices once you gave them half a chance.

"Oh dear, you sound dangerously serious. And I know how bullheaded you are once you get going."

"I'm not bullheaded, I just do what I think is right."

Henry laughed. "So you do. I just hope poor Ariella knows what she's in for."

Ariella was attempting to butter toast while checking messages on her phone, when she saw seven messages in a row from Scarlet that must have come in while she was at the gym. She put down the butter knife and punched in Scarlet's number.

"You're not going to believe this." Scarlet was breathless with excitement.

"Try me." She could barely believe anything that happened to her lately. Every time she thought about that kiss, she was assaulted by a rush of starry-eyed excitement and a burst of salty regret. What had they started?

"We've been asked to put in a bid on the Duke of Buckingham's wedding. In England!"

"That's great." Her mind immediately started whirling with plans for a side-trip to Ireland to find her mother.

"Could you sound a bit more excited?"

"I am, really."

"You know how we're trying to branch out into Europe. This will be our fifth party over there. I'd say this is some kind of landmark. And now that you're intimate with royalty, we have an excellent chance of being chosen to plan the event."

"You're not going to say anything about me, are you?" Her adrenaline spiked.

"Why? Is there something going on that's secret?" Scarlet's voice grew hushed with anticipation.

Could she lie to Scarlet, her close friend and business partner? She sucked in a breath and braced herself. "I kissed him."

"Ohmygod. You kissed Prince Simon?"

The truth was out. She strode across her apartment, trying to stay calm. "I still can't believe it happened, but it did. Can I swear you to secrecy?"

"My lips are sealed. So you guys have a...a thing going?"

"I don't know what we have going, but I'm seeing him for dinner tomorrow." Already her heart fluttered with anticipation—and fear of where this would lead.

"You're dating a prince. Wow. It's a crying shame that I can't put out a PR release about it. Can you imagine how much we could raise our prices if people knew you were practically a princess?"

"Would you stop! I'm not practically anything, except late for work."

"You're totally going to London to pitch this."

"Fine. Can I eat my toast now and we'll talk when I come into the office?"

"Oh, okay. Make me wait for details. You're cruel like that. I'll see you in a few."

Ariella put the phone down and tried to distract herself by spreading some more butter. She only liked real butter but it was annoying to wait for it to melt enough to spread. She unscrewed the lid of her favorite organic apricot jam, and the phone rang again. What now? It wasn't even eight-fifteen in the morning yet.

She glanced at the number. Unavailable. Frowning, she picked up the phone. "Hello."

"Is that Ariella?" She didn't recognize the voice. It sounded very far away.

"This is Ariella."

"Oh, hello." The line crackled with static.

"Who's this?" She was growing impatient, trying to spread with one hand.

"It's your, it's...Eleanor. Eleanor Daly."

Her mother. Her breath caught in her throat and she dropped the knife with a clatter and gripped the phone tighter. "I'm so glad you called. Thank you so much for writing to me. You have no idea how much that letter meant." So many thoughts unfolded in her brain and she tried not to panic.

"The agency didn't think it was a good idea for me to contact you when you were a child. They wouldn't tell me who adopted you. I never stopped thinking about you. Never."

The emotion in her mother's voice made her chest constrict. "I've always wanted to meet you. Could we get together?" She spoke fast, afraid that at any minute the call would drop and she'd lose the fragile new connection.

"I live in Ireland."

Ariella's brain was racing, as she tried to mentally organize the long-awaited meeting with her birth mother. "I have to come to England soon for work. Would it be okay if I came to visit you in Ireland?" The words rushed out, and suddenly she was terrified Eleanor would say no.

Why did she think of her as Eleanor and not her mother? Of course she wasn't "Mom" to her. That title would always be held by the woman who'd raised her and who she still missed every day. But she wanted to meet Eleanor so much it was a dull ache inside her all the time now.

After a long pause, Eleanor spoke again. "I'm in a remote rural area. Perhaps I could come to England to visit you while you're there?"

"I'd like that very much." Exhilaration roared through her and her hands started shaking, causing her to press the phone against her ear. "I don't know the exact dates I'll be there yet. What works for you?"

"Oh, anything, really. I'm widowed now, and I do baby-sitting for income so I don't have any real commitments." Eleanor suddenly sounded more relaxed.

"I can't wait to meet you. It doesn't seem fair that I don't know what you look like. You can see pictures of me in the papers all the time."

She laughed. "I'm afraid I'm not very glamorous. I probably look like a typical Irish housewife. I've lived in Ireland since the year after I…had you. I haven't been back to the States since. I was trying so hard to run away from everything. From you and Ted and the mess I'd gotten myself into."

"I'm so glad you wrote to me."

"It was a hard letter to write. I knew I had to reach out

to you and I didn't know how. I was afraid. I am afraid.
I know everyone thinks I made the wrong choices back
then and I..." Her voice trailed off.

"You made the choices you had to make. No one blames
you for them."

"There wasn't a day where I didn't think of you and
wonder what you were doing right at that moment."

"I had a great childhood." She couldn't believe she was
finally having this conversation she'd waited so long for.

"I'm so happy to hear that." She could hear tears in her
mother's voice. "I did worry. I tried to imagine that you
were being well taken care of and were happy."

"I could show you photos if you'd like. My dad was
an avid photographer and there are really far too many of
them." Then she wondered if she'd said the wrong thing.
Would Eleanor find it painful to see all this evidence of
someone else raising her child?

"I'd like that very much." Emotion heightened the pitch
of her voice. "I've missed so much. I never did have another child. You're my only one."

She couldn't believe she was actually talking to her
mother after all these years. So many questions flooded
her mind. Things she'd always wanted to know. "Do you
have brown hair?"

"I do, though I admit to coloring it now to cover some
gray. And I can see you have my green eyes."

"Those are from you? People have always asked me
about them. Green eyes are quite unusual. I wonder what
other characteristics we share? Oh, I wish I could leave
for the airport right now."

"I'm so glad I'll finally meet you after all these years.
I do feel terrible guilt about what happened. That poor
Ted never knew he had a beautiful daughter growing up

all that time. I don't think I'll ever forgive myself for that. Have the two of you become close now?"

She hesitated. "Actually I haven't met him yet. Since he's the president he's surrounded by all sorts of high security and no one entirely believed the story that I'm his daughter until the DNA test results came out. I don't think the White House knows quite what to do with me."

She rambled on. "And I suppose he's busy running the country. And dealing with that mess in the Middle East. They're thinking of sending troops." Every time she watched the news now she felt each domestic and international event a bit more keenly, knowing that her own flesh and blood had to make decisions about how to handle each crisis.

"Oh, I just thought that since you were both in Washington…"

She shoved a hand through her hair and tried to keep her embarrassment out of her voice. "We're going to meet very soon. ANS is arranging a televised special and we're going to appear on camera together." She wanted to sound happy and excited, not terrified.

"You won't tell anyone that we're going to meet, though, right?" Eleanor's voice had shrunk again.

"I promise I won't tell a soul. Is it okay if I call you sometime?" She'd already scribbled down the number, afraid it might disappear into the recesses of her phone or get accidentally deleted.

"I'd like that very much."

They ended the phone call with much excitement about the planned meeting. Ariella then managed to wolf down the toast and dash to work before her first appointment, adrenaline pounding in her veins like a dangerous drug. The receptionist handed her a message that Francesca wanted to chat about the upcoming ANS special that would bring her together with her famous father.

"It's lucky I thrive on being busy," she muttered to herself, as she opened the door to her office. She had umpteen phone calls to make about events happening this week, and now her mind was being tugged between the prospect of meeting her mother, doing a TV show with her father and, of course, seeing Simon again. There was way too much going on for everything to work out smoothly. That was something she'd learned early on in her years as an event planner. Too many balls in the air meant broken pieces on the floor, and soon.

But which ball would crash first?

On the evening of her date with Simon she left work early so she'd have time for a shower. She was about to climb in and wash her hair when she remembered she'd run out of conditioner. Great. Frizzy hair for her dinner with a prince. She'd have to head to the deli around the corner and pick some up.

She tied up her hair and put on jeans and a jacket. There was no more running to the store in shorts and a tank top now that reporters lurked in every crevice.

She strode into the shop and picked up a bottle of some harmless-looking generic conditioner—the store didn't carry her rather esoteric favorite—and marched up to the counter, fishing in her pocket for cash. A magazine behind the counter caught her eye. *Royal Watch* was the title, emblazoned in yellow letters.

Simon's gorgeous face almost totally filled the front cover. The rest of it, unfortunately, was hogged by the shiny, overly made-up face of a young blonde woman pressing her cheek against his. A young woman who was most decidedly not Ariella Winthrop.

"Two ninety-nine." The cashier's voice tugged her back to the present.

She handed him a twenty. "And I'll take that magazine, too." Her voice came out hoarse. She pointed at *Royal Watch*. "Research for work." Because of course she was just buying it to see if there was any information about what the Duke of Buckingham might want for his wedding decorations. Yeah. That was it.

She hurried back to her apartment with the magazine rolled tightly. She certainly didn't need any press coverage of her buying *Royal Watch*. Once inside she locked the door and walked slowly to the kitchen counter, now almost afraid to look at the cover again. Was she jealous? She'd only just met Simon. He must have an entire history of romances that had nothing to do with his feelings for her.

She risked another glance at the girl on the cover. Blue eyes, heavily outlined with dark eyeliner. The text over the photo said *Prince Simon Engaged!*

She frowned. He couldn't be in love with someone else and kissing her—could he? She flipped to the "article," which consisted of two paragraphs accompanied by a lot more pictures. All the photos appeared to be from the same outdoor sporting event—some kind of horse race—with all the women in big hats.

The article said that Lady Sophia Alnwick and Prince Simon had told their closest friends of their planned engagement, and that the queen was thrilled to welcome her new daughter-in-law into the family.

How come she hadn't seen any of this in the more mainstream press? Prince Simon wasn't as much in the public eye as his older brother, who was heir to the throne, but the entertainment press still picked up on stories about him quite often. Could *Royal Watch* simply have made it up?

Apart from the cover picture where they appeared to be cheek to cheek, they didn't look that intimate. Still...

She showered and dressed with considerably less excitement and more trepidation than she'd been feeling before she saw *Royal Watch*. How could she bring this up without seeming like a jealous harpy? On the other hand, she certainly didn't want to kiss a man who was engaged—even unofficially—to another woman.

When Simon's driver opened the rear door of the car thirty minutes later, she was surprised to find it empty. Did she now expect one of the crowned heads of Europe to arrive in person to pick her up? She was definitely getting a big head.

The car slid through the more exclusive streets of the city. She had no idea where they were going, but somehow it seemed embarrassing to admit it to the driver, so she didn't ask. Before long, they pulled up in front of a classical façade. The driver opened the door and she stepped out. The building looked grand and impersonal, like an embassy or an exclusive law office. She walked up the front steps and a suited man opened the door and murmured "Good evening." Still no sign of Simon. If her life wasn't so unpredictable and over the top already she'd probably be growing alarmed by now.

"Ariella." His deep, smooth voice called from down a marbled hallway. Immediately her body heat rose.

He walked up to her and kissed her softly on the lips. *Who's Sophia Alnwick?* she wanted to ask, but now was not the time. Her mouth hummed under his kiss and she wanted it to deepen, but the man who'd opened the door must be nearby, and maybe others, too. She didn't want anyone to find out about their clandestine affair.

An affair? That sounded so...sexual. And it wasn't. At least not yet.

"What is this place?"

"An unofficial annex to the consulate. There's no one here in the evenings so I've requisitioned it so I could entertain you *at home,* so to speak. We'll just have to pretend we're at Whist Castle, since you won't do me the honor of visiting me at my real home."

His teasing hurt expression made her laugh. He always managed to diffuse any tension in the situation and make her feel like they were just two people who happened to get along well. "As it turns out, I might be planning a party in England soon."

He picked up her hand and kissed it, which made her fingers tingle with pleasure. "Then perhaps I'll have some beefeaters intercept you and whisk you up to Whist." His eyes glimmered with humor.

"You wouldn't."

"Wouldn't I?" One brow rose as if he was asking the question of himself. "You don't ever really know what you'll do in any given situation until you're faced with it. That's something I learned during my time in the military. You can only hope you'll do what you know is right."

"Speaking of which, are you engaged?" There, it was out. And ringing boldly through the marble-clad hallway. Any staff who were lingering in the corners had just seen them kiss, making the question really embarrassing.

"Engaged as in busy?" He gestured for her to enter a room.

Which she did, glad to get out of the echoing hallway. They were now in a large sitting room, with damask curtains and big armchairs. "Engaged as in betrothed." She managed to stay fairly calm while she waited for his response. Was he going to deny it?

"Most definitely not."

He did deny it. "I saw a cover story about it in a magazine in my local deli."

He didn't look the slightest bit flustered. "Do you believe everything you read in the papers?"

Her face heated slightly. "No. Especially not if it's written about me." She felt a smile creeping across her mouth. "I should have known it wasn't true."

"But you had to ask anyway." His gaze challenged her.

"Yes." She lifted her chin. "I don't kiss men who belong to someone else."

"I'm relieved to hear it. And I love the way you came right out and asked. I get so tired of people beating about the bush. You're a breath of fresh air."

"I'm not sure how fresh I am. I've had a rather long day. I just learned that the Saudi prince whose wedding we're planning for next month requires that the men and the women celebrate in different rooms."

"We princes can be quite high-maintenance." His cute dimple appeared. "Though that does rather seem like it would take the fun out of the occasion."

"So the queen isn't thrilled that you're to wed Sophia Alnwick, as the magazine proclaimed."

He shrugged. "I suspect the queen would be more than thrilled if I was to wed Sophia. I, on the other hand, feel differently."

She giggled. She loved his dry humor. "So the palace is trying to set you up with her because she's suitable royal bride material."

"Yup." He sighed. "Blood as blue as a robin's egg, pretty as an English rose and not terribly bright. All the makings of a royal bride."

"But not your cup of tea."

"I prefer women with keen intelligence, even if that

makes them more troublesome." A smile tugged at the corner of his mouth.

"I can't be that intelligent or I wouldn't be spending time with you when I'm trying to avoid media attention. I think you might be the most eligible bachelor in the known world."

"You'd think they could find something more compelling to write about. Global warming, for example."

"Nah. Too serious. Handsome princes are more fun to read about. Especially when they're kissing the wrong woman."

He'd closed the door and now stood in front of her. His expression was serious, brows lowered and eyes thoughtful. "I'd much rather be kissing the right woman."

Uh-oh. An inner warning signal flashed inside Ariella. *Getting in too deep.* His steady gaze held her like a vise. She could feel her breathing quicken and her body heat rise. Her mouth itched to kiss him and her fingers to sink into his shirt. Isn't that why she'd come here?

His gaze lowered to her lips, which quivered with awareness.

Where was this going? This was obviously some kind of vacation fling for Simon and he'd fly back to England and be dating English roses again before the end of the month. She didn't usually embark on any kind of relationship unless she saw some kind of future in it, which might explain why she was usually free to work events on Saturday nights.

She'd been jealous of some strange woman called Sophia whom she'd never even met. She was still jealous of her, truth be told, because the queen wanted her and Simon to be a couple.

What on earth did the Queen of England's opinion have to do with her love life?

Did she even have a love life?

Her thoughts ran in all directions like rats fleeing a sinking ship, but her body didn't move at all. Simon's face grew closer until his lips touched hers. A flash of desire rose through her and her eyes shut tight as they kissed. Sparkles flashed across her brain and danced in her fingers and toes as chemistry rushed between them.

What was happening to her? She was the sensible one who drove her wilder friends home from parties. She didn't get into scrapes with their celebrity guests or have skeletons tucked behind the coats in her closets. Well, not until it turned out that she was the president's unknown love child. Everything seemed to have spiraled downhill since then.

Or was it uphill?

Simon's hands fisted in her blouse as their kiss deepened. Her fingers roamed into his thick, short-cropped hair. The rough skin of his cheek and his simple masculine scent thickened the arousal building inside her. His erection had thickened to the point where she could now feel it pressing against her belly. A pulse of thick, complicated desire throbbed and urged her to tighten their embrace.

Until a knock on the door made them fly apart.

Flushed and breathless, she smoothed her blouse as Simon strode to the door. He pulled it open a few inches and murmured that he preferred not to be disturbed. The invisible person on the other side mentioned something about an urgent phone call from Her Majesty.

Simon turned to her. "I'm afraid I must take this call. I'll be back in a moment."

The door closed and she was left alone in the strange sitting room. For the first time she noticed the painting above the fireplace, a clipper ship sailing across a stormy sea, tossing on the waves. An expensive-looking collection of porcelain lined the top of the mantel. What was she doing in this strange room—some kind of official den—groping a man who might one day be King of England. Had she lost her mind?

The queen must be calling to remind Simon of his royal duties and to urge him to keep his hands off strange American women.

Simon's absence did little to diminish her state of arousal. She wanted to hold him again. To kiss him. To rip his clothes off and make hot crazy love with him on the pale pink striped brocade of the sofa. She shoved a hand through her hair, only to discover that it was tangled from his fingers. She was madly smoothing it when the door opened again and Simon reappeared.

"Now, where were we?" Amusement glimmered in his eyes, along with desire.

A flame leapt inside her. She didn't remember ever feeling an attraction this strong. Her whole body seemed to gravitate toward him. Even while her brain issued warnings about how this liaison had no future and would likely end in disaster, her fingers snuck around his collar and into the hair at the nape of his neck, as their lips played together.

"What are we doing?" she managed, when they both came up for air. Her head spun from the intensity of the kisses.

"I'm not entirely sure but I know I like it." He nibbled her earlobe gently, which made her shiver with pleasure.

"Don't you think we should both be sensible?" She inhaled the scent of his skin and her fingers pressed into the muscle of his back.

"What's sensible?" His eyes were closed and his lips trailed over her face. Her skin hummed under his touch, under his breath, making her long to be closer to him than ever.

"I'm not sure I know anymore." She exhaled, longing to let go of her doubts and lose herself in Simon. He projected such confidence and self-assurance it was hard not to simply do what he said. He must have been a very effective army officer. "But my life is very wacky right now and I'm afraid of making it worse."

He laid a line of kisses along her neck, which had a frightening effect on her libido. "Am I making it worse?"

"Absolutely," she breathed. "Don't stop."

He chuckled, then kissed her full and firm on the mouth, embracing her with a caress that mingled power and strength with the utmost tenderness. So many emotions and sensations roamed through her that she almost wanted to cry.

When they finally stopped kissing and pulled apart, a deep sadness fell over her. The tiny separation foreshadowed the time when they'd say goodbye for the last time, because this relationship—if it even was a relationship—had no future. "If we have to keep this a secret, then it must be wrong." Her voice sounded thin and sad.

He opened his eyes and looked right at her. "Then let's not keep it a secret."

Five

Ariella paced around her apartment. Her phone had been ringing off the hook all morning. She couldn't ignore it because any call could easily be from an important client, but she was getting quite cagey about screening callers. The *Examiner* had printed a series of pictures of herself and Simon strolling through Georgetown the previous afternoon, so one more cat was out of the bag. She glanced at the familiar number with more than a little trepidation.

"Hi, Francesca."

"Ariella, you keep knocking it right out of the park."

"I know you're not talking about my softball swing."

"No, I'm talking about your ability to garner amazing publicity for the upcoming TV special. Liam says it will have the highest ratings of any show this year."

"Oh, yes. That." She went between regretting ever agreeing to it, and wanting to hurry up and get it over with. "Is there ever going to be a confirmed date for the taping?"

"They're still trying to get a firm commitment from the White House. That's about as easy as booking a date for the outbreak of a war. He's hoping for next week or the week after though. How about bringing your new royal boyfriend?"

"No way." She shoved a hand through her hair. "Besides, he has to go back to England for a bit." Her gut clenched. He'd phoned her only half an hour ago to say he'd be flying back that afternoon on urgent family business. How long would he be gone for? He did live there after all. Maybe he wouldn't come back and she'd be left to mop up one more scandal all by herself.

"You're a very dark horse."

"I totally am not. I'm the same person I've always been. It's the rest of the world that's crazy. Simon's a sweet man who happens to have been born into a famous family."

"Just like you happen to have been born to one."

She hesitated. "I guess you're right. He's not at all like you'd expect. Very unpretentious and genuine."

"And dead sexy."

"Yes. That, too." He seemed to grow more handsome every time she saw him. Or was that just because she was falling in love with him?

Her thoughts screeched to a halt. She was absolutely not allowed to fall in love with anyone on such short notice. Love was a big, long, lifetime thing that had to be carefully planned so that no one's heart got broken. She and Simon both agreed they didn't know where their... thing was going, and that they'd take it one step at a time.

"Didn't you realize the photographers would see you together?"

They had. In fact the photo opportunity was planned. They wanted to get it over with so they could stop meeting only in dark private corners surrounded by armed guards.

"Photographers see everything I do lately. They're always lurking about somewhere." It was a relief to shed the cloak of secrecy, but also alarming to give people one more thing to gossip about.

"Well, I'm so impressed with how you seem to take everything in stride. Anyone would think you'd been born in the public eye and handling it all your life."

"I suppose I'm like a duck where everything looks calm and smooth above the water, but underneath I'm paddling like mad." She needed to get to the gym so she could run off some energy on a machine. Otherwise she might explode.

"No way you're a duck, Ari. You're a swan. A royal swan."

She paced back into the kitchen and poured herself a cool glass of water. "There's nothing royal about me. I hope Simon's family aren't having a cow now that the story's broken in the press over there."

"How could they possibly not like you?"

Simon flew into Cardiff so he could drive directly to Dysart Castle in the Welsh Marches. The estate was the seat of his uncle Derek, the Duke of Aylesbury. It was Derek who had insisted in the strongest terms that he return to England and confront the "noxious" rumors about his affair with an American commoner.

Derek strode into the drawing room in his shooting jacket shortly before the usual lunch hour. He was damp from the mist of rain and had probably been out killing things since dawn. "Ah, you're here."

Master of the bleeding obvious, as usual. "You said it was urgent."

Derek peered at him from beneath his bushy salt-and-pepper brows. "Her Majesty is beside herself at the ugly stories splashed all over yesterday's papers. Your visit to the States has obviously grown overextended if the American press has the time and energy to invent silly stories about you."

"It's not a story. Ariella and I have grown close." And he looked forward to growing a lot closer. It had taken all his self-control to stop at kissing her. He'd managed because he knew there was something special about her, and he didn't want to do anything to endanger their budding relationship.

"Well, you'd better grow distant, immediately. You're second in line to the throne, man. You can't kiss any girl with a pretty smile who happens to cross your path."

Simon stiffened. "Ariella is not just anyone. She's intelligent, charming and has more poise than most of us royals put together."

"Don't be ridiculous. She's American. You remember what happened last time one of our family got involved with an American. He gave up the throne of England! Madness." Derek shrugged out of his jacket and tossed it over a gilded chair. "Break it off with her immediately and pray that she doesn't make a big fuss in the media."

"Ariella would never do such a thing. And I most certainly am not going to break it off with her."

Derek's already bilious face reddened further. "I thought your irresponsible and reckless days were behind you. Your older brother is married to a delightful and entirely suitable woman. Look upon him as an example."

"I honor and respect my brother and look forward to saluting him as my monarch. I feel confident that he will enjoy Ariella's company as much as I do."

"Don't be ridiculous. And she's the daughter of the president. We have enough trouble negotiating the maelstrom of American politics without you allying yourself with the daughter of one party's leader."

"She has never even met her father and politics plays no role in our relationship."

Derek had poured himself a stiff whiskey and swigged it. It was doubtless his third or fourth of the day despite the early hour. "Never even met her own father? Oh, yes. She's some kind of unwanted bastard who was given up for adoption. Perfect royal bride material."

Simon wanted to remind his uncle of the many "royal bastards" who had contributed to the country over the centuries, but he restrained himself. "Ariella and I are both adults, and quite capable of managing our affairs with dignity. I don't need any warnings or lessons or instructions in how to behave." Derek's miserable wife, Mary, was a pale shadow of the pretty, bright girl she'd once been. If there was any dire warning on how not to operate a relationship, Derek was it.

"Listen, Simon. If you get into some embarrassing international scrape it will be bad for all of us. Monarchies are in a battle for survival in the twenty-first century. An affair with this girl is tantamount to abandoning your duties. Next thing we know you'll be moving abroad."

Simon's hackles rose. "I'll never leave England. I know my duty to my country as well as to my own conscience."

His uncle's beady eyes narrowed. "The way you're acting you may well be asked to leave."

"You'd have to boot me out of the family first."

The older man sipped his whiskey and studied a painting of dead pheasants, bound by the neck into a lifeless bouquet. "Nothing is impossible."

The early morning air in England smelled fabulously exciting to Ariella. Even the fume-choked atmosphere around the taxi rank at Heathrow Airport. She had a roster of back to back appointments stretching over the next four days. Most of them had to do with the Duke of Buckingham's extravagant wedding. She had scheduled meetings with florists, caterers, makers of the finest crystal and porcelain for the handcrafted tableware, the list was almost endless.

But one appointment loomed in her mind above all the others. At three-forty-five on Wednesday—two days away—Ariella would finally meet the woman who gave birth to her twenty-eight years ago. Her heart pounded whenever she thought about it. How odd that this stranger had carried her in her belly for nine long months.

And of course Simon was here. She'd told him of her visit but warned him that she was very busy. She was here to work and just because she'd kissed a prince did not mean she could abandon her career and throw caution to the wind. Her friends at home had warned her that the British press were far more aggressive—and often crueler—than the press at home, so she should watch her step. Still, hopefully they could manage a meeting. Her skin tingled every time she thought about him. What would her mother think?

The question made her laugh aloud. The mom who raised her, the sensible Montana housewife, would probably be full of dire warnings, issued in the most kind and heartfelt way. She'd have much preferred to see Ariella with the owner of a solid car dealership in Billings, or perhaps a kindly bank manager in Bozeman.

But now she had another mother to think about. What would Eleanor think about her relationship with Simon? She was obviously concerned about her own privacy and shrank from the spotlight, so she wasn't likely to be thrilled.

Ariella's phone vibrated and she checked the number.

Think of the devil. "Hi, Simon." She couldn't help smiling as she said his name.

"You must be on British soil." His deep voice sent a flood of warmth to her belly.

"I am. Traveling over it in a taxi, to be precise."

"Where are you staying?"

"The Drake. It's a small hotel near Mayfair."

"Perfect. Right near St. James's Palace, my haunt when I'm in town. I'll pick you up at seven."

Temptation clawed at her. But her sense of duty won out. "I wish I could, but I'm meeting a potential client to pitch the most magnificent wedding in history. It will probably go quite late."

"I suppose asking you to come over after dinner isn't appropriate."

She smiled. "No, I suppose not."

"Lunch tomorrow at Buckingham Palace. Come meet the queen. She's never in town for long so it's a great opportunity for you two to get to know each other."

Ariella clutched the phone in a panic. "Oh, gosh, I have appointments all day tomorrow."

"That's a shame because she's heading to Scotland in the afternoon. But there'll be other times to meet her."

"I'm sorry I can't make it." Was it rude to say you'd rather spend the night in a meat locker than brave a lunch with one of the world's longest-reigning monarchs? Of course if things persisted with Simon, she'd eventually have to meet Her Majesty, but right now everything was very new and tentative and she had a feeling that no one would be rolling out the red carpet for her at the palace.

Not that she wanted them to. She didn't know what she wanted. "I'd love to see you, really I would, but…"

"Dinner tomorrow. My driver will pick you up with exquisite discretion. No one will know you're with me."

"I can't. I have a dinner meeting."

"That won't take all night."

She swallowed, and attempted a laugh. "I need to sleep, too. I wish I had more time for…fun, but this is a business trip." A pause made her nervous. Was he offended? It certainly wasn't good for business to snub a prince. She didn't want to book anything for after her mom's visit, as she was hoping they'd hit it off and spend hours together. "My last appointment is Thursday afternoon at three and my flight isn't until the next morning."

"So you can squeeze dinner with me into your busy schedule on Thursday?" Was he teasing or mad?

"I could, if that works for you. Of course if you're too busy, I quite understand." London whipped by outside her window, as rows of identical suburban houses gave way to more office buildings and shops.

"I'd clear my schedule in a heartbeat for the mere chance of laying eyes on you."

Okay, now he was kidding. "I don't think that will be necessary. Let's make plans closer to Thursday, okay? I hope nothing crazy happens between now and then, but you never know." She could hardly believe she was telling a prince that she couldn't commit to anything firm.

"I'm penciling it in." She could hear the irony in his voice. "And call me at once if there's anything you need. Our entire nation is at your disposal."

"Thanks." She grinned. "Much appreciated."

She shook her head as she put her phone away. How had her life changed so much in six short months? There were even photographers at the airport, though she doubted they'd get much money for photos of her in jeans and with her hair in a messy bun, carrying her luggage to the taxi rank. There was so much to be excited about, sometimes it was hard to remember that she had plenty to be afraid of as well.

Meeting her reclusive mother, hopefully meeting her famous father and now a romance with a man who made her smile each time she thought of him. It was all just a little too fabulous. Rather like teetering on a tightrope between two skyscrapers. She had to keep her chin up, her eyes forward and put one foot in front of the other, and hopefully in another six months she'd be in an even better place, where everything wasn't quite so strange and precarious.

"You come from America?" The cab driver's loud Cockney voice jolted her from her thoughts. He didn't wait for an answer. "You 'eard about this girl who's supposed to be the daughter of your president?"

She froze. Did he recognize her? He looked in his side mirror and changed lanes. "I'm not sure who you mean."

"Pretty girl. Long brown 'air. Looks a bit like you." His eyes fixed on hers again in the mirror. She blinked. "Papers say she's 'avin' an affair with our Prince Simon. Some people have all the luck, don't they?"

"Oh, yes." She pretended to text on her phone, keeping her head down. Maybe he was fishing for information he could sell to the London tabloid that always had a bare-breasted woman on page three. "Very lucky."

She kept her head down until they pulled up in front of her hotel. Mercifully there wasn't a photographer in sight and she checked in and changed, telling herself to be prepared for anything.

Frustration made Simon spring from his chair and pace across the room. How could Ariella be right here in his own country and too busy to see him? Their few days of separation had him in an agony of anticipation. Now he had to wait until Thursday to see her?

He called her on Monday night, hoping that her dinner meeting would be over and they could plan a moonlit tryst. No dice. She was still in consultation with a client, and she wouldn't even reveal the person's name. He rather suspected it was his schoolmate Toby Buckingham, and he tried calling him to intercept from another direction, but Toby didn't even answer.

On Tuesday morning he tried again, hoping for a quick tea, only to be politely brushed off. Restless as hell by Wednesday afternoon, he threw on a panama hat that covered his face and decided to stroll the short distance from St James's Palace to Buckingham Palace. Maybe he'd go for a ride on one of the queen's horses. He told his driver, who doubled as security, to head there without him so he could get some fresh air. David didn't make a fuss. He knew that nothing was likely to happen on the quiet streets between the two palaces, and Simon had his phone if needed.

He was walking briskly, trying to banish the vision of Ariella's intoxicating beauty from his mind, when a girl walking along the other side of the street, in the opposite direction, caught his eye.

She walked exactly like Ariella. Long-legged, and graceful as a gazelle, with the slightly loping stride of someone in a hurry. But this woman had shoulder-length blond hair. Large dark glasses hid her face. He turned and stared after her as she passed.

That was Ariella's walk. And those were her shoes. The sight of those simple black ballet flats she favored sent a jolt of adrenaline to his own feet. He turned, following her, still on the opposite side of the street.

Why would she be in disguise? The hair must be a wig. The neat black skirt did nothing to disguise the elegant swing of her hips. He'd recognize that walk anywhere.

Who was she hiding from? She had no reason to conceal her movements to plan the big wedding she was here to organize. She was used to photographers tracking her and mostly ignored them, as he'd witnessed on several occasions in D.C.

She was doing something that she didn't want anyone to know about. Including him.

She crossed the road to his side and he slowed his pace and hung back a little. Not that she even glanced at him. She was lost in a world of her own, barely noticing the other people on the pavement. She walked fast, but he had no trouble keeping up.

Why are you following her?

Because I want to know where she's going.

Something in his gut told him that this was wrong. She had a right to privacy. In fact they'd had several long discussions about how much they valued their right to privacy, which was often under siege. Somehow, that didn't stop him.

She turned left, down a small side road. She hesitated and pulled a phone out of her pocket, causing him to stop in his tracks. A man walking behind him bumped into him, and by the time he'd apologized she was walking again. Talking on the phone.

He couldn't hear what she was saying, but her singsong laugh was unmistakable. Which confirmed what he already knew. Ariella Winthrop was walking through Mayfair in disguise, and he was going to find out why.

Why hadn't she told him where she was going? Fresh from defending her to his suspicious family, he found doubts sneaking into his mind. He knew she wouldn't leak stories of their romance to the media. Would she? Not that there was anything to leak, though he intended to change that as soon as humanly possible.

Could it be something to do with her famous father? They hadn't spoken much about him. She seemed to find the subject awkward, considering that she'd never met him.

Or was there another man in her life? His mind and body recoiled from the idea and he didn't believe it for a moment. But where was she going?

She turned left and he hurried to keep up, in case she disappeared into one of the tall Edwardian buildings lining the street. She'd tucked her phone back into her purse and strode on, looking intently ahead. Then she stopped.

This time he glanced behind him before halting, to avoid a collision. She pulled out a piece of paper and glanced up at the plaque on the house. Then she climbed the steps, rang a bell, and entered through a pair of heavy wood doors.

He approached the building a full minute later and paused as discreetly as possible in front of the doorway. The Westchester Club. He had no idea what that was, only that he wanted to gain entry. He strolled to the end of the block, pretended to casually consult a No Parking sign and considered his options.

Ariella's heart pounded as she climbed into the elevator and pressed a button. It was the old-fashioned kind of elevator with the sliding iron gates, and hearing the porter slam them behind her didn't help her nerves. Her mother was waiting for her on the fifth floor.

Scarlet had suggested this private club as a venue. Rooms were available for rent only to the most exclusive groups, and Scarlet had called in a favor to secure one for this afternoon, since it was near Ariella's hotel so she could get there without attracting attention.

She pulled off the cheesy blond wig she'd bought to keep photographers off her scent, and loosed her hair from its bun. The elevator jerked to a halt on the fifth floor. She hauled back the iron gate and stepped out onto a polished wood floor. The hallway contained three tall doors, and she was wondering which one was number 503, when one of the doors opened.

"Ariella?" The tentative voice came from a slender, pretty woman with curly light brown hair.

"Yes?" There was a question in her voice, as if she wasn't quite sure who she was any more. She wanted to greet the woman as "Mom," but that seemed presumptuous. Her heart beat so fast she could hardly speak. "You must be Eleanor."

Eleanor's hands had risen to cover her mouth as tears welled in her big green eyes. Eyes almost exactly like her own. "You're so beautiful. Even more so than in the photos."

"You're sweet. And you look far too young to be the mother of a twenty-eight-year-old." She looked like she was still in her thirties, with smooth pale skin and a girlish figure.

"I am too young to be the mother of a twenty-eight-year-old." She shrugged and smiled. "That was the problem, really. I got pregnant when I was too young to be ready." Tears ran down her cheeks. "And I missed out on so much."

Eleanor seemed ready to lose it, and Ariella wanted to comfort her, but didn't know how. She ushered her back into the room, which was a large drawing room with several graciously upholstered sofas. "Shall we sit down?"

"Oh, yes." Eleanor pulled out a tissue and wiped her face. "I'm sorry I'm making such a fool of myself. It's just that…I've waited so long for this moment and I wasn't sure it would ever come."

"Me, too. I can hardly believe we're finally getting to meet." They sat next to each other on the plush sofa, and she took Eleanor's hands in her own and squeezed them. Her skin was cool and soft. Cold hands, warm heart. The cliché popped into her mind. "Thank you so much for coming to London to see me."

"It's my great pleasure. I'm too afraid to travel to the States. I feel like they'd know who I was when I go through airport security and there'd be a big to do." Eleanor had picked up an Irish lilt to her voice. "I'm very shy, really. That's one of the reasons why I knew I wouldn't be good for Ted. He was always so outgoing and friendly and loved to be around people."

Ariella realized that Ted was the man she still thought of as the president of the United States. "Was he your boyfriend?" She only knew what she'd read in the papers, and she knew from firsthand experience they weren't always a reliable source.

Eleanor sighed. "He was. We dated our junior and senior years in high school. I was so in love!" Her soft eyes looked distant. "Even then he had big plans and intended to go away to college. He dreamed of being a Rhodes Scholar and studying abroad, and then he wanted to join the Peace Corps and travel. He always had such grand ambitions."

"Well, he's achieved the highest office an American can attain."

Eleanor nodded. Her mouth tightened for a moment, her lip almost quivering. Ariella ached to put her arms around this delicate and nervous woman, but didn't want to frighten her. "I never did really understand what he saw in me. He said he found me very peaceful." Her eyes twinkled with the memory.

"I'm sure an energetic and outgoing man needs peace more than anyone."

She smiled at Ariella. "Maybe so. My husband, Greg, was a quiet man. Not as exciting as Ted but a good man who I shared a happy marriage with for twenty-three years. He died of a heart attack. Far too young, he was." Tears welled in her eyes again.

"I'm sorry. I would have liked to meet him."

Eleanor's gaze focused on her. "Did you tell me that you've never met Ted?"

Ariella swallowed and shook her head. "Not yet, but..." She paused. It sounded pathetic really. Embarrassing. How could they have gone all this time—nearly two months since the DNA test results were released—without any contact at all?

"I'm sure Ted wants to meet you. I know it in my heart." She squeezed Ariella's hands. "They must be keeping him from you. You must reach out to him."

"I've been talking to ANS about doing a taped reunion. It should take place soon."

"On television?" Eleanor's eyes widened into shock.

She nodded. "My friend Francesca's husband is president of the network. Apparently the White House is almost ready to agree to a date."

Eleanor winced. "A private meeting would be so much nicer."

"I know, but the president isn't a private person, really. Not to the point where I could call him up and introduce myself. Somehow it seemed more...doable."

"You're outgoing, too, aren't you?" She smiled slightly.

"I suppose I am. I plan parties for a living. I love getting people together and making it an occasion to remember."

She smiled again. "You must get that from Ted. You have his cheekbones, too. And that sparkle of determination he always had in his eye."

"I think you and I look alike, too." She drank in the precious sight of her birth mother's face. "Our faces are similar shapes, and we're both tall and slim."

"Will o' the Wisp, Ted used to call me. Said a strong breeze would blow me away one day. I suppose in a way he was right. It blew me over to Ireland and I didn't dare to look back."

"I'm sure he'd love to see you again."

Her eyes widened into a look of panic. "Oh, no. No. I'm sure he'd never forgive me for what I did. I thought it was for the best but looking back I can see that not telling him he had a child was a terrible thing to do. An act of cowardice. I won't forgive myself and I wouldn't expect him to, either."

Not knowing her famous father, Ariella wasn't really in a position to argue with her. "Why didn't you tell him?"

"I knew he'd do *the right thing.*" She said it with mocking emphasis. "Not the right thing for him and the big career he'd dreamed of, but the right thing in the eyes of our parents and pastors and neighbors. He'd settle down in our small town in Montana and live a tiny fraction of the live he'd imagined, because he'd be forced to support a family instead of going off to the big college he'd won a scholarship to. I could never let him throw away his future like that."

"You could have let him make the decision himself."

"I know. Now I know that." Tears welled in her eyes again. "I didn't want him to grow to hate me so I did the one thing that should truly make him hate me. I gave away our child and never told him she existed." She broke down into sobs.

Unable to hold back any longer, Ariella wrapped her arms around Eleanor's slim shoulders and held her tight, her own tears falling. "Everything happens for a reason," she said softly. "Maybe we'll never even know the true reason, but I believe that all the same."

"You're a very clever girl. I can see that in your eyes."

Eleanor dabbed at her own eyes with a tissue. "You have your dad's keen intelligence. I bet you have a university degree, don't you?"

Ariella nodded. "In history, from Georgetown."

"It's such a coincidence that both you and Ted wound up living in Washington, D.C." She blew her nose.

"It is strange."

At that moment the door opened and their heads swung around. Ariella gasped when she saw Simon standing in the doorway.

Six

"Ariella." Simon had a hat clutched in his hand and a curiously intense expression on his face.

Eleanor gasped and brought her wet tissue to her face as if she wanted to hide behind it.

"What are you doing here?" Ariella's voice came out sounding stern.

"I…" He hesitated. A sheepish expression crossed his handsome features. "I confess that I saw you on the street and followed you."

"What?" Anger surged inside her, warring with the sharp sting of attraction. "What made you think you could follow me into a private meeting?"

He shrugged. "I'm embarrassed to say that I didn't examine my motives too closely." He looked at Eleanor, as if expecting an introduction.

"You need to leave." Ariella rose to her feet. She could feel Eleanor, desperate to preserve her privacy, shrinking back into the shell that she'd started to emerge from. "You may be a prince but that doesn't mean you can march in anywhere you feel like."

"You're absolutely right, of course. My sincerest apologies." He nodded and bowed to Eleanor, and started to back out the door.

"Wait!" She couldn't just let him go. Damn it. Angry as she was, she wanted to see him too badly. She turned to Eleanor. "This is my...boyfriend." She dared Simon to argue with her word choice. "Is it okay if I introduce you?"

Eleanor gulped, but nodded shyly.

"Simon Worth, this is Eleanor Daly. My mother." Her throat swelled with emotion as she said the word *mother.*

Eleanor stared. "*Prince* Simon Worth?"

Simon bowed. "At your service. It's an honor to meet you, Mrs. Daly." He swept forward, took her hand and shook it warmly, while she gazed at him in shock. "I know Ariella's been looking forward to this for a long time."

"Goodness." She stared from one of them to the other, as if she wasn't sure what was going to happen next.

A feeling shared by her daughter. "Simon encouraged me to meet you. I wasn't sure you'd want to."

"I'm so glad the two of you are finally getting together." Simon glowed with confidence and good cheer, as usual. "It seems a wonderful thing to come out of the wiretapping scandal."

Eleanor still looked shell-shocked. "I saw a headline about the two of you at the newsagent and I just assumed it was more made-up rubbish."

"Sometimes there's a grain of truth in the wild stories the press invent." Simon smiled. "I'm happy to confirm that this is one of them."

"So you two are actually...dating?" Eleanor stared from Simon to Ariella.

"We're not quite sure what we're doing." Ariella jumped in, not wanting Simon to be put on the spot. She couldn't even imagine how the royal family might be reacting to news of their romance. Simon hadn't mentioned the topic, which wasn't too encouraging. "We enjoy each other's company."

"Oh." Eleanor's brow furrowed with concern. Ariella got the sense that she'd love to issue some stern warnings, but was too polite. She probably wasn't happy that her newfound daughter was embarking on a relationship that wasn't likely to end in a glorious happy-ever-after.

Because really, did she expect Simon to marry her?

The whole idea was ridiculously premature. They hadn't even done more than kiss yet. She glanced at Simon, whose eyes met hers and sent a zap of heat straight to her core. It would have been so much easier if she could have avoided him. This week was hectic enough already.

"I'll leave the two of you in peace." Simon must have read her thoughts. He nodded nobly to Eleanor, and squeezed Ariella's hand, then turned and disappeared out the door. Ariella couldn't manage to think of anything polite to say, so they both stared after him in silence until the door closed behind him.

"Goodness." Eleanor looked dazed.

"Life has been pretty intense this year." They both sat back down on the sofa. "Sometimes I wonder what else could possibly happen."

"Don't tempt fate." Her mother patted her hand. "But I do hope you get to meet your father soon. I'm so proud of him for being elected president, and I know he's going to do a wonderful job running the country. He's off to a great start already. Almost makes me think I should move back."

Adrenaline surged through Ariella. "You should. It would be so wonderful to have you near. Come live in

D.C.! Georgetown, where I live, is quite peaceful really. Lots of trees and lovely old buildings."

"You make it sound very inviting. Perhaps I have been living in the back of beyond for too long. Hiding away, I suppose."

"You don't have to hide from anyone now."

Eleanor looked doubtful. "I don't think I could face all those reporters the way you and Ted have. I'd be tongue-tied and embarrass both of you."

"You couldn't possibly embarrass either of us. I bet it would be a huge relief to come forward and get it over with. Why don't you come back to the States with me at the end of the week? I'm leaving on Friday and I can probably get you a ticket on the same plane if I call in a favor or two."

Eleanor's hand stiffened. "I…I'm not ready for that." Once again she felt her mother shrinking away from her. "But I'd very much like to stay in touch with you by phone, and maybe I'll gradually pluck up the courage to at least come visit you there. And maybe take a trip up to Montana to see all the old friends I've avoided for so long. I never told a single soul there about my pregnancy and I'm sure they all wondered what happened when I just disappeared. I stayed in a special home for unwed mothers way outside of town until I was due, and then I took all my saved pennies and left for Chicago after the birth. I couldn't face any of them knowing I'd given away my own child. Ted's child. I met Greg there. He'd come from Ireland for the summer to work as a roofer and he swept me off my feet." Her sad eyes sparkled a little when she spoke about him. "With him I started a new chapter of my life. I never looked back. I felt that if I did I'd fall off some cliff and get swallowed by all the emotion I tried so hard not to feel during that time." Her pale eyes grew glassy with tears again.

"It's not good to avoid your true feelings. Sooner or later they'll come back to bite you. I learned that after my adoptive parents were killed. All that pain is scary, but once you come to terms with it you can move forward. Until then you're stuck in a place of fear." She squeezed her mother's hands, which had softened again.

"You're very wise, Ariella."

"I wish I was. I just try to handle one crisis at a time. In my job there's always another one coming so there's no point in getting ahead of yourself."

They laughed, and, taking a cue from the sudden intimacy, Ariella hugged her birth mother for the very first time.

Simon refused to let Ariella leave England without visiting his home. He promised that he wouldn't stalk her around London or corner her in private drawing rooms as long as she'd agree to postpone her return flight until the following Monday so she could spend the weekend with him at Whist Castle. He insisted that, in her line of work, staying at one of England's great country houses counted as research and client cultivation. After a little persuasion, and a conversation with her business partner, Scarlet, she agreed.

He had the staff prepare his mother's favorite bedroom for Ariella, ostensibly because it had such beautiful views over the lake, but mostly because it had a door connecting it with his own bedroom. It had taken all his gentlemanly self-control to keep all their activities above the neck so far, and he intended to steer them both into unexplored territory this weekend.

His driver brought Ariella up from London on Thursday evening. He had a full schedule of activities planned to keep her entertained and give her a slice of English country life, and he intended to introduce her to the family at a charity polo match taking place nearby on Sunday. This weekend would be an excellent taste of the pleasures and realities of life in the royal family.

The realities, of course, might scare her. There was no denying that his family had rather fixed ideas about whom he should marry. Someone British, with aristocratic heritage and a featureless past that could not draw comment in the press. Of course he'd informed them that he would marry for no reason other than love, but he wasn't entirely sure they'd listened. He'd been raised to believe that duty trumped all other considerations, including happiness. So far he'd managed to find his own happiness within the confines of his duty, creating opportunities where he saw them. There was no denying that choosing Ariella as his bride would likely draw censure and disapproval.

On the other hand there was no good reason for them to oppose her, and sooner or later they usually saw reason. He just hoped they wouldn't frighten her too badly.

He tested the handle on the connecting bedroom door, and pocketed the key. No sense filling his head with plans then finding himself locked out. His body throbbed with anticipation of being alone with Ariella. From the first moment he'd seen her, across the ballroom at that gala event, he'd had a powerful sense that she was the one. So far he'd managed to battle all the forces standing between them, and now he was within reach of holding her—naked— in his arms. The prospect heated his blood and fired his imagination.

He hovered at the front windows looking for the approaching car, fighting the urge to phone and see how far away she was, then practically ran down the stairs when it finally nosed up the drive. He couldn't remember being this eager to see anyone, ever.

Ariella looked radiant, as usual, in a simple black dress, with her long hair flowing over her shoulders. A smile spread across her pretty face as she saw him, and he felt his own face reflect it back. "Welcome to Whist Castle."

"It's every bit as beautiful as I'd imagined."

"I'm glad you think so, too, and you haven't even seen the grounds yet. Come in." He fought the urge to slip his arm around her waist, which took a great deal of self-control. "How did your meeting with your mother go?"

"It was amazing." He glanced at her and saw her smile. "I'd been so worried that she'd seem like a stranger, that maybe we wouldn't even recognize each other. But I felt an instant connection with her."

"That's fantastic. Do you think you'll see her again soon?"

She hesitated. "I don't know. I really hope so. She's still deathly afraid of publicity and the criticism she'll face for giving me up and not telling Ted Morrow about me. I got all carried away and started trying to convince her to move to D.C."

He laughed. "That sounds like the kind of thing I'd do."

"Too much, too soon?" She smiled. "And then I tried to talk her into visiting Montana with me. I hope I didn't scare her right away."

"I'm sure she's privately thrilled that you're so glad to meet her and that you want to spend more time with her."

"I hope so. I really liked her. I plan to call her regularly, and hopefully we'll build the relationship and take it from there."

Words to live by. He counseled himself to take the same course with Ariella. Just because he felt a deep conviction that they were meant to be together did not mean that she felt the same way. Gentle persuasion and thoughtfully paced seduction would be the sensible path for him to take, no matter how loudly his more primitive urges begged him to take her in his arms and kiss her hard on the mouth.

He showed her to her room, glancing at the door to his own, but not mentioning it. There would be time for that later. Then he took her on a brief tour of his favorite place in the world—the great hall that had once been a Saxon throne room, and had hosted many riotous dinner parties during his reign there. Then they walked to the oldest part of the building, which held the gallery of paintings collected over the centuries by his ancestors, which included works by Raphael, Titian, Rembrandt, Caravaggio and El Greco, among others.

Ariella was suitably poleaxed. "I think you have a better collection than most museums."

"I know. I do lend them out to museums from time to time so they're not entirely hidden away in my lair. I am lucky to have had ancestors with such good taste."

"Have you ever had your portrait painted?" She glanced up at a majestic Van Dyke portrait of a young Charles II.

"Never. They'd have to nail me down to keep me still enough."

"I think that's a shame. I'd love to be able to stare at a magnificent painting of you."

"Why, when you can eyeball the real thing?" They'd been unabashedly eyeing each other since she walked through the door. Their days apart had created sexual tension thick enough to fog windows.

"What kind of setting do you think would suit you?" She looked him up and down, as if wondering whether a landscape or interior might be better. His skin heated under his clothes as her green gaze drifted from his face, to his torso, and lower...

"Definitely the outdoors. Hanging off a mountain, maybe."

"That's a great idea. And these days they can snap a picture to work from so you only have to stay in the same place for a microsecond. Think of all those poor starving artists who would love to become the royal court painter. I think it's your duty to be a patron of the arts."

"I hadn't looked at it that way."

She swept down the hallway, and he hesitated for a moment to enjoy the swinging motion of her hips inside her fitted dress, before striding after her.

Simon's castle was very ancient, but with wear from centuries of loving use, it felt like a home rather than a monument. And Simon thought of everything to make her comfortable: tea and scones on the terrace overlooking a lake with water lilies in full bloom, an art collection that could make you weep with its magnificence and a sunlit bedroom with a view of the lake.

Still, she wasn't entirely relaxed. This weekend would undoubtedly take their relationship to a new level, one way or another. She was on his turf, at his mercy. She had no idea what he had planned for the weekend and he'd told her not to worry, she was in good hands. Which made her very nervous. She was used to being in charge and making plans and booking the entertainment. What if he decided to spring the queen on her as a surprise? With Simon around she knew she'd better be prepared for anything.

"I told the staff we'll fend for ourselves at dinner." Simon led her back from the art gallery into a sweeping living room with a high wooden ceiling. "I make a mean spag bol."

"Is that a British way of saying spaghetti bolognese?"

He winked. "And they say Americans don't bother to learn other languages."

He was actually going to cook? She'd tell her beating heart to be still if she thought it would do any good. Dressed in khakis and a white shirt, he looked classically handsome. And the ever present twinkle of mischief in his eyes always sent her pulse racing. "I'll have you know I speak Spanish and French, and I intend to study Chinese as soon as I can find the time."

He smiled. "I'm impressed. Of course I'd have expected no less of you. You're disturbingly perfect."

"I am not." She felt her face heat. Now he was making her blush? So much for her famous cool and poised demeanor. "I have many flaws."

"Name one. No, wait." He walked across the room to a wooden cabinet, then pulled out a bottle of wine. "I think we'll enjoy an excellent wine while we discuss your flaws." He uncorked the bottle with muscular ease, and poured the rich red wine into two glasses.

Her flaws? Was this like a job interview where she was supposed to have flaws like being too much of a perfectionist, or excessively punctual? Or could she be honest?

It's not like she was trying to get him to fall in love with her.

Their fingers touched as she took the glass from him, sending a jolt of warmth to her core. "One flaw. Hmm. I'm a terrible speller. I always have to get someone to reread important documents. I'm quite capable of spelling my own name wrong."

"That's nothing. I'm dyslexic."

"Are you really? I had no idea."

"So you'll need a more impressive flaw than that, I'm afraid." They settled into a wide leather sofa. He peered at her as he sipped his wine. "A fatal flaw, perhaps. Or else I'll just keep insisting that you're perfect."

"I can be quite impatient."

"Nonsense. Look at how you've handled the press. Most

women would have had a tantrum or two by now. Next!"
His eyes sparkled.

"Hmm…" What could she say to shock him out of his
amused complacency? "I'm a reformed nymphomaniac."

His eyebrows rose slightly, but the rest of his expression
didn't change. "Not too reformed, I hope."

"You're terrible." She couldn't help laughing. "The truth
is I'm probably the opposite. Too uptight. Maybe that's
my flaw."

"That can be fixed." Heat flickered between them as
their eyes met in silence. A couple of buttons were open
at the neck of his shirt, revealing a tantalizing sliver of
rather tanned chest. His neck was thick and muscular, like
an athlete's, and she was pretty confident that the rest of
him would be, too.

He shifted closer to her on the sofa. Their thighs touched
and she wondered what he'd look like naked. Then she
wondered if she was going to find out tonight. Anxiety
crept through her, along with the steady pulse of desire.
Having sex with a prince wasn't something you could easily forget. Yet that's what she'd have to do, eventually, as
she was hardly going to become a member of the royal
family.

"Your brain is going a million miles an hour." His face
drew close to hers.

"There's another flaw. I think too much."

"No one's ever accused me of that. I'm known for acting first and thinking later." He grinned. She could smell
his intoxicating musky scent. "It's gotten me into some
scrapes over the years."

"And I have a feeling it's about to get you into another
one unless we put our wine down." Their lips were moving inexorably closer.

"You do think of everything." He took her glass and placed it on the floor next to his. "Now, where were we?"

She didn't have time to think of an answer, as his mouth closed over hers and his big arms wrapped around her. A sigh escaped her as she fell into his embrace. The days apart had been torture. Trying to stop herself from thinking about him, from wanting to see him. Then behaving appropriately in front of the drivers and the butler and all those other people constantly hovering around.

Now it was just her and Simon. Their kiss deepened and his tongue flicked against hers. The throb low in her belly grew more urgent, her nipples straining against the cups of her bra. But surely there was security or someone nearby? "Should we go somewhere more private?" she whispered. At night she was haunted by visions of photographers peeking in her windows, trailing her to the most mundane places and pouncing on her.

He didn't answer, but swept their glasses up and nodded for her to follow. They strode through the silent house. It wasn't dark outside. It stayed light until late in England in the summer, so it felt oddly like midafternoon though it must be at least eight. Why was she thinking about the time?

Because at this very moment she was about to climb into bed with a prince. At least she assumed it would be a bed. Knowing Simon she could well be wrong.

She followed him upstairs, and she felt a flush of relief when he turned into his own bedroom.

Condoms! Was now the right moment to mention the need for contraception? Or was that presumptuous? She took one look at the large bed. "Um, I have some condoms in my luggage."

He turned around with a smile. "Hmm. Maybe you

weren't lying about being a slightly reformed nympho-maniac."

"Or is it just that I'm annoyingly prepared for everything?"

"I suspect the latter. And don't worry, I have some specially purchased for the occasion."

"How does a prince buy condoms? I mean, you can't wander into Boots the Chemist on your local high street and slam them down on the counter with a smile."

"Why not?" He pulled a packet of Trojans from an elegant mahogany chest.

"Um, because everyone would know what you're up to."

"And they'd be jealous." He stepped toward her and stole her breath with a hot, urgent kiss. "But don't worry. My secretary purchases them in a cunningly anonymous fashion."

His fingers worked their way around the zipper on the side of her dress. Then he seemed stymied. Her breasts tingled at the thought of him touching them. "I have to lift it over my head," she rasped.

"No." He looked thoughtfully at the garment. "*I* have to lift it over your head." He lifted the hem and she held her breath and raised her arms as he pulled the dress up and off. With her dress crumpled like a tissue in his broad hands, he surveyed her—wordless—for a moment. She should feel self-conscious standing there in her bra and panties, but she didn't. Simon's desire was every bit as naked as her body.

She kicked off her shoes and tackled the buttons on his shirt, while he undid his belt and stepped out of his pants. Good grief. His chest was thick muscle, highlighted by a line of sun-bleached golden hair that pointed to the fierce erection seeking freedom from his conservative boxer shorts.

"Let me help you with that," she murmured, tugging the cotton down over his thighs. She realized too late that she was licking her lips. It had been a long time since she'd had sex and her entire body sizzled with anticipation. His legs were sturdy as the oak trees on his estate, with knees scarred by countless adventures, and she enjoyed the movement of his muscles as he stepped out of his underwear.

He unsnapped her bra before she had even stood up again, and her breasts pointed at him in accusation of arousing her past the point of decency.

At long last.

Together they pulled off her panties, then their bodies met, his erection fitting neatly against her belly. They breathed heavily, skin heating as they managed a very tentative kiss: a wisp of tongue, a graze of teeth, the tiniest, smooth, teasing and taunting until they couldn't stand it anymore. Then they fell onto the bed and Simon crawled over her, covering her with his body, with his kisses, tasting and testing her skin until she moaned with urgency.

He rolled on the condom and entered her carefully. Their eyes met for a moment, and the look of concern on his handsome face made her smile. She lifted her hips to welcome him and enjoyed his expression of rapture as his eyes slid closed and he sank deep inside her.

Pleasure coursed through her at the feel of his big, strong body wrapped around hers. She moved with him easily, enjoying sudden and intense relief from all the tension that had built between them in the short time they'd known each other.

"Ariella." He rasped her name with a hint of surprise, as if discovering it for the first time. Somehow it jerked her back to the reality of who she was. Ariella Winthrop, whose life had been turned upside down by the scandalous circumstances of her birth and now by a shocking international romance. Even as she writhed in Simon's arms she couldn't help wondering if this was all a crazy mistake. Would she wake up soaked in regret at compounding the madness that was her life lately?

If the press found out she and Simon had slept together they'd have a field day. They'd be clamoring for snapshots of the "royal smooch" or any casual indiscretion.

She'd let this whole thing spiral out of control. In D.C., she could have easily kept Simon at arm's length until he went back to Britain, instead of embarking on an ill-advised romance that would have people whispering and gossiping behind her back.

"Ariella." He said it again.

"Yes?" Was he asking a question?

"I just like saying it. Celebrating it. That we're here together at last."

She chuckled, then carefully maneuvered them until she was on top. "You're a hard man to resist." That was the truth. You couldn't say no to Simon. At least she couldn't.

She leaned forward to kiss him, then her hair trailed over his chest as she rose and moved over him. His eyes closed and his face wore an expression of sheer bliss as she rode him. His hands wandered over her chest, enjoying the curve of her breasts and circling her waist. Then he deftly changed positions again and took back the lead.

Thoughts slipped away as he drove her deep into a world where worries didn't exist. Nothing mattered but their two bodies, moving in sync, holding and clutching at each other, their breath mingling and their skin sticking together as they edged closer and closer to the inevitable climax.

Afterward they lay in each other's arms, as countless other couples must have done over the years in this same grand chamber. Dukes, princes and earls, wives, mistresses and probably a few comely servant girls as well.

"What are we doing?" She breathed into his ear. It wasn't the first time she'd voiced the thought aloud.

"We're in the throes of a passionate romance," he answered.

"You make things seem so simple."

"Usually they are simple, and people go out of their way to make them complicated."

"But how long can it go on for? You live here and I live in D.C. It's silly."

"It's wonderful." He stroked her hair, his eyes soft.

She exhaled slowly. "It is."

"So we need to enjoy our passionate romance one day at a time and see where it takes us."

"With the press breathing down our necks?"

He shrugged. "They'll do what they want to do, regardless of what we want or hope for. I try to ignore them in general. Unless I need some PR for World Connect. Then I'm all smiles and pithy sound bites." He grinned.

"I need to cultivate that attitude." She rested her head on his broad chest. "They're just doing their job. As you said before, they're not likely to leave me alone any time soon because of the president being my father, so I might as well get used to them."

"Good, because on Sunday we're going to a charity polo match and there will be plenty of press there." He had that mischievous look again.

"Uh-oh."

"It'll be fun. And you'll get to meet my family."

Anxiety spiked through her. "Your older brother and his wife?"

"They're away on a tour of Australia, but you'll meet

my grandmother and assorted cousins, aunts and uncles. And my younger brother will be there."

She swallowed, trying not to let her panic show. "Your grandmother...the queen?"

"Don't be intimidated. She looks fierce from a distance but up close she's very warm and easy to talk to."

She blew out a breath. "I hope I won't stutter like an idiot."

"You are the last person on earth to feel flummoxed in the presence of royalty. Especially since you're already sleeping with it."

She chuckled. "There is that." Then her gut churned. "Does the queen know? I mean, about us?"

"If she reads the papers she will." He stroked her cheek. "Don't worry. My family will love you. It will be fun."

Fun. Ariella very much doubted that it would be fun. Intimidating, alarming, fraught with potential pitfalls? Yes. Fun? Not so much.

Either way, in less than two days, she'd find out.

Seven

Ariella tried everything she could think of to get out of attending the polo match. The Duke of Buckingham had officially hired them for the wedding so she really should be in London scouting out suppliers for the party. But, yes, it would be a Sunday and in England most things were closed on Sunday. She should get back to the U.S. and… well, yes, it would still be Sunday.

So on Sunday morning she found herself combing her hair with shaking hands.

Simon opened the door dividing their rooms and looked in. He smiled when he saw her. "Just checking that you haven't climbed out the window."

"What if they all hate me?"

"They'll love you." His ebullient confidence did nothing to soothe her frazzled nerves.

"I don't know anything about polo."

"You don't need to. Clap when our team scores and you'll be good."

"What if a reporter asks probing questions?"

"They won't. It's a very exclusive event and there are unwritten rules that keep them at a respectful distance."

"What if I become hysterical and make a big scene?"

He grinned. "Then we'll call some nice men in white coats to come take you away. Would you like a glass of Pimm's to soothe your nerves?"

"No, thanks. I really don't like to drink before noon. Especially on Sunday. It affects my aim." She brandished her mascara wand.

"Quite understandable. I should probably warn you about my uncle Derek. He's likely to be three sheets to the wind by noon and isn't shy about expressing himself."

Uncle Derek? She'd never heard of him. Her confusion must have shown in her face.

"He's my mother's brother, so not royal by birth, but he's latched on to the family and is hanging on with a death grip. He tries to be more traditional than anyone so he's not likely to approve of me dating an American."

She sighed. "It's not like we're…serious." Was she trying to convince herself? Their weekend together had been so easy and fun. She and Simon really clicked. They could talk about anything. And the sex…

"Says who?" He sauntered into the room. "I can be very serious when the occasion calls for it." He walked up behind her where she stood at the mirror and slid his arms around her waist. His lips pressed hotly into her neck and sent heat plunging to her toes. "And I seriously like you."

She blinked, looking from her startled face to his relaxed one in the mirror. "I like you, too, but it is a strange situation, you have to admit."

"My entire life is a strange situation, by most measurable parameters." He nibbled on her ear, which made her gasp. "I don't let it bother me."

"I guess when you put it that way…" Her words trailed off as their eyes locked in the mirror. His managed to sparkle with amusement and desire at the same time. His hands roamed over her hips and belly, setting off tremors of desire. Last night's lovemaking still reverberated in her mind and body. If she could just get through this afternoon without any drama they'd be back in bed together, tonight. Their last night before her flight back to D.C. tomorrow.

Without making a decision to, she turned and kissed him, smudging her carefully applied makeup and gripping him in a forceful embrace. If this was all they ever had it would be well worth it. No regrets.

At least she hoped not.

"And this is my grandmother." Simon smiled encouragingly. People milled around them in the royal enclosure, laughing and clinking glasses. Photographers were at a discreet distance. Mallets thwacked against balls somewhere in the background.

The queen looked so tiny up close. Ariella began to curtsey, but the queen stuck out her hand, so she took it. Cool and soft, the fingers closed around hers with surprising strength. "A pleasure to meet you, Miss Winthrop. Simon tells me you've never been to a polo match before." Steel-blue eyes peered into her very core.

"No, this is my first."

"Simon also informs me that President Morrow is your father." The queen's cool grip trapped her hands.

"Um, yes." Did she realize they'd never met, or even spoken? "Rather a surprise to both of us."

"Surprises do keep life interesting, don't they?"

"They do indeed."

The queen bombarded her with information about the various polo ponies, their breeding and track records and finer qualities. She was clearly skilled at holding the entire conversation with little participation from others. Ariella decided she'd work on that skill herself. It seemed a safe way to keep conversations on the right track.

Simon smiled and nodded and generally seemed delighted at how things were progressing. Ariella smiled and nodded while thinking, *Omigosh, I'm chatting about horses with the queen. And I don't know anything about horses. And I'm sleeping with her grandson.*

She was definitely ready for a Pimm's by the time a new arrival interrupted their conversation to greet Her Majesty. Simon procured her a large glass of the tea-colored drink with its floating mix of strawberries, apples, orange and cucumber. She knew the sweet taste hid a base of gin, so she sipped it gingerly, not wanting to find herself giggling and falling over in her stilettos as some of the younger guests were already in danger of doing.

Simon's younger brother Henry was at the center of the group of more rambunctious partygoers, and Ariella felt a sense of apprehension as Simon led her over to meet him.

As tall as Simon, but with curlier hair and bright blue eyes, the youngest prince had a reputation as a hard-partying playboy.

"I see you convinced her to step into the fray." He fixed his eyes on hers as he kissed her hand, which felt very awkward in front of the gathered crowd of guests. Young girls, spilling out of their expensive dresses, stared at her with curiosity.

"My brother, Henry, Ariella Winthrop." Simon made the introduction.

"I think everyone in the developed world knows who

Ms. Winthrop is. And she's even lovelier than her photographs."

What did you say to a comment like that? "It's nice to meet you."

"But is it? You haven't known me long enough to be sure."

"Don't scare Ariella." Simon was smiling. "She's just heard the pedigrees of the entire equine half of the polo team from Gran."

"I hope you showed a suitable degree of fascination. Gran is very suspicious of anyone who doesn't share her passion for horses."

"I freely admit that I know almost nothing about horses."

"I thought Montana was cowboy country?" Henry was obviously enjoying this.

"Some parts of it are, but not where I lived."

"I think Ariella would make a marvelous cowgirl." Simon slid his arm around her waist. She tried to keep a straight face. Did he really want to do that in front of all these people? She felt eyes boring into her from all directions. "But I intend to make her fall in love with England."

Henry raised an eyebrow. "He must be serious. Usually he can't wait to get on a plane and go somewhere looking for adventure."

"Ariella has me thinking about adventures closer to home."

Ariella could hardly believe her ears. He was all but declaring himself. Maybe this was some kind of ongoing joke between him and his brother. She had no idea how to react. "I like England very much."

"Well, thank goodness for that. There's one thing I can't change about myself, and that's my homeland." Simon squeezed her gently, which sent a ripple of confused emotions through her.

"I'm not sure you can change all that much else, either." Henry teased Ariella. "He's very bullheaded and opinionated."

"I am not." Simon shoved him gently. Ariella could see the brothers had a friendly sparring relationship, but that they cared for each other deeply. As someone who'd never had a sibling to rib her, she found their closeness touching.

"Ariella came up with the idea for an outdoor concert to raise money and awareness for World Connect."

"I like." Henry grinned. "The lawns in front of the Washington Monument would be a great spot."

"I agree." Ariella smiled. "No harm in aiming high."

"Especially when your dad is the president." Henry winked. "We royals aren't averse to a little nepotism when the occasion calls for it. It's how we pass on the throne, after all."

Ariella's stomach clenched slightly. Everyone seemed to assume that she had a relationship with her father, when nothing could be further from the truth.

"Uh-oh, here comes trouble." Henry's nod made Simon turn.

"Too true. Let's head it off at the pass." He turned and led Ariella away from Henry and his gaggle of blushing admirers toward a tall man in baggy tweeds, approaching fast through the knots of glamorous polo-goers.

"Your uncle?" The man's bushy brows sank low over slitted dark eyes and his cheeks were the florid pink of a smacked behind.

"Good old Uncle Derek. Here to pour gasoline on untroubled waters."

Derek marched up to Simon and launched into a conversation about the polo team, totally ignoring her. She counted the burst blood vessels in his cheeks and wondered if he intended to simply pretend she didn't exist.

"Uncle Derek, do hold your fire a moment so I can introduce you to my honored guest, Miss Ariella Winthop. Ariella, this is my mother's brother, Derek, the Duke of Aylesbury."

"Just visiting England, are you?" His haughty voice grated on her ears.

"Yes, I'm going back tomorrow."

"Oh." He turned back to Simon and launched into a tirade about poor sportsmanship at his shooting club. Simon caught her eye as he nodded and yessed his uncle. Ariella sagged with relief when Derek finally finished his monologue and sauntered off.

"He's irritating but harmless. I try to ignore him." Simon's whispered words in her ear made her giggle. "One thing you learn to do as a royal is present a united front. We don't need the public to know that behind closed doors sometimes we drive each other insane."

"Quite understandable." She admired his ability to play the role he'd been born to. Such responsibility and the strict code of conduct would be too much for a lot of people she knew. It almost invited rebellion and debauchery, but Simon handled his unique life with ease and good humor.

Which only made her adore him more.

There was a brief commotion as one of the players fell off and, unable to support weight on an injured ankle, was helped to a medical tent.

"Simon, we need you!" Two of the other players beckoned from their horses. "Hugh couldn't come today and Rupert's still down with the flu so we're short. You know Dom would be happy for you to ride his horses."

Simon glanced at Ariella, then back at them. "I can't, I'm afraid. It would be rude to desert my guest."

"Oh, that's okay," she protested. "I'm sure I can take care of myself for a few minutes." The game had been going on forever, it seemed. It must be nearly over. "You go ahead." She knew his side was winning and she didn't want everyone blaming her if things went south because Simon couldn't leave her side.

"You're a brick." He kissed her cheek softly, which made her gasp and glance around as he jogged off to change.

Great. Now she was adrift in unfamiliar waters. And her glass of Pimm's was empty, mint leaves clinging limply to the remains of the ice cubes. She decided to go off in search of another, and hope someone scored the winning goal while she was at it.

"Ariella." A voice startled her as she headed down the side of a marquee. She turned to find Simon's uncle Derek right behind her. "A word, if you please."

Actually, I don't please. But she didn't dare say it. She paused, still half turned toward the drinks tent.

"Simon's young and impressionable." Those frighteningly large salt-and-pepper brows waggled up and down. "Enthusiastic and charming but not terribly bright, I'm afraid."

Her mouth fell open. "I find him highly intelligent."

"I'm sure you do." He swigged from a glass of clear liquid. "A coronet has that effect on women. The fact remains that a dalliance with you could destroy his future."

"I hardly think that…" She didn't know what she was about to say but it didn't matter because Derek blazed ahead.

"We all know what happened the last time a member of the British royal family lost his head over an American. He abandoned his country and his duty in the name of love. Not because he wanted to, but because he knew it was an *absolute requirement*." His emphasis on the last two words was underscored with a hiss.

"Why?" Now she was curious to hear his answer.

"Because he knew she could not possibly fit in."

"I thought it was because the monarch can't marry a divorcée. For starters, Simon's not a monarch, or very likely to be one. And second, I'm not divorced." Her own boldness shocked her. Pimm's must be powerful stuff.

The monstrous brows shot up. "Times are different now, but not that different. Her Majesty holds very traditional views, and each of her grandchildren has been groomed from birth to follow a specific path. Simon will marry a member of the British nobility, and will raise his children here to be members of the British aristocracy. Lady Sophia Alnwick will be his future wife and the wedding invitations are all but printed. She'd be here with him today if she wasn't holding vigil at her esteemed father's deathbed. Within the next day or so she'll inherit all his lands and wealth and be the richest woman in England."

Ariella blinked. "I hardly think Simon needs to marry for money or prestige."

"Those two things are never a negative." Derek's beady black gaze chilled her. "You are a…a nobody. The illegitimate daughter of an American upstart who's clawed his way into a temporary position of power. Don't delude yourself that you can compete with the thousand-year history of the Alnwick family. Like his brother's, Simon's life path has been planned since birth. The estate he lives in, the so-called charity he's so enamored of, these are all part and parcel of his role. If you get your claws into him and cause him to do something foolish, he'll lose both of them."

"I don't believe you."

"No? The estate isn't his. It belongs to Her Majesty. That silly charity is funded almost entirely by the royal coffers. Simon's role in the family is a job like any other. His employment is contingent on Her Majesty's largesse, and can be rescinded at any time. Think about that when you kiss him."

He hissed the word *kiss,* and spittle formed on his bulbous lips. Then he turned and marched away. She wilted like the mint in her Pimm's. Was this true? Was Simon really a royal puppet whose strings could be cut at any time?

Part of her wanted to encourage him to tell them all to shove it and live his own life. Then she thought about how much he loved his home at Whist Castle. And how proud he was of the achievements of World Connect. Could she really be responsible for causing him to lose them both?

Her legs were shaking and her hand sweating around her glass. She hurried to the drinks tent and got another Pimm's, then walked around the perimeter of the royal enclosure, pretending to watch the match. She cheered wildly, heart pounding with pride and happiness, when Simon scored a goal. Then glanced around, wondering if she should have pretended more disinterest. He looked so dashing and handsome on top of the muscled bay horse, who listened to his every move and galloped for the ball as if its life depended on it.

"He's a fine player." The distinctive voice startled her.

"Yes, Your Majesty." The queen must have walked right up to her while her eyes were glued on Simon and she hadn't even noticed. Her attendants hovered at a discreet distance. "He obviously enjoys the game."

"Simon's been playing polo since he was about eleven. He'd already been riding for years at that point, of course. Do you ride?"

"No. I've never even sat on a horse. I suppose that seems

funny when I come from Montana, but we lived in town and I never had the chance."

"Ah. What did you do for entertainment in Montana?"

Ariella swallowed. This seemed dangerously personal. And she was to blame for bringing up her roots. "My dad used to take us to watch football games almost every weekend in season. And we went fishing at the lake."

"How nice." She didn't seem especially interested. And why should she be? "Do you plan to go back to Montana?"

"I have a business in Washington, D.C., so I'm not sure if I'll ever live in Montana again. Never say never, though."

"And when are you returning to Washington?" A hint of steel shimmered in her voice.

"Tomorrow, actually." Sadness mingled with relief. She'd have to leave Simon, but she wouldn't be stuck trying to make small talk with a monarch. "I was here on business. Simon's helped make it a wonderful trip."

She looked at the queen's face. She couldn't resist throwing in that last part.

"Simon tells me you're a party planner." The cool blue eyes had narrowed behind her glasses.

"Yes. I'm here to plan the Duke of Buckingham's wedding." She had no doubt the queen and the duke were old pals.

"How wonderful. Everyone's so happy to see him marrying Nicola at last. They've been chums almost since nursery school."

"I'll make sure it's an event to remember."

"I'm sure you will. Did Simon tell you he'll be getting married soon?"

She frowned. "What?"

The queen smiled sweetly. "A similar situation, really. A childhood friend who we all love. Perhaps he can get some wedding ideas from you."

Ariella's lung capacity seemed to shrink until she could hardly breathe. The queen was warning her off Simon. Telling her he was already spoken for and that she was not wanted on the voyage. A roar of clapping rose through the crowd and she joined in enthusiastically, though she wasn't even sure which team had scored a goal.

"I'm sure Simon's wedding will be an affair to remember," she managed at last.

"Indeed. Do have a good trip back to the States." The queen smiled thinly, then turned and walked slowly away.

Ariella felt like she'd just been slapped. She'd now been warned off Simon by two members of the royal family. They must feel quite threatened by her, which wasn't surprising given that Simon had allowed the press to get wind of their romance. Sophia Alnick was probably throwing a tantrum somewhere, too, if she was in on this whole aristocratic marriage scheme.

Standing there with her drink, she felt like a single tree in a tempest, while well-dressed people in big hats—she was hatless—swirled around her, going about their glamorous lives. Her role was to make those lives a little more glamorous by creating extravagant events for them, not to come play their own games with them. Clearly she was losing her grip on reality lately.

She counted the minutes until the match ended and Simon jumped down from his horse. He shared some congratulatory fist pumping with his teammates before jogging across the grass to her. "I hope everyone looked after you."

"Oh, yes."

He was even more handsome with his hair tousled and his chiseled face glowing with exertion. Shame he would never really be hers. "See? I told you they don't bite."

She didn't want to mention the tooth marks they'd left

on her psyche. Not while they were still here, at least. "I'm rather exhausted by all the excitement. Would it be okay if we left?" She certainly didn't want to find herself having to be polite to Uncle Derek, or even the queen, who'd practically shoved her toward her plane.

"Of course." He waved to a few people and escorted her to the car as if she really was the most important person there.

"Don't you need to say goodbye to the queen?" She didn't want to be blamed for him neglecting his royal duties.

"No worries. I'll be seeing her tomorrow after I take you to the airport."

"Oh." And why wouldn't he? She was his grandmother, after all. She probably wanted to go over wedding venue ideas, or discuss the ring he'd soon give to Sophia. Her heart sagged like a deflated balloon.

They talked about the game on the drive back to Whist Castle. Simon obviously loved his life here, surrounded by people who cared about him, and the excitement of his jet-set existence. He was born for it.

She wasn't.

They enjoyed a hearty dinner in the castle dining room, this time served by staff who were obviously trained to ignore the fact that he'd had a woman to stay for the weekend. They must know there was a connecting door between her room and Simon's, and she was pretty sure they knew she and Simon had been using it. It was embarrassing having so many people know her business. They'd all be whispering about her soon as Simon's last hurrah.

"You seem very thoughtful tonight." Simon spoke softly. They were still sitting at the dinner table, sipping coffee.

"Am I? I was just thinking about the Duke of Buckingham's wedding." There was some truth to it. This weekend had given her insight into the British upper crust that would help with the planning. "I hope I'm not being too dull."

"Impossible." His warm smile was so encouraging it almost melted her anxiety. "Let's go relax upstairs."

She gulped. How could she make love to him again, knowing that his family fully intended to keep them apart? "Okay." She'd always known this was never going to be a long-term thing. It was a crazy affair, something they'd both fallen into by accident.

He took her hand as they climbed the stairs, and the way he glanced at her sideways and squeezed her hand gently was so sweet and romantic, it stole her breath. Why did he have to be a prince? Why couldn't he have been a regular guy with an ordinary job and a house somewhere in the D.C. suburbs?

"You seem...worried." He closed the door to his room after they were both inside. The door to her own room was wide open. Apparently there was no pretense that they were sleeping apart.

"I am." It was hard not to be honest with him. He was such a straight shooter himself. "I'm going to miss you."

"Then we'll just have to make sure not to stay apart for too long." He gathered her in his arms and laid a warm kiss on her lips. Her anxiety started to unspool as she kissed him back.

"Yes." She said it but she didn't believe it. It would be better for both of them if they kissed and wandered back to their regular lives. Less media frenzy, less royal disapproval. Less fun.

Their kiss deepened until she had to come up for air. Simon's hands plucked at the zipper near her waist, and soon she was shimmying out of her dress and struggling with his belt and undressing him. Even though everyone in the outside world seemed to think he'd soon be marrying Lady Sophia, right now she knew he wasn't interested in anyone but her. Alone in this room they were two people who cared about each other. It felt so good to shrug out of the trappings of society and press her skin against his. His naked body was so sturdy and capable. She had no doubt he could leap tall buildings in a single bound if he wanted to. She felt so confident in his presence, like together they could accomplish anything. It would be hard to be back in her D.C. apartment, alone.

Simon nibbled her jaw and neck, his breath hot and urgent. "I don't know what I'm going to do without you."

So she wasn't the only one thinking it. They slipped under the bed clothes together. "You'll do what you did before you met me. You know, climb mountains, jump over waterfalls, that kind of thing."

"You're probably right. At least until my next trip to D.C." He maneuvered himself on top of her and his erection nudged her belly.

She inhaled a shaky breath. "Who knows what will happen between now and then?" No doubt the royals would warn him to stay away from her. If he had any sense, he'd probably listen. She'd be busy with her own dramas—meeting her father on national television, her frantic work schedule, dodging photographers.

"Let's not think about the future. We don't want to waste a single precious second of our last night together." Arousal thickened his voice. He raised his hips and entered her.

Desire and relief crashed through her as she felt him deep inside her. Sheer physical pleasure was a welcome change from all the thinking and plotting and scrambling she did during the day. Simon's powerful arms felt like the safest place to be in the whole world.

They moved together effortlessly, drawing to the brink of madness and back, as they tried to wring every last ounce of passion out of each other, only to find there was an inexhaustible well of it bubbling somewhere deep inside them.

When her orgasm came, Ariella wanted to cry. The feelings inside her were just too much. Desire and fear and pleasure and panic and wanting to stay right here in Simon's hot and hungry embrace until the world ended.

Simon gripped her tight, as if he was afraid she'd drift off into the night breeze. "Oh, Ariella," he whispered in her ear. She loved the way he said her name, with his formal sounding British accent and such conviction. She was sure no medieval knight ever serenaded his lady with such intensity.

She simply breathed, holding tight to the precious moments where she felt at peace, before she'd be spat back out into the world and have to fend for herself.

In the morning an alarm sounded, reminding them both that she had a plane to catch in a little over four hours. It was odd that you could be sleeping in a royal palace, with a prince, no less, then have to battle your way into coach and cram your bags into the overhead bin and hope your neighbor didn't drool on you while he slept.

She wanted to laugh, but nothing seemed too funny right now.

"Did you like my family?" Simon's odd question came out of nowhere.

It startled her into a fib. "They were very nice."

"Except Uncle Derek." His voice sounded curious.

"Yes, except him."

He sat up. "Did he say something to you?"

She hesitated for a moment. Why hadn't she told him about this already? She didn't want to spoil their last night together. And she knew it would upset him. "Kind of." Simon took her hand and peered into her face. She wanted to run from his thoughtful and caring expression, not hurt his feelings by telling him what his uncle had said to her. "I have to get ready."

"What did he say?"

"Oh, nothing really." She tried to get up, but he held her hand firm.

"I don't believe you. Come on, word for word or I'll have to start in with the medieval torture techniques." He acted like he was going to tickle her. But neither of them laughed.

"He said you're going to marry Sophia Alnwick soon."

"Which you already know is not true."

"And he reminded me of what happened the last time a British royal got involved with an American."

"You're hardly Wallace Simpson."

"I told him that. Not that it matters, anyway, since we're barely even dating. It was silly. I didn't think it was worth mentioning."

"Did anyone else say anything?"

"Not really. Though the queen did seem fairly interested in when I was going back to the States. I suspect they'll all be glad to see the back of me so you can go back to dating some nice, suitable English girls." She smiled and tried to sound jokey. That was what would happen after all.

But Simon's face was like stone. "I'll have a talk with them." He frowned. "I'm sorry they made you feel uncomfortable."

"I was fine, really. It was fun. I've never been to a polo match before and I loved watching you play."

"I shouldn't have left you alone. I'll sort them out."

"There's no need, really!" Her voice sounded too loud. Would they tell him what they'd told her? That he'd lose Whist Castle and his charity if he dared not to toe the royal party line? "I need to get dressed and throw my stuff back in my bag. And do you have the number for a taxi?"

"A taxi!" He wrapped his arms around her and hugged her tight. "There's no way anyone but me is driving you to that airport. And it'll be a miracle if I don't make you deliberately miss your plane."

"Then my partner, Scarlet, will kill me. She's been holding down the fort by herself all week."

"She can't kill you if she can't find you." He raised a brow and mischief twinkled in his eyes again.

"She can send out a hit man. They're good at tracking people. They can probably trace my cell phone."

"They'd have to get past the palace guards." He kissed her face and cheeks and lips. She shivered, hot pleasure rising inside her. "It can be handy living in a fortress."

"I see that." Her hands roamed over the muscle of his back. "I think I could get used to it." It was so easy to talk to him and tease him. He never made her feel like he was a prince and she was a commoner. With him she felt they were on the same team and could take on the world together.

The alarm sounded again. She pushed him back, very reluctantly, and leaped out of bed. "Duty calls."

"Being in the army I know all about that, so I suppose I'll have to go along with it."

They dressed and had a quick breakfast, then Simon drove her to Heathrow. They kissed in the car where no one could see, but he insisted on walking her into the terminal. She saw a photographer's flash out of the corner of her eye as they said a chaste goodbye.

Move along, she wanted to say. *There's nothing to see*

here. She felt numb as she checked her bag and moved through customs. Would he really come to D.C. to see her? Or would the queen and Uncle Derek make him give her up and turn his attention back to his royal duties?

Somehow she had to go from the most intense and wonderful romance of her life to…nothing. Maybe she'd never see him again except on the pages of a glossy magazine. She sank into her airplane seat feeling hollow and deflated.

Until she checked her phone and discovered that she was about to finally meet her famous father.

Eight

A brief text from Liam Crowe, the head of ANS, told her the taping was scheduled for Tuesday, only two days away, and everyone at the network was scrambling to pull it together. Ariella had barely arrived home and unpacked before Francesca, Liam's wife, came over to help her prep for the taping.

"It seems shallow to ask, but what do you think I should wear?" They both sat at her kitchen table, sipping herbal tea. Her nerves were firing like bullets. "I usually wear black but I've heard that doesn't look good on video. It disappears or something. I don't want it to vanish and leave me stark naked on national television."

Francesca's bold laugh filled the room. "It looks a bit flat, that's all. But colors do usually work better. Let's go look at your wardrobe."

They walked into the bedroom. Ariella opened her closet door sheepishly. The apartment was old, from an era when people had maybe five to ten outfits. Her collection of clothes looked ready to burst out and start running.

"How do you find anything in here?"

"My first boss used to have a sign on her desk that read, *'This is not a mess on my desk, it's a wilderness of free association.'* I took it as inspiration."

"It's a wilderness, all right." Still, Francesca dove boldly in and pulled out a knee-length red sheath. "Red portrays confidence."

"That I don't feel. I think I should go low-key."

"You? You're practically a princess. How about this royal blue?" She held up a matching top and skirt in an intense shade.

"I am sooo not practically a princess. Believe me. I was way out of my league with his family."

"You met the queen?" Francesca grabbed her arm.

She nodded. "We made small talk. It was scary." Ariella reached in for a quiet gray jacket and skirt. "How about this?"

"Way too mousy." Francesca shoved it back. "I can't believe you met the queen. I love her. She's so old-fashioned."

"Exactly. The kind of person who's horrified by the prospect of her grandson dating an Amerrrrican." She managed to roll her *R*s. Then sighed. "He's sweet but it's one of those things with no future."

"I'll have to read your tea leaves when we're done picking your outfit."

"Does that work when you're using a tea bag?"

"It does require more creativity, but I have plenty of that."

"Let's just stay focused on getting me through this taping in one piece. How about this lilac number?"

Francesca surveyed the dress. "Perfect. Fresh and young, yet sophisticated and worldly."

"I'm glad that's settled. Will I get to meet the pres— I mean, my father, before the taping starts?"

Francesca hesitated. "Liam and I did talk about that. He wants you to meet for the first time on air, for maximum dramatic impact. I told him this isn't a primetime special—well, it is—but it's your real life. If you don't like the idea of meeting him under the studio lights, I'll beg and plead until he gives in."

"Don't worry about it. I don't mind meeting him on camera. In a way it might help as I'll have to keep a lid on my emotions."

"Oh, don't do that. It's bad for ratings." Francesca winked.

"Liam would rather have me blubbering and calling him Daddy?"

"Absolutely."

She blew out a breath. "Yikes. That's not really me. I'm known for being calm under pressure. I'm afraid I won't give good TV."

"You just be yourself, and we'll let Liam worry about the ratings."

Ariella's usually calm demeanor was trembling. Her hands kept shaking as she tried to apply her mascara. Her lips quivered as she smoothed on her lipstick. Even her hair seemed jumpy. In seventeen minutes—not that she was counting—she'd be sitting on a sound stage with the man who shared half her DNA. She wasn't that nervous about the television cameras, or even the audience of millions that would supposedly be tuning in. She was nervous about what she'd see when she looked into Ted Morrow's face.

Would his expression encourage her to build a relationship that could shape the rest of her life? Or would he be wearing that mask of genial competence that had helped him clinch the election? She knew that mask. She wore it herself a lot. In fact, she planned on wearing it tonight.

She hoped that this meeting might be the start of a relationship between them, but she was keeping her hopes in check since he didn't know her well enough to trust her. He might not want to get close to anyone new. He was in a position of power and influence that made him strangely vulnerable. He probably didn't want to share intimacies and feelings with a stranger who might turn around and repeat them to the press, or even to her friends. Still, she knew she'd be disappointed if she didn't feel even a little bit closer to him after tonight.

"We're on in five!" The perky production assistant stuck her head around the corner. "Are you ready?"

"Ready as I'll ever be." She stood up on shaky legs and smoothed out the skirt of her lavender dress.

"You can come sit in the green room. The president is chatting with Liam so you won't meet him until we're on air."

"It's going to be totally live?" There'd been some back and forth about whether it would be taped and then edited, but the ANS producer had reassured her that if it was live she was actually more in control of the final output than if it ended up in the hands of directors and editors. Apparently live was also better for ratings.

"Yup. No delay. No one expects either of you to start cursing or doing anything else that needs to be tweaked before it goes out." The PA squeezed her arm. "You'll be great. Just remember not to talk too fast and try not to look at the cameras."

"Okay." She said it to reassure herself as much as the PA. What if she froze and couldn't speak? What if she passed out in a dead faint? Whatever happened would be seen live by millions of curious onlookers.

She followed the PA into the green room, which wasn't green at all but mostly gray and had two sofas and some chairs. A jug of water, glasses and a basket of muffins. She certainly didn't have any appetite. She sat on one of the sofas and smiled weakly.

The PA looked at a sheet of paper in her hand. "Barbara Carey will be going in first to introduce you, then the president will come in." Celebrity journalist Barbara Carey was known for her ability to make all her interviewees cry. They'd probably picked her just for that reason. No matter what happened, Ariella was sure she wouldn't cry. All she had to do was stay calm, be polite and survive the half-hour ordeal.

A light went on near the door marked Studio C. "Has the show started?"

"Yup, they're taping. Get ready." She ushered Ariella over to the door, and opened it quietly. The lights blinded her as she stepped onto a big sound stage with cameras on all sides. Barbara Carey was sitting in a set that looked a bit like a living room, with soft chairs and a potted plant. There was an empty chair on either side of her. In a few seconds she'd be sitting in one of those looking at her father.

Her heart clenched and unclenched and she tried to keep her breathing steady.

Barbara Carey's voice filled the air. "…a young woman who's been plucked out of obscurity and thrust onto the world stage by the startling revelation that her father is none other than the president of the United States. Ariella Winthrop." The PA had maneuvered her just outside the scene, so she plunged forward. Barbara stood and she shook her hand, then she sat in the seat indicated. Where was the president? She fought the urge to look around to see if he was standing offstage somewhere.

"Did you have any idea at all that your father was Ted Morrow?" Up close Ariella could see that Barbara Carey was wearing a tremendous amount of makeup, including long false eyelashes.

"Not until I read it in the papers like everyone else."

"Had your parents told you that you were adopted?" She leaned in, sincerity shining in her famous blue eyes.

"Oh, yes, I always knew that I was adopted. They told me my mother was unmarried and too young to provide for me and that she gave me up so that I could have a better life." Her thoughts strayed to Eleanor, so nervous and desperate to hide from the limelight. She'd rather die than be here on this stage.

"And did you ever hope to meet your birth parents?"

"I didn't." She frowned. People probably thought it shallow, but it was the truth. "I considered my adoptive parents to be my mother and father."

"But they died in a tragic accident. Surely you must have wondered about the man and woman that gave you life?"

"Maybe I didn't let myself wonder. I didn't want to try to replace my mother and father in any way." This was turning out to be more of an interview than she expected, and making her nervous. She wished they'd hurry up and bring Ted Morrow out. She probably wasn't giving them the emotional yearning they were hoping for. "But I'm glad of the opportunity to meet my father."

No one knew she'd already met her mother. She'd sworn to keep it a secret, and she'd stand by her promise.

"And you shall." Barbara Carey stood. "Let me introduce you to your father, President Ted Morrow."

A hush fell over the room as she rose to her feet, peering into the darkness just beyond the studio lights. The familiar face of the president emerged, tall, handsome, smiling. He looked at her and their eyes met. Her breath stuck in her lungs as he thrust out his hand and she took it. His handshake was firm and warm and she hoped it would go on forever. His eyes were so kind, and as she looked into them she saw them brimming with emotion. "Hello, Ariella. I'm very happy to meet you." His voice was low and gruff.

Her heart beat faster and faster and her breathing grew shallow. "I'm very pleased to meet you, too." The polite words did nothing to express the deep well of emotion suddenly rushing inside her.

His pale blue eyes locked with hers, and she could see shadows of thoughts flickering behind them. "Oh, my." His murmur almost seemed to have come from her own mouth. Overwhelmed, their hands still clasped together, they stared at each other for a long time that seemed agonizingly short and then she felt his arms close around her back.

The breath rushed from her lungs as she hugged him back and held him with the force of twenty-eight years of unexpressed longing. She could feel his chest heaving as he held her tight. Tears fell from her eyes into the wool of his suit and she couldn't stop them. It was too much. Feelings she'd never anticipated rocked her to her core. When they finally parted she was blinking and pretty sure that she wouldn't be able to talk if someone asked her a question. The president's—her father's—eyes were wet with tears and his face still looked stunned.

He helped her to one of the seats, then took his place in the other, on the opposite side of Barbara Carey, who tactfully remained silent, letting the moment speak for itself. At last the interviewer drew in a breath. "It's been a long time coming." She looked from one of them to the other.

Ariella's father—it didn't feel crazy to call him that

now, which didn't really make any sense, but then none of this did—stared straight at her. "I had no idea you existed." His voice was breathless, as if he was talking just to her, not to Barbara Carey, or the cameras, or the viewers.

"I know," she managed. She'd known he existed, of course, but not who he was.

"Your parents have obviously done a wonderful job of raising you. I've learned of all your accomplishments, and how well you've handled the avalanche of events these last few months."

She smiled. "Thanks."

"I should have met with you before now but I was foolish enough to take the advice of strategists who wanted to wait until we knew the truth from the DNA testing." His eyes softened. "I was a fool. I only have to look at you to know you're my daughter. And you have your mother's eyes."

Those same eyes filled with tears again, and she reached for one of the tissues from a box that had miraculously appeared on a small coffee table in front of them. Suddenly she could see herself in the jut of his cheekbone and the funny way he wrinkled his nose. They'd been living their lives often only a few buildings apart here in D.C. but might have never met.

"I suppose we have to be grateful for the nosey journalists who uncovered the truth." She said it to him, then turned to Barbara Carey. "Or we might have lived the rest of our lives without ever meeting."

"We have a lot of lost time to make up for." Ted Morrow leaned forward. "I'd like very much to get to know you."

"I'd like that, too." Her heart swelled until she thought it might burst. "I've been longing to meet you since I first learned you were my father. It's not easy getting an appointment with the president."

He shook his head. "I've been anxious to meet you, too. It's usually a mistake to let other people tell you how to run your life, and it's one I won't make again. I have a strange feeling we'll find we have a lot in common."

She smiled. "I've wondered about that. And I'd like to learn more about your life in Montana."

Something flickered across Ted Morrow's face. Maybe he was thinking back to his high school days, where he'd become involved with Eleanor. She wondered how he felt about being deceived for all these years. Would he forgive Eleanor for keeping her secret?

"I had a wonderful childhood in Montana. And I was very much in love with your mother." He spoke with force, eyes still shining with emotion. "It's been a strange journey since then, for sure. Who knows how different it would have been if she'd told me she was pregnant with you?"

"You might not be sitting here as president of the United States," suggested Barbara. "Your life might have taken a different course."

"I might have accepted the assistant manager position I was offered at Willey's Tool and Die." He chuckled. "They paid time and a half for weekends."

"But you had bigger dreams." Barbara tilted her head. "You'd just accepted a scholarship to attend Cornell University."

"I wanted to get out of my small pond and see if I could swim in a larger one." Then his eyes fixed on hers again. "I never intended to abandon Ellie."

Barbara Carey leaned toward him. "Ellie is Eleanor Albert, your high school sweetheart?"

"Yes. I wrote her letters and we'd made plans to spend the summer together." He frowned. "Then one day she stopped responding to my letters. She didn't answer the phone. Her mother hung up on me." He shook his head. "I guessed that she'd met someone else. I had no idea she'd been bundled out of town to hide a pregnancy."

"And you never saw her again." Barbara's famous voice added drama to the pronouncement.

He looked right at her. "Never. I've certainly thought about her over the years. Wondered where she was and hoped she was happy."

"But you never married anyone else."

"I guess I just never met anyone I loved as much as Ellie."

His usually granite-hard features were softened with emotion. Ariella's heart ached at the thought that Eleanor—Ellie—was out there and deathly afraid of him. Thinking he'd be angry and would hate her for her choice to keep her secret. She vowed that once she got to know him she'd convince Eleanor to meet him in person.

"Well, we have a surprise for you, President Morrow."

He lifted a brow. "I'm not sure how many more surprises I can take. It's been quite a year for them."

Barbara stood and peered off into the darkness beyond the studio lights, and both Ariella and her father instinctively stood as well. "It wasn't easy to convince her, but I'm happy to tell you that Eleanor is here with us tonight."

Ariella gasped. She tried to make out her mother's face but it was too hard to see. She glanced at Ted Morrow, but he simply looked shocked. At last she made out Liam Crowe, the head of ANS, walking toward them with Eleanor on his arm. Her hair was carefully coiffed, and she wore a simple burgundy dress, and looked young and pretty, and very, very nervous.

Her eyes were riveted on Ted Morrow like she'd seen a ghost.

"Ellie." The president breathed her name like a prayer. "It's really you."

Blinking, she walked into the glare of the lights. "Hello, Ted." Her voice was tiny, barely audible. He enveloped her in the same bear hug he'd greeted Ariella with, but there was something…tentative about the way he held her.

Stage hands quietly appeared with a chair for her to sit on, next to Ariella, who she greeted nervously.

Barbara leaned toward Ted. "I have to tell you that Eleanor approached us. She had heard of the special from Ariella, and she decided it was time to face you and tell her side of the story."

Ted stared at Eleanor in a daze as if he couldn't believe she was really here.

"Ariella and I met in London." She spoke quietly. "Meeting her meant so much to me. I don't suppose I realized how much I gave up until I saw her beautiful face and talked with her. After that I knew I had to face you again, too, Ted."

"I never knew what happened to you. I pestered your mother for years but she never told me. She said you'd gone to live abroad."

"It was true. I met my husband, married him and moved to Ireland all within a year of giving birth to Ariella. It seemed easier for everyone if I just disappeared."

"It wasn't easier for me," Ted protested. "Why didn't you tell me? You know I'd have married you."

She looked at him in silence, her lip trembling. "I knew that's what you'd do. That you'd give up your dreams to do the right thing. I couldn't let you do that."

"Ellie." Tears filled his eyes. "Maybe there were other things that were more important to me than building a big career."

"I'm so sorry." Eleanor's voice was higher. She was beginning to look as if she regretted coming. Ariella grabbed her hand and squeezed it. "Looking back I can see I made a terrible mistake. I was in a panic. My family said that the scandal of an unwed pregnancy would ruin your prospects. It was a different time. I was young and stupid and alone. I didn't know what to do and I followed bad advice."

"The important thing is that we're all here today." Ted Morrow's voice sounded presidential for the first time since he'd come on set. "We've all done things we'd do differently if we had the chance to do them over again. Instead of looking back and saying 'if only,' I suggest that we embrace the present."

"Well said," chimed in Barbara. "And we here at ANS are thrilled to be a part of bringing you all together again."

After the taping, they filed into the green room. Ariella felt shell-shocked. They'd all watched an edited montage of childhood photographs and background interviews and answered a few more questions. She was relieved it was over but also anxious to make sure she didn't miss the opportunity to get to know her father and mother better.

Ted and Eleanor stood together, awkwardly silent, staring at each other. She wondered if she should say something to break the ice, but then she wondered if it wasn't ice but something far warmer and maybe she should stay out of the way.

"You haven't changed at all." The president's usually commanding voice sounded gruff with emotion.

"You, either. Though the gray at your temples makes you look more distinguished." Eleanor's eyes sparkled. "I wasn't at all surprised to learn that you were running for president. I even obtained an absentee ballot for the first time so I could vote for you."

Ted laughed. "It was a close race. I'm glad of the help." He looked like he wanted to say so much more. He took her hands. "I know you did what you thought was best."

He spoke softly, as if they were all alone, though Ariella stood only a few feet away and production staff moved in the background.

"It doesn't seem that way now, but you know what they say about hindsight."

"I never loved anyone else." Ted's soft words shocked Ariella. She felt embarrassed to be eavesdropping, and wanted to disappear. But she knew how hard it was to engineer this meeting in the first place and who knew when she'd get another chance to spend time with her father. "I probably shouldn't tell you that. I know you were married."

"Greg was a good man." Ellie didn't seem so nervous and skittish anymore. Being in Ted's presence seemed to calm her. "He was always so kind to me and we shared a good life together, even though we were never blessed with children."

"I'm sorry to hear that he died."

"Yes, it was very sudden and unexpected." Their gazes were still locked on each other and they held hands as if afraid circumstances might suddenly tug them apart again.

It made her think of Simon. Circumstances certainly conspired to keep them apart. In fact it was odd that they'd ever met and managed to forge a few moments of intimacy. Some things just weren't meant to be. She was almost at peace about it. It had been a fun fling, a wonderful whirlwind romance, and now she needed to get back to her regular life—whatever regular was these days—and try to forget about him.

"Do you think we could...have dinner together?" Ted Morrow asked with a touchingly hopeful expression.

"I'd like that very much." Eleanor glowed. She looked so young and lovely standing there with Ted. Ariella would barely have recognized her as the white-lipped, anxious woman who'd met her in their secret London hiding place. "We have a lot to catch up on."

They both seemed to suddenly remember her. "You will join us, won't you?" Ted reached out and took Ariella's hand, so that they were all linked. "It would mean so much to me to finally get to know you after all these years."

"I'd be thrilled."

The dinner was very emotional. Their happiness at meeting was thickened with sadness at all the things they'd missed sharing together. Ariella arrived home feeling literally sick with exhaustion, emotional and physical. She'd had her phone turned off since before the taping, and when she finally turned it on she saw that Simon had left a message.

"Great news. I've managed to engineer a series of meetings in D.C. next week. I'd like to put in my application now to take you out for dinner on Tuesday. Call me."

Her heart constricted, partly with the familiar thrill of hearing his voice, and partly with the ugly knowledge that she needed to start weaning herself off him, not getting excited about dinners. Feeling dizzy, she lay down on her sofa, clutching the phone to her chest. She listened to another message from her partner, Scarlet, asking her to call and fill her in on the details. She decided that could wait until tomorrow because Scarlet had probably watched the taping like everyone else.

Her phone rang and she didn't have the energy to come up with a strategy, so she answered it. "Were you ever going to call me, or what?"

"Hi, Scarlet." Her voice sounded far away, like it belonged to someone else. "I'm wiped out."

"I bet you are. That was quite a live reunion. I do believe your parents are still madly in love with each other."

"Was that obvious on television, too? I felt like a third wheel."

"You don't sound good. Are you okay?"

"I'm feeling a little queasy. I'm probably dehydrated or something." They'd been out for a big fancy dinner but she'd found herself barely able to eat. "And I need a good night's sleep."

"All right then. Don't forget we have the Morelli meeting in the morning."

Ariella groaned. She'd totally forgotten they were meeting with the extended Morelli clan to plan a huge fiftieth wedding anniversary. "Ten o'clock, right."

"Call me if you're not up for it, okay? I can handle it."

"I'll be fine."

But she wasn't.

When her alarm went off at eight her comforter felt like a lead blanket. Her eyes didn't want to open. "Coffee. I need coffee," she tried to convince herself. But the moment she managed to get her feet on the floor, a wave of nausea hit her.

Her phone rang on the dresser on the far side of the room, and she leaped to her feet to go answer it. Or at least she tried, but her ankles didn't seem capable of holding weight so she found herself flopping back onto the bed, her breath coming in unsteady gasps.

After about five minutes of deep breathing she got the nausea under control, and managed to walk like a zombie to her phone. Scarlet had called again, so she dialed back without even listening to her message. "You know what you said about doing the meeting without me?"

"Not a problem. You sound terrible."

Her voice did sound rather raspy. "I must have come down with something. I'd better lie in bed for a bit."

"You stay right there and I'll keep you posted on everything that happens."

Ariella stayed in bed all morning. Every time she tried to do something useful the room started spinning or her stomach began to heave. She hadn't been sick in so long she'd forgotten how miserable it was. It was probably from all the stress and anxiety leading up to the TV special. She probably needed a day or two in bed to recover.

Not that she had time for that. She had phone calls to make, menus and décor to approve and clients to meet. But maybe she could lie down for a few minutes first.

Ariella awoke with a start to the sound of the doorbell. A quick glance at the clock revealed she'd been asleep for four hours. She staggered to the door and opened it.

Scarlet stood on the threshold with a concerned look in her face. "I brought some chicken soup." She thrust forward a container from the expensive bistro around the corner. "It has antibacterial properties."

"What if it's a virus?" Ariella couldn't resist teasing her.

"Ah, so you're not as sick as I thought. Let's put it in bowls anyway. I need to grab some lunch before I meet with the manager of that new venue near the river."

"I feel a lot better now. I think I've just been burning the candle too fast lately."

"And Prince Simon has been helping you do it." Scarlet lifted a brow. "But you had a few days to recover from your British romp before the taping."

"Not enough, I guess." She led Scarlet into the kitchen and pulled out two bowls and two spoons. "I usually fight everything off but maybe it's catching up with me. At least I made it through the televised reunion."

"What's he like?" Scarlet poured the soup into both bowls. "The president, I mean."

Ariella paused. "I liked him." She looked right at

Scarlet. "I mean, I liked him before, enough to vote for him—which is lucky, I guess—but he's very genuine and unpretentious in real life. You could tell he found the whole situation rather overwhelming, and that really touched me."

"I saw you guys both weeping."

"And I'd sworn I wouldn't do that." She grabbed a paper towel and wiped up some spilled drops of soup. "I can usually put a lid on any emotion."

"I know. I've seen you in action with the nuttiest clients and guests."

"But the whole thing blew me away. He's my father. We have the same genes. We probably have some of the same likes and dislikes, and he has the same funnily shaped earlobes as I do."

Scarlet peered at her earlobes. "Cool."

"It's frightening to think that I might never have met him. Simon was so right that this is a big life-changing opportunity for me."

"I hear ya. We can plan some White House parties now." Scarlet winked.

"You know what I mean. I have a new set of parents. They'll never replace my parents who raised me, of course, but we'll have new experiences together. We've already made plans to go up to his house in Maine for a few days in the fall."

"Without consulting me?" Scarlet put her hands on her hips in mock indignation. "Just because your daddy's the president and you're dating a prince doesn't mean we're not still partners."

They both laughed. Ariella shook her head. "What next?" A wave of nausea rolled through her. "I need to sit down."

Scarlet followed her into the living room, brow furrowed with concern. "Have some soup." She held out the bowl. "Have you eaten anything at all today?"

Ariella shook her head. Her throat slammed shut at the sight of the soup. "I have no appetite."

"Maybe you're pregnant." Scarlet smiled. She was kidding.

"Sure, if Simon and I had sex."

"You have though, haven't you?" She leaned in. "Even though you won't share the juicy details."

"Barely a week ago. I couldn't possibly be pregnant."

"It only takes one time. And my mom said she started feeling symptoms right away. She took a test and it was positive less than two weeks later."

"We used condoms." Ariella's nausea was getting worse. Scarlet was kidding, wasn't she?

"Don't they have a five percent failure rate?"

"What?" Her grip tightened on her unused spoon.

"That's why most people use something else as well. Still, you're probably not pregnant. You've had a lot on your plate." Scarlet leaned back into the armchair and spooned some soup into her mouth. "Don't worry about it."

Ariella stared at the bowl of soup Scarlet had placed on the coffee table. There was no way she could eat that. There was also no way she could be pregnant.

No. Way. It simply wasn't possible.

Was it?

Nine

Simon paused outside the building where his meeting was to take place and punched Ariella's number into his phone. She was proving very elusive since she'd gone home to D.C. If he were more sensitive he might think she was trying to avoid him. The phone rang, and he leapt to his feet when he heard her tentative, "Hello."

"How are you?" He managed not to ask where she'd been. Didn't want to seem too oppressive.

"Um, fine. How are you?" She sounded oddly formal.

"I'd be a lot better if you were here." He glanced around the busy London street. His imagination wanted to picture her darting along the pavement as she had been when he'd followed her on her secret assignation to meet her mother. "I can't wait to see you next week."

"Yeah." Her voice was barely audible. "Me, either."

"Are you okay?"

"I'm fine." The words shot into his ear so fast he almost jumped. "Great. Really busy with work. You know how it goes."

"Absolutely." There was so much he wanted to say to her but he knew now wasn't the right time. He'd probably come on too strong already, and he was pretty sure that introducing her to his family had been a tactical error. He'd been so sure they'd be bowled over by her charms like he was that he couldn't wait to get the introductions out of the way. Henry had been right. Poor Ariella. There was hardly anyone on earth who wasn't intimidated by the queen, and Uncle Derek was a force of nature akin to a sinkhole. He should have introduced her to one or two family members on a one-on-one basis and let her get to know them before plunging her into their midst. "I did rather shove you into the middle of things here. I could tell you were a bit dazed by your visit."

She laughed. "Was it that obvious? I was way out of my league."

"You were fantastic. I'm sure they'll adore you when they get to know you." He'd caught a lot of flack for bringing her to such a public event with no warning. Pictures of the pair of them had been all over the papers for the next week and there'd been a lot of flapping about suitable relationships and time to settle down and stop playing the field.

He tried to ignore the naysayers. You couldn't hold a sensible argument with fifteen hundred years of tradition so he'd learned to pick his battles and go about his business. If they wanted him to settle down, fine. But not with Sophia Alnwick. And if not her, then why not a fun, sexy, intelligent American girl? He generally preferred to just do stuff and explain it afterward, not get people all fired up over something that might not happen. "I can't wait to see you." Her face hovered in his mind all the time. He wished he could reach out and squeeze her. Traffic weaved along Regent Street in front of him, but time seemed to be standing still until he could see Ariella again.

"Me, neither." She didn't sound her usual self. Maybe she was in a room with other people, or rushing between appointments.

"I miss you."

"I miss you, too." For the first time she seemed to be speaking directly to him. "But I'm worried we're getting into something that's...too big."

He froze. "That's impossible." Then he realized that he was pushing things along the way he tended to, and he tried to rein himself back. "We're dating. That's a perfectly normal thing for two healthy adults to do, don't you think?"

"Well, yes, but...we're both in the public eye. And your family, I don't think they..."

"Don't you worry about what they think. Sometimes they need a little convincing but believe me, I have years of experience in that department."

"I don't want things to move too fast."

"I know. I've been telling myself to slow down. Sometimes I'm like a steam locomotive in motion, but I'm putting the brakes on, I promise you." He was running late for his meeting. "When I get to Washington, we'll do everything so slow it will be downright kinky." He glanced about, suddenly remembering he was in a public street.

She chuckled, but again, it wasn't her usual enthusiastic laugh. She must be getting cold feet now that they were apart. Which only made him more impatient to get there and warm them up for her.

"I've got a board meeting for UNICEF, so I have to go, but I'll talk to you soon," he said after a pause.

"Great. Thanks for calling." She sounded a bit like she couldn't wait to hang up. He was tempted to call her on it, then reminded himself not to be pushy.

"You're more than welcome." Telling her he loved her would be waaaay too much pressure, even if he was convinced it might be true. That could wait for a more intimate moment, preferably one where no one but Ariella was in earshot.

Ariella hung up the phone with her gut churning. In the last three days since Scarlet had planted the idea in her mind, she'd become more and more convinced that she was pregnant. She hadn't paid much attention to her menstrual cycle before, but based on the last period she could remember, she was due for another one, and it wasn't showing up.

Talking to Simon and trying to pretend everything was normal was agony. She could barely get words out of her mouth, let alone make polite conversation. How would his snooty family feel about the exciting surprise of an unplanned pregnancy? She'd bet that wouldn't go over too well.

If she was pregnant, of course. There was no way to be sure until she took a test. Scarlet had brought one over for her yesterday and told her to take it whenever she felt ready. It sat on the shelf in the bathroom, in its unopened white-and-pink box, mocking her.

Was she too chicken to find out the truth? Possibly. If she confirmed a pregnancy, she'd have to deal with how to tell people. Scarlet, for a start. She had enough money saved to take some time off work, but you didn't run a small business with someone then announce that you'd need a year of maternity leave. Then there was Simon....

She walked slowly into the bathroom and looked at the test. Picked up the box and read the directions. It sounded easy. Maybe she wasn't pregnant? Maybe the nausea was just from stress and exhaustion as she'd first suspected. Or maybe she'd eaten something funny.

Her nipples had become very sensitive, but that could happen when she was expecting her period. Same with the sudden swings of emotion that made her weep over television coverage of the fund drive at a local dog shelter. She could simply be losing her mind. People had cracked under less extreme circumstances than she'd found herself in lately.

Her stomach contracted as she picked up the box and ripped it open. She was a big girl and could handle the consequence of her choices. She'd willingly had sex with Simon, and sex could lead to pregnancy. Everyone knew that.

But for some reason it hadn't crossed her mind even once during those steamy nights in Simon's bed. In his castle.

Go on. Do it.

She picked up the stick and followed the directions, waiting the exact amount of time listed while watching the long hand of her watch. If she were pregnant, a line would appear. If she weren't the little circle would remain blank. She'd never wanted to see a blank space so much in her life. Her eyes started to play tricks on her during the agonizing wait, so she hid the stick under a tissue while the time was passing. When she reached the full five minutes she held her breath and lifted the tissue....

To see a thick pink line bisecting the white circle.

"Oh." She said the word aloud, and startled herself. Then she ran from the room as if she could run away from the whole situation. Which, of course, followed her. Apparently—and she still couldn't believe it—there was a baby growing inside her belly, right now. She glanced down at the waistband of her jeans. Her snug T-shirt sat against a totally flat stomach. Though of course at this stage the baby probably wasn't larger than her pinkie nail.

Suddenly she felt dizzy and plunged for the sofa. How could it all happen this fast? She'd slept with Simon for the first time less than two weeks ago and now her entire life was about to change forever. It didn't make sense.

She jumped out of her skin when the phone rang. A quick glance at the number revealed that it was Francesca. Normally she shared everything with her. She'd even taken her mother's very private letter to show Francesca when it had first arrived and she needed to share it with someone. But her friend was now madly in love with the head of the most powerful television in network in the country, and this was quite possibly the scoop of the century. What if Francesca tried to convince her to announce it on air? After meeting her father for the first time in front of the entire country, it seemed anything was possible and her own privacy, even her feelings, were of little importance.

She let the call go to voicemail, as guilt trickled through her. More secrets and subterfuge. She wouldn't tell Simon until he got here. It wasn't the kind of news you should break over the phone and she'd see him in a few days. She'd have to tell Scarlet right away, especially since the nausea came and went in waves and she wasn't sure how useful she'd be on the floor at events if she might have to rush to the ladies' every few minutes.

And then there were the reporters. The TV special had reignited interest and she'd had a harrowing couple of days trying to smile and answer journalists' questions every time she left the house. The creepy bearded guy who practically camped on her block had been joined by a few other camera-laden competitors, all vying for a money shot of her doing something newsworthy, like having a bad hair day. Maybe she could sneak away and run off to Ireland? It had worked for her mom, though of course she'd had her baby before she left.

The similarity in their circumstances smacked Ariella across the face. On instinct she picked up the phone and dialed the number of her mother's D.C. hotel room. Ted Morrow had persuaded Ellie to stay in D.C. at least until the end of the month, so they could all have a chance to get to know each other again. Ellie's now-familiar soft voice answered.

"It's Ariella." A strange wave of relief rushed through her, which was crazy as she'd barely met Ellie, but already she knew in her gut she had someone to confide in. "Something really strange has happened. Can I talk to you in person?"

"Of course, dear. Would you like me to come to your house?" Ellie had grown increasingly confident at navigating her way around D.C. despite an entourage of reporters.

"I'll come to your hotel if that's okay. I'll be there in twenty minutes."

Ellie glowed with warmth as she opened the door, and Ariella felt oddly relaxed in her presence despite her dramatic news. This one person would know exactly how she felt.

Ellie ushered Ariella into the large suite that ANS had reserved for her, and they sat on the sofa. "What's going on? You look white as a sheet."

"I'm pregnant."

Ellie drew in a breath. "Oh, no."

Ariella's throat closed. This was not exactly the comforting response she'd been hoping for. Though she had to admit it was her own initial reaction. "It's okay. I'm perfectly healthy and I'm in a pretty okay financial situation to have a baby." Now she was trying to soothe her mother, not the other way around. The irony of the situation made her want to laugh.

"Do you love him?" Ellie's question shocked her.

"I don't know. We've only been seeing each other a few weeks. It's Simon, who you met in London."

"Oh, dear." Ellie's face crumpled.

Ariella put a hand on her arm. "What's the matter?"

"I feel like history's repeating itself. Why couldn't you be pregnant by a nice ordinary man who could marry you and live a comfortable ordinary life?"

"Simon's surprisingly ordinary for a prince." She tried to smile. "Okay, maybe not ordinary but he's very warm and down to earth."

"But his family. Those royals are absolutely bound by tradition. That's why Prince Charles couldn't marry Camilla in the first place like he should have."

"He's married to her now, isn't he?"

"Yes, but." She sighed. "So much sadness happened in the meantime. I'm still not sure they're ready to welcome an American into the family."

"Me, either, to be quite honest." She lifted her brows. "I socialized with them at a polo match last weekend and I felt like any of them would have happily driven me to the airport right then and there."

Ellie stroked her hand and looked softly into her eyes. "So they're not going to be too happy about you having his baby."

Ariella's breathing was steadily becoming shallower. She stopped and drew in a deep draught of air. She certainly didn't need her baby to be deprived of oxygen at this crucial stage in his or her development.

She laughed.

"What?" Ellie's eyes widened. She was probably wondering if Ariella had lost her mind.

"I was thinking about my baby. I wonder if it will be a boy or a girl."

Ellie's eyes brightened. "I always knew I was having a

girl. I dreamed of little girl dresses and dolls and all kinds of frilly pink things over and over again."

"And you were right." Though Ellie had never had a chance to enjoy dressing her daughter in fluffy dresses or buying her Barbie dolls with extravagant wardrobes.

Ellie's blue eyes suddenly shone with tears. "You won't give the baby up, will you?"

"Not a chance of it. I'm lucky that I've had a good career for a few years now and I have some savings. I can work right through the pregnancy, and probably hire a nanny soon afterward and work from home a lot. It's very doable." She was trying to convince herself as much as her mother.

Ellie smiled through her sudden tears. "You're much more confident and capable than I was. That's a blessing." Then her face grew serious. "Have you told Simon yet?"

Ariella shook her head. "I haven't told anyone yet. You're the first."

Ellie gasped, and suddenly their arms were around each other. "That's a great honor."

"An honor?" Ariella buried her face in her mother's soft hair. "You were the first person I thought of when I needed to tell someone. I can't even begin to tell you how happy I am to have you back in my life."

"Back in your life?" Ellie pulled back a little. "They took you from me as soon as you were born. They never even let me see you." Her eyes still glittered with tears. "They said it was for the best, but even then I knew they were wrong."

"You took care of me for the nine months that I was growing inside you. During that time we formed a bond that could never be broken. Not really."

Ellie breathed in slowly. "I thought about you every day for all of those twenty-eight years."

"See? In a strange way we were always connected, and you came back into my life just when I need you the most."

Her chest heaved as she held her mother tight. It was going to be okay. But first she had to tell Simon.

Simon couldn't stop whistling. It was midmorning and he'd been floating on air ever since he got off the plane in D.C. the previous evening. He had some urgent business to attend to and now Ariella was on the top of his agenda. She had invited him to her apartment, and he took that as a very promising sign. She'd been cool on the phone lately—when he could even reach her. Suddenly she wanted to see him, and as soon as possible. Apparently meeting his family hadn't scared her off as much as he thought.

The sweet and gracious way Ariella had handled his large and intimidating family further confirmed that she was the perfect woman for him. He'd trusted his instincts when he first saw her across that crowded ballroom, and so far they had been dead-on. She was *the one they talked about,* who came along once in a lifetime. He felt it deep in his gut. Or was it his heart? His whole body sang with emotions that he'd only read about in books before. He didn't plan to waste his once-in-a-lifetime chance at happiness. Now all he had to do was convince Ariella herself that they were meant to be together.

His jacket pocket bulged slightly with the tooled leather box delivered just before he left. Nestled in white satin was the loveliest ring he'd ever seen. He had to admit he hadn't paid too much attention to engagement rings before, but once he'd decided to propose, he did extensive research among his female friends.

He made up the elaborate excuse that he might be interested in helping promote the sale of African diamonds to help his charity, and he wanted some feedback on designs. He wasn't entirely sure they fell for it, but he got a lot of great information anyway: not too bulky; flashy is fine but not for everyone; steer clear of color unless you know it's one she adores. There was a long list he'd carried in his mind to the jeweler.

With the help—and promised discretion—of the queen's appointed jeweler, he'd chosen a stunning, very pale pink diamond with a provenance dating back to the maharajas of India. Together they'd designed a setting of tiny diamonds and, since she always wore silver jewelry rather than gold, a simple platinum setting. The jeweler's workshop had put the ring together almost overnight and he was convinced that it was the perfect ring for Ariella and that she'd adore it.

If she'd agree to be his wife.

He wasn't nearly so confident about that part. Ariella wasn't the type to accept just because he was a prince—which was one of the many reasons he loved her. He'd missed her so much since she'd returned to D.C. Playing it cool and not bombarding her with phone calls had been torture. He ached to see her again. To put his arms around her and kiss her as if the world was ending. He'd never felt even a fraction of this passion for a woman before. He knew his intense feelings meant that Ariella was the only woman for him.

The car pulled up in front of Ariella's tidy Georgetown house and he got out. A sizzle of anticipation ran through him as he saw the lights were on in her first-floor apartment. He intended to build up to the proposal. He'd woo her and get the mood romantic before he plunged in with the question of a lifetime.

She'd had cold feet the last time he saw her. He'd be sure to warm them up and reassure her that even the most intractable members of his family would come to their senses. The monarchy hadn't survived for so many years by being inflexible. No one was going to force him out of the country or make him give up his position in the royal family because of whom he loved. Together they'd slowly but surely win them over and make them realize that an infusion of fresh energy from across the Atlantic was just what they all needed. He'd kiss her until she was weak in the knees and maybe even make love to her until they lay spent in each other's arms—then he'd ask her.

His driver handed him the big bunch of pink roses he'd ordered. No doubt any nearby photographers would have a field day, but soon enough they'd all be scribbling the story of their engagement so it didn't really matter what they were speculating. In fact he welcomed them heralding the happy news that he and Ariella would spend the rest of their lives together.

He climbed the steps to her building with glowing anticipation and rang the bell a little too long. The first sight of her face after a two-week absence almost made him shout. She was unquestionably the most beautiful woman on earth, with her long dark hair tumbling about her shoulders and those big, soulful eyes fixed right on him.

When he flung his arms around her, still clutching the roses in one fist, he noticed she seemed a little stiff. "It's so good to see you again."

"Yes." Her answer seemed a little less than enthusiastic.

"I brought you some roses. I thought they might remind you of our English rose gardens."

She smiled. "Your country does have the most beautiful gardens in the world."

They were talking about gardens? He was dying to propose to her and get it over with, as the suspense was killing him. But something wasn't right. She looked pale. "How are you?"

She ushered him into the apartment. Wordless, her shoulders slightly hunched, she seemed very tense. "Please sit down."

He frowned. "I feel like you're about to drop some kind of bombshell. I'm not going to fall down like an old granny."

That gentle smile hovered about her mouth again. "I'm sure you wouldn't, but just in case."

"You do have a bombshell to drop?" His mind ran through the possibilities. Her father had asked her to go live in the White House and forbidden her from dating? She couldn't take the press anymore and had decided to go underground? Aliens had invaded and...

"I'm pregnant."

Ten

Ariella watched as Simon's amused expression faded to a blank. "What?"

"I know it's hard to believe, but I took a test and it was positive."

"We didn't have sex until…two weeks ago. Is that even long enough to know you're pregnant?" He stared at her in astonishment and confusion.

"Apparently so." Did he think she was pregnant by someone else and had decided to pin the blame on him in the hope of a big royal payoff? Indignation stirred in her chest. "Don't worry, I don't expect anything of you. I know the timing is terrible and it's the last thing we expected, but it's happened and I intend to raise the baby. I'm financially well off, so you don't need to worry that I'll ask for money."

"That's the last thing I'm worried about." He blinked, staring at her. "We used a condom."

Apparently he still didn't believe it was possible. "It could have leaked or broken or who knows what. They're not very effective. At this point it doesn't really matter. I'm definitely pregnant." She'd done another two tests. Different brands, same result.

"Wow." He climbed to his feet and came toward her. "Congratulations."

She laughed. "You don't have to congratulate me. We both know it was a big accident."

"Still, it feels like an occasion for celebration." He reached into his pocket and pulled something out.

Oh, no. A leather box. Her heart seized as she realized what he was about to do. Could she refuse a proposal before it was even made?

He got onto one knee, confirming her worst fears. "Ariella." His eyes were smiling, which seemed downright strange under the circumstances. "Will you marry me?"

She bit her lip, hoping to hold back sudden and pointless tears that threatened. She couldn't seem to get words out so she simply shook her head.

He frowned. "You won't? Why not?" His sudden indignation would be funny if she didn't feel so sad. This must be one more sign that they weren't meant to be. It didn't seem to cross his mind that she might have her own opinion and it could be different from his. Probably being a prince trained you to think that everyone was on your side and wholeheartedly agreed with you.

"It would never work." Her voice came out broken and raspy. "Your family would be horrified. They made it abundantly clear that they intend for you to marry someone else."

"They'll get over it." His gaze turned steely.

"No they won't. I've seen enough press coverage of your family to know they're very set in their ways. I don't want to be the outcast and black sheep for the rest of my life. Nor do I want the queen to take away your beloved estate or kick you out of your charity. You've built a life that you love and marrying me would ruin everything, so it's not going to happen."

The truth of her words echoed inside her. She truly didn't want those things to happen, for Simon or for herself.

"Why are you talking about everyone else? I want to marry *you*. Now that you're pregnant there's all the more reason to do it, and soon." He was still on one knee in front of the sofa where she sat. The whole situation seemed ridiculous. Especially as his words were undermining her conviction. Could they really just forget about his family and the reporters and the British public and her presidential father and do what they wanted?

No. They couldn't. Life didn't work like that.

He smacked his head suddenly. "In all this talk about a baby and my family, I think I forgot to mention the most important thing." He took hold of her hands. "Which is that I love you. I never knew what love was until I met you. Every minute I'm not with you I'm wishing I was. When I am with you I don't want to leave. I want to spend the rest of my life with you, Ariella. I need to spend the rest of my life with you. I love you."

Her chest tightened as he tried to put such strong feelings into mere words and those words rocked her to her core. What hurt most was that she felt the same way. Since Simon came into her life nothing else seemed very important any more. But the truth was that the world was still out there, and hoping and dreaming wasn't enough to build a life on. "Love doesn't last forever. It's a brief flash of excitement and enthusiasm that brings people together. The rest of it is work. I know my parents—the ones who raised me—worked hard to keep their marriage strong in the face of all the tiresome details of life. My birth parents obviously couldn't manage to do that."

She frowned and stood up. She needed to put a little distance between them so she could think straight. It was hard to even speak with his big, masculine presence looming over her and his rich scent tugging at her senses. "There's a fierce attraction between us." She walked away from him, with her back turned. It was easier to speak when she couldn't see his bold, chiseled features. "It takes hold of me and makes me forget about everything else when I'm with you." Then she turned to face him. He'd risen to his feet and seemed to fill the space of her living room. "But that will fade. You were born with your whole life planned out for you. You're already married to your family and your country. You can't abandon them to marry someone who they disapprove of and who will never fit in. It was disastrous for your ancestor Edward VII and it would be disastrous for you." Tears fell down her cheeks and she couldn't stop them. "It's better for all of us if we break it off right now."

Simon exhaled loudly, like he'd been bottling up words and emotions inside him. "You're right. I am married to my family and my country and I'd never give them up. I know it's a lot to ask of you to embrace those things and love them as I do, but I am asking that." He strode toward her and took her hands. She wanted to pull away and attempt to keep some distance and objectivity, but he held them softly, but firmly, and she wasn't able to break free. "Marry me, Ariella."

Her gut churned. Her nerve endings cracked with an effusive "Yes!" but her brain issued loud warning signals. "I don't want you to marry me out of a sense of duty, because I'm pregnant."

"I'm not asking you because you're pregnant." Amusement sparkled in his eyes. "I bought the ring before I knew about the pregnancy. I was planning to build up to my proposal and do some romantic beating about the bush before springing the big question on you, but your surprise announcement made that seem superfluous. I want to marry you, pregnant or not, Ariella Winthrop, and I'm not leaving until you say yes."

"You're planning to bully me into it?" She stiffened. Sometimes his boundless enthusiasm and confidence were appealing, and sometimes it was a little scary.

He softened his grip on her hand. "No." He spoke softly. "There I go, running roughshod again. I apologize. I truly wish to embrace a lifetime of your moderating influence on my overly ebullient personality."

He said it so sweetly that her heart squeezed. She did believe him. "I don't think anyone could squash your bubble too much." She chuckled. It touched her deeply that he'd congratulated her on carrying their baby. For the first time it occurred to her that maybe he wanted to be congratulated, too. "I'm sure you're going to be a wonderful father, even if we aren't married."

"That's true, I will be." He hesitated. She could almost feel him bursting to insist that they would be married, but holding himself back, trying not to offend her.

"You're a wonderful man, Simon. I'm totally overwhelmed right now with all the publicity about my father, and my mother and the TV special. It's almost ridiculous that I met you at the same time. It would be crazy to leap into an unplanned marriage without thinking long and hard about the consequences. Perhaps at some time in the future we can discuss it again and…who knows?" She trailed off, running out of words. Part of her wanted to run screaming away from Simon and everyone else and hide from reality.

The rest of her wanted to rush to him and throw herself into his strong arms and let him take care of her the way he so confidently intended to.

"I'm not leaving, if that's what you were trying to hint at." That familiar gleam of humor shone in his eyes. "Me and my ring will sit quietly in the corner until you come to your senses."

"As if that was possible." She couldn't help smiling. "I doubt you could sit quietly anywhere for more than about three minutes."

"Three whole minutes?" He rubbed his mouth thoughtfully. "You could be right. In the meantime, you should be eating for two so I think we need to go out for a hearty lunch."

She laughed. "You're impossible."

"I'm all about making the impossible possible. They said I couldn't raft up the Zambezi or ascend the north face of Mount Everest. They laughed when I talked about internet access in the Masai Mara. I proved them all wrong. If they say an American isn't a suitable bride for a British prince, then I'll spend the rest of my life proving them wrong about that as well, and have fun doing it."

His passion made her heart swell. But he was talking as if she was just another mountain to climb. "You do make a compelling case for your own convictions, but you don't seem to be listening to me."

"How?" His look of confusion made her want to laugh again.

"I said I'm not ready to commit to anything right now. I've had the biggest shocks of my life these past few months and I barely know which end is up."

His expression grew serious. "Point taken. I'll stop pushing my agenda. Now, how about that lunch?"

"That, I'll agree to." And she let him take her hand and

help her up from the sofa. His skin sparked arousal as it touched hers. She hid a silent sigh from him. Why did her life have to be so complicated?

She frowned when Simon's driver pulled up in front of Talesin. The navy awnings created cool shade in front of one of the most exclusive restaurants in D.C. Unease trickled through her. "Are we eating here?"

"Their steaks are world famous. You need iron rich foods."

"Why does everything you say make me laugh?" Then she glanced about. "Did you know it's the president's favorite restaurant?" What if they ran into him here? She hadn't seen him since the dinner they'd shared after the taping, though he'd sent her several warm emails and they were talking about a weekend together at Camp David, the presidential retreat in Maryland.

"Is it really?" He helped her out of the car. "I've been meaning to eat here for ages."

"It's probably hard to get a table without a reservation." She remembered one tense afternoon of scrambling to book a room for an important client's dinner there.

He leaned in and whispered. "Not when you're a prince."

She chuckled. "Oh yes, I forgot about that."

"Welcome to Talesin, Your Highness." The imperious maître d' nodded and gestured warmly. "A table for two?"

"Thank you." Simon shot her an amused smile. "See what I mean?"

She arched a brow. "Don't get cocky."

"I'll do my best."

The maître d' led them through the main dining room and out onto a shady patio with a view over the river.

"Ariella." The now-familiar voice made her turn to find the president standing behind her.

"Oh, hello. How nice to see you." She felt a surge of panic. "Simon, this is President Morrow, my...my father. And this is Simon Worth." Should she have used the word *prince?* She hadn't researched the correct way to address him. Luckily, being Simon, he wasn't likely to mind.

Ted Morrow smiled at Simon. "Would you both do me the honor of joining me in my private dining room?"

"I... We..." She glanced at Simon.

"I suspect we'd be delighted." Simon glanced at her, a question in his eyes.

"Yes. Yes, we would." She swallowed. Simon *and* her father, the president? An odd nagging feeling suggested that this was a little too much of a coincidence.

They followed the president back inside the building through a doorway that led into a bright room with tall windows and elegant furnishings that were a mix of eighteenth century and modernist Italian design. The professional side of her brain wondered if it could be rented out for special occasions, while the personal side of her brain wondered what the heck they would talk about.

The restaurant's most trusted staff waited on them hand and foot, recommending dishes and bringing bottles of wine. She learned that the president had a policy of only drinking American wine, and it made her like him more, considering the other options that must be available in the White House cellars alone. She managed to refuse the wine by saying she didn't drink during the day, but the moment did serve as a reminder that there was a fourth person in the room—her unborn child. And Simon's unborn child. Ted Morrow's grandchild. Her whole life seemed like an elaborate spider web that kept expanding to encompass more of the people around her.

Simon kept the conversation going with easy banter about traveling and the parts of America that he hadn't

seen yet but wanted to. Ariella was constantly amazed by
how naturally he could talk to anyone. No doubt it was
the chief requirement of his role in the royal family and
if she were his boss she'd give him a raise. She'd actually
started to relax by the time they finished their delicious
appetizers and three gleaming steaks arrived, accompanied by mounds of fresh vegetables. Even her shaky pregnancy appetite felt revived by the sight.

"This is turning out to be the most extraordinary year of
my life by quite a long way," said her father, after a pause
while they all chewed their meals. "I thought last year with
the run-up to the elections would be hard to beat, but it has
been, and hands down. And the best thing of all has been
learning that I have a beautiful daughter."

He gazed at her with such warmth that she felt emotion
swell in her chest. "It does seem like a wonderful thing
now that the media frenzy is dying down and we can finally get to know each other."

"And if the press hadn't found you, I might never have
seen Ellie again. I had no idea she'd moved to Ireland, and
if it wasn't for this whole brouhaha, she might never have
come back to the States."

"I think she's considering moving back here for good."

He smiled. "I know. And she told me that the two of
you are becoming close."

Ariella blanched. Ellie hadn't told him the secret of her
pregnancy, had she? No. She knew her mother would never
do that. She'd kept her own secrets for so long she could
be trusted. Suddenly she hated herself for the subterfuge,
but she knew it was too soon to tell anyone. At least until
she and Simon had a few things figured out. "We are just
getting to know each other but already she's becoming one
of my favorite people on earth. I'm trying to convince her

to stay in the D.C. area for now, so she we can all try to make up for lost time."

The president paused and took a sip of his white wine. "Making up for lost time is something that's been on my mind a lot." He put down his glass. "I loved your mother with all my heart, Ariella. I would never have let her go. She just didn't know that at the time. I was being a typical man and bottling up my emotions, trying to act cool."

Ariella glanced at Simon. He wouldn't do that. He was the last person to keep anything bottled up. It was one of the things she liked best about him. There were no guessing games with him. "Have you told her how you felt?"

"You'd better believe it." He smiled wistfully. "It was the first thing I did when we had a few moments alone. I apologized with all my heart for the fact that she felt so alone back then, and was forced into a choice she later regretted." He frowned and looked down at his glass, then looked up at her again. "I still love her, you know."

Ariella's eyes widened. She was mostly astonished that he was saying all this in front of Simon, who—as far as she knew—he'd only just met. "Have you told her that?"

"I most certainly have. I think she was astonished rather than delighted." He smiled. "We've been spending a lot of time together."

"That's wonderful." Her heart filled with gladness at the thought that her mother and father could rekindle their love after all these years. What a shame that they'd had twenty-eight years apart. "Is she the reason you never married?"

He nodded. "I tried to talk myself into loving other women, but when it came to the crunch none of them compared to my Ellie and I could never marry a woman I didn't feel wholeheartedly committed to."

"That's my opinion entirely." Simon chimed in. "I think

that choosing your mate is the most important decision you'll make in your entire life."

"Quite right, son. It's not a decision to be taken lightly." Her father looked at Ariella with a twinkle of amusement in his eye. "Which is what I told this young man when he demanded an audience with me to request your hand in marriage."

Ariella's jaw dropped. So they had met before. And this meeting was preplanned. Simon had been sneaking around behind her back. Indignation snapped inside her and she turned to Simon. "What were you thinking?"

"In our country, it's traditional to ask the father of an intended bride if he objects to the marriage. Given the sensitive circumstances of your father's position, I felt I should listen to any objections he might have."

The president laughed. "And you'd better believe I had them." He reached out and took Ariella's hand across the table. "I told him he'd better direct any important questions of that nature to the lady intended, not to me. Since I've been in your life for less than two weeks I don't feel I should have any say whatsoever over who you marry or don't marry." He squeezed her hand. "He's got a lot of chutzpah, I'll say that for him."

Simon smiled. "He told me to stop beating about the bush and go ask you. Which I did. So now I've asked both of you."

"Oh." Ariella's heart clenched as she realized the president was waiting to hear what answer she'd given Simon.

Ted Morrow looked at Simon. "Could I have a few moments alone with my daughter?"

"Certainly, sir." Simon rose from the table. He'd already finished his meal while they were talking. He smiled at Ariella. "I'll be on the balcony."

The door closed behind him, and Ariella frowned.

Should she tell her father she'd said no to him? Should she confess the truth about her pregnancy? It was all too much and her tired and emotional brain couldn't handle it.

"Well, isn't that something. I'm a guy from a small town in Montana and I just told a member of the British royal family to leave the room."

"And I'm a girl from a small town in Montana and I'm having lunch with the president of the United States."

He nodded and smiled, and his blue eyes sparkled. "I guess it proves we're all just people once you look past the pomp and circumstance." His expression grew serious. "Do you love him?"

She twisted her water glass in her hands. "I think I might."

"You don't sound too sure."

"We really…click. I guess that's the best way to put it. I have so much fun with him and I always feel relaxed in his company, which is really weird under the circumstances." She did not feel the need to mention the intense sexual attraction. "I like him very, very much. But the fact is, we only met a few weeks ago and they've been some of the craziest weeks of my life and I don't know what to think about anything anymore."

"Well, I'll give you a piece of advice that might be worth exactly what it'll cost you." He inhaled. "Don't wait around for the 'right time' when everything falls into place and feels perfect." He fixed his eyes on hers. "In my experience, which is considerable at this point, that time never comes."

She nodded slowly.

He leaned forward and took her hand again. His hands were big and warm and soft. "If you love this young man— and from what I see in your eyes, I think you do—don't blow the love of a lifetime because it doesn't fit your calendar. I went off to college naively assuming that Ellie and the whole life I had planned out with her would still be there when I got back." He shook his head. "Instead I got back to find that she'd left town and no one knew where she was. My entire future evaporated overnight just like that. Sure, I got the college education I wanted and then started the big career I'd always hoped for, but the soul of my life, the really important part, had got on a train one dark night and skipped town without me."

His eyes were now soft with tears. "I missed Ellie so much those first few years. Then I suppose I grew numb, or grew used to the dull ache of living without her. When I think of the memories we could have shared it infuriates me that I missed out on all that through my own stupid fault. I should have married her and taken her to college with me instead of stupidly insisting on waiting until the time was right. Yes, times would have been hard and we would have had to scrimp a bit, but we would have had each other, and that's the important thing. If you love this young man, then don't miss out on the opportunity of a lifetime." He squeezed her hand softly. "I don't want you to live to regret it like I did."

Ariella's chest was so tight she could hardly breathe. "I'm having his baby. I just found out this week." She had no idea how he'd react, but she knew she couldn't keep it to herself any longer.

His mouth made a funny movement, like he wanted to say something but was too choked up.

"I told Ellie a couple of days ago and she urged me not to hide it from Simon. I took her advice today. It almost feels like history is repeating itself, doesn't it?"

Her father shook his head. "No, Ariella. History isn't repeating itself because you and Simon are braver and stronger and maybe a little more bullheaded than Ellie and I were." He laughed. "Simon's quite a young man. I don't think you could go far wrong with him in your life."

She smiled. "I know. He's pretty amazing." Then she swallowed. "But then there's the rest of his family. And we'd have to live in England."

He shrugged. "England's just across the pond. A short plane flight. Simon told me he'd already introduced you to the whole family."

"Did he also tell you they were all trying to pack my bags and get me on the next flight back to D.C.?"

Ted frowned. "He didn't mention that part."

"He glosses over it like it's no big deal. He thinks they'd all come around. I'm not so sure."

"Well, I'm inclined to agree with Simon since he knows them better than you. And it probably doesn't hurt that your father is commander in chief of their largest ally." He winked.

She smiled, but then her stomach lurched as she remembered his uncle's cruel threats. "His uncle Derek warned me Simon could lose his estate and his charity if he doesn't follow the party line."

Ted laughed. "I wouldn't worry about that old coot. He has bigger problems to worry about than an American in the family. The CIA chief just informed me that he was involved in brokering an arms deal with a South American dictatorship."

"What?"

"Yup. I don't think he'll be hassling you too much after that scandal explodes in the press."

Ariella stared, speechless.

"Greed. That's what made him do it. Apparently he doesn't have the income of the rest of the bunch but he's trying to live like an emperor. The insecure ones are usually the meanest. That's what I've noticed."

"You've made me feel a lot better." She did feel like a weight had lifted. The queen had been stern, but not actually hostile. Derek was the only one who'd told her to get lost in no uncertain terms. And now he was going to be public enemy number one himself. She couldn't help smiling. "I think I can handle Uncle Derek."

"I suspect you can handle a lot more than one narrow-minded Limey, though I suppose I should stop calling them that if there's going to be one in the family. Shall we invite him back in for dessert?"

"Yes." She grinned. "Let's do that."

Ted opened the door to the balcony and called Simon back. He arrived with another woman on his arm—her mother.

Ariella gasped. "What kind of conspiracy is this?"

Ted Morrow kissed Ellie on both cheeks. "I asked Ellie to join us for coffee because I can't stand to be away from her for more than a few minutes."

Her mother was transformed from the pale and harried woman she'd first met in London. A soft jade-green dress hugged her girlish figure, and the light of passion shone in her green eyes. "And I feel the same way. It's embarrassing for someone my age." She blushed sweetly. Ted Morrow took her hand and led her to a chair right next to his. He seemed besotted with her. Ariella watched in astonishment.

"Did your father tell you how annoyed he was with me seeking his opinion before I asked for yours?" Simon slid his arm around her waist.

"Not really." Heat rose through her as she felt his body through their clothing. "He told me not to blow what might be the love of a lifetime."

"Excellent advice," Simon murmured. His breath stirred

the tiny hairs on her neck and sent shivers of desire running through her. "I hope you listened."

"I did. Did someone mention dessert?" She pulled away from him and reached for the hand-written dessert menu. It felt embarrassing to be romantic in front of her parents.

Though come to think of it, they were getting rather romantic themselves. Ted held Ellie's hands in his and they gazed into each other's eyes as if the rest of the world didn't exist.

"No, I don't believe anyone did mention dessert, but we don't want you starving, so let's get the trolley brought in." He smiled and looked at her belly.

Ariella's eyes widened. Then she realized that everyone in the room knew her secret, so it wasn't really a secret. "I am rather starving right now. Maybe there is something to the old wives' tales."

"Did you tell your dad whether you intend to marry me?"

"I did not." Ariella scanned the menu. Then she looked up, trying to keep her expression neutral while her heart swelled with emotion. "Though I'm pretty close to making up my mind."

"Torture is banned by the United Nations." Simon's imploring gaze made her want to laugh and touched her deeply at the same time.

She glanced at her parents, then tugged her eyes away quickly as they kissed each other softly on the lips, eyes closed in a rapture of togetherness. They'd lost twenty-eight years of happiness together, because they weren't ready to commit all those years ago. Because the timing wasn't right, they almost lost everything.

She drew in a long, slow breath, as conviction filled her heart, mind and lungs. "Yes, Simon Worth, I will marry you."

Epilogue

Three months later

Ariella woke up to the familiar sight of Simon's handsome face next to hers on the pillow in their shared bedroom in Whist Castle. He had scoffed at the notion that they should pretend to live apart until the wedding, and somehow the British public thought his honesty and disdain for tired etiquette was part of his charm. She'd been sharing his bed for a solid month now, since she'd finally packed up her D.C. apartment and her life in the States.

They hadn't told anyone about the baby yet. Somehow it made sense to keep the secret until after the ceremony, so the wedding preparations had to be rushed. She still wasn't showing, at least not in a way she couldn't pass off as the aftereffects of a large meal.

Their bodies were pressed together almost from chin to ankle. Somehow she always wound up on his side of the bed in the morning. It would be embarrassing if he didn't clearly enjoy it so much.

"Morning, gorgeous." Simon's husky voice sent a shiver of awareness through her.

"Same to you." Helicopters buzzed outside the windows, sending adrenaline streaking through her veins. "Is it really our wedding day or is this just a long, fantastical dream?"

"I'm not sure." He smiled, still resting on the pillow. "What do you think?"

She pretended to pinch herself. "I'm lying in a luxurious bed in a castle and getting ready to marry a prince. Sounds like a dream to me."

Simon leaned forward and planted a soft kiss on her lips. "How does that feel?" he murmured.

"Mmm. That feels real." Passion and warmth swelled in her chest and she slid her arms around him under the covers. "Breathtakingly real. But wait. You're not supposed to see me on my wedding day!" She pulled back, suddenly panicked. What else would she do wrong today?

Simon pulled her closer again. "There are some traditions best left by the wayside." He nuzzled her neck, which made her smile. "I'm probably not supposed to make love to you on the morning of your wedding, but luckily I have a rebellious streak."

"We can't. Can we?" Arousal trickled through her like music. "We have to get ready." She said it more as a question than a statement.

"We'll be ready when we need to. You're not planning this one, thank goodness."

She'd turned the reins of the wedding over to Scarlet and her new partner, and they'd done a spectacular job pulling together what promised to be the wedding of the century in less than three months. "It's hard for me not to worry about the details, though. What if the caterer can't get through the crowds to deliver the food?"

"Someone else's problem." He kissed her lips again.

Relaxation soaked through her veins. "You're very good at distracting me." She kissed him back, letting herself sink into his arms. Nothing ruffled Simon's feathers, at least not for long. He was so confident and capable that it was hard to be anxious around him.

His hands roamed over her chest, sparking trails of excitement, and she could feel his arousal thickening against her. "Uh-oh, are we really going to do this?"

"It's starting to look inevitable," he rasped.

"But we have a thousand guests coming. And our friends staying here at Whist are probably downstairs having breakfast right now."

"We'll see them soon enough."

He squeezed her backside, and she responded by pinching his gently, with a giggle. "You're a bad influence."

"I love you." He said it simply, and the truth of it punched her in the gut.

"I love you, too. I think I knew it from the first night I met you, which doesn't make any sense at all."

"Love isn't supposed to make sense." He smiled, looking into her eyes. "That's why it's so wonderful."

Her heart filled to overflowing. "If you weren't the most persistent and persuasive man on earth, I might never have dared to let myself fall in love with you."

"Tenacity has its virtues." He nibbled her earlobe, which made her gasp, then laugh. "Thank goodness I had your parents to help convince you to take a chance on me."

"And now they're getting married, too." She grinned, thinking about the rapturous looks Ellie and Ted always had on their faces when they were together. A president had never married while in office before, and the event,

planned for a month's time, was to be the American equiv-
alent of a royal wedding. She couldn't wait to be there and
watch them finally pledge their vows to each other after
so many wasted years.

A long steamy kiss sent blood racing through her veins
and arousal trickling to her fingers and toes, and other
parts.

"Come here, madam." Simon climbed over her, and slid
his fingers over her hot, ready sex.

"Yes, Your Majesty." Her back was already arching,
ready to receive him. Her fingers pushed into his thick hair
as he entered her, making her gasp with pleasure. Wedding
anxieties shriveled and floated up to the sky like embers
as they moved together under the soft covers, reveling in
each others' bodies. The sweet relief of their climax left
them relaxed and ready to face anything.

"I can't believe we get to do this whenever we want for
the rest of our lives," breathed Simon heavily, as they lay
spent, with their heads on the same pillow again. "I'm the
luckiest man on earth."

"We are lucky, aren't we? This year started out with all
the shocking press revelations that I was the president's
daughter, and spiraled out of control from there. I seem to
have landed in a very soft place."

"Are you trying to say my body is soft?" He poked her
gently.

"No one could accuse you of being soft. Well, except
your heart."

"Okay, that I'll admit to. I'm just glad I found the right
woman to give it to."

A knock on the door made them jump. "Sorry to dis-
turb you," called a tentative voice. "But the dressmaker
requires your presence for an urgent fitting."

"Oh, dear," she whispered. "I think we'd better get up."

"If we must." He nuzzled her face. "The best part is that tonight we'll be right back here together."

The ceremony took place in the estate's thirteenth-century chapel. Since the chapel was only large enough to seat immediate family, Simon and Ariella's vows were simultaneously broadcast to the gathered crowd of guests on the estate lawns and an eager viewing audience on both sides of the Atlantic. When they were declared man and wife, the newest royal couple joined the guests outside on a glorious summer's day.

Scarlet had planned and executed the wedding with skill and courage worthy of a major battle. Tables and chairs were arrayed across the rolling lawns, each decorated with fresh flowers, and, in a green touch that Ariella especially loved, an assortment of beautiful tableware and linens borrowed and bought from collections, antique stores and markets, for a spontaneous yet luxurious, country garden picnic feel.

Given the estate's large size and the volume of the crowd, they decided that one band wasn't enough, so in addition to the traditional orchestra, they had an African ensemble, a bluegrass band and a group of singers from the Westminster Abbey boys' choir, who wandered the grounds serenading guests as they mingled on the lawns and nibbled delicacies at their tables.

Ariella saw Scarlet rearranging a Meissen jug full of roses, and hurried over to her. "Hey, lady, you're not supposed to be working today. You're here as a guest, remember?"

Scarlet spun around, red curls flying. "Old habits die hard, though the team we hired is doing a great job. I'm surprised you're not rearranging the glasses yourself."

"It's taking a lot of discipline." She grinned. "But I'm working hard to retrain myself."

"I'm still ticked off that you're leaving DC Affairs. You could have been our British office."

"I'll have my hands full arranging events for the palace."

"Lucky you." Scarlet sighed. "The most magnificent venues in England at your fingertips. And the most sought-after guests as your family. How did the queen feel about Simon choosing you as his bride?"

"I was very nervous about it but weirdly enough she was lovely to me from the first moment Simon told her he'd proposed to me. She said she could see how perfect I was for him and she welcomed me into the family. Probably the biggest surprise of my life. And with her on my side everyone else welcomed me, too. Simon's brothers are so sweet—it's like having brothers of my own."

"How did you talk them into letting you plan their parties?"

"I could see they needed someone with an imagination to take over. They were still throwing the same parties that seemed fun during post-war rationing. I told them I can provide ten times the flair for half the money, so they're letting me go wild. British people really know how to party when they get a chance."

"So I've noticed." Scarlet glanced around with a grin.

"And some of the Americans are getting crazy, too. I saw you and Daniel dancing like demons to the bluegrass a while ago."

"Daniel's definitely mined my fun-loving streak. Before, I always enjoyed watching other people have fun at events. Now I'm realizing how great it is to be one of them." She glanced up. "Cara's just as bad as me. She's only supposed to be managing PR for the event, but look, she's trying to retie the bow on that table skirt even though she's so pregnant she can barely bend." They hurried over to her. "Drop that bow or we'll send you on enforced maternity leave."

Cara had recently left the White House press office after she fell in love with a network news reporter, and now worked with DC Affairs. She had that famous maternal glow already, her eyes shining and her chestnut hair glowing. "I have more than a month left before I'm due. You should indulge me now as I may not be capable of anything once I'm only getting two hours of sleep a night."

Cara's husband, Max, appeared, glass of champagne in hand. "Max, darling." Ariella kissed his cheek. "You need to rein your wife in. She's trying to do everything again."

"I've talked to her about that and she's still unstoppable. She should never have agreed to work with DC Affairs. You and Scarlet are a bad influence."

"It must be killing you that ANS is getting the scoop on the wedding." Ariella and Simon had decided that ANS should have exclusive coverage of the wedding as a reward for Liam skillfully orchestrating her reunion with her parents. Until recently Max had been the popular anchor of a rival TV network and still worked for them behind the scenes.

"I'm over it. It's a nice change to be able to enjoy a royal wedding instead of barking about it while standing on a street corner somewhere. I notice Liam's busy dancing with Francsesca. Isn't he supposed to be manning the scoop of the century?"

"Nope." Ariella crossed her arms. "None of my friends is allowed to work today, by royal command. Anyone caught working will be thrown into a dungeon."

Max glanced up at the ivy-covered walls of Whist Castle. "Hmm, that sounds like an interesting experience. Maybe I could do a live feed—"

"Oh, stop." Ariella laughed. "Have you seen my husband? We've only been married forty minutes and I've already lost him."

Scarlet nodded toward the area near the champagne bar. "He's locked in conversation with my husband. I think Simon's trying to convince Daniel to expand his network into Africa." Daniel owned a social networking site that had helped spread the word about the concert for World Connect. "I still can't believe you guys managed to get Pitbull, Beyoncé and Jay-Z and Eric Clapton all on the same stage, and only two weeks before your wedding, no less."

"Uh, hello, don't forget Mick Jagger and Aretha Franklin." Ariella still glowed with pleasure at how incredible a success the concert had been.

"Seriously, you guys are a force to be reckoned with."

"The concert was for an awesome cause so it was easy to get people excited." She smiled. "I'm going to Africa with Simon next month to raise awareness of his projects there."

"Look out, Africa." Max grinned. "There's no question that you and Simon are the most popular couple in the whole world. I didn't think his older brother's romance could be outshone but you've proved me wrong."

"At least they don't seem to hate me." Ariella shrugged. "I wasn't at all sure how the British people would react. I can truly say they've welcomed me with open arms. Not that they had much choice with Simon around." From where they stood she could see the queen in apparently intent conversation with her father.

"How could the British people not love you?" Lucy had strolled up with her husband Hayden and his curious toddler. She was a former reporter for ANS where she and Hayden had discovered that her own stepfather, then head of the network, had approved the illegal phone tapping that had revealed Ariella's parentage. Lucy became friends with Scarlet and Ariella after hiring DC Affairs to arrange her own wedding. "I know Liam takes full credit for reuniting you with your dad, and for getting Ted and Eleanor back together."

"All of our ears are burning." Ted Morrow walked up behind Ariella with Eleanor on his arm. He looked both statesmanlike and warm at the same time, and Ellie looked radiant in a stunning Narciso Rodriguez dress Ariella had helped her choose.

Liam was hot on his heels. "I'm shamelessly trying to negotiate exclusive coverage of your father and mother's wedding. A president hasn't married in office since 1915."

Ted Morrow beamed. "I told this nice young man that I'm far too busy enjoying my daughter's wedding to think about my own just yet." He turned and kissed Ellie softly on the cheek. "Though we freely admit that it will happen this year." A big fat rock sparkled on Ellie's slim hand. "We have a few other things to do first. After this shindig winds down we're heading to Ireland to visit the village where my beautiful Ellie was hidden away for so long."

"They'll be really happy to meet Ted." Ellie gazed at him adoringly. "After my husband died five years ago, people started pestering me to date again, and I never wanted to. I seem to have changed my mind."

"Thanks to my efforts, of course." Liam beamed. "Everyone told me you'd never come on air for the reunion, even Ariella. But I've never been one to take no for an answer. If I had I wouldn't have won my own bride." He squeezed Francesca, who grinned. She wore a stunning ruched dress that made her look like an Italian bombshell. "She would have told me the stars weren't aligned right, or something. Speaking of stars, here comes Prince Charming."

Simon walked over and waved. "You all know my cousin Colin, right?" He gestured to the tall blond man walking next to him. "He's the diplomat who negotiated the privacy rights treaty that brought me to the U.S. in the first place."

"Where I found my wife, Rowena." Colin squeezed the pretty woman at his side.

Rowena waved hello. "I'm having the time of my life here in Colin's home country. Everyone's so sweet." She held the hand of her toddler son. Ariella had made sure that all children of the guests were invited as well. Who would want to go away for a weekend to a foreign country without their children?

"Ah, we're not always that sweet." Simon kissed Ariella on the cheek. "My wife can tell you that sometimes we're as stubborn as mules."

"I like to think of that as part of our charm." Colin smiled. "It certainly can be an advantage in foreign diplomacy."

They all laughed. Simon raised his glass. "I hope you'll all be regular guests here at Whist Castle. We intend to travel back to the States as often as possible so it's only fair that you all return the favor."

Ted Morrow lifted his glass. "I'll drink to that. As long as you don't start trying to tax our tea, we'll get along just fine."

"You Americans barely even drink tea," Simon protested. "One time I ordered tea in a D.C. restaurant and they brought me an ice cold glass of dishwater with a slice of lemon in it. Very uncivilized."

Ted chuckled. "We'll be sure to have some of that dark

witches' brew you British enjoy on hand when you and Ariella come to stay at the White House."

"Don't forget the biscuits," Simon teased. "And they're not the big puffy ones dripping with butter that you Americans eat, either."

"I know." Ted smiled. "They're what we call cookies. Since my beloved Ellie has now lived on both sides of the Atlantic, she's helping me navigate the language barrier. It's wonderful being part of a big, international family."

Ariella beamed with pride as her handsome husband wrapped his strong arm around her waist. In a few short months she'd gone from being a lonely orphan to finding herself at the center of a large and growing family, with two loving parents, a sexy and adorable husband and a network of friends stretching around the world. Could anyone be luckier?

"Three cheers for Their Royal Highness," chimed in Colin. They all lifted their glasses. "Hip, hip!" called Colin, and the crowd roared a deafening, "Hooray!"

Ariella laughed. It would take her a while to get used the sometimes antiquated customs in her newly adopted homeland.

"Hip, hip!" yelled Colin.

"Hooray!" roared the guests.

But she'd have fun doing it, and sharing her life with the most caring and loving man she'd ever met.

"Hip, hip!"

The cheers had spread through the crowd and the final "Hooray" boomed across the lawns like rolling thunder.

* * * * *

HER PERFECT
CANDIDATE

CANDACE SHAW

For my girlfriends Brenda, Kenyatta, Lisa, Mary and Tonya for their love and support as I embark on this new chapter in my life.

Chapter 1

"Great!"

Megan Chase plopped her forehead on the steering wheel. It was early evening in rush hour traffic, and her SUV had just gotten a flat tire on Interstate 85 in Atlanta. Luckily, she was in the far right lane and was able to inch the vehicle over to the shoulder. She lifted her head, breathed deeply and eased open the door to survey the damage. But before her 4-inch heel could hit the pavement, she quickly drew it back in observing the cars zooming by at high speeds.

Shutting the door, she moved her laptop bag and purse from the passenger seat into the back, before climbing over the gearshift. The flat was on the back passenger side. She figured she could change it and then be on her way to meet her twin sister and her best friend at a scholarship fund-raiser event one of her clients had invited them to.

She hopped out of the SUV and walked carefully along the rocky pavement.

"Of all the days to dress up," she said, pulling her short black dress down to barely touch her knees. She stooped down to look at the damaged tire. The tires were new, so she wasn't quite sure why she had a flat. A nail, probably, she thought.

Earlier that day, she'd put the finishing touches on decorating a model home in a new subdivision outside of Atlanta. Houses were in the process of being built, and Megan had toured the subdivision to see the homes. She figured she'd run over a nail in the process.

As she popped the trunk to retrieve the tire, she heard her cell phone blaring from her purse in the backseat. Climbing through the trunk of her SUV to reach the phone, she knew who was calling before she even looked at the display. Now, glancing down at the caller ID to confirm her suspicion, she saw Sydney Chase's name flash on the screen. Megan knew if she didn't answer the phone, Sydney the worrier, would probably have the FBI, CIA and the SWAT team scouring the city for her within the hour.

The sound of a horn and tires on the gravel behind Megan stopped her from answering the call. She grabbed the mace she always carried in her purse and began to climb backward out of the SUV. Her finger placed firmly on the spray button.

As she turned around to step down, a fine-looking

tall man was standing in front of her opened trunk, with his hand out to assist her. She blinked twice and stifled a "Goodness he's gorgeous" with a slight gulp. The sun was going down behind him radiating an aura of bright yellow and orange.

"Need some assistance, pretty lady?" the sexy, baritone voice offered.

Megan tossed the mace spray over the backseat and placed her empty hand in his. His touch on her skin, although brief, sent a warm shiver through her veins. Once settled onto the pavement, she squinted her eyes and placed her right hand straight across her forehead to see him better without being blinded by what was left of the sun.

She looked up in amazement at the most handsome man she had ever laid her eyes upon. He was quite tall, at least a few inches over six feet. His hair was neatly trimmed with black wavy ripples. The evening sun was bringing out the color of his smooth, milk chocolate skin, and she fought back the urge to run a hand over his hairless, chiseled face. He had thick eyelashes that supermodels would give up purging their dinner for. His charming smile displayed pearl-colored teeth between his inviting lips. While he had let go of her hand, she could still feel the warmth of it on her skin. She wondered how his strong hands would feel on the rest of her body.

For a moment time stood still. She didn't notice the cars zooming by them or the April sun bearing down on her. Instead, she thought about how he reminded her of the man she always dreamed about.

The man who would one day rescue her on his white horse and love her forever.

Suddenly remembering that he'd asked her a question, she blinked several times before coming down from cloud nine.

"Do I know you?" she asked, studying his captivating face.

A delicious grin crossed his mouth causing her to almost sigh out loud. *Stay composed, girl. You see handsome men all the time.*

"I don't think so. I would definitely remember you if we knew each other," the sinfully sexy gentleman stated in a tone that caused another wave of heat to rage through her.

What the heck is wrong with me?

"Oh, sorry for staring so hard, but you look familiar," Megan replied, studying his face carefully. Megan wasn't good with names, but she never forgot a face, especially one as intriguing as his. She couldn't help but stare at the yummy dimple on his right cheek that appeared every time he smiled.

"What's your name?" Megan asked.

"Steven."

"Nice to meet you. I'm Megan."

"Do you need some help changing that tire?" he asked, nodding his head in the direction of the flat. "It's too dangerous for you to be out here alone."

"Oh, yes. I…" she stuttered, glancing toward the tire. *This man is making me forget why I'm standing out here in the hot sun in the first place.* "I was just about to change it."

His left eyebrow rose. "Really?" His gaze traveled the length of her body. "Wearing Louboutins and a very…um…sexy little freak'um dress. Are you trying to cause accidents? Seeing you bent over trying to change a flat tire will cause a ten car pileup," he teased, taking off his blue suit jacket along with a red tie and handing them to her. "I'll take care of it, while you call back whoever keeps calling you." He nodded down to the cell phone in her hand that kept vibrating. "Your man is probably worried."

She shook her head and glanced at the caller ID. "It's my sister. We're supposed to meet for an event…" She stopped to glance at her watch. "I'm thirty minutes late and big sis is concerned," she said, watching Steven take the spare tire and jack out of her trunk. He then slammed it shut and turned to look at her.

"I completely understand. My brother is always checking on me and he's younger. How many years apart are you?"

"Two minutes," she answered. "We're twins."

"So there are two of you?" A cocky grin formed on his lips. "Nice," he commented, barely loud enough for her to hear as he rolled the spare tire over to the flat one. "You're more than welcome to sit in my SUV and wait. The sun is going down, but it's still hot. Crank the ignition and turn up the air conditioner if you'd like."

Megan looked past him at the white Range Rover. *He seems like the type to own such an elite SUV. Tai-*

lored business suit, expensive watch and a powerful, masculine presence.

"Thank you. I'll call my sister and let her know I'm fine." She walked steadily on the gravel toward the passenger side of his Range Rover. Once settled in the plush leather seat, she cranked the car as he suggested and was pleasantly surprised to hear Sade singing "Smooth Operator" through the speakers. She turned the volume down when she saw the light flash on her cell phone again.

"Hello?"

"Megan, where are you? I've called you like five times!" Sydney exclaimed.

"Syd, I'm sorry. I had a flat tire, but I'll be along soon," Megan answered quickly. She was too busy gazing at the jaw-dropping man who was now peeling off his dress shirt to reveal a white undershirt. The shirt did little to hide the gorgeous muscles of his arms, chest and back. A thin sheen of sweat glistened on his forehead. *He looks so damn hot and fine.* Megan reached over and turned the air conditioner to full blast.

"Are you listening?" Sydney asked in an impatient manner.

Who could listen at a time like this?

"Huh? What did you say?"

"I said do you need any help? Or are you changing it yourself?"

"No, this kind man is changing it for me." Megan continued to watch as Steven lifted the flat tire off, showcasing the toned muscles of his arms. *Oh, my goodness!*

"Kind man? You mean strange man! Where are you?"

"Calm down, Agent Chase. I'm sitting in his Range Rover watching him change my tire. He's almost done," Megan said, a little disappointed. "Poor thing, he's sweating. I think I have some bottled water still left in my lunch cooler. Syd, this man is so gorgeous!"

"Um…is this the same Megan that swore off *all* men almost two years ago when her ex-boyfriend cheated?"

"I didn't swear off all men, I just said I needed a break from dating and that mostly included all of the blind dates you, Jade and Tiffani had been arranging for me. I don't have a problem being single." She frowned as Steven replaced the last lug nut. He looked up and flashed a million-dollar smile, causing her to suck in her breath and become slightly turned on.

"He's done. I'll see you in a few." Megan abruptly hung up the phone to avoid any lectures from her sister about being safe. Sydney was a criminal profiler with the Georgia Bureau of Investigations, and in her book, everyone was a suspect.

Megan hopped out of the passenger seat and walked over to Steven who was wiping the sweat off of his forehead with his dress shirt.

"You're going to ruin that shirt," she said, opening the back door of her SUV and reaching over to pull out a small, unopened bottle of water from a small ice cooler. She opened the cap and handed him the water.

"Thank you, pretty lady." He gulped down half of the bottle before taking a breathing break and then downed the rest of the water. "The shirt will be fine. I'm headed home to change clothes anyway."

Megan watched him intently as she thought of something else to say. She knew in a minute they'd be back in their own vehicles, going back to their already scheduled day. She didn't notice a wedding ring—just a college ring. But that didn't mean he wasn't seeing someone.

"Thank you so much for changing my tire for me. I must've run over a nail today while driving around a subdivision's construction site."

"Having a home built?"

"No. I'm an interior decorator. I just finished a project in one of the model homes and decided to drive around the subdivision." She hoped to find some way to keep the conversation going, but he was already buttoning his shirt and checking his Rolex. She decided not to delay him any longer. He needed to go, and she needed to leave as well before Syd assumed she'd been kidnapped.

He stepped toward her as she closed the back door. She leaned against the SUV as he stood directly in front of her, literally in her personal space. The woodsy scent of his cologne swirled in her nose, sending tingles through her body. *I wonder what his scent would smell like intertwined with mine?*

Her lips parted slightly as he stared down at her, she thought surely he was undressing her with his eyes as they raked over her.

"Thank you again. I hope I didn't inconvenience you, Steven."

"No, not at all. I'm very glad I pulled over to help you," he stated in a sincere tone, running his eyes over her body one more time before they settled back on her face.

She smiled up at him before stepping over to the passenger door. He opened it for her and she slid in, crossing her legs and turning her body to face him.

"Bye, Megan," he said hesitantly before shutting the door. He gave her one last smile before strolling back to his car, whistling.

Steven watched as the loveliest vision he'd ever laid his eyes on drove away. When he first saw her in the trunk bending over the backseat of her Acura MDX reaching for something, he couldn't help but wonder if her toned caramel-coated legs and thighs matched the rest of her. The way her little black dress hugged her bottom and hips as it rose up, stirred his manhood. He had decided to take a chance. Plus, he couldn't possibly leave a female on the side of the highway with a flat tire.

Her long, curly brown hair with subtle blond high-lights flowed down her provocative bare back in an utterly sexy manner. He would've given anything to run his fingers through her soft curls, or better yet, spread them out on his pillow as he looked down at her.

He'd been pleasantly surprised when she turned around to acknowledge him. Strikingly stunning, she had a pleasant smile, high cheekbones and wore very little makeup. Her almond-shaped eyes were cinnamon in hue and when he stared into them, he felt a sense of overwhelming peace.

Steven admired all women, but Megan stirred feelings and emotions he'd never felt before in the thirty-three years of his life. Her pleasant personality and warm demeanor were a breath of fresh air.

While changing the flat tire, he couldn't get the image of Megan's short black dress and shapely legs in black heels out of his head. He had let his eyes roam all over her breathtaking body while he tried to make polite conversation. It was hard to do, considering she had the perfect hourglass figure. Her perky, rounded breasts and small waist were followed by hips that settled snuggly but tastefully in the dress she wore.

He had tried to move his eyes back up to hers so she wouldn't realize he was checking her out, but instead they'd rested on her inviting lips. Sexy, luscious lips painted in a reddish shade that he enjoyed watching move. He didn't care what she was saying, he just wanted to devour them. He felt a rise in his briefs again as he thought about the possibility of being kissed by the sexy interior decorator.

He didn't mean to step into her personal space, but he'd needed to see her supple lips up close once more.

It took everything he had in him not to drag her body close to his and kiss her senseless right there against her SUV. The way he noticed her checking him out as well, he wouldn't have been surprised if she had responded. However, he was shocked at his thought. Kissing was something he didn't do. Sex, yes. Kissing, no. It was too emotional, and he wasn't looking for an emotional relationship with anyone. Yet, kissing the beautiful Megan was all he could think about.

As he drove toward his penthouse in Midtown, it dawned on him that she didn't recognize him as the Georgia state senator Steven Monroe, son of Robert Monroe, United States senator. Coming from three generations of politicians and Harvard Law School graduates, the Monroe family were considered to be the black Kennedys because of their millions, power and influence in the political world. Because of who he was, most women usually flirted with him and did any and everything possible to garner his attention.

Steven leaned his head back on his seat and inhaled the sweet scent of the intoxicating perfume lingering in his SUV. *Damn, why on earth didn't I ask for her phone number?*

Megan searched through her console between the seats for her Sade CD with her right hand as she kept her left hand steady on the wheel. She needed to hear "Smooth Operator" one more time as thoughts of Steven filled her head. She was surprised at her thoughts but couldn't help but smile. She then glanced at herself in the rearview mirror to see how she looked when he met her. Upon finding the CD, she slid it into the CD player and waited anxiously while it loaded. She skipped the first few songs until she heard the beat of "Smooth Operator" and turned the volume up.

As she was singing the song for the second time, she saw Syd's cell number flash on the dash. She had the Bluetooth hands-free function connected to her car, which made it safer for her to talk to clients while driving. She turned off the music and pushed the cell button on her steering wheel.

"I'm almost there, Syd," Megan said as she exited the interstate. She then turned toward Atlantic Station, an outdoor mall in Midtown Atlanta that housed the swanky hotel Twelve, where the fundraiser gala was being held.

"I'm just making sure the stranger who changed your tire didn't kidnap you."

"Whatever."

"So tell me about this *kind stranger.*"

She blushed at the thought of him, and then giggled like a high school girl. "His name is Steven and that's all I know. Oh, and he looks simply amazing in a suit."

"Did you get a last name? I can do a background check."

"No, I didn't, we didn't exchange information. But I'm fine with that."

"Well…you seemed as if you were beaming so I just thought you may go out with him."

"Syd, for the last time, I'm happy being single.

My main concern is expanding my business. I'm focusing on my career right now."

Megan turned her car into the valet parking area and grabbed her purse from the backseat as the valet guy opened the door, greeted her and handed her a ticket. "I'm here, Syd. I'll see you in a few minutes."

Thirty minutes later, Megan sat at her reserved table after she gave her donation and chatted briefly with her client and mentor, Chelsea Benton, who had invited her to the gala. Megan loved to dress up and hang with her girlfriends in intimate or casual settings but big bashes weren't exactly her cup of tea. However, it was for charity, plus Chelsea had promised to introduce her to some potential clients.

She glanced over at her twin sitting beside her, who seemed to be having a great time people watching.

"Let me guess. You're watching everyone and figuring out what they're thinking just by their body language."

Sydney nodded. Her bob hair cut swished forward in the process. Their hairstyles were the only way people knew who was who. Plus their personalities were like night and day. Megan was the more whimsical, bubbly twin whereas Sydney was the serious-minded and logical one.

"Yes, but not on purpose. It's just a habit. Like right now I can tell by your pursed lips and the way your hand is resting under your chin, that you're ready to leave."

"I am, but I'll stay for a little longer. Chelsea wanted Jade and I to meet some potential clients."

"And where is your best friend?" Sydney glanced around the room.

"Right here, Tia and Tamera," a sassy voice behind them said. "Thank you for saving me a seat."

Jade Whitmore was Megan's best friend from college. Together they owned Chase and Whitmore Designs, an up-and-coming boutique decorating firm for the past six years.

Jade slid into the empty seat on the other side of Megan and placed a glass of champagne on the table. "Sorry I'm late. I had to meet with the Cannadys to pick up their last payment. Glad we're done with that project."

"Me, too," Megan agreed but her attention was diverted by the commotion at the entrance of the event. The ladies and other guests all placed their eyes on a man flanked with bodyguards and an entourage of people strolling into the gala. The man in the middle turned his back to the crowd as he stopped to shake hands and chat with a few people who approached him.

"Must be someone important," Megan shrugged and sipped her champagne as she stared at the back of the tall man clad in a black tuxedo. He turned to the side to greet a lady with a too-short dress on who in return gazed up at him as if he were the most handsome man in the world.

Megan cocked her head to the side and raised an eyebrow as a smile inched across her face and her heart and stomach began to flutter uncontrollably.

"Oh, my goodness!"

Sydney and Jade placed their attention on her, and Sydney waved her hand in front of her twin's face. "I've never seen you smile like that before. I know he's gorgeous, but stop drooling."

Megan shook her head as she tried to calm her smile and excitement down, but it was no use especially when he turned his head as if he sensed her staring at him. Their eyes locked, and a charming smile crept across his breathtaking, chiseled face. He nodded knowingly as he took a step in her direction but a couple stepped in his path for conversation. Even though he conversed with them, his eyes on hers never faltered.

Jade tapped her on the shoulder. "Megan, do you know who you're making goo-goo eyes with?"

She nodded. "Yes, that's him. The man who changed my flat tire."

"That's who changed your tire?" Sydney questioned in a surprised tone.

"Yes and apparently he *is* someone important since everyone seems to know who he is except me."

"Um…yes…" Jade started. "That's Georgia state senator Steven Monroe, self-proclaimed lifelong bachelor and one of Atlanta's most notorious playboys."

Chapter 2

"I'll call you next week about that," Steven promised, shaking his associate's hand as he tried to move away from the crowd of people that were beginning to form around him. His eyes couldn't tear away from Megan's lovely face. He was quite surprised to see her when he entered the ballroom for just some moments ago he'd taken a cold shower as he thought of her. Of course he told himself the cold shower was to cool down his temperature after changing her tire in the blazing evening sun, but he knew that was a lie.

He hadn't been in the mood to attend the fundraiser, but considering it was in the same building he lived in, all he had to do was ride the elevator down to the first floor. Plus, his best friend and campaign manager, Shawn Bennett suggested Steven at least should show his face, shake hands and give a considerable donation. But most importantly stay away from the ladies. His reputation couldn't handle any more bad press considering he had been on local blogs and news channels with a different woman nearly every week. And considering Steven's father wanted him to eventually run for the U.S. Senate seat he was retiring from at the end of the year, Steven needed to first clean up his image. While he would be a shoo-in to win the nomination because of his intellect, clean political slate and charismatic nature, the Monroe campaign team was more concerned that Steven's playboy image would cost him the opportunity to win.

So he'd made a promise to stay low-key and out of the limelight with the ladies and therefore opted not to have a date that evening. However, there was something about Megan that was drawing him to her like a magnetic force. When he entered the room earlier, he sensed the same calming peace he had when he'd initially met her. Was it her perfume in the atmosphere or her cute giggle that made him turn her way, only to find her inquisitive eyes on him? She bestowed her beautiful smile as she had when he'd changed her tire, but this one was accompanied with a look of promise that he couldn't explain. He had a feeling his smile matched hers.

Steven continued to nod and shake hands with people who approached him all the while keeping his eyes glued to Megan and her table. He briefly glanced on either side of her to make sure she didn't have a date. On her left was a woman who looked just like her, which must've been the twin sister she'd mentioned. And the other lady at the table, while drop-dead gorgeous, did nothing for him, either. There weren't any men in their presence, and he was grateful. "Hello, Megan," he said casually. "And ladies." He nodded at them but kept his eyes on Megan. "Nice to see you here. I was hoping to run into someone I know."

She chuckled with a head tilt. "Weren't you just bombarded with people *you know?* We just met an hour ago."

"Hmm...I know, yet we keep running into each other. Maybe we're supposed to be in each other's lives."

She released her signature cute giggle again, and he was glad when her friends excused themselves but not before the both of them winked at Megan. He sat in the chair across from her and dismissed his bodyguards who were actually his campaign manager and his brother, Bryce. They'd tagged along to make sure he stayed out of trouble. And he sensed their hesitancy before they strode away.

"I must say, I'm quite glad to see you. You drove away without me getting any of your information. I don't even know your last name."

"It's Chase. Megan Chase...Senator Monroe," she stated knowingly with a grin.

He threw his head back in laughter. "Does that bother you?"

"Nope. I'm forever grateful. Could you imagine me changing a tire in heels and in this dress?"

His eyes traveled over her body settling on her shapely legs and a glimpse of the side of her exquisite thighs peeking out from her dress.

No, but I can imagine you only in those heels with your legs over my shoulders. He blinked his eyes a few times and cleared the frog in his throat. At first he thought he'd spoken his private thoughts out loud.

"So that means I have your vote in the next election?"

"I don't know," she said in a teasing manner. "What makes you the perfect candidate?"

"I'm a regular down-to-earth guy who likes to help people less fortunate than myself and ultimately make a difference in my community."

"I'm sold. When does your current term end?"

"I just started my second term as a senator for Georgia so not for another two years. However, I'm considering running for a U.S. Senate seat within the next year or so, but let's keep that between us for now. It's my father's seat, and I'm sure there're a few people who would love to have it if they caught wind of my dad retiring."

"Your secret is safe with me," she said sincerely.

Steven couldn't believe he'd told her such secret information so easily. Only he, his father, brother and best friend were aware of Senator Robert Monroe's retirement plans. But for some reason he trusted the lady sitting in front of him.

"So how long have you been in the interior-design business?"

"Well unofficially since I was seven years old." She paused to laugh. "I redesigned my side of my childhood room by using watercolors and markers on the wall. I also cut up some old drapes my mother was going to toss to make throw pillows and a duvet cover. I loved it but much to my mother's dismay, she wasn't pleased with the mural on the wall. But officially when I graduated with my undergraduate degree, so six years."

"I currently live in a penthouse here at Twelve, but it was already furnished. However, I'm looking into buying a home soon and would love to hire a professional decorator."

"I'm always looking for new clients, which is one of the reasons why I'm here. Just let me know when you're ready."

She opened her evening bag and handed him a business card.

He knew it would be months before he would close on a home. He wasn't even officially looking for a house yet although he had an agent. It was just something he was considering, but he couldn't let months go by without seeing her.

"Well, do you have any appointments available this Monday? I would love to see your portfolio and talk to you about some of my ideas."

She nodded and pulled her cell phone out of her purse. "I have Monday around noon available. Is that a good time for you? If not… Friday."

He actually had an appointment on Monday at the exact same time, but he couldn't possibly wait until Friday. He didn't know if he could wait the two days until Monday. "Noon will be fine. How about we meet at a restaurant and have a business lunch?"

"That sounds good. My office is located in the Buckhead area. How about Café Love Jones? It's a jazz club, but they're open for lunch, as well. I have business meetings there quite often."

"That's a great spot. Delicious food and atmosphere."

"Glad you think so. My big brother Braxton is the owner."

"Cool. I don't know him personally, but I met him briefly at an event there a few years ago. Brother can play the hell out of a piano."

Steven then unconsciously glanced up to see Shawn tapping his watch which meant it was time to move on. He was supposed to stay focused, mixing and mingling with the crowd, not flirting with the most beautiful woman at the fund-raiser. But he remembered his promise, and reluctantly stood as the smile on Megan's soft face sank a little.

"It was nice seeing you again, Megan. I look forward to our meeting on Monday."

"Me, too." She held out her hand to shake his, but instead he raised it to his lips and kissed it tenderly. The feel of her silky, warm skin on his lips and the scent of her perfume on her wrist shook him to the core. He let his mouth linger on her hand longer than he should have, as he stared into her cinnamon eyes.

She let out a soft sigh and slowly withdrew her hand from his. He regained his composure and tried to remember where he was before he did something impulsive like pull her into his arms and kiss her until her knees buckled.

Steven cleared his throat and shoved his hands in his pockets to restrain them. "I'll see you later."

For the rest of the evening he socialized with the other guests, discussing politics all while keeping his eyes on Megan. Every now and then he'd catch her glance in his direction as Chelsea Benton escorted her and her friend around. He assumed Chelsea was introducing the women to possible clients since they were eagerly handing out business cards.

An hour later he felt a tap on his shoulder and was pleasantly surprised to look down into Megan's adorable face.

"Hey, pretty lady." He leaned over and whispered in her ear. "Having fun? I saw quite a few gentlemen trying to get to know you better."

"Um…yes, but I'm not trying to date at the present moment. However, I met some potential clients. I just wanted to say thank you again for changing my tire, and I look forward to our meeting on Monday."

"Me, too. Why are you cutting out so early?"

"I'm not really one for social events even though I should be. However, Chelsea insisted that I come."

"How do you know Chelsea Benton?"

"She's one of my mother's best friends from college. And you?"

"Her husband is golf buddies with my father, and

she did some fashion consulting for me both times I ran for the state senate."

"She's the best." Megan then let out a yawn, which caused him to yawn, as well. They both laughed, and he stepped closer toward her.

"Good night, Ms. Chase." His voice was low. Serious. He hoped the stir in his manhood stayed at bay. He wasn't in the mood for any more cold showers that evening.

If she was any other woman, he would've invited her upstairs to his place, but he knew Megan wasn't the type to say yes to that and he was glad she wasn't. Out of all the young women at the fundraiser aside from her twin and girlfriend, Megan was the only one that hadn't either batted her eyelashes and twirled her hair or slipped her phone number in the front of his pants' pocket.

"Good night, Senator Monroe."

He hesitated to leave, but just then her sister arrived to let her know the valet had pulled their cars around, and the two ladies walked away.

"Who was that?" he heard Shawn say as he approached from the side as they both stood in place staring after Megan and her sister.

"The one woman who could possibly make me settle down."

The next morning Megan awoke to the sounds of birds chirping outside the window ledge of her loft apartment and a splitting headache. Usually the echoes of birds soothed her nerves, but not this morning. She wasn't able to sleep last night. Every time she closed her eyes, she fantasized about the handsome Steven Monroe and his strong hands roaming over her figure. Or his lips moving from her hand and wandering over every inch of her body until she passed out from pure ecstasy. She'd almost swooned last night when the caress of his warm lips pressed against her skin sent her to a point of oblivion while she tried to remain composed on the outside. No man had ever stirred her like that before. But she knew getting involved with a politician was out of the question. Or any man for that matter. Right now her focus was her career and a serious relationship was out of the question.

After tossing and turning, Megan had gotten up in the middle of the night and spent a few hours online researching Steven. She'd heard of him before but because she wasn't all that interested in politics, she never paid him much attention, and she didn't read the gossip blogs. She discovered he was divorced but with no children. No mention of a dog, but it was a possibility. Men like him usually had a dog for companionship.

As Megan continued her research, she learned that Steven was a politician that believed that his constituents should be able to voice their opinions. He based his platforms on their concerns as well as his own moral and personal beliefs. As a state senator, he held monthly meetings with the citizens of his district to discuss their needs in the community. Steven had opened a children's after-school center, organized community gardens and raised funds for new roads in poverty stricken areas as well as more funding for the schools in his district. He wasn't afraid to speak his mind, which made him well liked by his constituents though frowned upon by some of his fellow politicians.

The only negative news Megan discovered was that he was dating several different women at the same time. The media labeled him as both an eligible bachelor and playboy. She found that hard to believe considering he was a perfect gentleman the night before and paid no attention to other gorgeous women who threw sexy smiles his way and dirty looks at her. However, there were plenty of pictures of him and beautiful women on the gossip blogs so apparently it was true.

Megan rose from her bed to put on a pot of coffee. Percy, her Persian cat, was staring at her from his heated cat bed on the floor. She was surprised that he wasn't in the bed with her, but sometimes Percy needed his own space. *Just like a male.* She laughed.

Megan sipped on hazelnut-flavored coffee seated at her kitchen's island and reviewed paint colors for her latest project for Chelsea. Chelsea was her role model and mentor. It was because of her that Megan had a steady flow of clients lately. She was supposed to meet Chelsea to look at fabrics in the next hour. Luckily, the store was only within ten minutes of both her loft and office. She decided since it was a lovely April day, she would walk and clear her brain.

After her shower, she threw on some jeans with

a fuchsia T-shirt and pulled her hair into a bouncy ponytail. She glanced at the clock and realized she was ahead of schedule. Grabbing her cell phone, she was surprised to see over twenty missed phone calls and text messages from her cousin Tiffani Chase, Sydney and Jade all within a span of ten minutes. The phone then rang while it was still in her hand. It was Sydney.

"What's up Syd?"

"Wow, don't you sound calm."

"Why wouldn't I be?"

"I guess you haven't seen today's paper or the local gossip blogs this morning."

"I just got up. Haven't been online yet."

"Turn on your computer and go to the Atlanta Social website.

Megan went into her living room where her tablet sat on the coffee table. She opened the website Syd mentioned and almost dropped her tablet on the hardwood floor. On the screen were pictures from the fund-raiser last night, but the main picture of the article was of her and Steven when he kissed her hand. The accompanying caption read, "Who's the senator's new lady of the week?"

"Oh, no." Megan sighed and sank onto the couch. "This can't be happening." She scrolled through some more of the event pictures, and there were four more of them laughing and having a good time.

"Girl, those aren't the only pictures of you two. I'm at the GBI office and one of the agents just brought me the social section of the newspaper.

There's another one where Steven is leaning over whispering in your ear, and you're staring at him like a lovesick puppy with your eyes half closed."

"We were just talking. I'm not dating the senator. Why would they print this?"

"Calm down, sis. This happens to him all the time. You just don't keep up. It'll all blow over I'm sure. He'll be on the same blog tomorrow with a different woman, and no one will give you a second thought."

"But this has never happened to *me* before. I don't want my reputation ruined with my clients because they think I'm dating a playboy politician. No, wait. It says 'lady of the week.' That's even worse." Megan looked at a few more local blogs she found through Google, and the same pictures with similar captions popped up.

"Try not to worry about it," Sydney said in a sincere tone. "They don't even know your name."

Megan's phone beeped with another phone call. *Perfect.*

"Our mother is calling me on the other line."

"Now you can worry. Don't answer."

"I'm not. I can only imagine what she's going to say."

"Chin up, sis. I have a meeting, but call me if you need to."

After hanging up, the phone rang again but this time from a number she didn't recognize. She decided to answer it anyway just in case it was a potential client.

"Hello?" she answered cautiously.

"Hey, Megan this is Steven."

"Oh, joy. It's the playboy politician," she said sarcastically as she walked to her bedroom that was separated from the living room with a sliding wall. She grabbed her purse and keys from the bench in front of the bed. She needed to head out soon to meet Chelsea.

"I guess you saw the blogs this morning."

"Yes, I did, and I'm not amused at all. I don't even know you! We just met yesterday."

"I'm so sorry this has happened. Trust me last night I was supposed to mix and mingle and not flirt. I'm trying to clean up my image if I'm going to run for my dad's seat, but whenever the media sees me with a woman they assume I'm seeing her...which sometimes I am."

"Maybe if you stop kissing women's hands and whispering in their ears, your photo won't get taken as much," she snapped.

He chuckled, and her breath caught in her throat. She was supposed to be mad, but how could she when his seductive voice was in her ear reminding her of the tossing and turning she did last night over him?

"You have a point, but my team sent a statement to all of the blogs and news outlets that have the pictures that we aren't dating, and that you're an interior decorator who will be working on some projects for me in the future, all of which is true."

She let out a sigh of relief. She knew it wasn't his

fault that this had happened. He was a politician from a very prestigious family so naturally he would be in the limelight. Too bad his playboy past was getting him in trouble even when the situation was innocent. While she had just met him, he seemed like a cool, down-to-earth guy. Maybe the media blew his reputation out of proportion.

"Thank you for releasing the statement. I know it's not your fault, but it did shake me up because I live a simple, drama-free life. And I like to keep it that way."

"I completely understand. I wish my life was simple at times. So, are we still on for this Monday?"

"Yes, of course. Remember, I'm not really the lady of the week, I'm the interior decorator you'll be working with." She laughed.

"I'll keep that in mind. Besides, you aren't 'lady of the week' material. More like the lady forever, and I would hate for anyone to think otherwise."

The heat in her cheeks began to rise, and she had a feeling they would be burning red if she looked in a mirror.

"Thank you. I hate to cut this conversation short, but I have a meeting in a few minutes."

"On a Saturday?"

"Normally I wouldn't schedule a meeting on a Saturday, but it's Chelsea."

"Cool. Give her my best."

After saying their goodbyes, Megan grabbed her tablet and purse and headed out the door. She felt somewhat better since Steven called.

While browsing through material in the fabric store, Sydney sent her a text that a statement had been released about her and Steven's platonic relationship and the blogs had been updated. She decided she wasn't going to worry about it. Like her sister said, it would all blow over, and some other woman would be in a picture with him tomorrow. The thought of that made her a little sad, but she knew he was the last man she should be involved with even if the very thought of him caused her to go weak.

Her main focus was expanding her business and taking it to the next level. Her and Jade were in the process of landing a guest spot on the famed show *Decorator's Dream* on the Fabulous Living Channel. They'd sent in pictures of all of their decorating jobs over the past few years and their audition video. Now they were on pins and needles waiting to hear back. Plus, much to her family and friends' dismay, Megan actually enjoyed being single at this time in her life. She shook her head to wipe the thought of dating Steven out of her mind. From now on, she would think of him as a potential client. Nothing more.

Chapter 3

"Steven, we have one more topic to discuss," Shawn Bennett said uneasily to his best friend.

Steven sat at the desk in his downtown office while Bryce and Shawn sat in the leather wingback chairs in front. They'd been discussing the latest comments about Steven from the media including gossip blogs and social media. He had begun to tune them out after a while considering it was the same conversation that'd been had over and over.

Instead, his thoughts began to wander to Megan. He couldn't seem to get her bubbly personality, cute smile, flirty eyes or whimsical voice out of his head. He didn't know which was cuter: the way she spoke or the sparkle in her eyes when she laughed. He was eager to leave for their lunch meeting just to resolve which one.

He glanced at the clock on the opposite wall and then back at the two men in front of him that he'd momentarily forgot were there. *Maybe if I pay attention to them we could speed this boring meeting up.*

"What else do we need to talk about?" he asked nonchalantly.

Bryce cleared his throat, stood up from his seat and positioned himself in front of his brother.

"Ok, big brother. It's like this. We feel that you have a wonderful platform and a good chance of winning the nomination for Dad's seat. There are constituents who will vote for you because of who you are plus they agree with your views on certain issues. You're a great senator. But because of the way you've been portrayed in the media, people may not take you seriously as a U.S. senator," Bryce said as he paced back and forth around the room. "Your escapades have caught national attention lately since there's a buzz going around about Dad retiring at the end of his term."

"Man, maybe you need to slow down some with the ladies," Shawn added. "You know…save some of the action for me and Bryce."

Steven looked at his brother and his best friend. He'd been friends with Shawn since their days at Harvard, and he always had his back. Steven knew they were both right. He wasn't trying to have a reputation as a playboy, he just happened to enjoy the company of different women. Some spent the night and some didn't. And after the last incident at the ski resort in Colorado with an alleged threesome, the media was following his every move.

"Steven, is there someone in your life you can date exclusively?" Bryce asked.

"No, not really. They were mostly one-nighters. And I don't mean one night stands, necessarily. Just one date and then I wasn't interested anymore." Steven thought over the list of women he'd been out with or slept with lately. Even though only one woman was occupying his mind at the moment.

"What about the interior decorator you were photographed with?" Shawn offered. "You two were having a grand time at the fund-raiser event. The shutterbugs couldn't get enough."

"We have a meeting at noon to discuss her possibly decorating my house... Once I find one and buy it, of course. But I doubt she would want to go out with me. She's already called me the playboy politician."

"This is exactly our point. You can easily lose the female vote if women only see you as a playboy," Bryce said.

Steven thought about what Bryce said for a moment and then gave a cocky smile.

"Or the opposite. You know, some women will vote for me because they think I'm a good-looking playboy. Have you seen these dimples? Women go crazy!" Steven said trying not to brag and more so lighten the mood of the room.

"Oh, you find this funny?" Bryce asked in an irritated tone. "The Monroe name is on the line. Our family has worked hard for generations in order to become established and to be taken seriously in the political world. Dad has groomed us for this, and you're not going to ruin my chances of becoming a district attorney one day. Plus, Jacqueline is considering going into politics, so don't ruin this for our baby sister. Shape up and get it together."

Steven nodded as he listened to his brother. He knew he was right. Fun and games were over. He was a grown man. He was a Monroe man. He knew his family was influential in politics thanks to his grandfather and father.

"What do you need me to do?"

"Cut out this playboy persona and settle down with one woman to improve your chances to win the nomination. You need to be seen in the media as a good guy and a devoted boyfriend. Ever since your divorce, you've been on this wild roller-coaster ride for the last ten years. It's time to get off."

His divorce. It should have been an annulment, but his ex-wife, Veronica, wanted the prenuptial agreement to stand so she could receive her settlement should they ever part. After only six months of marriage, Steven knew it was hopeless. Veronica had only married him because he was a Monroe. When he realized that she never loved him, he was crushed. He thought she was the one when he saw her studying in the library while both law students at Harvard. Apparently she'd done her homework and was determined to be his wife. Over the years, they remained cordial running into each at events or speaking engagements. She was now a law professor at a college in Washington, D.C., thanks to his last name that she refused to drop no matter how many millions she was offered during the divorce settlement.

Since they'd parted ways, he dated, but nothing serious ever came out of it. And once he realized they were only interested in the Monroe name, he dropped them, thus igniting his persona in the media.

"I hear you, Bryce. Which one of my past conquests should I consider?"

"Actually, Megan Chase would be the perfect candidate. You've already been photographed with her, and you two appeared quite cozy."

"Yes," Shawn said as he grabbed a folder from his briefcase. "We did a little research as always when you're photographed with a new woman. She's twenty-seven years old. According to her DMV records, she's five feet six inches and weighs 125 pounds. Her father is a principal at a local high school and her mother is a first grade teacher. They were high school sweethearts and have been married for thirty-five years. Ms. Chase has never had any arrests, and has only had one speeding ticket. She won a full scholarship to Clark Atlanta University and started her interior-decorating business out of her parent's basement along with her best friend when they graduated from college. But now they have an office in Buckhead.

"Ms. Chase's twin sister is a GBI agent and their older brother is a musician who owns a jazz club/

restaurant here in Atlanta. Her uncle on her mother's side is Dr. Francis Arrington, a world renowned heart surgeon in Memphis and all his children are doctors, as well. She likes hanging with her family and her girlfriends. Her ex-boyfriend is a doctor here in Atlanta. She helped him start his practice, but they broke up about a year and a half ago once she found out he was cheating with one of his nurses."

"Wow. Do you know her blood type, too?" Steven asked sarcastically. Shawn had done research before but never to this extent.

Shawn glanced through some papers in his folders. "Yes. She's AB."

Steven chuckled. "I was just joking."

"We aren't," Bryce stated in a firm tone. "This is serious."

"Anything else I need to know about Ms. Chase? Is she lactose intolerant? How does she like her eggs prepared?"

"Yes. She's trying to get a spot on the show *Decorator's Dream*." Shawn closed the folder and laid it on Steven's desk.

Steven then glanced down at it and shook his head in disbelief. "Well, I'm not sure if I'm totally on board with this absurd idea, but I'll give it some thought."

Megan sat nervously in the parking lot of her brother's restaurant on Peachtree Street downtown. She'd called Braxton ahead of time to tell him she was coming because she wanted to make sure her favorite booth was available because it overlooked the stage. It was the perfect spot for when jazz bands played in the evenings and occasionally during lunch.

She tapped her steering wheel nervously, trying to decide whether or not she should restart her SUV and drive home before Steven showed up. She knew it was just a business luncheon, but for some reason she felt as if they were going on a first date. Taking a deep breath, she checked her hair and makeup in the visor mirror before stepping out of the car and walking toward the front door of the restaurant. She saw her reflection in the glass doors and stopped briefly to make sure she looked presentable. She had decided to wear a pair of dress jeans with a white tee, a pink seersucker blazer and wedged sandals. Her hair was curly and swooped to one side over her shoulder. Huge gold hoop earrings and a charm bracelet completed the casual look.

She tried to tell herself that this meeting wasn't a big deal but deep down she was nervous. He made her nervous. Not because he was a politician or a millionaire. She'd dealt with people of his social status before. She was nervous because she knew somewhere inside of her, she wanted him and that scared her. She'd been on quite a few dates thanks to her girls playing matchmaker but none of the men had flustered her to this point. None of them had kept her up at night with sinful thoughts that made her cheeks turn pink like Steven had. His scent. His smile. The seductive way he gazed at her when he kissed her hand, were all imbedded in her brain.

"Megan!"

She looked up to see Steven walking down the elegant staircase of the restaurant. He, too, had dressed casually in khaki dress pants and a red golf shirt. His smile was simply charming, and she couldn't help but return it as she walked toward him. She began to get a little wobbly in the knees, and she couldn't stop smiling at the magnificent man in front of her. *Heaven help me!*

When Steven saw Megan looking up at him from the bottom of the staircase, he was captivated. He thought the dress she'd worn when he met her was sexy, but there she stood in jeans even sexier, and she wasn't even trying.

"Wow, you look great," he said, reaching out his hand to her to lead her back upstairs. "Our table is up here. I was told it's your favorite."

Once seated, the waiter took their drink and lunch order. Thirty minutes later, they were eating shrimp po' boys and fries and laughing at all of the blind dates Megan had been on lately.

"So let me get this straight," Steven said, amused, "This dude was on a date with you trying to sell you a time-share?" He laughed again, taking a sip of his tea. "Did you buy one?"

"No, I declined. Then he tried to tell me about some other get-rich-quick scheme. I have tons of stories."

"Why do your family and friends keep setting you up? You're breathtaking. I would assume men ask you out all of the time."

She lowered her head and tried to stifle a smile when he mentioned she was breathtaking. He didn't want to embarrass her. He was merely speaking the truth. She twirled a French fry around in the ketchup before looking back up and answering him.

"They do, but I always cancel at the last minute or find some reason not to go on a second date. My girlfriends say I'm just being picky so they set me up with guys that they think would be perfect for me."

"So how many dates are we going to go on before you decide to dump me, too?" he asked jokingly.

"This isn't a date. We're supposed to be discussing decorating your future home. You haven't even looked at my portfolio yet." She reached into her oversize leather tote bag and pulled out her tablet and slid it across the table to him.

"To be honest, I'm having such a great time that I forgot this was supposed to be business luncheon. My meetings are usually with old men discussing politics, investments and golf. Not with an adorable woman cracking me up with her blind-date history."

"Trust me they weren't that funny to be on, that's for sure. I've asked my friends both politely and rudely to stop."

"Why do they keep setting you up? Did something happen in a past relationship?" he asked, thinking about what Shawn read earlier.

"Ever since my last long-term relationship ended, they think I'm lonely for a man because all I do is work. But what they fail to realize is that I'm happy being single. I enjoy my freedom. I was with my ex for almost four years and my world was centered on him. I helped him start his medical practice right after I started my interior-decorating business with Jade. I began to lose sight of my dreams and ambitions that he wasn't even being supportive of in the first place. After I found out he was cheating with a nurse in his office, I dumped him and focused on me and building my business. I'm not lonely, but no one seems to understand except me."

"They sound like my brother and campaign manager. Just earlier today, they were telling me to settle down with one person. They think that would somehow improve my image and give me a better shot of winning the nomination for my father's seat."

"Well, you are a self-proclaimed playboy," she said, shrugging her shoulders and rolling her eyes away from his with a grin.

He chuckled at her sarcasm. "The media says that. Truth is, I've been married before—didn't work out. Like you, I enjoy my single life. No strings. No attachments. No hearts to break."

"I wish I could just tell my family and friends I have a boyfriend so they can stop harassing me." She threw the cloth napkin from her lap into her plate and sat back in her seat.

Steven studied her angelic face, which at the moment appeared disturbed. He knew what she was going through. But now that he'd had met Megan, he wanted to get to know her better. Even though, it seemed as if she wanted to be single and free. Heck, so did he, but he knew he needed to settle down his dating habits and clean up his image if he wanted to win the nomination. Most of the potential candidates for his father's seat were either engaged or married with families, summer homes and of course a beloved dog. He didn't even have a dog.

As he watched Megan, he saw the epitome of what he wanted in a woman. Graceful, refined, sexy without having to try, successful and independent. He was ready to learn about her other qualities, as well.

"You know Megan, you could just tell them you're dating me."

"But that would be a lie," she answered, shaking her head.

"It wouldn't have to be."

"Steven, that's ridiculous. We can't do that."

"Think about it. Your family and friends want you to date and be happy. My campaign team feels I need to stick with one person. Why not?"

"Because it wouldn't be right. It would be dishonest, and I know despite your escapades with women, you're an honest politician. You're a good man, Steven."

"Thank you, but I need someone like you and…" he paused as he thought about something else Shawn said earlier. "You need me."

She leaned over the table toward him and whispered, "I don't need to date you in name only to please my family and friends. Besides, I have a blossoming career thanks in part to having more free time to concentrate on it instead of cater to an ungrateful man."

"Really?"

"Yes, really." She sat back against her booth seat.

He leaned forward and whispered, "I can get you more clients and a chance to meet with the bigwigs of the Fabulous Living Channel. You can showcase your work on an upcoming show they're doing this summer."

She blinked her lashes several times and stared in disbelief. *"Decorator's Dream?"* she asked, leaning in toward him again with her eyes wide. Steven grabbed her hands in his when he thought he heard her heart beating faster.

"Yep, that show."

"How do you know about that show? They're only in the early-production stages."

"I know the creator."

"Justine Monroe? Jade and I sent her a copy of our portfolio and the audition video three months ago…" She stopped. She seemed to be pondering something, and Steven hoped it was a yes to his question. "Monroe…? Is she your ex-wife?"

"No. First cousin. I could put in a good word for you if…"

"If I agree to date you…in name only."

"Why do you keeping saying in name only? Am I not to get any *special* benefits?"

"You'll have the benefit of me on your arm, no more."

"So, that's a yes, Ms. Chase?"

"If I decide to do this, are you still going to see other women on the side?" Megan asked seriously.

"No, I don't intend to date anyone else. Unlike what you've read or heard through the grapevine about me, I don't have dozens of girlfriends."

"I'm sure the word *girlfriend* isn't in your vocabulary. So why me?"

"Because I need a successful, intelligent and classy woman such as yourself on my arm," he said. "Plus, you're the quintessential girl-next-door, which is the type of woman I need in order to clean up my image."

"Don't you have plenty of other female friends to ask? I read the gossip sites. There are tons of pictures with you and drop-dead gorgeous women. Supermodels, actresses, singers…someone more on your level."

"I don't want a woman like that. They get boring. They only care about fame, material things and spending my money. I want someone I can talk to. Someone to stimulate my mind. Someone to laugh with like you've made me do for the past hour. And I can save you from more horrible dates. So, yes I'd say you're the perfect candidate."

"Perfect candidate? I'm not the one running for office."

"But will you be by my side when I do?"

Chapter 4

The next morning Megan woke up earlier than normal. She wasn't a morning person, but she could no longer sleep after tossing and turning with Steven's request on her mind. He told her to think about it, and if they chose to go forward with their plans, they agreed to tell no one.

She decided to jog on her treadmill and listen to some music. She was nervous about what the future held. But at least she wouldn't have to worry about any blind dates for a while because she would be in an exclusive relationship with Senator Steven Monroe.

Her main fear was that he'd sleep with women on the side, but it wouldn't be cheating because they weren't in a real relationship. Though, he had said he wouldn't, and she believed him. Megan wondered how her ex would feel about her dating a senator. He probably wouldn't care. He definitely didn't care about her feelings when he lied and cheated on her for almost four years.

She was going to get on with her life and if that meant helping a senator clean up his image, then that's was what she was going to do. Plus, if it meant having a shot to land a guest spot on *Decorator's Dream* then it was well worth it. Satisfied with her decision, she jumped off of the treadmill, showered, dressed and headed out the door to Chase and Whitmore Designs.

When Megan arrived, Jade was speaking to the intern, Lucy, in the mostly all-white reception area that Lucy had recently remodeled for a class project. Megan, who loved antiques, was quite impressed with Lucy's mixture of modern and Louis XVI–style furniture. Light blue and lavender toss pillows laden the white chairs and couches in the client waiting area. Fresh calla lilies and orchids sat on end tables along with decorating books.

Megan smiled as she looked at her best friend. She was truly the diva of fashion and style. Her makeup was flawless which added to her large brown eyes and her auburn-colored skin. Her shoulder-length layered dark hair was curled without a strand out of place. She wore an off-white pantsuit with stilettos making her even taller than her already five-foot-seven-inch height.

"Are you forgetting our job today?" Megan inquired looking down at her khaki capris, tennis shoes and a sleeveless pink T-shirt. Her long hair was pulled back into a bun at her neck. "We're hanging wallpaper."

"I have a change of clothes in the car. Besides, that appointment isn't until this afternoon, and I have another appointment in an hour with Wade Greene, you know the sportscaster." Jade looked up from the file she was reading. "Chelsea introduced me to him at her cocktail party last month. After seeing what we did with her home, he now wants me to redo his dining and living room areas. Still, I promise to be at the Brown's to help you hang wallpaper. I just need to show him some fabric swatches for his dining room."

"And get a date?" Megan questioned her single friend.

"If I'm lucky." Jade winked and then sashayed back to her office.

"I'm going to run down to Starbucks for a caramel macchiato," Megan said, heading toward the door.

"I can go get it for you, Ms. Chase," Lucy offered. She was an eager-to-please intern. Lucy had one more semester before graduation, and Megan was contemplating hiring her full-time.

"No, I need to run a quick errand, as well. I'll be back in a few." She really didn't have to go to Starbucks considering they had a Keurig in the kitchen, but she wanted to go ahead and call Steven with her answer before she changed her mind. And she didn't want to do it in her office. She rarely closed her door when she was there because Jade and Lucy were always in and out. She didn't want them to think something was wrong, and she definitely didn't want anyone to else to know about her arrangement with Steven.

When she walked into the Starbucks, she found an empty table near the back. She figured she would order enough coffee and pastries for everyone before she left. She then nervously dialed Steven's cell phone number. She couldn't believe what she was about to do.

At exactly seven that evening, Megan's phone rang. She was sitting on the floor brushing Percy, a weekly ritual that he hated. She glanced at the caller ID and saw Steven's name. He was in a meeting earlier when she called him with her decision. They agreed to talk that evening, and he was punctually calling at the time she'd suggested.

She stood up to grab her notepad that she had earlier jotted some general questions in to ask Steven. Free from Megan's hands, Percy darted out of the bedroom to escape the brushing ritual.

"Hello?" Megan plopped down on the bed.

"Hey, it's Steven. How are you doing this evening?"

"Fine, Stevo. And how are you?"

"Stevo?" he asked taken aback.

"Well, I figured you need a pet name for me to call you. You don't like Stevo?"

"No, it reminds me of my days in high school when the nerds would call me Stevo or worse Stevster."

"I see. Well, I guess we'll think of something else. In the meantime, I have some questions that every girlfriend should know," Megan said getting her pen ready.

"Yes, I have big feet and great hands to give body massages with," he joked.

Megan felt her face getting hot at the thought of his great hands giving her a body massage with hot oil. A man with big feet could only mean one thing, at least most of the time. She smiled at the thought.

"I already have my list of questions."

"That's fine. How was your day?"

"It was good, and yours?"

"I spent most of the day reviewing a possible campaign budget with Shawn just in case I receive the nomination. I need to do some fund-raising if I'm to have a successful campaign."

"I thought all you needed was a great platform and a speech," Megan said, sounding a little naive on that subject. She was never one for keeping up with politics.

He chuckled softly before answering her.

"That's part of it, but I also have to rent the headquarters, pay people to work there or find volunteers, buy materials, pay for advertisements, but that's not my biggest dilemma at the moment. The community center that I started and help fund is losing one of its grants, therefore losing about ten college students that would normally assist with events with the children during the summer camp."

"Can you do a fund-raiser?"

"Yes, I'm considering hosting a fund-raiser party and then writing a check to match whatever is raised. The grant funded quite a bit."

"Well, maybe I can help." Megan was always one for volunteering her services or expertise if the need arose. "I'm the assistant graduate advisor for one of the undergrad chapters for my sorority. I'll check to see if some of the girls would like to volunteer their services this summer. A lot of them are education majors so they need the experience of working with children," she said, taking notes. The undergrads were having their last meeting of the semester the following evening, and she could approach the ones that were staying in Atlanta for the summer.

"That is very thoughtful and supportive of you."

"No problem. Also, I have a few clients and friends that could possibly give a donation. And I'm sure Braxton won't mind you using the mezzanine level at his restaurant. Let me make some phone calls tomorrow and work my magic, that's if you want me to." She hoped she wasn't overstepping her bounds. Though she was only supposed to play the make-believe girlfriend, planning and organizing were her specialties.

"No, that's wonderful. Thank you," he said in amazement.

"No problem. Isn't that what girlfriends are for?" she asked jokingly.

"Yes, they are. There're some other things girlfriends are good for, as well," Steven said in a sexy tone.

"If you're going to continue talking like that, the

deal is off. Now on to my list of questions," she said getting back to the real business at hand. As much as she liked Steven, Megan knew that sex was one road she couldn't travel with him. For if she did, she'd never want to let him go.

Over the next hour, Megan learned that Steven liked to fish, and listen to jazz, classical, R&B and hip-hop. He played the guitar and gave lessons to the children during the summer camp. He was a running back during his freshman year of college but got hurt and decided not to play anymore. He never wanted to go professional, but he enjoyed football. His parents were relieved he could no longer play, especially his father who wanted him to follow in his footsteps and go into politics. He loved seafood especially shrimp, and he liked Bruce Lee movies. His pet peeve was people who complained about issues but did nothing to make a change. It was also the reason he decided to go into politics and not become a practicing attorney like Bryce. He had a brownstone in Washington, D.C., that he shared with his brother and a townhome in historic Savannah.

"Do you feel that you really know me now?" he asked in a low, deep voice that sent goose bumps down her arms. This man was driving her insane, and she didn't know how much longer she could stand having his voice in her ear.

"Overall." She put down her pen and notepad as Percy jumped into her lap. "I'm sure I'll learn more in the months to come. But I just thought of something else. When I was online looking at pictures of you, I only saw you with a bunch of females. There were only a few family pictures and some of you giving speeches during your last campaign. However, there was nothing with you and the good you do for the communities in your district such as the center and the gardens. Why is that?"

"Well one reason is that all the media and gossip blogs tend to care about is who I'm dating. Plus, I do what I do for my community because it's my passion. I'm not doing it for the publicity. I do it because I care, and I'm in the position to make a change. Everyone wasn't born wealthy like me, but it doesn't mean they can't have the same advantages. There're some articles out there though, about some of the things I've done, but unfortunately my past lifestyle outweighs the good."

"We're going to change that, Steven. It'll help with cleaning up your image. They need to see you playing the guitar with the children and getting dirty in the community garden. They need to see your philanthropy side not the philandering one. I have a reporter friend at one of the local news stations. I'll see if she can come to the fund-raiser."

He laughed. "Wow. Are you an interior decorator or an image consultant?"

"I'm the woman who believes in you and what you stand for."

"Thank you. That truly means a lot to me. Out of all of the women I've dated, including my ex-wife, you've been the only one to say that, and you're not even my real girlfriend. I don't know what I'm going to do without you when this ends. Promise me we'll always be friends."

"Of course." A lump formed in her throat. She didn't want to think about the end. Clearing her windpipe, she glanced at her notepad to see was there anything else she forgot to ask.

"I read somewhere that you don't drink alcohol. Is that true?"

"I may have an occasional glass of wine or champagne, but only when I'm in the comforts of my own home. I wouldn't want the media to snap a picture of me holding a drink. Then I'd be labeled as an alcoholic."

"Makes sense." *I guess he already has enough labels.*

"And you?"

"Occasionally a glass of wine or some girlie drink like Sex on the Beach."

"You like having sex on the beach? Me, too. I own some beachfront property if you ever want to…" Steven said in a teasing manner although she knew he meant it. She tried to ignore his comment even though a picture of them making love on the beach popped into her head.

"Steven, if we're going to do this, you have to refrain from flirting so much." *Because its making me want to jump through the phone and onto your lap.*

"I can't help it. If I can't flirt with you, who am I going to flirt with? You're my girlfriend, but I'll try to keep it to a minimum if it's making you want me."

"Want you? Who says I want you?"

"I know you have to be attracted to me to even do this and that goes both ways. I was going to ask you out anyway. Who knows? Maybe this is a way for us to be a couple and get to know each other in the process. You know, skip the courting part. Besides, you don't like dates."

She laughed sarcastically. "You know, you're funny. If you don't get the nomination, you can always go into comedy. Anyway, a little about me. I was born and raised here in Atlanta. My dad is a high school principal and my mother is a first grade teacher. My hobbies are reading suspense and romance novels, going to the movies and comedy shows. I also listen to most music genres and my favorite singer is Beyoncé. Anything else you care to know?"

She was ready to get off of the phone. She had three meetings all before noon the next day. Plus his low, sexy voice in her ear was starting to wreak havoc on her thought process, and she was beginning to wish he really was her boyfriend. And his sex-on-the-beach comment had made her rather hot in a certain area, and she needed a cold shower. *Fast.* He was quite flirtatious all of sudden, and she didn't know how she was going to make it the next few months if he was constantly flirting with her. He may just receive a special bonus after all.

"What's your favorite flower?" he asked.

"Pink roses and red tulips."

"Why tulips?" he asked curiously.

"My grandfather used to plant them in his garden when I was a little girl. When he died, they bloomed so beautiful that year. But after that they stopped coming back," Megan said getting teary eyed. "Please continue with your questions. I get emotional sometimes thinking about him."

"I completely understand. What's your favorite color?"

"Pink but I also like purple."

"You are such a girlie girl. And favorite perfume?"

"Amarige by Givenchy."

"Is that what you were wearing the day I met you?"

"Yes, it was. That's all I ever wear. Anything else? I really need to get going to type up a budget proposal for a client." She really didn't mean to get that personable with him. She'd never even told her ex the reason why she loved tulips. Perhaps because he'd never asked.

"Yes. That's all for now. Have a good evening, Megan."

"The same to you, Mr. Monroe," she answered hanging up the phone quickly.

A minute later, the phone rang again. *What now?*

"Yes?" Megan answered in an annoyed tone. She was lying on her bed still trying to get the image of sex on the beach out of her head. However, all she kept fantasizing about was lying naked with Steven on a beach towel with those strong hands of his roaming over her body and his lips placing hot kisses on her neck.

"I sometimes wish caller ID hadn't been invented. That way you wouldn't have to answer the phone with such an attitude," Steven said jokingly.

"But answering machines do exist," Megan said impatiently getting up and walking over to her sewing room. She needed to get away from her bed especially with his voice in her ear.

"You still have an answering machine?"

"No."

"I won't keep you on the phone. I just wanted to tell you thank you for helping me. I sincerely appreciate it."

"You are a good man and an honest politician despite your jaunts with women. The only thing I ask of you is that you remain honest with me," Megan said to him seriously.

"That's a promise I can keep. However, by the end of this, you're not going to want to let me go. Good night, Megan."

She sat at her sewing machine and dropped her forehead on it. His words played in her head like a broken record. *What I have I gotten myself into?*

Megan was supposed to be working on a project board for a presentation next week. However, she'd found herself unable to concentrate at home, so she'd headed to the office thinking that her thoughts of Steven wouldn't follow her there. But as she sat in her office staring at a blank board, she was so wrong.

It had been a week since Megan had agreed to be Steven's girlfriend. She hadn't seen him and a part of her was happy about that. However, she found herself missing him and that scared her. Whenever the phone rang, she hoped it was him and in some instances it was. He was out of town on business, but they spoke every day because she was planning a Jazz Wine Down Wednesday fund-raiser for the community center. She was able to reserve space in Braxton's restaurant, which was donating the food and wine. She was also able to invite people from the media. She had secured eight of the undergrads from her sorority, and six undergrads from Steven's fraternity had signed up to volunteer during the summer. Megan had negotiated that the fraternity and sorority members wouldn't be paid, but Steven would write letters of recommendation when they graduated from college, and he would attend a voter's registration drive on campus sponsored by his fraternity.

Megan hadn't told her parents she was dating Steven yet. But she figured they would know by tomorrow morning considering that night's fund-raiser event would be their first outing in public. She did tell Jade, Tiffani and Sydney that she was helping Senator Monroe plan a fund-raiser for the community center. She also casually told them she was his date for the evening. They were excited for her especially since they were invited. Jade only went to A-list events and Tiffani was glad to get out of the house and away from her four-year-old son and his recent tantrums. Ever since Tiffani's husband died of a heart attack almost a year ago, her son had been acting out. Sydney even voluntarily cancelled the date she had set up for Megan to go on the following week, much to her relief.

Megan sat at her desk contemplating her decision to date Steven. While she was indeed attracted to him, the fear of falling for him had weighed heavily on her mind since the day she accepted. Every time she thought about him, her heart thumped hard against her chest and her mind wandered to a place of lust and fantasy with him.

Lucy tapped on the ajar door interrupting Megan's amorous thoughts.

"Ms. Chase, you have a special delivery!" Lucy excitedly announced zooming into the office with her bouncy red hair and blue eyes sparkling brightly. She took Megan by the hand and pulled her out into the reception area. On Lucy's desk, were two dozen pink roses with red tulips scattered throughout in a sparkling crystal vase with a pink-and-lavender chiffon ribbon tied around it.

"Open the card. Open the card." Lucy jumped up and down like a little schoolgirl.

Megan remained speechless. Jade tapped her foot impatiently and placed her hands on her hips giving Megan a "hurry up" look.

"Girl, open the card and stop looking surprised! You know it's from the senator!" Jade demanded handing Megan the card from the bouquet.

Megan really wasn't sure if she wanted to open it in front of them. *Why is he sending me flowers in the first place? This isn't a real relationship!* But she opened the card anyway, if only to appease Lucy and Jade.

"Can't wait to see you tonight. Yours truly, Stevo." She giggled at the way he'd signed his name. *I guess he liked the nickname after all.*

She tried to act overwhelmed in front of Jade and Lucy even though she really didn't have to act at all. She was flattered.

"Oh, these are so beautiful. He remembered my favorite flowers," she said, pleasantly surprised by his gesture.

Now she realized why he asked what her favorite flower was. She was rather pleased that he had sent them and was even more elated of the added extra details of the color of the ribbons. For once, she had found a man that knew what she wanted. *Too bad he's not really my man,* she thought. Too bad her ex never thought like that. She remembered when he sent her yellow roses for her birthday after the fact because he was too busy with patients. She later discovered he was rather getting busy with his nurse at a hotel downtown.

Blushing, Megan took the arrangement to her office and placed it on her desk.

"Ms. Chase," Lucy called after her, "You have a phone call holding on line three. It's Justine Monroe from the Fabulous Living Channel."

Megan ran out of her office and collided with Jade as they immediately locked wide eyes, and then headed straight to the conference room and closed the door.

Jade sat down and stared at the phone. "Girl, this could be it! I'll pray while you answer the phone."

Megan took a deep breath before answering. She pushed the speaker button so Jade could hear, as well.

"This is Megan Chase here also with Jade Whitmore."

"Good morning, ladies. This is Justine Monroe with the Fabulous Living Channel. I have some fabulous news to share with you."

The women locked eyes again, and Jade stood up above the phone and placed her hand over her heart.

"I'm happy to say after reviewing your portfolio as well as the audition video, we would like to offer you and Ms. Whitmore the opportunity to have a segment on *Decorator's Dream.*

"Oh, Ms. Monroe, I… Thank you. We're very excited." Megan sat in the chair in front of the phone and tried to remain composed as she and Jade squeezed hands.

"Craig, my production assistant and I look forward to working with you this summer in Hilton Head. I have to go, but Craig will be in contact with you within the next few days with all of the necessary information you'll need."

"Thank you so much for the opportunity, Ms. Monroe."

After they hung up, the women gave each other huge hugs before running out to the reception area to inform Lucy.

"Now Lucy," Jade, began in a serious tone. "We'll

be gone for a couple of weeks this summer. Think you can hold down the fort while we're away?"

"Yes, Ms. Whitmore. It'll give me a chance to do some projects on my own."

While Jade and Lucy conversed, Megan thought about how quickly Justine called so soon after she spoke to Steven about the opportunity. She made a mental note to call Steven and thank him. She sighed, he had already lived up to his part of the deal, but now she had to do her part. *Why does mine seem so much harder?*

Chapter 5

The evening of the fund-raiser arrived sooner than Megan realized. She left a voice mail on her parent's home phone explaining her plans for that night so they wouldn't be in total shock if there was a picture of her and Steven in newspaper the next day. They had seen the other pictures but once they saw the statement Steven's team had released, her parents had admitted they felt better. She knew they wouldn't be home because of PTA meetings, so a voice mail was perfect. She knew sooner or later they would find out about him so she opted for the later.

Megan stood at her vanity putting the last touches of her makeup on. Steven was sending a car to pick her up, which was to arrive in thirty minutes, and she still hadn't decided on which dress she was going to wear. She'd just gotten out of the shower, but she felt herself perspiring with anxiety. She went into her bedroom and turned on the ceiling fan even though she already had the air conditioner on full blast and tossed the bathrobe on the bed. Percy just stared at her and purred.

"What am I going to wear?" she asked the cat who was now licking his paws. She walked back into the closet and looked at her evening wear and opted for a fuchsia, spaghetti strap dress with a flared, flirty skirt that stopped at her knees showcasing her smooth, freshly waxed legs.

She buckled her heels and then smiled. She was glad that Jade had convinced her to go to the spa with her after Justine Monroe's call. Megan's toes and fingernails were freshly French manicured and her hair was straight down her back with loose curls on the ends. Her hairdresser added a few strawberry blonde highlights that matched her caramel skin and brought out her cheekbones.

Looking through her antique jewelry box, she picked a simple gold necklace and big gold hoops. When she was done, she surveyed her classy and elegant outfit in the full-length mirror. She looked like a senator's girlfriend should look, she thought.

Then she decided to lose the hoops and wear diamond studs instead. She didn't want to look too flashy and draw any more attention than necessary to herself. Megan was sure the attention would be on her more so than Steven when it came to the press. That was her only worry about agreeing to date Steven. While Megan was a people person at work, she really preferred privacy in her personal life. Megan laughed at herself as she realized that her private life was about to be flipped upside down.

After she was completely dressed, Megan added a little bit more makeup and sprayed on some Ama-rige. She looked at the grandfather clock that once belonged to her grandmother as she walked into the kitchen. She had a few more minutes, so she decided to drink a glass of cold water to calm her nerves even though a shot of whiskey would probably work better. While she was in the kitchen, her buzzer sounded. *Let the games begin,* she thought as she answered her intercom.

"Yes?"

"Hello, Megan. Are you ready to go?" It was Ste-ven. She hadn't realized he would be picking her up. She assumed he was only sending a car. At least the driver would be in the car, she thought. But that wasn't good either. She would have to start pretend-ing before the party, and she wasn't ready for that yet.

"Yes. Just surprised to hear your voice. I was ex-pecting a driver."

"Change of plans. I'm driving."

Great. Now it will just be us together. I think I need that shot of whiskey now.

"Okay. I'll be down in a minute," Megan an-swered. She ran back into her bedroom and glanced in the mirror one last time. As she walked out the room, she said to Percy, "Wish me luck!" The cat just blinked and jumped on her bed. She knew he would stay there all night.

Megan grabbed her black evening purse and a shawl and headed down to the front lobby. When she arrived she saw Steven standing alone. He was on his cell and hadn't realized she was there. He looked handsome in a dark blue suit with a light blue dress shirt and a paisley tie. Megan's heart began to beat fast again, and her lips slightly parted as her stomach churned. As she watched him, she began to remember just how important a man he really was. He was a politician, a man with power and status. He was serious-minded. He had authority and a way of taking total command of any situation. Megan was impressed and it was a solid part of what made him one sexy man. Megan smiled when she realized that like her father, Steven spoke with his hands.

Steven was in a deep conversation with Bryce. He put his hand to his head in disbelief. Another main donor for the community center decided not to offer their usual amount for the summer program because of budget cuts with their company.

"Speak with Shawn and let him…" His voice trailed off. He knew Megan was behind him. He could smell her tantalizing perfume. He slowly turned and saw her sitting on one of the Victorian-style chairs in the lobby. She gave him an encouraging smile, and he took the phone away from his ear. He was pleased at her lovely appearance and for a quick second had forgotten why he was angry. Just looking at Megan sitting there so elegantly with her legs crossed wearing four-inch heels sent his mind on a journey to speechlessness.

Bryce was still talking, but Steven hadn't heard a single word. He had more important business to tend to at the moment. He regained his composure just long enough to get off of the phone.

"I gotta go, talk to Shawn. I'll see you fellas in about twenty minutes," he rather hurriedly told Bryce and pushed the end button on his cell phone screen. He rushed over to Megan as she stood up.

Megan took a deep breath as he approached her. She was suddenly feeling nervous and nauseous about the situation she placed herself in. *How can I play make-believe girlfriend for a handsome man that I could find myself falling for? No correction. That I am falling for.*

"You look beautiful," he said and kissed her on her cheek.

"Thank you. You look nice as well," she said, thinking the games had begun. She almost backed away when he kissed her cheek, but remembered that they were in public. She would later remind him however, only kisses on the cheeks and no lips. She could only imagine how his lips would kiss other places on her body.

"Ready?" he asked, holding out his hand. She put her hand into his, and they walked out to his car. He opened the passenger side of his black Mercedes convertible for her and she slid in, and he closed the door. When Steven got into the car, she noticed the strain on his face. As he started to drive, he stared straight ahead as a Sade CD played.

"Is everything okay?" she asked him. She was concerned. She wanted tonight to be special for him. There would be possible donors there as well as the media, and he had to put on his game face.

"Another donor that donates to the summer program backed out today." He glanced in her direction and then back on the road. "You know what I think?"

"That your reputation is beginning to catch up with you?"

"Yep. Bryce said the same statement earlier."

"Remember when I told you I may have some clients who may donate to the community center? They are coming tonight with checkbooks. Let me work my magic for you," she said patting his leg. As she tried to move her hand he grabbed it and held it tight.

"Thank you for supporting me, Megan." He held on to her hand until they pulled into the parking lot at the event. Before they got out of the car, Megan told him of her kissing rule. Steven agreed unless it was absolutely necessary. Megan gave him her "I don't think so look" as Steven drove the car to the front door for valet parking.

Once inside, Steven introduced Megan to his colleagues including Bryce and Shawn who both nodded approvingly. She gave a beautiful smile and said a lot of nice-to-meet-yous and thank-yous for coming to support Steven and the community center. She was glad when Tiffani, Syd and Jade arrived. They all gathered at Megan's table while Steven spoke with his guests.

"Girl, I'm so happy for you. You two look hot together!" Tiffani said with her cute dimples displaying on her smooth, sienna face.

"Yes, girl," Jade chimed in. "So glad you finally got a man and a wealthy one at that."

"I had a feeling there was something going on between you two," Sydney said. "You were just too giddy after he changed your tire. And the way you two were looking at each other all night at the gala, I just knew you would end up together. So happy for you, sis."

"Thank you. Now, if you ladies would excuse me, I need to go raise some money. Oh, and when I return please have your checks waiting," Megan said as she bounced away.

For the next hour, Megan indeed worked her magic with her clients that she invited including Chelsea and her husband, attorney Richard Benton, as well as a few others. Real-estate investor Broderick Hollingsworth was one of Megan's top clients. She had recently redone all of his rooms in a bed and breakfast he owned in Rome, Georgia. Because he trusted her judgment, he agreed to donate a large amount and offered a free weekend for her and Steven to relax at the inn. She thanked him for the free weekend although she knew they would never use it together. She would give it to Tiffani instead who could use a weekend away, and Megan would baby sit Keith Jr.—or KJ as he was affectionately called—considering he was her godson.

While she was speaking with Sharon Diamond, a romance author, she noticed Steven looking at her with the same strained look he had earlier. Megan wasn't sure why he appeared stressed, so she quickly ended her conversation with Sharon. Besides she already had her donation. She said thank you and walked over to Steven's side.

He was deep in a conversation with a gentleman who wasn't sure if he totally agreed with Steven's views on certain issues and said he was too wet behind the ears to run for his father's seat. She was about to walk away when Steven grabbed her hand and held on to it.

"Mr. Brown, this is Megan Chase, my girlfriend," Steven said. "Mr. Brown is one my father's colleagues."

"Nice to meet you, Mr. Brown. I'm sure you're as excited about Steven possibly running for the U.S. Senate as I am," she said warmly as she shook his hand looking him straight in the eyes. "Steven can you please be a dear and get me a bottled water. I'll stay and keep Mr. Brown company."

A few minutes later Steven returned with the bottled water as Mr. Brown and another gentleman who approached the conversation were writing checks and handing them to Megan.

"Steven, you've definitely found an angel. Where have you been hiding her? About time you settled down with *one* woman," Mr. Brown stated as he and the other older gentleman walked off to the buffet table.

"Ms. Chase, you've raised a lot of money for the community center. What have you been telling these people? You didn't make any promises I can't keep did you?" he asked teasingly.

"I told them you would give them your firstborn son if they donated." She paused to giggle. "I simply told them the truth. That you're the perfect candidate for the position and even though they might not agree with all of your political views, the children at the community center were more important than your political differences," she said, smiling up at him.

A sincere grin crossed his face. "Well, I certainly found the perfect candidate, as well. Oh, by the way, did you receive the flowers I sent earlier to your office?"

"Yes, I did. They were lovely. Thank you." She turned away. She didn't want him to see how truly happy she was about receiving the flowers. "Also, thank you for contacting Justine for me. She called today."

"She did?" he asked with a puzzled expression.

"Yes. She offered Jade and I a spot on the show this summer."

"Congratulations, except I never spoke to her."

Megan shook her head in disbelief. "Wait. What?"

"I called her and left a message, but I didn't tell her what it was about and she hasn't returned my call yet. Looks like you didn't need my help."

She smiled and then laughed. "Oh, my goodness. I'm shocked."

"Why? I saw your portfolio. You're a very talented and creative decorator. You deserve more than just a guest spot. You deserve your own show."

"Well that's the ultimate goal one day."

"Now, I know our agreement, but you aren't going to back out, are you?"

She shook her head and chuckled. "No, I want to help you clean up your image and help you win the seat." Megan stopped speaking as a reporter approached wanting to interview Steven about the community center and the rumor about him running for his father's seat. Megan left them to scout out Braxton who she hadn't had a chance to thank in person. She asked one of the waitresses who told her that he was downstairs. Megan peeked over the banister and saw her brother moving from table to table conversing with the patrons as the smooth sounds of the jazz band on the stage reverberated throughout the restaurant. She waved to get his attention, and he gave his charming smile that matched their father's. He jetted up the stairs as the group of women he had been speaking with checked him out. Megan didn't blame them. He was handsome in his dark gray suit that fit his muscular six-foot-four-inch frame. His bald head glistened under the dim lights, and Megan saw a few women fanning themselves. She shook her head and smiled as he approached and led her to an empty highboy table.

"Is everything set up how you wanted it?"

"Yes. Everything is perfect. Your staff did an awesome job. Are you playing tonight?"

"I may sit in with the band for a while but definitely on Friday and Saturday because my band is playing."

"I'm sure all of the women down there would love to hear you on the keys tonight."

"We'll see. So my baby sister is dating Senator Monroe. Have you told our parents? I can just hear Mother now."

"They don't know officially yet, but I'm sure they will by tomorrow."

He flashed a smile and Megan caught one of the waitresses looking his way blush. Her brother was indeed handsome with his perfectly trimmed mustache and goatee sitting on his chiseled, mocha face.

"Our mother will be calling you. I suggest you tell her first."

She simply nodded. Megan and her mother didn't always see eye to eye. She chatted with her brother for a few more minutes before one of the hostesses called him away.

"Hey," a deep voice said in her ear from behind her. "Having fun?" His lips skimmed the top of her ear causing her to feel faint. The emotions he made her experience in a split second were uncanny, and she needed to get out of there before she forgot they weren't really a couple and turned around to lay a juicy kiss on his inviting mouth.

She turned around slowly to face him. His handsome face no longer wore the tense expression from earlier. He looked more relaxed as he held a plate of appetizers in his hand. He dipped a shrimp into the cocktail sauce, popped the entire thing into his mouth and then ran his tongue along his bottom lip. It was such a seductive gesture that she knew she really needed to leave and quick.

"I believe the evening went well. I think we have received donations from most of the people here. I'm going to go home with Syd in a few minutes," Megan said, turning away from him to scan the room for Syd. She found her in a deep conversation with Bryce. Megan could only hope Syd wasn't telling him how she really felt about a case where Bryce had represented a man who the GBI had arrested. Syd had been certain the man was guilty although he was found not guilty. However, Bryce Monroe was one of Atlanta's top criminal attorneys and rarely lost a case.

"Oh, are you sure? The night is young, and we haven't even danced yet. Plus, if you think about it, this is our real first date since you refuse to count the lunch meeting," Steven said grabbing her hand as she turned back around to look at him. He placed his plate on the nearest table as the band began to play "Hello" by Lionel Richie.

"Well, luckily this is one of my favorite songs otherwise, I would say no," Megan said as he pulled her out onto the dance floor.

He placed her arms around his neck and his own hands around her waist.

"Are we putting on a show for the audience?" she

asked as her lips brushed against his ear by mistake. She felt him freeze for a second.

"Yes," he whispered back. They had plenty of spectators Megan noticed. *Good.* She'd made up her mind that evening that Steven would make an excellent U.S. senator. She intended to make sure that it happened, even if it meant slow dancing with him and holding his hand in public, which is something her ex never did when they were together. He didn't like public displays of affection. Even though Steven was just pretending, it still felt nice be in his warm embrace even if it was all one big lie.

The scent of his woodsy cologne whiffed into her nose. She wished it would rub off on her body so she could smell it later when she was alone in her bed. She wanted to dance with him for the rest of the evening but the song was almost over, and she hoped the band would play one more slow song so Steven would hold on to her just a little longer. She knew her brother was on the piano because she knew how he played that particular song. She tried to transfer her thoughts to him thinking that maybe he'd play one more slow song. She almost laughed at the idea but her and Sydney had their twin senses so maybe she could have it with Braxton, as well.

"Is my dancing that bad?" he whispered. "You're not smiling anymore."

She looked up at him with a smile. "Your dancing is on point."

"That's my girl," he said as he brushed the hair

over her ear that had fallen in her face. "What would you do if I kissed you right now?"

"Kiss you back and slap you later," Megan said seriously, while a heat wave rushed through her when he asked. She then found herself half wishing he would kiss her, but she knew it was all for show.

His smoldering gaze was seductive. Sexual. Dangerous.

Her breathing had become uneasy, and she suddenly became aroused, and she noticed he had, as well. She could feel his slight bulge against her pelvis area, and backed up a few inches. But he pulled her close again against his hard body. She began to wonder how it would be if they were naked and entangled in her sheets but quickly shook her head to clear her mind. Sexual tension was the last thing she wanted with Steven. He wanted to simply win the nomination, not her.

"That's a chance I'll have to take," he answered in a sexy, arrogant tone. He ran a finger alongside her cheek to her lips as they parted on command. He lowered his mouth to hers and caressed her lips with a slow, sensual kiss. A low moan escaped her throat as his tongue pushed deeper into her mouth, and she matched his seductive strokes in the same sweet rhythm.

Her hands journeyed up his neck and around to his face as he continued his passionate assault on her lips, showing no mercy. Not that she minded. In fact, she craved more than just a kiss and judging from the fervent groans he made, she could tell they were on the same page.

Megan was somewhat surprised he kissed her. She honestly didn't think he was serious, especially after she had threatened him with a slap in private. But she couldn't push him away with all of the people in the room thinking they were a couple. So of course she kissed him back. What else could she do as his pulsating tongue flicked along her bottom lip as if it belonged there? Every cell in her body was on an electrifying passionate ride that he was in control of.

He lifted his lips from hers as a protest cry escaped her mouth, and her eyes opened. Why on earth had he stopped? She could go on and on. Through the haze she was in, she could see Steven staring at her with a weird expression, and then she glanced around the room and saw all eyes on them as well as a few cheers and whistles.

"Everyone is staring," he said through a clenched smile. "Please don't slap me."

Remembering the premise of their relationship— for she had certainly forgotten for a moment—she smiled, as well. "Of course not. It's all for show."

"You think we were convincing enough? I saw a few shutterbugs, but I'm not sure. My eyes were closed, and I was too busy concentrating on your divine mouth."

"Good. You need the media to see you in a committed relationship and considering we've been in the blogs already, I'm sure tonight's pictures will have them convinced."

She knew she was convinced. Convinced she was falling for him. Hard. She tried to pull away from his embrace, but he placed a kiss on her forehead and slid his hands tenderly down her waist to her hips and finally off of her body. Megan rushed away from him and back over to where Sydney was sitting alone.

"Looks like someone is having a great time," Sydney said with a smirk.

"We were just kissing. So I saw you speaking to Bryce Monroe?" Megan said wanting to change the subject and get her mind off of the kiss.

"Yes, unfortunately. He's such an ass."

"He seems like a nice man." Megan glanced in his direction as he spoke with some of the guests. He was about the same height and build as Steven, except Bryce's hair was curlier and his complexion was more of a butterscotch shade. He had a strong jawline and a charismatic smile under a neatly trimmed mustache and goatee. He would make a great catch for someone.

"Not in the courtroom and definitely not with me." Sydney ran a hand through her bouncy bob.

"You ready to go, sissy?" Megan asked.

"I know I said I would take you home, but I just received a call from my partner. Big case and I need to head to the GBI office. I'm sure Steven can take you home. After all he did pick you up."

"But Syd..." Megan started. She didn't know if she could be alone with him again in the car especially after that crazy kiss that meant nothing to him and everything to her.

"Girl, you'll be fine. Just ask Steven now," Sydney said, nodding toward him.

Megan slowly turned around to find Steven directly behind her.

"Of course I can take you home, precious. Just give me a few minutes to say goodbye to Bryce and Shawn." He darted away before Megan could protest. Megan sat down with her lips pressed together.

"What's wrong with you? He is your man. Shouldn't he take you home?" Sydney inquired.

"Oh, sure. I just thought he needed to stay longer."

"The fund-raiser is pretty much over. Now, you know I'm the body language expert. I can tell that he is really into you and the way you almost galloped over here with that flushed face after your kiss, clearly suggests you want him, too. I thought surely you two were about to make love on the dance floor. So let him take you home and finish what he started," Sydney said.

"You sound like Jade."

"I'm just speaking the truth. Here he comes. Have a nice evening."

A few minutes later, Megan sat numbly in Steven's car fiddling with her purse. Luckily, Steven was on his cell phone talking to Shawn.

Megan stared out the window trying to concentrate on something else. Even though all she could manage to do was inhale his cologne and listen to his deep voice. She had no idea what he was saying but the angrier he became the sexier he became, and her mind kept travelling back to the kiss.

She stole glances at him wondering how long she could keep up this charade that she wasn't really attracted to him. She was becoming highly upset at the fact that he had been on the phone the entire time, which made it clear he had no interest in her. Megan shook her head angrily and then gave him an ice-cold glare. She couldn't believe she thought that kiss could've meant something to him, as well.

When they arrived at her parking garage, Steven was still on the phone in a deep conversation with Shawn. Megan reached to open her door, but Steven placed his hand on her arm and shook his head. Megan looked at him and realized his facial expression was one of annoyance but not for her.

"Shawn, I can't keep going over and over on this issue with you. You know my view and it's not going to change. So let's just drop it." Steven breathed heavily and hung up his phone without saying goodbye. Keeping his hand on her arm, he loosened his grip and then rested his head back on his seat. He turned to face Megan.

"I apologize for being on the phone and ignoring you. Trust me that wasn't my intention, baby. Shawn can be so…what's the word…?"

"Annoying?" Megan asked, feeling a little better that he wasn't trying to ignore her. Did he just say *baby*?

"Something like that. He keeps trying to change my mind about certain things. He's not in my shoes and doesn't understand the pressures politicians have to face. I'm sorry for complaining to you. I know you probably don't want to hear me babble about my political stuff."

"That's what girlfriends are for right? To listen and support their man?" Megan said, teasingly and punching him lightly on the shoulder.

Steven smiled at her comment. "I'm beginning to think perhaps that's what they're for." He chuckled and patted her hand. "I forgot to tell you thank you for tonight. You really did work your magic," he said touching her face tenderly with his hand. He moved closer to her and pulled her face close to his, resting his head on her forehead.

"Just one more little kiss?" he asked in a sexy voice that sent a tremble through her body.

"But…" Megan started.

"But what? Didn't we have a good time on our first date?"

"It wasn't a date."

"So you didn't feel anything with that kiss on the dance floor?"

"No." She couldn't tell him the truth. The last thing she wanted to do was to get caught up in a fairy tale that she knew would end sooner for him than it would for her.

He slid back to his side. "Well, let me walk you up to your loft," he said seemingly taken aback.

"I can manage by myself," she said, opening the door and stepping out of the car. He got out and pushed the remote to lock the car.

"I said I would walk with you, Ms. Chase."

"Ms. Chase? I thought we were on first name basis, Stevo," she said, giving him a sincere smile. However, he remained silent. She continued to walk ahead of him to the elevator. They remained quiet on the ride up and when they got off, he continued to follow her to her door. Megan unlocked it, but she didn't open it. She turned to face Steven and smiled at him. She stood on her tippy toes and reached up to kiss him lightly on the cheek.

"Good night, Steven. I had a lovely time on our first date."

Megan went inside and leaned her back against the door. *Boy, that was close,* she thought as Percy greeted her by rubbing around her legs.

"How did I ever get myself into this mess?" she asked herself out loud, picking up the cat and walking toward her bathroom to take a refreshing shower. Steven Monroe was making her feel things she had never felt before. She just hoped she could get through the next few months without completely falling in love with him.

Chapter 6

A week had passed since Megan had seen Steven but she'd spoken to him a few times while he was out of town. Their relationship was growing into a comfortable friendship that she pleasantly enjoyed. She was genuinely concerned about his senatorial duties, and she could tell that he loved to hear her opinions. Although politics had never sparked an interest in her before, she was up all night reading his platform, speeches and emailing him her thoughts.

The day after the fund-raiser, tons of pictures hit the internet on gossip blogs, Twitter, Instagram and Facebook. However, there was one she couldn't get out of her mind. *The kiss.* It had been snapped from so many different angles that there were at least twenty different pictures, but they all conveyed the same thing. That the senator was finally in love and had tossed aside his playboy ways for her. Of course that's what they wanted the media to think. Unfortunately when she looked at the pictures, she saw herself falling in love with a man that would never want her in that way. Sure, she figured he was attracted to her, and she sensed he wanted her but more than likely only for sex. Since it was Friday, she decided to work from home instead of going into the office. She'd brought home the duvet, toss pillows and shams she was working on for Chelsea, but Megan wasn't in the mood to work. Her thoughts were still on last Thursday night at the fund-raiser. Dancing with Steven felt nice. It had been a long time since a man made her feel special. It reminded her that she would find love again and that all men weren't like her ex.

She glanced at the clock. It was a quarter to seven. She got up and walked across the room to turn off the alarm that would sound in a few minutes. She wasn't in the mood to jog on the treadmill, so she opted to do one hundred stomach crunches on her yoga mat.

Afterward, Megan walked barefoot to the kitchen with Percy following closely behind her. He was hungry, otherwise he would still be on her bed. She took out his food and noticed the roses and tulips on her island. They still looked beautiful even after a week, and she hoped they would stay alive for just a little while longer. It had been a long time since she had flowers in her home that she hadn't bought for herself.

After giving Percy his food, Megan decided that

a cup of coffee followed by thirty minutes of yoga and meditation would help her relax. While she was rinsing out her coffee pot, her phone rang, and she already knew who it was. Her dad was the only person who would call this early in the morning. He was always at his school by six-thirty to make sure he had everything in order for the day.

Megan had been avoiding her parents. Her mother had left a very distraught voice mail yesterday about her dating Steven. But she finally decided she might as well get it over with and speak to her dad. He was more understanding. Megan didn't bother looking at the caller ID as she answered the phone.

"Hello, Daddy," Megan sighed.

"Daddy? I thought my nickname was Stevo, but I can get used to Daddy. How about Big Daddy? Big Poppa? S. Diddy, you know, like P. Diddy? No wait, it's just Diddy now." He paused, but continued when she remained silent. "Well, I was hoping to get a laugh or a smile from you this morning."

"Steven, I thought you were my father!" Megan said embarrassed. "He's the only person to ever call me this early."

"I wanted to catch you before you went to work."

"I took the day off, but I still have a project to finish and an appointment this afternoon with a potential donor for the community center." Megan walked to the kitchen table to double-check her schedule on her tablet.

"I have to go to Washington, D.C., today. I wanted to know if you could go with me."

"I didn't know I would have to travel," she said, wrinkling her brow.

"I know its short notice, but I have a black-tie charity function to attend on Saturday night that I hadn't planned on going to, but Shawn is insisting I go. Other congressmen and senators will be there with their wives and girlfriends. I thought it would look nice to have you on my arm. You can fly out on the private plane that Bryce and I share."

Private plane?

"I see. When are we returning?"

"You could come back on Sunday or Monday. But I have to stay for some meetings, so I'll return on Wednesday."

"Steven, this is such short notice. I don't have anything to wear to a fancy function in Washington, D.C.," Megan said truthfully.

"I knew you would say something like that. That's why I arranged for you to go shopping with Chelsea today at Barneys. She's already in New York City meeting with some other clients."

"But I have an appointment at two with an executive from Coke about donating to the community center."

"Shawn can go. What other excuses are you going to come up with?"

"What time are we leaving? I have to finish a project," Megan said reluctantly. She couldn't believe she agreed to go with him to Washington, D.C.

"I've arranged for the plane to take you to New York City this morning and then to D.C. once you're done shopping. I have a function to attend this evening in Atlanta so I'll meet you later on tonight. I'm sending a car to take you to the airfield around ten, so get to packing."

"I don't have Barney's money," Megan answered, thinking about what she had in her closet to wear.

"But I do." Without another word, he hung up.

Three hours later Megan was in the limo headed to a private airfield that she didn't know existed in Atlanta. Since her conversation with Steven earlier that morning, she managed to finish her project, pack and drop Percy off at Tiffani's. Megan also had the misfortune of answering the phone without looking at the caller ID while packing. When she heard her mother's voice, Megan cursed in silence and hoped the conversation wouldn't last long.

Her mother wasn't happy about her daughter flying to Washington with someone that she hadn't met yet. She told Megan about her research on Senator Monroe and that she wasn't at all thrilled with the results. Her teacher friends even told her to tell Megan to be careful.

"Megan, it's not a good idea to date him. He doesn't care for you. You just got out of a long term relationship," Mrs. Chase fussed. "You're very vulnerable right now. Men feed off of that! Men like him love that! There is no challenge for him, and he's going to just use you and then throw you away like all of the others!"

"Mother, you don't know what you're talking about. Everything is fine. I'm not trying to start a serious relationship now. We're just dating. That's all!" Megan threw her clothes into the suitcase instead of folding them. Megan and her mother never saw eye to eye, and most of their conversations usually ended because of disagreements.

"Dating? It seems as if you're flying out of town with him! I hardly call that dating! He just wants to have sex with you and then move on to some other pretty young thang!"

"Mother!"

"Megan, you're my daughter. I love you. I'm only looking out for your best interests. And dating a senator, especially one like Steven Monroe, isn't just a regular relationship, honey." Her mother paused and was silent for moment. Megan hated that. She knew that meant her mother's mind was churning for more reasons as to why she shouldn't date Steven.

"Mother..." Megan started before she continued.

"Everyone will know. You'll be on television, in the tabloids. Your life will no longer be private. This is so embarrassing!"

"Embarrassing for whom? You? Are you scared of what your teacher friends will say to you or what they've already said to you? Mother, I'm a grown woman, in case you've forgotten. I know what I'm doing. Steven is a nice guy. Now I have to go finish packing. I love you, Mom." She then hung up before her mother could bicker more.

Megan decided to call her dad on the way to the private airport. It was easier to call him at work when she knew her mother wouldn't be around to snatch the phone and voice her opinion some more. She spoke to her father briefly in between him suspending two boys for fighting.

"How did you meet him? Isn't he out of your circle? Is this Syd's doing?" Dr. Chase sounded concerned. Megan had always been daddy's little girl, and she understood that her father didn't want to see his daughter hurt again by yet another man.

"We're just trying to get to know each other. It's not that serious," Megan told her father.

"Does he play golf? I'm sure he does."

"I think so, Dad," Megan answered making a mental note to ask him.

"When do I meet him? I have some political and personal questions for him."

"Soon, Dad. I'm going to Washington with him for a function this weekend. Maybe next weekend." She had no intentions of introducing them. She doubted Steven wanted to meet her parents.

"Your mother called earlier ranting. You just be careful. You know how those politicians are, and he's a playboy."

"People change, Dad."

"Yeah, and you said that about that punk exboyfriend of yours. He was too arrogant and only concerned about his status and not loving and taking care of my baby girl. You know I never liked him."

"Yes, Daddy, I know. Well, I'm going to let you get back to running your school," Megan said trying to get off of the phone. Once her dad got started on a tirade, he didn't know how to stop.

"I have some teacher evaluations to do this morning, so yes I need to go."

"I'm sure they're looking forward to seeing you arrive unannounced." Megan was glad she decided not to become a teacher. She loved being her own boss and not having to worry about someone always looking over her shoulder.

When Megan boarded the private jet, she was greeted by a flight attendant. The woman held out her delicate, manicured hand to shake Megan's.

"Good morning, Ms. Chase. I'm Susan, and I'll be your flight attendant for today. Senator Monroe has informed me to take extra special care of you. Would you like a mimosa while I give you a tour?" Susan stepped aside to let Megan walk in front of her.

Megan stood in awe. The main cabin of the jet had six plush, oversize white leather chairs on top of a very beautiful gold-and-white Persian carpet. She was used to flying coach or sometimes business class, but the Monroe family jet represented accommodations seen only in illustrious magazines.

"No thank you to the mimosa, but a definite yes to the tour. This is absolutely breathtaking." She looked at Susan. "I bet you love your job!" Megan exclaimed as Susan began to show her around. In the cockpit, she made a quick introduction of Captain Simmons.

The jet was about twice the size of a motor mansion, with the same luxuries, including a mini-kitchen, wet bar, a bedroom, and a bathroom in the back of the plane.

Megan walked back to the front. She hated taking trips on a plane and preferred to be asleep during the flight. Especially the last twenty minutes because her ears would always clog up, and she wouldn't be able to hear that well for at least three hours afterward. She'd brought a bag of jellybeans and a pack of gum to snack on to prevent excessive ear clogging

She decided to sit up front in one of the reclining seats and have a glass of orange juice from the wet bar to accompany the breakfast that Susan served. Captain Simmons informed Megan that there was a thirty-minute delay because they had to wait for a clear runway at the small airport. While Megan enjoyed her breakfast of French toast, shrimp and grits, and a spinach-and-feta-cheese omelet, she was interrupted by her cell phone ringing.

"Hello?"

"Hey, I called to check on you," Steven said.

"I'm fine. I'm eating a delicious breakfast."

"Shrimp and grits?"

"Yep, and it's so good. We're taking off in a few minutes."

"I have a meeting and then a fitting for my tux to wear on Saturday. My housekeeper Greta will pick you up from the airport."

"Oh. I didn't know you had a housekeeper."

"Greta is a sweetheart. She's been with the Monroe family since I was born. She's almost like a second mom to me and my siblings. By the way, I may not be in Washington until after midnight, so don't wait up." He hesitated for moment and cleared his throat. "Megan, I need to prewarn you. Greta is expecting you to sleep in the master bedroom."

"Wait! I can't sleep in the same bed with you," she said aloud, but then remembering she wasn't alone, Megan lowered her voice. "I'm sure your brownstone has a guest room!"

"It does, but Greta also knows me, and my female guests have never slept in the guest room. Don't worry, I have a California King bed. You won't know I'm there."

"Fine! Stay on your side!"

Once Megan arrived to New York, she met Chelsea in Manhattan. Chelsea had arranged with Barneys and a few other places for Megan to try on and purchase a dress for the evening.

Chelsea spoke on her cell phone a mile a minute, speaking in her usual "I'm in control and don't you forget it" tone. She smiled and winked at Megan while they walked down 5th Avenue.

Megan walked alongside her mentor, thinking about the upcoming weekend and what her father said earlier, even though Chelsea's conversation was much more interesting. Megan had always admired Chelsea since her mother had first introduced them at a sorority meet-and-mingle tea. The two of them immediately developed a mentor and mentee bond. She admired Chelsea for her wit, sassiness and for always knowing the right thing to say in any situation. She was truly fabulous at fifty with her pixie cut hairstyle, size six frame, and stunning appearance that always turned heads.

Chelsea was currently using her wit and sassiness to appease an irate client. She talked and walked fast in her Louboutin's as if they were tennis shoes. Megan increased her pace in her flat gladiator sandals in order to keep up.

"*Chérie,* my love. The awards show is a month away. I have already spoken to someone at Versace, and they're making five one-of-a-kind evening gowns just for you to try on." Chelsea paused and rolled her eyes, which made Megan giggle silently. "No one else will have the same dress. My assistant has already spoken to a rep from Harry Winston about a diamond choker with matching earrings. Have I ever let you down?" Chelsea shook her head at Megan. "Of course not, my love. Now go finish recording that number one song and let me handle the big things," Chelsea said before her client could oppose. She pushed the off button on her phone.

"Girl, these celebrities never know what they want. That's why they hire me to tell them." Chelsea tossed her phone into her purse and placed her aviator shades in her hair as they walked into Barney's.

Megan nodded her head in agreement.

"I understand completely. I have a celebrity client right now who keeps changing her mind about what type of rug she wants in front of her fireplace. Her home is being featured in a magazine next month, and she's a nervous wreck, which is driving me crazy. However, I'm excited that one of my creations will be in *House to Home Magazine.* Now if my client will just make up her mind before the photo shoot." Normally Megan made all of the decisions, but this particular celebrity client wanted to give her two cents. Luckily, Lucy was going to handle the rug problem on Monday.

"Probably the same person," Chelsea said. "Now let's get back to why we're here. You need an evening dress for a black-tie function. There're some gowns that I want you to try on as well as some other things."

"Other things?"

"I've already called ahead and had the saleslady take out several black gowns in a size six for you to try on," Chelsea continued as Megan looked at her questionably.

"But what other things?"

"I was thinking since you're dating Senator Monroe, you may want to invest in getting a few more items. Some suits, cute sundresses for the summer. No shorts or minis. Some nice summer slacks and blouses. I know you're only twenty-six, but we're going to have to get rid of the baby doll and peasant top look you've been wearing since college. No more Gap and Old Navy, my love," Chelsea said glancing at Megan's T-shirt and bootcut jeans.

"Chelsea, I'm only here to buy a dress," Megan complained not interested in an image makeover.

"Correction, Mr. Monroe is going to buy the dress and whatever else you want. He gave me a limit and trust me it's a nice one because there isn't one. It will all be charged to his Black Card. A whole new wardrobe for the summer. We'll do the fall one when the time comes. He said that personally. I guess his bachelor days are over with!" Chelsea said looking through a rack of sundresses, pulling out several and handing them to the saleslady. Chelsea continued while the brightness in Megan's face slowly faded.

"Next week I'm going to go through your closet and tag the clothes you're not to wear while out with him just in case you get photographed. What wife of a senator do you know that dresses like you? Sweetie, you dress really cute but remember you're dating a senator now."

"I'm not married to him, Chelsea."

"Not yet, my love. Not yet. And of course I'll help you pick out your wedding gowns. You must have one for the ceremony and another for the reception. I'm sure Vera will design something special just for you. Then you'll need a whole new wardrobe as a married woman. We can store your old clothes in your guest room closet or give them to charity. I'm sure you can use the tax write-off."

"Chelsea, let's go through my closet first before we begin buying other things. I own a lot of nice suits and dresses. I have to wear jeans and sweats when I'm doing a job. I have to be comfortable if I'm on a ladder painting, moving furniture or hanging wallpaper."

"Sweetheart, I'm only following orders from Mr. Monroe. He is paying me nicely to select clothes for you. Now, my goal is to give you a new look and style of your own. We want other politicians' wives, girlfriends and even their mistresses to be jealous of you plus set out a new trend. Remember Jackie O?" Chelsea inquired placing a dozen of dresses on the chair next to Megan and going back for more.

"The rapper?" Megan asked sarcastically.

"You know exactly who I mean. First Lady Jacqueline Kennedy Onassis. Her style was graceful, elegant and classy. Everyone wanted to look like her, dress like her. People still admire her sense of style and poise. That's what I want for you. I want people to see a sophisticated young lady on the arm of Senator Monroe. Do you understand, honey?" Chelsea asked seriously.

Megan groaned as she took several dresses into the dressing room. For the next three hours she tried on more outfits than she had that entire year. She tried to suck it up and have fun, but all she could think about was sleeping next to Steven that night and hoped she wouldn't have the urge to seduce him.

Chapter 7

Megan arrived in Washington, D.C., around eight in the evening. Her ears had finally regained most of their hearing as she stepped off of the plane, chewing her fourth piece of gum. She looked around and saw an older, kind-looking lady holding a sign that read Megan Chase in bold letters. She waved at the woman, who she assumed to be Greta, and walked hurriedly over to her.

"Good evening, Ms. Chase. I'm Greta Reid, Senator Monroe's housekeeper. Your bags are being put into the car. Do you need anything before we go to the house?" Greta had a Southern accent, a grandmotherly presence and a genuine smile. Her gray hair was in fresh curls around her warm, brown face and her pleasant demeanor made Megan comfortable.

"No, and it's very nice to meet you," Megan said, shaking Greta's hand. Greta looked rather surprised when Megan took her hand.

"Now, Ms. Chase…" Greta began.

"Please, call me Megan."

"All right, Ms. Megan. Is there anything you do or don't want to eat for breakfast in the morning? I can cook just about anything from A to Z, at least that's what the Monroe family says."

"No, whatever you cook is fine with me just as long as coffee goes with it." Megan enjoyed eating a hearty breakfast when possible, and she could sense that Ms. Greta seemed like the type to cook big meals.

"Well, I haven't seen Mr. Steven for almost a month, so I'm going to fix all of his favorites," Greta said as they walked to the car.

"If you need any help, let me know."

"Ms. Megan, that's sweet of you, but you just enjoy yourself these next few days. Mr. Steven said you're a hard-working interior decorator. I'm sure you can use the break."

"Do you have any children?" Megan asked.

"I have two daughters. Both married with kids. They live in Mobile, Alabama. That's where I'm originally from. I'm usually there until Mr. Steven calls me a few days before he arrives here in Washington or in Savannah. Mr. Steven is like the son I never had as well as Mr. Bryce," Greta said as they approached the car. It was a black Lexus LS 460.

"You don't live here all the time?"

"No, Ms. Megan. I'm sort of on call for Mr. Steven or anyone else in the Monroe family. I'm retired now. I've worked for the Monroe family for many years. Changed all of the Monroe children's dirty diapers."

"Well, you're a part of the family. Do you travel with him sometimes?"

"Sometimes, but Mr. Steven is a simple guy, if you can believe that. He knows how to cook and clean for himself, even though I spent most of the day cleaning." Greta opened the back door for Megan. "He said he wanted it to be perfect for you and now I see why."

"Ms. Greta, I'm not used to having people chauffeur me around. Can I sit up front with you?"

"Of course, sugar. You know, you're different from those uppity girls I see him with in the newspapers and magazines. When he used to bring them here or to Savannah, they wouldn't even acknowledge my presence. I think he has a keeper now." Greta winked.

When they arrived at the brownstone, Greta told Megan to make herself at home. It was a beautiful, three-story building with a studio apartment on the top floor that Greta mentioned she stayed in when she was there. The masculine decorations reminded her of Steven. Sturdy, strong furniture in dark colors. Greta took her up to the second floor to the master suite. It was a large room with a sitting area with a fireplace, and two big, brown-leather, comfy-looking chairs and an oversize leather ottoman. The bed was huge with cherrywood posts. It was so high off the ground it had matching steps on both sides.

"Right around the corner is your closet. I've already put away your things for you while you toured the brownstone. What a stunning dress you're wearing tomorrow evening. I'll steam it for you before you put it on tomorrow. It got a few wrinkles from the plane ride. You know those baggage handlers just throw people's stuff around."

"Thank you so much, Ms. Greta," Megan said thinking there was a "his" closet on the other side of the master bathroom. The one that was supposed to be "hers" was empty except for her things, a few African paintings, and a stack of about a dozen books sitting on the floor.

After Megan ate a delicious Southern dinner of chicken fried steak, mashed sweet potatoes and collard greens, she retired back upstairs to the bedroom and looked through the books that were on the floor in the closet. Reading was her favorite pastime. She found a Walter Mosley novel that she hadn't read yet and quickly read through the first few chapters in one of the big comfy chairs in the sitting area. She found herself yawning an hour later and decided to get up and walk around. She went into the master bath, which was an interior decorator's dream. A beautiful antique tub with four brass legs stood in the middle. The floor and countertops were marble. There were two vanities on opposite walls. The "hers" vanity had a makeup area with a timeless antique chair. There was a shower big enough for two.

Now that Megan was on her feet, she realized how exhausted she was. She decided to take a warm shower and climb into bed. Then it hit her again that she would be sleeping in the same bed as Steven. She'd almost forgotten. But he was right about one thing—it was an enormous bed.

After a refreshing shower, she walked into the bedroom, wrapped in her towel. She remembered Greta telling her she would put her nightclothes on the bed for her. When Megan walked into the room, the sheets on the right side were pulled back, but she didn't see her pajamas on the bed. Instead, Greta had laid out the little black slip that was in the same garment bag as her evening gown.

"Ha," Megan said out loud, walking to the closet with the slip to find the pajamas. She didn't see them anywhere. She knew she packed them.

"I was on the phone arguing with my mother, packing my suitcase. I folded up the shirt…" Megan realized that the pajamas were still lying on her bed in Atlanta. *What am I going to wear to bed?* Her only other choice was her workout clothes. *They will have to do.* She slipped on a tank top and pink velour shorts. The shorts had shrunk somewhat when she last washed them, but it was better than wearing the slinky black slip. She didn't want to give Steven any ideas.

Satisfied, Megan walked back into the room, only to discover Steven asleep in one of the leather chairs by the fireplace. Time flew, she thought. It was only midnight. She had planned on being asleep when he arrived.

She stopped abruptly in the doorway and stared at him. He sat somewhat slumped down in the chair with his legs apart. His hand rested on his forehead as if he had a headache. A loosened tie hung around his neck, and the first few buttons on his shirt were undone to reveal a glimpse of his smooth chest. Megan had the urge to straddle his lap and wind her arms around his neck and run her tongue down his skin. She shook her head at the thought and began to walk toward the bed, but the hardwood floor creaked, and his eyes flew open. He smiled and sat up straight.

"You're here early," she said, feeling awkward. She didn't know if she should climb into the bed or not.

"Yep. I was able to leave the gathering earlier than planned. Have you found everything you needed?" He began to unbutton his sleeve cuffs.

"Yes, thank you. Greta is wonderful." Megan decided to sit in the other chair across from him. "These are really cozy chairs," she said, rubbing her hands on the arms of the chair to feel the texture of the leather.

"Thank you. I just bought them and had them delivered when Greta got here. I used to have an old couch sitting here. When I saw these chairs in a magazine, I knew they would look nice by the fireplace. Greta did a good job picking out the comforter on my new bed." Steven looked admiringly at the gold-and-red comforter.

"New bed?" She was rather relieved that no other woman had slept in it. *But why should that matter? It's not as if we're a couple.*

"Yes, I ordered it at the same time as the chairs. I used to have a queen sleigh bed in here, but I had it moved to an empty room down the hall. I needed a change." He walked over and ran his hand over the comforter. "I haven't even slept in it yet, and now I can't wait especially since I get to share it with a sexy lady."

"Watch yourself, Steven. You better stay on your side of the bed."

"I promise. Scout's honor. Did you enjoy your shopping spree today?" He hopped up and sat on the bed. His longs legs barely touched the hardwood floor.

"Yes, I did. Thank you. Chelsea knows what she's doing. I also picked out a really nice tie for you, as well. Maybe you can wear it on Election Day," Megan suggested. "I hung it in your closet."

"Thank you. So you just know I'm going to win the primaries and then make it to November's election?"

"Of course. I've read the information about the other potential candidates vying for your father's seat. And I'm not saying this because I know you, but I really do think you're the best candidate. The only thing that may have been holding you back was your lifestyle. But the media loves that you've settled down... Well...sort of, I suppose. So, yes, I think you have a pretty good chance of winning."

"Megan, you keep blowing my head up like this, and I'll never let you go," he said in a sexy tone that caused her breathing to pause for a second and a sensual warmth rushed over her skin.

A heated, seductive stare passed between them and for a moment, Megan wished what he said would really happen, but she couldn't dwell on that. They were simply two people helping each other obtain their career goals. The media was finally warming up to him, and she'd seen a boost of phone calls from prospective clients after the event at Braxton's restaurant. Besides, she enjoyed her freedom of being single and so did Steven. After the election, they could return to their normal lives. But would it be normal or miserable because he would no longer be a part of her life?

"Well…I'm going to go take a shower," Steven said as he strode into the bathroom and closed the door.

Megan wasn't sure what to do next. She decided to get in the bed and try to fall asleep before he returned. If she wasn't, she would pretend she was sleep. She looked around the room again before getting under the covers. Greta had indeed done a wonderful job. Now all that was needed were new curtains and a few throw rugs on the hardwood floor and the bedroom would be complete. She thought of all of this as she drifted off to sleep between the fresh Egyptian cotton sheets.

Steven let the warm water from the shower wash over his tired body. He could still smell her scent in the shower, and it continued to arouse him. When he woke up to find Megan in a tank top and her very short shorts, he found himself at a loss of words. The way the shorts fit around her hips and bottom made him very happy to be a man. He couldn't believe he managed to talk about comforter sets and furniture. What he wanted was to run his hands on her smooth, freshly oiled legs and taste the scent that emanated from her body when she walked causally into the room and sat in the chair next to him. Even though she wasn't wearing lingerie, she was still sexy with her pink shorts and her hair pinned up on her head. He had to quickly escape to the bathroom so she wouldn't see his growing erection.

After his refreshing shower, Steven went back into the bedroom. He glanced over to the bed. He didn't want to make her any more uncomfortable than she already was, so he decided to sleep on the old couch in his spacious walk-in closet. Plus, he was still aroused and couldn't handle sleeping next to her without touching her. He watched her sleep for a moment before he turned off the lamp on the nightstand.

Saturday evening the celebrity stylist Chelsea had arranged to do Megan's hair and makeup, clapped his hands excitedly as Megan turned around twice so he could admire his creation.

"Girlfriend, you are absolutely fierce! You're going to make heads turn!" Keenan the stylist said admiringly, snapping two fingers in the air. "Especially the senator's."

Megan smiled at herself in the floor-length mirror on the wall in the foyer. Her long hair was piled up in a flowy updo with long, curly strands framing her face. Her makeup was light and flawless. Her straight black dress with a lace overlay hit her curves in all the right places, highlighting her curvy hips and small waist. The salesman at Barney's told her and Chelsea that no one else was able to really fill out the dress like Megan, including a lot of celebrities who had tried on the dress and didn't look as good as she did. Megan thought the guy was probably just trying to sell it and would say anything so she would buy it.

"Thank you so much, Keenan! I wish I could take you back to Atlanta." Megan gave him a hug and then a kiss on each cheek.

"Chile, please! When Senator Monroe wins the U.S. Senate seat, I'm sure I'll see you more often in D.C. Here's my card." Keenan handed her his business card and then turned toward the staircase to retrieve his styling materials from upstairs. "I'm sure you and the senator will be attending more functions in Washington for years to come." He ran into Steven on the first landing.

"Senator Monroe, it took me hours to do her hair. Please don't ruin it tonight after the event, but if you did, I wouldn't blame you. She looks ravishing, but don't tell my boyfriend I said that."

Megan gazed at Steven as he descended the stairs, still laughing about Keenan's comments. She was so glad to see him that she almost ran and jumped into his arms. But instead she stood still, her heels pressed into the hardwood floor. She hadn't seen him since he went to take a shower, and she fell straight to sleep after a long day. She woke up in the middle of the night to the realization that he wasn't next to her in the bed. At first she was relieved that he'd chosen to sleep elsewhere and then slightly disappointed. After he'd called her sexy, she was sort of hoping that he would just go ahead and seduce her. When she woke up, there was a note on what would've been his pillow stating he wouldn't be at breakfast and was going to play golf but that he arranged a day of pampering for her at the spa. Megan was relieved. She didn't want to play the devoted girlfriend around Greta. However, Greta was disappointed because she had made all of his favorite breakfast dishes.

Steven stopped on the last stair and a debonair smile inched across his face before he stepped into her personal space.

"You look absolutely lovely."

Warmth dissipated all over her body, and she couldn't help but offer a gracious smile. "Thank you and you look as if you just stepped out of *GQ Magazine*," she said as her eyes perused over his attire. He wore a black Armani tux with a cravat instead of a bowtie. His diamond cuff links sparkled.

He was indeed an exquisite-looking man. Megan felt overwhelmed to have such an amazing man as her escort. She just hoped she could get through the evening without ripping his clothes off. The way he stared at her made her feel sexy and wanted. He stepped closer toward her with a smoldering gaze, and her heart began to beat uncontrollably as his hand reached out to slide the hair out of her face.

"You're so beautiful." His voice was barely above a whisper.

Greta rushed into the foyer with a camera. Steven stepped away from Megan, and she turned to grab her purse from the credenza. She was relieved Greta came into the room. One more second and Steven's lips would be on hers. It was a chance she couldn't take. She knew just one more kiss from him would send her over the edge, and they would never make it to the Smithsonian.

"Oh, just look at my babies. Now let me get a few pictures of the two of you," Greta said, holding up her digital camera, pulling Megan and Steven to each other.

Megan felt as if she was going to her high school prom again, and her mother was making a big fuss. Except this time her date didn't look scared stiff because of the prom-rules talk with her father moments before. Steven and Megan scooted together and posed for several pictures. Greta beamed with sheer delight. Megan glanced at Steven, who seemed to be enjoying the photo session, too.

Steven was surprised at Greta's actions. In all his years of going to functions with women, including his ex-wife, Greta had never gone to this extent of being concerned about his dates. The most Greta would say was "have a nice evening, sir" and hand him his trench coat.

"Have a great time," Greta said opening the front door. "Are you sure you don't need me to drive you?"

"No. This event may not end until late. Just get some rest. I want all of my favorites in the morning." Steven chuckled and gave Greta a kiss on her cheek. "I promise, no golfing." He grabbed Megan's hand and squeezed it gently as they walked to the car.

"You seem nervous," Steven said once they were in the car headed to the Smithsonian. He didn't want her to feel out of place this evening. He knew she wasn't used to this type of event. However, because she was such an elegant and classy lady, he knew she would be able to handle herself with the other girlfriends and wives.

"Just a little. I've been to numerous events but never a dinner fund-raiser where the plates were $500.00 each. I don't spend that much in one month on groceries!"

"Yeah, the price is quite steep, but the money raised is going to the Save the Manatee campaign in Florida. They're slowly becoming extinct." He had a soft spot for the huge animals that were being killed by ships and boats.

"Hmm, interesting. I saw recently on a documentary that the propellers on the boats are striking them, leaving scars, or even worse, causing their death. That's so sad. I'm glad to see how concerned you are about the manatees."

"I'm an animal lover."

Steven tried to stare straight ahead but his eyes kept wandering to the beauty sitting next to him. Keenan was right. She was indeed ravishing, and it took everything in him not to pull the car over and mess up her hair. However, it was clear to him that Megan wasn't interested in being anything more than friends or at least she didn't want to admit to it.

Moments later, they arrived at the Smithsonian. There were cameras flashing as they walked the red carpet, and they stopped and posed for a few pictures before going inside.

He squeezed her hand. "Don't be nervous," he reassured her as they walked into the event. "I'm by your side."

After the hostess showed them to their table, they were offered a choice of wines. They both opted for an iced tea and lemonade instead. Some other politicians and their wives or girlfriends joined their table of ten. The men mostly talked about politics, sports and the president while the women discussed fashion and what clothes they were taking on their upcoming fabulous vacations. Steven could tell that Megan was trying really hard to join the conversation, but all of the women were so superficial. Megan was down-to-earth and not concerned with such nonsense.

"So where are you two vacationing this summer, Megan?" Mrs. Douglas, the wife of U.S. Senator Richard Douglas from Nevada, asked. He was one of Steven's golfing buddies from that morning.

"Not really sure. I have a lot of work to do this

summer." Megan glanced at Steven with a "help me" look on her face.

"What do you do besides look tenderly at Senator Monroe?" Mrs. Douglas asked.

Steven smiled at Mrs. Douglas's comment. If she thought Megan was looking tenderly at him, then she must've been doing a good job of faking it.

"I have my own interior-design business in Atlanta. This summer I'm doing a show for the Fabulous Living Channel as well as still finding time to spend with my Steven."

"Splendid! You two have to come to our place in the Hamptons this summer." Mrs. Douglas placed her hand on her forehead. "Megan, I'm in dire need of redoing some of the guest rooms and bathrooms there. Maybe you can give me some suggestions or better yet, just do it for me." Mrs. Douglas scooted closer to Megan.

"I'll have to check my schedule, but I'm sure a few days at your summer home would be lovely, Mrs. Douglas," Megan answered sincerely. "And I'd be happy to help you with your decorating needs."

After dessert, Steven and Megan said their good-byes. He could see the relief on her face when he announced they were leaving. As they walked to the door, he heard someone call his name in a familiar tone.

"Senator Monroe," a woman called after him. Steven cringed before he turned around. He knew that voice in his sleep. It belonged to his ex-wife, Veronica. He just hoped she was on her best behavior tonight. He'd known Veronica since college, and her vindictive ways hadn't, and probably wouldn't ever change.

"Hello, Veronica," Steven said, turning slowly around. He glanced at Megan, who remained her poised self.

"Oh, Steven, it's a pleasure to see you here. I had a feeling you would be here to support the manatees this year. And who is this lovely *young* girl?"

"This is Megan Chase, my girlfriend. Megan, this is Veronica Scott, my ex-wife."

Veronica's dark eyes stayed on Steven when she addressed Megan.

"Actually, love, it's Dr. Scott-Monroe. I never dropped his last name. I love the way it sounds."

"Nice to meet you, Veronica," Megan said nodding her head instead of shaking her hand.

"Steven, we must do lunch while you're in town. I'm no longer in Fairfax. I just bought a charming brownstone in Georgetown." Veronica turned her back completely to Megan. "Kind of like the one you bought when we first got married. That seems like eons ago, does it not Steven?"

"Still at Georgetown?" Steven said, walking around Veronica to stand next to Megan and wrapping his arm around her waist, pulling her close to him.

"Oh, yes, I simply love being there. After I got my doctorate from Cornell, I applied at Georgetown and a few other colleges. But you know I love D.C. Are you still in college, my dear?" Veronica's gaze finally came to rest on Megan.

"No. I've already finished my bachelor's and master's degrees." Her voice was calm and steady. Steven was pleased. Some of the women he'd dated who had the displeasure of meeting Veronica were always tongued-tied around her.

"Megan has her own interior-design company in Atlanta. She decorates homes for celebrities and other public figures," Steven said, squeezing her even closer and then placing a sweet kiss on her forehead. She tenderly smiled back at him just as Mrs. Douglas had mentioned.

"Oh, how cute. Is that how you two met? Well, I must run. I'm here with Judge Hill, and you know he's the jealous type. Call me about lunch." Veronica strutted away.

"We'll look forward to it," Steven said, calling after her.

"Well, that went well," Megan said, withdrawing herself from his embrace but placing her hand in his as they headed out the door.

"I hope Veronica wasn't too mean. She can be a real witch sometimes."

"No, really?" Megan said sarcastically with a laugh.

"You handled yourself pretty well. Most of the women that I've dated that have met Veronica usually freeze up."

"Well, I'm not most women. Besides, I didn't feel threatened. I'm not really your girlfriend remember?"

"Oh, yeah. I almost forgot."

He hoped she would just forget, as well.

* * *

They rode in silence back to the brownstone. Overall, Megan did have a nice evening. She met some potential clients with a summer place in the Hamptons and was able to give to a charity.

Her thoughts wandered to Veronica and how exotically beautiful she was. Her waist-length natural curly hair was a jet black that brought out her dark, slanted eyes. Her skin was tanned and smooth and her makeup was flawless. She was tall and slender and could pass for a supermodel. Her diamond choker with matching earrings sparkled. Megan could tell she wasn't dolled up for the evening— that was how she always looked.

The more Megan thought about all of the women in Steven's life before her, the more she realized they were all beautiful, high maintenance women who could walk the runways during fashion week in New York or Paris. Sighing, she knew he could never fall for her.

When they arrived back to the brownstone, Megan noticed that the light in Greta's room was on. It was nearly ten o'clock. She had figured Greta would be asleep by now.

"I guess Greta waits up for you?" Megan inquired when the garage door lowered behind them.

"No, not really. She likes you and probably wants to know how your evening went."

"I like her, too," she said, getting out of the car while Steven tossed something in the trash. "She reminds me of my grandmother who passed about five years ago." Megan waited by the door that led to the keeping room.

"Greta is a wonderful person. I really don't need a housekeeper, but I like having her around." He paused. "Well, I'm off to the study to do some work. Thank you for a great evening." Steven fumbled with his keys.

"Work? Do you ever relax? Take a break?" Megan offered.

"No. Then I wouldn't be where I am today. Jeez. I sound like my dad," Steven said, still looking at the keys.

"Do you need some help finding the right key?"

"Um…no. They're just…twisted," he said, still rummaging through them. "You know, it's only around ten on a Saturday night in Washington. How about we go out dancing or something fun? I know of a really cool place. I can teach you how to go-go dance."

"Well, if you don't count a fourth-grade field trip, this is my first time in Washington, so that sounds like fun." She finally grabbed the keys from him and opened the door, which happened to be already unlocked.

"Okay, well let's change clothes and get out of here. According to you, I can use some relaxation," Steven said as they walked up the stairs to his bed-room.

"Didn't you relax playing golf? My dad says it's a very relaxing sport," she said, kicking her heels off once they were in the bedroom. They were beginning to hurt her feet. Then, remembering she wasn't at home, Megan immediately gathered the shoes and placed them neatly in the closet. She went into the bathroom and took the hairpins out of her hair. She had asked Keenan to pin her hair so that it would fall after she took the pins out. It fell perfectly with soft curls on her back. She could hear Steven talking from his closet.

"Nope. We stand around and pretend to care about the other person's golf game. We're really trying to find out each other's opinions on current issues, bills that must be passed, who's running for what and when. So you see, Megan, playing golf with the good old boys wasn't relaxing. It's all politics."

"So is this," Megan whispered to herself, looking through the clothes she brought with her. The clothes from Barney's were being shipped back to Atlanta. Luckily, Chelsea told her to keep a few of the dresses just in case they went somewhere unplanned. Megan reached back to undo her zipper when she remembered that Keenan and Greta had zipped and clasped her gown. She wasn't able to unhook the first clasp. Megan knew that it wouldn't be a good idea to call Greta because she would wonder why Steven couldn't undress his own girlfriend.

"Need some help?" Steven asked, startling her. He had changed into black dress slacks and a yellow polo shirt.

"Yes, please. If you wouldn't mind just unhooking the first clasp. I think there may be another one at the end of the zipper." Megan turned around and lifted her hair off her back.

He undid the clasp, and his hands brushed against her bare back when he lowered the zipper. Heat rushed through her as his warm hands touched her skin. She wanted nothing more than to feel his lips where his hands were. That was when Megan remembered she wasn't wearing any panties because she hadn't wanted the line to show through her dress. She turned around immediately to hide her backside, but it was too late. She heard him whisper *wow* and stepped back, as if to admire the view in front of him.

"I'll be ready in ten minutes," she said, quickly pushing him out the closet and closing the door.

"Cute tush," she heard him say through the door.

Ten minutes later they were on their way down to the garage and backing out of the driveway.

"You look lovely tonight. Is that another Chelsea suggestion?" Steven asked. The strapless purple dress was short and hitting her curvy body in the right places.

"Yes, it is. Chelsea does her job well. She's the best fashion stylist and consultant I know."

"I agree. She referred me to an excellent tailor here in D.C. When I win my father's seat, I'll definitely need one here."

Megan looked out the window. He would win the election, move to D.C. and forget all about her. She decided to change the subject.

"You have a very nice car. It's my dream car."

"Really? You want to drive it? I can have some-one drive it back to Atlanta for you. It just sits in the garage for weeks at a time."

"No. Besides, you have to drive something while you're in D.C."

"I have a few other cars that just sit in the garage. I can have the Range Rover sent to D.C. easily."

"No, my SUV is fine." Megan said. She would love to drive the Lexus, but she'd never been a gold digger, and wasn't about to start. She rarely drove her ex-boyfriend's convertible Porsche or his Mer-cedes when they were together. But every now and then, she saw his nurse happily driving the Porsche around Atlanta.

"Well, if you change your mind, let me know."

They arrived at Capital Club about fifteen min-utes later. After giving the valet the keys, Steven took Megan by the hand and they entered the dance club. They found a table in the back and ordered bottled waters. *The atmosphere is sort of young,* she thought as she looked around. It was mostly college students or fresh out-of-college-students. The floor was packed with people doing all types of dances that Megan had never seen in the clubs in Atlanta. The music blared through the speakers. Strobe lights of red and purple flashed on the dance floor. The DJ played a top forty mix.

"Isn't this place kind of young for you?" Megan screamed over the loud music. She thought they were going to a more upscale location for professionals.

"Yeah. I guess you're right. I used to come here

when I was visiting friends. I was in college at the time," Steven screamed back, looking around. "I feel sort of overdressed looking at all these young men wearing baggy jeans."

Megan was getting tired of screaming, but she didn't have a choice.

"Well, I'm still in my twenties, so I feel fine," Megan answered smiling at him.

"Yes, you certainly are fine," he said, smiling back at her with a wink.

Megan thought she heard him but wanted to be sure. "What did you say? I couldn't hear you. It's rather loud in here," she screamed.

"Nothing. I guess this place isn't for talking," he screamed back.

"Well, since we're here, let's see what you can really do, old man," Megan said, pulling him out of the chair and on to the dance floor.

"We'll see about the 'old man' comment. I'm sure I can outdance you any day of the week!" Steven said, as he jokingly started to imitate some old '70s moves, including the robot and the twist.

They danced and laughed for the next hour straight. He taught her how to go-go dance and she taught him the latest moves from Atlanta that he didn't know. Finally, the DJ played a slow song. But before Megan could turn to walk off the dance floor, Steven pulled her close to him. She didn't resist. She was too tired.

Instead, she let him hold her close. She felt as if she had drunk more than just water. Her dance high was coming down, and she relaxed in his arms. His hands slowly caressed her waist and back. His intent gaze rested on her face. He lowered his head down to hers, and she caressed his neck with her hands as her breaths became heavy. With their lips only centimeters apart, a voice in Megan's head said, *Go ahead and kiss him.* Something told Megan it wasn't make-believe anymore, well unless he was a very good actor. When she realized he was lowering his head to kiss her, she didn't turn away.

Steven kissed her softly on the lips, just enough to taste the strawberry lip gloss she had put on over her lipstick. A hint Chelsea had given if she wanted to make her lips more noticeable and luscious. She wanted him to kiss her some more, but this club wasn't the place.

"Let's get out of here," he whispered to her.

"Okay," she said barely above a whisper. As they rushed out of the club holding hands, Megan still felt the warmth of his lips on hers.

They rode in silence back to his brownstone. He continued to hold her hand, rubbing the inside of her palm with one of his fingers. She had too many thoughts in her head about what had just happened between them. She closed her eyes and rested her head back on the seat. She wasn't sure how to handle her emotions.

Once the car was settled in the garage, neither of them spoke. They still sat holding hands. Megan looked straight ahead, but he was looking directly at her. She decided to let him speak first.

"So are you going to slap me now or later?" he asked jokingly.

"Do you want me to slap you?"

"No. I really want to kiss you again," Steven said, moving toward her and running his finger along her lips. Placing his fingers under her chin, he brought her face closer to his and once again kissed her supple lips, slowly. She responded in the same manner taking her time to taste every inch of his mouth. Warm sensations coursed between her thighs as she returned his kisses with the same passion and vigor that he displayed to her. Low moans of pleasure erupted from her as he kissed her even deeper, letting his tongue penetrate the inside of her mouth.

Her hands roamed over his face while one of his hands caressed the center of her back and the other one massaged her neck. He reached in between her legs under the seat to press a button that moved her seat back as far as it would go. He then reached around her and pushed the back of the seat all the way down, his lips never leaving hers as their kissing intensified and the car windows began to slightly fog. She pulled him on top of her, and he stopped the kiss for moment, taking off his shirt and tossing it in the backseat. His lips placed hot kisses on the side of her neck as she explored her fingers along his hard, muscular back. She could feel the pulsating of his erection through his pants.

Her moaning was unrecognizable as he pulled down the top of her dress, exposing her breasts, which hard hardened and yearned for his tongue, mouth and hands to entice them. He popped one nipple into his mouth, circling his tongue around it before gently tugging it with his teeth. She let out a cry of desire as he continued licking and teasing her breasts going back and forth between the two.

"Steven...that feels so damn good. Please, please don't stop."

"Don't worry. I won't." His voice was heavy, filled with passion. "Not until you're completely satisfied."

He captured her lips once more, thrusting and winding his tongue inside of her mouth. Every fiber in her body was ablaze, and she needed whatever he had to offer to put it out. A cold shower wasn't going to do the trick. She craved him. She had desired him for so long. When she wrapped her legs around his trim waist, he stopped for a second and looked into her eyes as if searching for a sign to go ahead.

She kissed him softly at first and then licked her tongue across his bottom lip causing his breathing to stifle. He slid his hand to the hem of her dress and pulled it up to her stomach. His hand lingered on the band of her panties and then pushed them to the side. He circled her clit with his finger as erotic moans emerged from her mouth. He traced his finger down between her folds as his lips kissed the side of her neck. When he inserted a finger into her slick canal, her breathing became irregular as she thrust her hips up to meet his in and out motion. His lips left her neck trailing down her chest and stomach until he was on his knees in front of her. She shook in anticipation of what she wished would come next, and when he replaced his finger with his warm, wet tongue, she almost exploded. He raised her legs up so that her shoes were in the seat and parted her thighs as he twirled his tongue around inflicting pure ecstasy on her.

"Oh, my goodness, Steven…" she said breathlessly, clutching his shoulders.

"You're so damn wet. You're dripping. I'm the reason. Right, baby?"

"Yes…"

"Who?"

"Yes, Steven."

"That's my girl."

He continued darting in and out of her, cupping his hands under her bottom as her hips moved with the same urgency as his tongue. Her emotions and feelings for him welled up as an orgasm slammed through her body with a force that left her weak and vulnerable yet craving for more of him. The moans and cries eliciting from her were foreign and out of her character, but she didn't care. With him she felt carefree. She could let go and be herself with him and that terrified her.

He lifted up and positioned himself over her. The screech of a zipper sounded, and it wasn't hers. And the conversation she had with her mother yesterday popped into her head.

She immediately pushed him away. "No. This is a big mistake, Steven. I can't do this anymore," Megan said, squirming from under him and pushing open the car door. She pulled her dress down, and rushed into the house and up the stairs to the master bedroom. She didn't know what to do. She was ready to return home to Atlanta and back to her normal life. She had been afraid this would happen. He wanted fringe benefits, as well.

Steven sat in the car for a few minutes before going inside to face Megan. He wasn't sure what had just happened. He thought he and Megan were on the same page. The way she kissed him was like no other kiss he had ever experienced. He'd never been the kissing type. Even while married to Veronica, he seldom kissed. But when he first laid eyes on Megan, the first thought that came to mind was how bad he wanted to taste her lips. And now that he had, he wanted to kiss her juicy lips—both sets.

Sighing, he got out of the car. The last thing he wanted her to feel was hurt, because it was never his intent from the beginning.

When he walked into the bedroom, he saw her packing her suitcase. She was shaken and distraught.

"Where are you going?" he asked quietly.

"Home. I have a credit card. I can pay for my own plane ticket," she said, stuffing her things in her suitcase.

"You can't leave now," he said, taking her by the shoulders and turning her around to face him.

"Why? Because you're scared you won't win the nomination? You're scared how the public is going to look at you?" Megan jerked away, going toward the bathroom. He followed her. "I knew this was a big mistake!"

"No. I..." He stopped midsentence. Now he felt bad. He didn't want her to think he was taking advantage of her, he was very much attracted to her. He couldn't believe it. He had found the one woman who could actually change him into a one-woman man, and she didn't even want him.

"I apologize, Megan. I guess it was the music and the atmosphere. Or it could've been the fact that I was holding a very beautiful woman in my arms, who smells and tastes just like strawberries. Please don't go. Not because of how the public may perceive me, but because it's late, and we've had a long day. Just leave in the morning. We'll tell Greta you had an emergency and had to fly back home early. I'll take you to the airport myself." He hoped she would accept his apology.

"I can take a taxi," Megan said, putting her suitcase down.

"I understand if you don't want to do this anymore," he said sincerely although he had the urge to reach out and pull her close to him.

He watched as Megan sat in the leather chair, contemplating her decision.

"No, I made you a promise. You're right, it's late, and the music and atmosphere played a part, as well. New clause—no more dancing."

"It's a deal," he said, and gently shook her hand.

Chapter 8

The following Monday after her Washington, D.C., trip, Megan was back at work and glad to be doing something to keep her mind off of her fantasy life. She needed to concentrate on her own normal life for a change. She had a million things to do before she headed to Hilton Head that summer to work on the project for the Fabulous Living Channel. She also needed to get her mind off of Steven.

She sipped on a cup of coffee Lucy had made for her. It was storming that morning and no one wanted to make a Starbucks run in the rain.

It had to be the dancing, Megan thought to herself as she took another sip. It had been a while since she'd had that much fun with a man, but Steven was just the wrong man at the right time. While she enjoyed the kiss—among other things—they shared in the car, she didn't want to get her emotions involved, only to be disappointed later. She was glad she was able to leave that Sunday morning to fly back home. Steven had arranged for her to fly first-class back to Atlanta.

Megan continued sipping on her coffee as it surprisingly calmed her nerves. She asked Lucy to refill her cup before her meeting. Chelsea was stopping by to finalize plans for her daughter's bedroom, but Megan knew she really wanted the play-by-play of her Washington weekend.

Chelsea arrived promptly at ten for their meeting. She sashayed into Megan's office wearing a pink Chanel suit. Her diamond earrings and matching tennis bracelet seemed as if they would be too much for someone to wear at ten in the morning. However, it was normal for her. Chelsea believed in being ready for any type of occasion at a moment's notice. The sleeveless dress under her suit jacket could easily be a cocktail dress. Her wristlet that she always kept in her bigger purse could easily double for an evening bag.

Chelsea sat in one of the leather wingback chairs in front of Megan's glass desk and shook her head in disapproval at Megan. "What is up with that white peasant-type blouse? That should be in the bag going to the Salvation Army. I'm sure some young college girl could make use of it." Chelsea rested her Prada bag on Megan's desk.

"Good morning to you, too, sunshine. Can I get

you some coffee?" Megan asked with a hint of sarcasm in her voice.

"No. Hot water, please. I have herbal tea bags in my purse," Chelsea stated, taking one of them out and setting it on the desk.

Megan buzzed Lucy to bring a cup of hot water for Chelsea and more coffee for her. *If the next hour is going to be like this, I may need more than just coffee.*

"I love everything you did to Madison's room. I had Julie put the comforter set on this weekend, and it's simply charming. She's going to adore it when she comes home from Vanderbilt this summer. The last thing will be a nice antique chair for her writing desk."

"Julie? What happened to Amanda?" Megan wondered.

"I had to fire her. She almost ruined my hardwood floors by putting bleach in the bucket. Luckily, I caught her pouring a cap into it and was able to stop her from mopping. A good maid is so hard to find!" Chelsea exclaimed, putting her hand on her forehead.

Megan smiled and thought about how Chelsea would have fit in with the senators' wives at dinner on Saturday night. "Well, I wouldn't know anything about that. I can't afford a maid."

"But, darling, you will once you marry Steven. Now, tell me all about your trip." For the next hour Megan told Chelsea about her trip, leaving out the car incident and argument.

Later on that afternoon Tiffani and Sydney joined

Jade and Megan for lunch at the Cheesecake Factory. The rain had finally stopped and the sun was shining brightly as if it had never rained. It had been a few weeks since they'd had lunch together and Megan needed to catch up on happenings in her girls' lives. Plus, Tiffani and Jade really wanted to hear about Megan's life with the senator. And Megan knew that Sydney needed a break from profiling a new case that kept her up most of the night.

Sydney immediately grabbed the bread basket and began buttering a roll. "Ladies, I'm famished. I haven't eaten since dinner last night, which consisted of two chili dogs, three cups of coffee and two doughnuts. Maybe three doughnuts," Sydney added, as the waiter left with their food orders.

"You were at the GBI office?" Jade asked.

"Since noon yesterday," Sydney stated, squeezing a lemon into her water. "This is the first time I've left. I can't talk about the case of course, but I can tell you it's giving me a headache."

Tiffani sighed and shook her head at Syd.

"Your headache probably came from eating two chili dogs. There's no telling what kind of meat was used to make them, and you stopped eating pork years ago. You know that processed meat is just ground up left over parts from pigs, chickens, and cows all mixed into one hot dog." Tiffani was very health conscious after she found out her late husband had high cholesterol. "We really need to be more aware of what we put into our bodies. We should treat our bodies like a temple and take care of them.

Remember, this is the only body we will ever have. Can't sell it and buy another one like a house."

"You know how to spoil a good time," Jade groaned.

Megan chuckled at Jade, who was actually more of a health nut than Tiffani.

"Tiffani, I'm so glad you could make it. I know you have your hands full. Where's my godson?" Megan asked.

"He's with his grandparents," Tiffani answered. "If it wasn't for my parents, I don't know how I could've gotten through this year. They've been wonderful, and so have all of you."

Megan placed her hand on Tiffani's and squeezed it. "That's what family and friends are for. How's your father doing after that car accident a few months ago?"

"His back has been bothering him again, so Alfonso prescribed something for him and told him to take it easy the next few days." Tiffani looked at Megan apologetically as soon as she uttered her exboyfriend's name.

"Tiffani!" Sydney exclaimed, and then looked sympathetically at Megan.

"Oh, girl, I'm so sorry. I didn't mean to mention his name in front of you," Tiffani said with a sincere smile.

But Megan didn't care anymore. It felt good to finally be over him.

"Girl, its fine. He was your father's doctor before we started dating," Megan replied.

"Besides, she's dating a Monroe man now. Forget the doctor. Our little Megan has moved up in the world," Jade reminded everyone.

Tiffani, who still looked sympathetically at Megan chimed in. "How was the fund-raiser in Washington? I read in the newspaper that the foundation raised over $300,000 dollars to save the manatees."

"It was nice. The tiramisu was delicious. I think I may order one today with my lunch, along with an espresso," Megan said, looking at her dessert menu and trying to avoid the conversation. Even though she knew it would come up eventually. She handed them the dessert menu. She knew the only reason Tiffani liked coming to the Cheesecake Factory was for the cheesecake.

"Good idea. I'll take some to go. Dad loves it. I'll probably order him something to eat, as well. I just hope he's feeling better. I worry about him," Tiffani said.

"You know, I have had acupuncture done to help with regulating my menstrual cycle. It also helps with other ailments such as back pains," Jade explained, taking out her doctor's business card and handing it to Tiffani.

"I was reading about acupuncture in one of my alternative health books. I prefer holistic approaches as well but, well, you know men. I don't know if my dad would go for it or not. He's old-school and would probably say it's for women. Megan, do you think Steven would do acupuncture if you suggested it?" Tiffani asked.

Megan remained silent for a moment to collect her thoughts. She didn't know if he would or not. She didn't even know his favorite color or if he was left- or right-handed, so she shrugged and said, "He's a man, what do you think?"

The ladies talked some more, and then Sydney suggested that they go look at the cheesecakes on display at the front of the restaurant. Once they were at the cheesecake counter Sydney said, "We haven't spoken since you returned from your trip, sissy. Did you really have a nice time in Washington?"

"Yes and no," Megan whispered.

"Wait a minute. I know that look. You've fallen in love with Steven!"

"No! Perhaps. Yes!" she finally admitted to her sister. "We get along great. He's really a nice, down- to-earth guy. One would think because of his status and his family's wealth that he would be arrogant and cocky, but he isn't. Well sometimes, but only when he's joking about something. He's a very simple and self-efficient guy. He's so different than what's-his- face who acted like he grew up with a silver spoon in his mouth and flaunted his money like it grew on trees."

"Megan, that's all Steven knows. He grew up having money so it doesn't matter to him. Men like your ex want everyone to know they have made it. A show-off. That's why Daddy never cared for him."

"Syd, when I see him, a part of me wants to rip my clothes off and have him throw me against the wall and make me scream his name."

"Up against the wall? Megan, that doesn't sound like you."

"My point exactly, but I can't stop thinking about having sex with him in all kinds of positions. It keeps me up at night."

"Girl, you got it bad. Real bad."

"What should I do?"

"Well, the best advice I can give is to simply follow your heart. You'll know if he's the right man. It's just a gut feeling that a person has when they know that there's no one else who can make them happy." Sydney spoke in a whimsical voice, which was way outside of her character.

"Syd, is there something you need to tell me?" Megan asked smiling, as they walked back to the table.

"No." Sydney shrugged. "Just speaking in general."

The ladies enjoyed the rest of their lunch for the next hour. Tiffani promised to be home by three to relieve her parents, and Sydney had to go back to the bureau. Jade and Megan rode back to the office in Jade's convertible BMW.

"Megan, are you all right? You don't look that well. Did something you ate not agree with you?"

"My stomach is a little queasy. Just a little jet lag, more than likely," Megan answered. The truth was, she was having confusing feelings about Steven, and it was making her sick.

"When we get back to the office, just get into your car and go home. Lucy and I can handle our appointment. You look like you need some rest," Jade stated.

"Thanks. I could use some more sleep. When I got home yesterday, I finished my project boards for Hilton Head and did laundry," Megan answered. *And I was up all night thinking about my so-called love life. Mostly, fantasizing about how many ways to make love to the Steven,* she added in her mind.

"Well, just go home and get some rest. I'm sure being the girlfriend of a politician can be quite busy and exciting," Jade said, as she parked her car in the parking garage.

Megan hugged Jade and then walked to her car. She didn't need anything from her office. She had work at home to catch up on. Anything to get her mind off of Steven. Luckily, he would be in Washington, D.C., until Wednesday, and then he was going to Florida before coming back to Atlanta next week. If she was lucky, he wouldn't call unless she needed to go somewhere with him, and she wasn't sure if she would be up to going anywhere with him anytime soon.

Megan wanted time to reflect and think about the decision she'd made to date him. If she was falling for him, she didn't know how much longer she could keep up with this charade, because the truth was, she was no longer pretending.

Chapter 9

Almost a week had gone by and Megan still hadn't heard from Steven. It was Saturday afternoon, and she was preparing to leave for her godson's birthday party. She wasn't sure if she should call Steven or not. She tried staying busy by going overboard on projects for clients as well as helping her sorority with a community-service project she hadn't originally signed up for.

She hadn't thought too much about him by the end of the week, at least not during the day. But once her head hit the pillow at night, thoughts of him resided until dawn. She saw him on CNN Thursday morning while she was jogging on the treadmill. The bill he was voting on had passed, and a reporter outside of the capitol in Atlanta was interviewing him. Megan could see that he was freshly shaven and had recently gotten a haircut. His dimples were present and his teeth were white and sparkling.

She had picked up her telephone to call him, but quickly decided not to. She had nothing to say. But in a way she sort of missed talking to him. He was very easy to speak with and was usually in good spirits unlike her ex. She used to have to make him listen to her and even then she knew he wasn't really listening at all. He never wanted to know how her day was, what projects she was working on or even the simplest of concerns like how she was feeling. Steven always asked those questions, and he actually meant them.

Well, I don't have time to sit around and worry about Steven, she thought as she tried to wrap KJ's birthday gift. She hated wrapping presents and would have preferred if she could put it in a gift bag. However, KJ was turning five, and her mother told her a long time ago that children like to unwrap their presents not look in a gift bag. Megan was trying to wrap the present as neatly as possible, but then she remembered KJ was going to just rip the paper off anyway. The finished product looked somewhat decent, but she placed it in a gift bag anyway and decorated it with colorful tissue paper.

"That's better," she said to Percy holding the bag up so he could see it. The cat raised a paw at it. She knew that meant he really wanted to play with the dark blue ribbon she tied on the handles.

Megan glanced at the clock and realized if she

didn't get a move on, she would be late to her god-son's birthday party.

Thirty minutes later she was dressed in a yel-low, flowery sundress with matching yellow wedges. Chelsea had insisted this sundress would be perfect for a Saturday afternoon luncheon with the senator. Of course, a five-year-old's birthday party didn't fit into that category, but she really wanted to wear the dress. Megan pulled her thick hair back into a pony-tail. She had been so busy trying to keep her mind off of Steven that she missed her hair appointment on Thursday and had to reschedule.

"Bye, Percy," Megan said, walking to the door with the gift bag in one hand and a grocery bag with homemade potato salad in the other. Megan wasn't much of a cook, but she was always praised for her potato salad.

It was Saturday, so she knew traffic would be a little hectic from Atlanta's Buckhead area to the suburbs in Stone Mountain where Tiffani lived. As Megan stepped off of the elevator, she literally ran into a familiar face with the yummy dimples that she immediately wanted to shower with kisses.

"Hello, Megan."

"Steven, what are you doing here?" she asked surprised that he was there. She had just thought about him when she was in the elevator. *Where was he when I thought about him in the shower? That's where he should've popped up.*

"Well, I was in the neighborhood and decided to stop by. No, that's not true. I just wanted to check on you." Steven raked his eyes over her body, settling them on her manicured toes.

"You could've called," Megan, suggested walking past him toward the parking garage.

"I know, but I just got back in town this morning. I've been so busy with meetings all this week. Plus, I wanted to give you some space."

"I see. Well, I have to go to my godson's birthday party. I'm running sort of late. I should be halfway there now," she said, putting her things in the trunk of her black Mustang.

"I thought you had a SUV?"

"I do. This is my weekend car. It was my first car straight out of college. An impulse buy, at least that's what my dad says. Syd has a red one just like it." Megan stood by the driver's door waiting for him to leave, even though she actually preferred to stay and talk to him.

"So Sydney has a SUV like yours, as well?"

"No. She has a motorcycle."

"Really? Bryce has one, too." He paused and looked around as if he wanted to say something else.

"I really need to go," she said even though she didn't want to.

"I guess I should've called first, but I wasn't sure if you were taking my calls after what happened last weekend."

"All is forgotten," she lied. She couldn't get it out of her head.

"I wanted to see if you wanted to hang out today. Grab some lunch or something. I remembered what you said about me needing to relax. I actually have some free time if you can believe that!" Steven said, opening the door for her.

"Really?"

"No, not really, but I am giving myself free time. I feel like I eat, sleep and dream about politics. There's always some bill I need to read over, complaints from constituents and don't get me started with the rumors in the press. Sometimes, I just want to have a normal day without distractions," Steven complained.

"Well, you can come with me to the birthday party if you want. I mean it's a kiddie party with the pony, face painting and the clown, but you can still come. Tiffani won't mind. She'll probably put you to work though," Megan offered, surprising herself.

"Cool. But I don't have a gift," he said, walking around to the passenger side of her car.

"Do you have cash on you?" she asked as she started the car.

"Why do you need some gas? I know the gas prices are getting outrageous, which is another issue we're dealing with," he said, shaking his head.

"No, this car is always on full. But Keith Jr. likes money and saves it faithfully in a tin box under his bed."

"Smart young man. It's best to start now. By the time he retires, there won't be any more Social Security, and he'll have to invest in the stock market or some annuities. But even all of that is questionable." Steven looked through his wallet. "Yeah, I have a few twenties to add to his investment portfolio." Steven took out two twenties from his old worn out wallet.

"One twenty will be fine. You can use the other one to buy a new wallet," Megan said.

"I like my old wallet. I have some new ones, but this one is special to me. It belonged to my grandfather," he said, patting it affectionately. "We were very close."

For the rest of the ride, Steven told her about his meetings at the capitol as well as the recent comments about him in the press. People liked the fact that he had settled down with one woman but most importantly, they liked Megan.

"So, how much longer am I supposed to be your girlfriend?" Megan asked wanting it to end soon so she could go back to her normal life and stop thinking she was in love with him.

"You know, I really hadn't thought about that. It's up to you. Why you have your eyes set on someone else? The ex back in the picture?"

"No. I just want to know so I can move on with my life, and I'm sure you want to get your life back to normal with the ladies," Megan said even though she didn't mean it. But she felt once they were no longer "dating" she would be over him.

"I guess we can cross that bridge when we get to that point. I hadn't thought about being without you. I still want to keep in contact with you."

"Of course. We can still stay in contact. You're a really nice guy, Steven." Megan smiled as they turned onto Tiffani's street. Her house was a beautiful two-story, cream-colored stucco in the middle of the cul de sac. There were plenty of cars already parked in the driveway. Megan hated parking on the street. She always feared someone would hit her car and drive away without leaving a note.

"You ready?" she asked once the car was parked.

"Yeah. Who's all here?" Steven asked, looking at all of the cars. "I can't believe there's almost fifteen cars for a child's birthday party."

"Jade and Syd are here. Kids from Keith's playgroup, karate class and cousins," Megan answered, taking her things out of the trunk.

"Great. I love kids."

"Good. I'm in charge of face painting. You can help me with that," Megan suggested as they walked around to the backyard.

"Wow!" Megan exclaimed as she saw the scene before her. There were about two-dozen kids lined up at different stations. Keith Jr. was on a pony with his grandfather holding the reins. There were kids in the moonwalk and the older kids were in the pool. Megan saw Tiffani and Syd grilling hamburgers and Jade was fanning herself on the deck and setting out the paper goods. Megan was surprised that Jade had even bothered to show up. She didn't care much for a lot of little screaming children running around. Megan set her present on the gift table that was overflowing with nicely wrapped boxes and colorful gift bags.

"Megan, Steven, great to see you two. Steven, I'm so happy you came. I didn't know you liked kids' parties," Tiffani smiled, taking the potato salad from Megan and hugging her at the same time. She then turned to Steven and gave him a big hug.

"I need a break from adults," he said, looking around at the children who were playing and running around.

"How is everything going so far?" Megan asked as they walked toward the grill.

Tiffani placed her hand on her forehead and shook her head as her curly ponytail that was sitting on top swung.

"Girl, terrible! My friend who knows how to make balloon animals was supposed to come, but he called an hour ago and said he wouldn't be able to make it. My dad has to do the pony station, which stinks by the way, and my mom is in charge of the moonwalk area. I can't have these kids getting hurt," Tiffani said in a flustered manner. Megan was used to Tiffani always remaining calm under pressure but at the present moment, she understandably couldn't control her frustrations.

"I can do the balloon animals," Steven volunteered.

"Steven, that's wonderful! The station is already set up next to the face painting," Tiffani said, pointing to the two stations by the back of the fence.

"All right, let's get started," Megan said, but she wanted to say hello to the birthday boy first.

"Godmommy!" Keith Jr. screamed as he ran to give Megan a big hug.

"Hey sweetie. Are you having fun?" she asked, picking him up and giving him a tight hug.

"Yes. Who's this man with you? Where's Dr. Alfonso? He always brings his stethoscope for me to play with. Why isn't he with you?" Keith Jr. asked as she put him down. He was no longer the little baby she used to carry around. Megan glanced at Steven who was snickering at the little boy's comment.

"This is Mr. Steven. He's a friend of mine." Megan hoped that would answer the curious child's question. "Remember, I told you that the doctor and I are no longer friends."

"Nice to meet you little fellow," Steven said, shaking the little boy's hand.

"Did you bring me a present?" Keith Jr. asked as his mother walked over to join the conversation.

"KJ, go play. That isn't a nice thing to ask," Tiffani scolded.

Steven reached into his worn wallet and pulled out the crisp twenty dollar bill and handed it to KJ. "As a matter of fact I do, young man. I heard you like to save money."

"Aww...cool," KJ exclaimed admiring the bill. "Thank you, Mr. Steven. I just got a new wallet, so this is going in there right away." He gave Steven a hug before he skipped away.

Tiffani then made an announcement on her megaphone that lunch would be served in thirty minutes. She also reminded her guests that the face painting and balloon stations were open.

For the next thirty minutes Steven made really

cool balloon animals for the children. His station was the most popular next to the pony. Megan watched him as she painted stars and hearts on the little girls' cheeks.

"So, birthday boy, what animal would you like for the great balloon master to make for you?" Steven asked KJ.

"A puppy!" KJ exclaimed jumping up and down.

"Okay, a puppy it is," Steven said as he began to make the puppy out of black and brown balloons. The children sat in awe as Steven twirled the balloons around each other. Sydney walked up behind Megan whose station was now empty.

"I'm surprised to see him here," Sydney whispered.

"Yeah. Me, too, but he stopped by my apartment as I was leaving. When I invited him, I never thought he would actually say yes. I was just being polite," Megan said as she watched Steven make the puppy for Keith Jr. The kids clapped loudly at the finished product and begged Steven to make more animals. He glanced over at Megan and smiled. She clapped her hands and smiled back.

"What was that?" Syd asked observantly.

"What was what?" Megan asked somewhat annoyed.

"The smile he just gave you and the one you gave him back. Megan you forget I'm a profiler. But most importantly, your twin sister. I know all your facial expressions because I have the same ones and usually for the same exact reasons. That smile and stare meant he loves you girl!" Sydney exclaimed.

"Syd, please stop always trying to read other people's minds. He did a good job on making the balloon puppy for KJ and that's why I'm smiling, so please let it go," Megan answered, agitated. She was never good at hiding her expressions from Syd.

"Well, I know what I saw. And I'm glad I saw it," Sydney said as Megan rolled her eyes.

Megan and Sydney walked over to the balloon station once they were done cleaning up the face-painting materials. Sydney picked up a few of the balloons that had popped.

"You did a great job with the kids and the balloons," Sydney said to Steven.

"Thank you. It was one of my duties when I was growing up. I used to entertain my younger siblings and cousins," Steven answered as he placed the unused balloons back into plastic bags.

Just then Tiffani made another announcement that lunch was ready and for the children to walk over to the round tables where Tiffani, her mother and Jade had prepared lunch.

"You know, Tiffani is so organized," Megan said as she watched her friend tell the children where she wanted them to sit. Jade walked around in her high-heeled sandals pouring fruit punch, looking completely out of place and uncomfortable.

"I hope she decides to go back to work now that KJ is going to kindergarten in the fall," Sydney said. "She never wanted to place him in day care, but I know she's running low on the insurance money now."

"Yes, I know. There are some openings at Mom's

school in the fall, and Dad wrote a recommendation letter for her, as well."

"That's good to know. Then KJ could possibly just go to work with her and save on day care."

"Yep. Just like we did when were growing up."

Sydney laughed. "And we hated every minute of it. I'm going to help Jade. She looks so uncomfortable with the children." Sydney said leaving Megan and Steven alone.

Steven leaned against the table and folded his arms across his chest. "You know I went to school with my mother, as well. I enjoyed it. Bryce and Jacqueline not so much. They stayed in trouble."

"Ha. Sounds just like Syd and Braxton. We went to elementary school with my mother and middle school with my dad. He was the assistant principal at the time."

"Jeez. I guess you couldn't wait until high school where you would be free from your parents," Steven said.

"No. My dad's brother, Tiffani's father, was the principal," Megan answered, thinking back to the times when she and Syd were in high school.

"I guess you and Syd had to be on your best behavior all the time," Steven said.

"Please! She stayed in trouble. My dad caught her smoking in the girl's bathroom in eighth grade. He suspended his own child for three days. My mother was livid at him for a week!"

"He suspended his own child? I don't want to meet him! He sounds pretty tough," Steven balked.

"Yes and no. I'm a daddy's girl whereas Syd is a mommy's girl. She said Syd was probably forced to smoke the cigarette. But the truth is she was the one teaching the other girls. Mommy was mad for weeks," Megan remembered. "Are you ready to go eat? Tiffani is serving hamburgers and chicken tenders for the children, but steaks and salmon for the adults. Syd grills the best salmon," Megan boasted about her sister as she grabbed his hand and walked toward the food area set up for the adults. They ate their lunch at the adult-only table. KJ's older cousins were put in charge of the children so the adults could take a break.

After lunch, the children were entertained again with more balloon animals, face painting and swimming. Five of the boys were spending the night, but Tiffani's father was in charge of that. Tiffani had worked hard all week to prepare for the party, and was going to relax for the rest of the evening. Megan and Steven said their goodbyes to everyone after they helped clean up.

"So did you have a nice time?" Megan asked as they were leaving the party.

"I did. Your friends are really nice," Steven said, looking through her CD case.

"You want the top down?" she asked.

"Sure, why not," Steven said, leaning back in his seat and dozing off as the sounds of Corrine Bailey Rae filled the car.

Megan looked over at him as he slept. Even in his sleep he was handsome. She kept thinking about what Syd said. Megan thought they made a nice couple as well, but she knew it was all business. She wasn't one of the fabulous glamour girls he was used to dating. Even though Chelsea had tried to give Megan a new image, she still felt like the same old down-to-earth Megan. She didn't know how she would even fit into his world.

"Wake up, sleepyhead," Megan said softly to him as they pulled into her parking garage.

Steven slowly opened his eyes and turned his head toward her. "Man, I was tired. I guess it has been a long week," Steven said as he stretched his arms and yawned.

"Yes, you were knocked out snoring over there," she teased.

"Snoring? I know I wasn't snoring."

"No, I'm just teasing. Although you were sleeping quite soundly. Perhaps you should go home and get some rest tonight instead of working," Megan suggested.

"As good as that sounds, I have some work to catch up on. I really enjoyed the party though. It was a way to leave my reality at least for a little bit. Thank you for inviting me," Steven said, getting out of the car.

"You want to come up for some coffee? I just bought some Mexican organic coffee I've been wanting to try. It will wake you right up!" Megan asked, not believing that she just asked him to come in for coffee. Men usually thought that was actually an invitation for sex.

"Yeah. That sounds great," Steven said.

When they were settled into the loft, Megan told Steven to make himself comfortable on the couch while she prepared the coffee.

"Nice place. You have it decorated beautifully. It's classy and elegant. Reminds me of you."

"Thank you. I like to come home to calm surroundings unlike all of the outrageous things my client's request. I just like to have things around me that mean something to me such as my grandmother's grandfather clock or my lamp I made out of sea shells I found on Pensacola Beach." She sat the coffee in front of him on the table and returned to the kitchen.

"It's very eclectic."

"Do you need cream or milk? Megan asked, taking both out of the refrigerator.

"Neither. I like my coffee black and just a little sugar. Anything else and the coffee loses its flavor," Steven answered, blowing the hot coffee.

"I see. Well, I like mine extra sweet with milk. I guess I will try your way eventually," she considered as she poured the milk into her coffee.

"This is delicious. I'm not really a coffee drinker. Only when I need a boost," Steven said.

"Well, I love coffee. I could drink it all day. Actually, sometimes I have, which explains why I'm up all night. Maybe I'm not a night person after all," Megan pondered.

"Yeah, maybe you just drink too much coffee," he said laughing.

"Well, it's hard to give a good thing up," she said.

"I'm beginning to believe that. So maybe you should drink decaf," Steven suggested.

"I'm supposed to. After my surgery a few years ago, I tried giving up caffeine," she said, sitting in the chair opposite him.

"What kind of surgery?"

"Nothing major. I had a benign lump in my breast. The surgeon suggested that I stop my caffeine intake. I did some research on it and a found some articles that agreed with his statement while other research stated it didn't matter. However, at that time I trusted him so of course I stopped drinking coffee with caffeine. Plus, my cousin Bria, who is an allergist, suggested I cut down on my caffeine intake. Only recently did I start again," Megan said as she glanced around the loft for a sign of Percy. She got up and looked under her bed. Sure enough Percy was laying down peeking out from under the dust ruffle.

"Do you like cats?" she asked, carrying the cat into the living area.

"I don't like or dislike them. I prefer dogs though. You can't play catch or go running with a cat, and they're too self-absorbed," he answered, rubbing the cat's head. Percy jumped down from Megan's hold and ran back into her room.

"Well, at least he let you pet him," Megan said, settling back in her chair.

"What made you get a cat?"

"It wasn't intentional. I found him as a kitten in the dumpster behind my office a few years ago. Jade and I heard this crying meow, so we got him out. Luckily, he'd managed to climb onto a bag, but he was very weak. I took him to a vet. Percy was dehydrated and very hungry, but he bounced back in a couple of weeks. I took him in only to find him a home, but grew attached, so I kept him. My ex was being a complete jerk around that time and Percy was a nice comfort."

"Megan, what happened between you and Alfonso, if you don't mind me asking you?" Steven curiously began. "I can't figure out why a man would let you go."

"Well, I don't know exactly. It's kind of hard to answer that question. I thought I was doing everything he wanted me to do. I was supportive and caring. His parents and friends loved me as well as my family and friends loved him except for my dad, that is," Megan began.

Steven walked over to the stainless steel coffeepot and helped himself to more coffee and then with a smirk on his face said, "Your dad isn't going to like anyone you bring home no matter what he does or how nice he is to you. That's how fathers are about their precious little girls, you know."

"You're going to be up all night if you have a second cup of that coffee. I told you it's very strong," Megan said, shaking her head. Men never seemed to listen, she thought.

"I'll be up late working. Now, finish telling me about Mr., I mean excuse me, Dr. Alfonso," Steven corrected sarcastically, settling on the floor beside the unlit fireplace and grabbing some oatmeal cookies Megan had placed on the coffee table.

"Well, everything was fine until right before Christmas the year before last. We started spending less time together. We were always together. Even when he was busy with his work, he would try to make time for me. He is a very popular surgeon here in Atlanta with a lot of patients. A lot of women would refer their friends because they thought he was handsome. So he had plenty of female patients, but that never bothered me. Anyway, around Christmas time we scheduled a trip to go to the Bahamas for a week and to return on Christmas Eve so we could spend Christmas with our families. Well, he had an emergency surgery to perform right before we left, and I went alone. He flew down two days later to meet me there, with a tan by the way. Now, explain to me how he got a tan in Atlanta during the winter time? The man was always bundled up! He hates being cold. Well, two days before we were scheduled to leave, he got an emergency phone call and he flew back to the States to perform yet another emergency surgery. And being little naive me, I believed him. I mean things do come up with his patients all of the time. However, when Alfonso is on vacation Dr. Bobb always covers for him if necessary, and he covers for her," Megan said and then paused.

"So, when did you finally realize that he was probably in the Bahamas the whole time with another woman?"

"Well, when I returned back to the States, of

course he was the first person I called. My car was at the airport. I called him to see if I could come straight to his house, but he didn't answer the phone. So I drove to his house anyway because, well, I did have a key. However, my key was to the front door only. When I pulled up, I remembered that Jade and I had his double doors changed out, and I didn't have the new key. I rang the doorbell and called his phone again. I could hear the phone ringing from inside of the house, but still no answer. I left a note on his door and a voice mail that I was back from the Bahamas," Megan said tired of going over this story again with someone. At least this time she wasn't crying like the time she told Tiffani and Jade.

"So what happened next?"

"Well, the next day he came over about 8:00 in the morning with breakfast and a present. He said he had been out with Curtis who is his best friend and didn't get my note until he returned home at 4:00 a.m. I later found out that Curtis and his family were in Denver, Colorado on a ski trip. He did see Curtis that night, but only to drive him to the airport."

"Interesting," Steven said, stretching out on the floor.

"Yes, very interesting considering whenever Al went out with his friends, he always called me no matter what time of night to come over or sometimes he just showed up at my door. Well, like I said, I was still being Ms. Naive, and I believed him except that his tan was much darker than it was when he left me in the Bahamas. But I didn't question him. We exchanged gifts and had breakfast. I thought surely we were going to make love afterward considering one of the gifts I gave him was a purple sheer night-gown with matching lace panties. Usually, if I gave him a gift like lingerie that meant I was definitely in the mood, but he said let's save it for later. That man had never turned down sex!"

"Megan, I don't know a man that would unless he was on his death bed and even then he would prob-ably ask for a Lewinsky or something," Steven said sarcastically.

Megan laughed at Steven's comment as she walked to the kitchen to pour the rest of the coffee into her mug and turned off the coffeemaker.

"That coffee is going to keep you up all night, Miss Lady," Steven said, teasing her.

"Yes, I know, but that's fine. I have a lot of work to do, as well. I have some drapes to make. But let me finish telling you about Dr. Alfonso. So any-way, a few days went by before I saw him again. We were having lunch at his house, mostly leftover Christmas dinner from my parents' dinner party. I was opening the refrigerator to take out some juice when I noticed a brochure about a medical conven-tion in Chicago on the refrigerator. I asked him about it and he casually said it was in a few months. So I said cool. Just let me know the details so I can rear-range my schedule. Whenever he attended a medical conference I always went. He never had to ask me, it was always understood that I would go because he wanted me to go with him. Well, at first he was silent and then he said that I didn't have to go because it was in March and I was always busy in March with decorating homes for the spring. I still insisted, and he said don't worry about it and quickly changed the subject. Then the doorbell rang."

"It was the girl he was seeing behind your back?" Steven asked, sitting all the way up.

"No, it was Dr. Bobb and her husband. She said they were in the neighborhood and they wanted to drop off Alfonso's gift. Well, he didn't look happy to see them at all and tried to rush them out. I gave Dr. Bobb and her husband a hug and told them to come and sit down in the living room. Alfonso had gotten a call on his cell and went to another room to take it. I asked the Bobbs about their Christmas trip and she said they didn't go anywhere for Christmas. But that they were going to Memphis for New Year's Eve to visit her husband's family and wanted to make sure that Alfonso could return the favor since she was on call for him while he was in the Bahamas. I decided not to mention that he flew to the Bahamas later because of an emergency surgery because obviously, by the way the pieces of the puzzle were fitting together, there wasn't an emergency of any kind. So I simply said we had a lovely time. They left a few minutes later to finish delivering other Christmas gifts," Megan said, taking a break from her long story.

She was trying to shorten it, but she felt that certain details were important. But she remembered a man's attention span wasn't that long, especially when Steven said, "Okay, so when did you confront the pig?"

"I'm getting to that. So later on that evening we were in his study. He was writing out some bills, and I was pretending to proofread a medical article he wrote. I decided to ask him about the medical convention again in Chicago. He said don't worry about it and that he wasn't sure if he was going to go or not anyway. I knew something wasn't right. I stood up and decided it was time for me to leave. In doing so, I straightened up the pillows on his couch. And that is when I found my evidence."

"What? What did you find? An earring that wasn't yours?" Steven questioned sitting up from his comfortable position by the fireplace.

"No, worse. A pair of red panties that weren't mine!"

"Damn! You know that girl left them there on purpose for you to find. If it was earrings he could've lied and said they were his mother's or something like that," Steven said. "Not that I would know," he added sheepishly with shrug.

"Ha. Yeah, right. Anyway, he was stunned to see them and claimed that they must be mine, but I wear a small and those panties looked a lot larger. Plus, I don't own anything red and he knows that. Anyway, he decided to tell me the truth about him and his nurse, Shelia. I had a feeling it was her. She was always trying to be overly nice to me when I stopped by the office to visit him. After an hour of arguing, I walked out thus ending our four year relationship."

"So, he didn't try to stop you or beg for your forgiveness?"

"No. He was relieved. In fact, he wanted to end our relationship anyway to be with her, and they're still together now. She lives in his home that Jade and I decorated for him before the breakup. But I've moved on. Alfonso leaving me just left the door open for the right man to come into my life," Megan answered, taking their empty mugs back into the kitchen.

"I'm so sorry to hear all of this. What a fool he is. You're a very special lady, Megan. I'm sure the right man will come along if you just let him," Steven responded, walking to the kitchen behind her.

"Yes, I know," Megan said, loading the dishwasher and trying to hide her face. She knew if he looked at her now, her facial expression would give away her true feelings for him. She was ready for him to leave so she could be alone with her thoughts.

"Do you need some help? I did drink all of your coffee and eat all of your cookies. The least I can do is clean your kitchen," Steven offered, taking one of the dish towels and wiping down the counter.

"No, Steven. It's getting late. I have bored you enough tonight."

"Are you kicking me out?"

"Yes. If you're going to be our next U.S. senator you need to go home and work on your campaign," Megan said, not really wanting him to go. Although, she felt that they were getting too close again, which was something she didn't want to do. Plus, when he mentioned eating all of her cookies, she had a different type of visual.

"You're right. I didn't realize it was almost ten," he said, walking back to the fireplace to retrieve his car keys and cell phone. Megan watched him. He was indeed the perfect man. Handsome, successful, compassionate and determined. He had all of the qualities that she wanted in a man, but she knew it was pointless to dwell on it. A relationship with him would be out of the question.

"What's wrong?" he asked, interrupting her thoughts.

Megan was startled. She hadn't realized she was staring at him so hard. She smiled and brushed it off. "Oh, nothing. I was deep in thought I guess." She turned away to hide her embarrassment.

"Hey, Meg I'm sorry if I brought up old wounds from the past. I won't mention him again," Steven said, walking toward her.

"Oh, I wasn't thinking about him," she said, walking toward the door to let Steven out. "I'm truly over him now."

"Well, I hope I had something to do with it. I mean I know this isn't a real relationship, but I hope I've brought some sunshine to your life," Steven said with his hand on the doorknob.

"You have. Good night, Mr. Monroe," Megan said smiling and opening the door for him. He lightly gave her a kiss on the forehead and left. Once the door shut, Percy ran out from under the bed and rubbed his body on Megan's legs.

"Percy, what am I doing? I have gone and fallen in love with a man I can never have," Megan said as she picked up the cat. She held Percy close as the tears started to roll down her cheeks.

Chapter 10

It was the Monday morning following KJ's birthday party. Megan, Jade and Lucy sat in their staff meeting going over the upcoming week's agenda. Lucy was finally going on her first assignment with Jade to look for vintage furniture for a client that loved antique dressers and wanted four, one for each of her bedrooms. Megan's mind was wandering during the meeting. On Sunday morning while making coffee, she had decided to try it Steven's way and drink it black with just a little sugar. She'd smiled as she realized he was right. It had in fact retained the flavor.

Megan had picked up the phone to call him but hung up before dialing. She was so used to sharing everything with her ex-boyfriends that it seemed natural to call Steven, but she'd had to remind herself that he wasn't really her boyfriend.

"Megan, are you ignoring me?" Jade asked in her usual sassy tone.

Lucy waved her hand in front of Megan's zoned-out face. "Earth to Megan. Are you there?"

"Oh, ladies, forgive me. I spaced out. What were you saying?" Megan asked remembering where she was.

"Did you want to go the furniture store with us?" Jade asked standing and grabbing her belongings from the table.

"No...I'll be at a client's home all day waiting for and arranging furniture."

"Okay, we'll be back this afternoon."

Moments later, Megan sat at her desk contemplating what she needed to do before she left. Then the phone rang. She glanced at the caller ID and saw it was Steven. She hadn't spoken to him since Saturday night. She took a deep breath and answered the phone, "Chase, Whitmore and Associates, how can I help you?" she asked in a cheery tone.

"Hey, Megan, it's Steven. How are you doing this marvelous Monday morning?"

"I'm fine, Steven. What can I do for you?"

"I just wanted to tell you that I had a nice time with you and your friends on Saturday. KJ is a good kid. I see him being an investment broker or maybe Hugh Heffner the way those little four-year-old girls were crowding around him in the moonwalk. Did you see the one that kissed him on his cheek when she was leaving? That was really cute. I like children. They say and do the darnedest things. Do you want children?" he inquired.

"One day. I have to find the right man first," Megan answered. Even though she felt as if she had found the right man, she knew that soon after he received the nomination, their relationship would be over, and she would be alone again.

"I also wanted to tell you that I'm going out of town tomorrow on the campaign trail this week to help out a friend in another state. Anyway, I'll be back on Saturday morning. If you need anything, just leave a voice mail or text on my cell."

"Will do."

"I was hoping to see you tonight. How about I bring some Thai food over, and we watch movies together, unless you'd rather be alone."

Megan didn't want to be alone, and she was looking forward to seeing him considering he would be gone for the rest of the week. She took a deep breath and said, "That would be nice. Thai food and you, of course, are more than welcome to come over this evening."

"Great. I'll see you later."

The rest of the day passed by slowly as Megan remodeled a dining room and a living room for a client. She was looking forward to Steven coming over that evening, and she could barely concentrate on her job. Once home, Megan changed into a pair of jeans, but then decided to slip on a polo shirtdress and pulled her hair back into a loose ponytail. She vacuumed her hardwood, cleaned the kitchen and hung up all of her clothes that were scattered on the bed. Megan kept glancing at the clock. He'd texted her earlier and said he would be over around seven.

Megan sat on the couch and watched her grandfather clock slowly tick by. A little after the hour, her intercom buzzer sounded.

"Yes?"

"Delivery for Megan Chase," Steven said trying to disguise his voice. A few minutes later he was standing in her living room carrying two big bags of Thai food.

"Wow! Did you bring enough for the whole building?" Megan teased as she took the bags from him and placed them on the island in the kitchen.

"Well, I wasn't sure what you liked so I bought different things we can sample. There's a bottle of wine in that bag. I'll put it in the freezer for a few minutes to chill."

"Great!" Megan exclaimed as placed the takeout boxes on the table and then grabbed plates and wineglasses.

"So, do you have any good DVDs? I see you have about two hundred of them over there."

"Yes, but you've probably seen them all," Megan said crossing the room to read off the titles.

"Baby, I rarely go to the movies. I don't have time. Besides, I prefer to watch movies at home. Do you have any nongirlie movies?"

"Yes. But I don't have any scary movies unless you count Scary Movie one, two and three as scary.

I have a lot of comedies." Megan scanned through her collection.

"Let me see what you have. Comedy movies are my favorite next to suspense and drama. *Crimson Tide* is my all-time favorite," Steven said kneeling down on the floor beside her.

"Well, I don't have that, but how about *Kiss the Girls* with Morgan Freeman? It's a suspense movie. I read the book before the movie came out. I couldn't put it down! However, I was picturing Denzel Washington as Alex Cross not Morgan Freeman. Do you want to watch it?" Megan asked, holding up the DVD.

"You know," Steven said, moving closer to her, "I was just thinking about that."

"Cool. I'll put it in," she said, still looking through her collection of movies trying to ignore the fact that he was so close to her that she could feel his breath on her neck.

"I wasn't referring to the movie," Steven replied. Tossing the DVD case on the floor, he kissed Megan passionately on the lips. Megan responded willingly as he laid her down on the floor next to the DVD stand. Steven kissed her hungrily while reaching his right hand under her dress to feel her thighs. His other hand fiddled with her ponytail. He tossed the scrunchy across the floor and dug his hands into her hair.

Passion surged through her as he kissed her, sinking his tongue deeper into her mouth as muffled moans caught inside her throat. His kisses were like the fairy-tale kisses she had always imagined, but never experienced. Passionate. Erotic. Sensual. When his lips left hers she let out a loud cry as he kissed her on her ears and then her neck. His hand trailed down her body and then back underneath her dress, kneading her thighs. When his hands began to pull down her panties, all her senses rushed back into her head, and she pushed him off of her.

"Wait we can't do this," Megan interrupted before jumping up and running to the bathroom with Steven closely running after. She closed the bathroom door before he could come in. She splashed some water on her face as Steven opened the unlocked door.

"Damn it, Megan! Stop running away from me. From us."

"Steven, this is all wrong. You don't want a real relationship with me. This is just pretend until after the election," Megan cried.

"What? You honestly think that? You mean to tell me you didn't feel anything a minute ago? Or even when we were in Washington? Or, hell, when we first met? I'm tired of pretending. I want a real relationship with you, I want to be with you, Megan Chase," he said standing behind her looking at their reflection in the mirror. He placed his hands on her shoulders, but didn't turn her around. "Don't we look good together? We make the perfect team. I knew we would the minute I laid eyes on you," he whispered into her ear, his lips lightly brushing it. She flinched as his lips touched her. Megan looked at their reflection in the mirror.

"Steven…" She turned around to face him with happy tears filling her eyes.

"I think, my lady, we've done enough talking for one night," he said as his lips came crushing down on hers.

Steven lifted her up in his arms and carried her to the bed laying her down gently on the comforter. He placed his body on top of hers, kissing her gently on the lips, trying to savor every inch of her delicious mouth.

Steven had never felt so intense and passionate about a woman before. He knew this was the woman who he wanted to see as he closed his eyes every night and couldn't wait to wake up to the next morning.

"Can I help you out of your dress?" he asked, sitting up to take off his shirt to bare his smooth rippled chest and abdomen. Megan smiled as she ran her fingers and then lips over his chest twirling her tongue around one of his nipples. While she continued to arouse him further, he quickly lifted the dress off of her, throwing it across the room with his shirt.

"Damn, baby. You're so beautiful," he complimented as he raked his eyes over her fuchsia lace bra and panties. He licked his lips as he pulled her toward him to feel her hot bare skin under him.

Once she was nude, he lifted her off of the bed and guided her against a nearby wall.

"I had a fantasy about you pushing me against

this very wall," she said, unbuckling his belt. "And having your way with me."

A cocky half grin crossed his mouth. "Oh, really?"

She nodded, displaying a sexy, lazy grin, and kissed him lightly on the lips as she removed his belt and unbuttoned his slacks.

"Well...I am..." He paused as he returned the kiss and licked her lips. "Here to make all your fantasies come true, precious."

He turned her away from him and placed her hands on the wall causing her to let out fervent moans of pleasure. "Part your legs."

He began slowly gliding his tongue from the base of her neck down her back until he was at her center. Megan moaned loudly as his tongue licked and drank her womanly juices. He squeezed her butt and then slapped it, sinking a finger into her as she squirmed and pleaded with him.

"Oh, Steven, please don't stop," she yelled out, pressing her head on the wall as he continued to tantalize her insides with his tongue and fingers. His answer to her was putting his fingers in as deeply as possible, causing the first of many orgasms that night.

Her legs, and her balance, became undone as he lowered her to the floor and held her in his arms as he massaged her clit. Her cries of passion and desire shattered across the room. He kissed her damp forehead and rubbed her hair until she came down from her high.

"Do you have protection?" she whispered.

"Be patient, my love, we have all night."

"Can't we just skip the foreplay? I've waited so long to have you, Steven," she begged, putting her hand on his very erect penis and massaging it through his pants.

"My insatiable, little Megan," he whispered with his lips hovering over hers. "You want it right now?"

"Yes," she cried out.

"Right here up against the wall like in your fantasy?"

"Wherever you intend to."

"Oh, I intend to make love to you in every possible position tonight, in every possible place in this loft. If we run out of rooms, we may have to go to my place."

"I think I have some condoms somewhere."

"Are they Magnums?"

"Um…no."

"Then that won't work." He took her hand and placed it directly on his penis that was now fully erect and ready thanks to her pleading. "Don't worry, my love. I came prepared."

"Go get it."

He stood them up, placing her back on the wall. He obeyed, taking a few packs of condoms out of his back pants pocket and held them up much to her delight. He wasn't used to a woman barking orders at him. Smirking, he stared at her exquisite body leaning on the wall and stepped toward her, pulling his pants and boxer shorts down at the same time and stepping out of them. "Let's get one thing straight.

I'm in charge and in control," he said placing a condom over his firm rod.

She gulped with wide eyes as she glanced down and then back up at him with a wicked grin on her face.

"Oh, really?" she asked sarcastically.

"Yes, really," he said as he picked her up by her buttocks as if she were light as a feather and slid her up the wall. She wrapped her legs tightly around his waist, and he immediately entered her, wasting no time with his strong thrusts causing her to scream out his name in ecstasy. He pounded her harder and harder while she dug her nails deeper into his shoulders. He knew he would have scars later on but he didn't care. The warmness and wetness of her made him sink further into her spirit and mind. She was causing him to feel things he'd never felt before, and he wanted to make sure that all of him was in tune with her. The more she cried out his name, the more he gave it all to her.

Megan wrapped her legs and arms tighter around him as he carried her from the wall and placed her on the bed. She stared up at him with loving eyes as he filled her even deeper. They rocked back and forth concentrating on each other intently. He moved her legs around his neck and held her hands to the bed, as he went all the way in and then all the way out. Her hips met his strokes at the same cadence.

As they screamed out together, he felt all of the emotions bottled up in his heart rush out of him. He grabbed hold of her tightly as he panted her name and a few curse words over and over in the crook of her neck. As his breathing slowed down, he lifted his head and kissed her lightly on the lips.

He was satisfied yet ready for round two with her. The room was quiet except for the soft sound of the ceiling fan above. Neither of them spoke and there wasn't any need. Their lovemaking had spoken louder than any words they could have uttered to each other.

An hour later, they were still intertwined together lying on top of the comforter. Megan tried to wrestle away from his hold to grab the blanket at the end of the bed. Steven pulled her closer into his body so that her back was completely pressed against his muscular chest.

"Where are you going?"

"To grab the blanket."

"I'm not keeping you warm enough?"

"You are. I just feel weird lying naked on top of the comforter."

"I want to see and feel your sexy little body next to me," he said and then kissed the base of her neck. She let out a soft sigh at his touch and technique. She could feel the hardness of him urgently bearing against her bottom and then the tear of a condom wrapper.

"I need to be inside of you again, Megan," he heavily urged in her ear causing her to feel a shooting sensation as he dived into her once again. He turned her over on her stomach as he continued long strokes, in and out, making her dig her fingers in the mattress. Each time it was more intense causing her to release shuddering orgasms one after the other.

After the fifth orgasm, Megan was so out of it, she barely knew where she was. All she knew was that the man she loved was making her feel so damn good.

He pulled her up so she was on her knees. He placed his hands on her round bottom to guide her.

"Am I making you feel good, baby?"

"Oh, yes. The best," she truthfully said.

As he came inside of her, she swore she heard a roar of a lion escape him.

Megan fell limp on the bed as he rolled off of her. She could still feel him pulsating through her as she laid on her back staring up at the ceiling trying to catch her breath from their escapade. She could tell by the aching in her legs, she may be sore the next day, but it was well worth it.

He lay next to her on his back with his head turned toward her.

"Do you smoke?" she asked.

"Um…no? Why, do you smoke?"

"No, but if I was to start, this would be the perfect time to," she said laughing.

"I agree," he said, pulling her close to him.

Chapter 11

Megan was floating on cloud nine. She had heard of the expression and was now experiencing it. She'd never been happier in a relationship. Steven was kind, thoughtful and honest. He sent flowers, texts on her cell phone and voice mails when he was away from her. He was still busy, but he always found time for her. Megan was also happy because her dad finally liked someone she brought home. Steven and her dad had already played golf at the golf course in her parent's subdivision, and they were planning a weekend trip to see Tiger Woods play.

One evening, Megan was looking over some swatches at her office. She didn't like to work late at night but she had to prepare for the beach house she was decorating that would be featured on the

Fabulous Living Channel. Jade and Lucy had already left and Steven was in meetings all day. They were supposed to have dinner, but at around 4:00 p.m. he'd called and cancelled. He said that he had a lot of work to catch up on and would be at his office all night. She decided to stay late and catch up on work as well since she would be at a client's home for the rest of the week. After work, she decided she would stop by his office and surprise him with dinner. She knew he wouldn't mind since she'd done it a few times before, much to his enjoyment.

She called one of her favorite places to dine and ordered two dinners to go. She wanted to spend as much time with Steven as she could before she left for Hilton Head in a few days.

Megan parked her SUV next to Steven's Range Rover. She noticed another car in the parking lot that didn't look familiar. She hoped he wasn't in a meeting. It was nine at night. Her goal was to convince him to eat and then follow her back to her place for a little romantic time. She walked around to the front of the building. *The door is unlocked so he must be in a meeting,* she thought. She walked into the empty "showroom," as Shawn called it. Ten cubicles were in the middle of the room. On the walls were the copy machine, faxes, water cooler and the worktables. In the back were Steven's and Shawn's offices, a conference room and break room with a bathroom. Steven would usually hold any meetings in the conference room. So she decided to wait in his office.

As she walked back to his office, she noticed the

door was ajar and the light was on. Megan went to the door and stuck her head in. She saw Veronica sitting in Steven's chair and Steven sitting on the desk facing Veronica with his back to the door. Veronica saw Megan peeking in and smiled sweetly at Steven rubbing her hand on his knee.

"I enjoyed catching up over dinner tonight," Veronica said loudly enough for Megan to hear and rubbing her hand back and forth. "We must do this again real soon."

Megan entered the office.

"Oh, hello dear," Veronica said sweetly to Megan. Steven turned around quickly and stood up. He looked surprised and guilty.

"Hello, Veronica. I didn't know you were in town," Megan stated still remaining poised.

"Yes, Veronica came into town this morning. She's speaking at Atlanta Memorial College for a Women's Day program tomorrow," Steven answered calmly.

"I must run now. I need to read over my speech again." Veronica stood, displaying a very short red dress that was clinging to her figure like a glove. "Thank you for a lovely time tonight. Call me and let me know if you can escort me to the banquet on Saturday. You know I only prefer to have a handsome man on my arm, and Judge Hill is unavailable. But you and I always look good together at black-tie affairs," Veronica said kissing Steven on the cheek. She then turned her tall frame toward Megan.

"Bye, Maggy, It was nice to see you again," Veronica said. She then grabbed her purse off of Steven's desk and sashayed out of the office smiling.

Megan waited until she heard Veronica open and close the front door

"I thought you were here working late?" Megan asked in a composed tone.

"I am. I intend to be here until midnight, if not later. Shawn will be back at ten. We have some things to go over. Is there something wrong?" Steven said sitting down in his chair and looking over some papers on his desk, avoiding eye contact.

Megan felt the anger rising in her, but she decided to remain poised and listen to his side of the story of what she'd just walked in on.

"You cancelled our dinner plans this evening," Megan said. She walked over to where he was sitting and stood over him with her right hand on her hip. "And then had the audacity to have dinner with your ex."

"Megan. I didn't just have dinner with her. The president of Atlanta Memorial College was there as well to persuade me to speak at the Woman's Day ceremony tomorrow," Steven said as he stood up and placed his hands on her waist.

Megan stepped back. She was too upset for him to touch her. She didn't want to lose trust in him, but if he was beginning to act like Alfonso, then she was in the wrong relationship once again.

"Really? Are you speaking at the program?" she inquired.

"Yes. I told her I would attend the opening session in the morning."

"You and Veronica looked really cozy when I came in. Are you also escorting her to the banquet on Saturday?"

"No. What's with all of the questions tonight?"

"You lied to me, Steven."

"I didn't lie to you. She called after I cancelled our dinner plans. It was all business. Veronica means nothing to me." Steven grabbed her hands.

"And I guess I don't either if you can't tell me the truth." Megan stormed out of his office and into the showroom.

"Megan, I don't have time for the jealous girlfriend act. I'm in a very serious time in my life right now," Steven said following after her.

"You know what? I don't have time for the ex-wife act right now either. Steven, I heard the way she was speaking to you!"

"She only did that because you were here. This evening at dinner, she barely spoke to me. She was on her cell phone most of the time. Trust me the only man she is after right now is Judge Hill. He's trying to make it to the Supreme Court one day. You've seen the stories on the news about that. Veronica is all about gaining prestige. I know you realized that when you met her in Washington."

"What if someone got a picture of you at dinner tonight with her? It could be all over Twitter and Facebook by now."

"The dinner was at the president's home. There

was definitely no one there to snap any pictures. It was just an innocent dinner. Trust me, there is nothing going on between Veronica and I."

A thought popped into her mind. "Why was Veronica even here at your office if you had dinner at the president's home?"

"We rode together, and she came inside to use my computer for a work-related issue. That's all."

Megan knew he was telling the truth, but she was still uncomfortable with his ex-wife being in his life, especially one as beautiful and vindictive as Veronica. Megan walked over to Steven and put her head on his chest.

"Our first fight," she said staring up at him. He bent down and kissed her tenderly on the lips.

"Well, I guess we need to do some making up," he said walking her back to his office.

"Here?" she asked surprisingly. "Shawn will be here in about thirty minutes." She said looking around.

"Just real quick," he said, kissing her on the neck.

"Okay. But you're never real quick," she said as he carried her back to his office and laid her down on the couch for their make-up session.

"So are you going to hang out with me and Shawn tonight? I know you have some work in your car. You can use the conference room," Steven suggested once they were done and sitting on the couch in his office.

"No, baby. Just come over when you're finished. You have a key. Besides, I'll still be up working on some sketches for the *Decorator's Dream* project. We can make up again when you come over," Megan said, grabbing her to-go bag off the table. She hadn't eaten since lunch.

"It's a deal. I promise," he said.

Steven didn't come over until two in the morning, but they were both too exhausted to make love again. Instead, they cuddled while Percy watched from his bed. Steven also suggested a possible minivacation when she returned from Hilton Head.

Before Steven left that morning, he reassured her he wasn't going to take Veronica to the banquet.

The rest of his week was full with visiting different colleges in the state to discuss his plans for the continuation of the Hope Scholarship. In addition to some other educational programs beneficial to college students.

According to a pole in the Atlanta Newspaper, Steven was in the lead by 75% as a favorite to run for the U.S. Senate now that his father had officially put the rumors to rest that he was indeed retiring at the end of the year.

Steven decided he would announce his plans to run for the U.S. Senate seat soon, as the primary deadline was approaching. He was happier however, that he no longer had to pretend with Megan. They were an official couple. There was a picture of them in the paper with a caption that read, "Has the senator finally settled down or is this just a publicity stunt?" The article went on to comment on his progress and compared his views with other potential candidates.

After Steven returned from speaking at Atlanta Memorial College, he looked over the itinerary Shawn had left for him for the rest of day. He was supposed to have lunch with his father and Bryce and spend dinner and the rest of the evening with Megan. She was leaving the next morning for Hilton Head, and he wanted to spend as much time with her as possible before she left for a week, possibly longer.

As he sat at his desk, Steven thought about lunch with his dad and brother and knew it wouldn't be pleasant. His father was in town to discuss the upcoming election. Steven checked his watch. It was almost one, and he knew if he didn't leave his office now, he would be late for his lunch meeting at the French Peasant.

Arriving twenty minutes late, Steven saw his father and brother sitting in a booth at the back of the restaurant under a skylight. Mr. Monroe always made sure he was given the best table in any restaurant. The art on the walls was intricately wood-carved flowers. Megan had told him that she had designed a client's dining room to replicate the restaurant. The young couple had their wedding reception there and wanted the same atmosphere in their home. Steven suggested the French Peasant to his father because he knew his dad enjoyed intriguing artwork and would appreciate his son being considerate of him. His father stood up to shake his hand, but Bryce stirred his ice tea with his straw and smirked at Steven.

"Son, you're late. That's not a good trait for a politician. They're watching you all of the time, even when you don't realize it. Don't forget you're a very important man. Have been since the day you were born," Mr. Monroe stated, shaking his hand. Steven sat down and glanced at Bryce who was still smirking. Steven wondered who "they" were while he looked at the menu.

"So, Dad, how's Washington?" Steven asked, hoping to sway the conversation off of him. He really wanted to enjoy a relaxing lunch with his father and brother, although he could sense from Bryce's facial expressions that their father had a lot to say.

"My son's political career is at stake. Let's order. We have a lot to discuss."

Steven glanced at Bryce who continued reading the menu, probably glad the heat wasn't on him for a change.

For the next hour, Mr. Monroe drilled and debated Steven on every issue that would come up during the election. When they were done with lunch and his mock debate, Mr. Monroe sat back in his chair looking proudly at his son.

"You're definitely a Monroe man. You both are. We never let anything stand in our way of getting exactly what we want." He leaned over the table toward his sons and whispered. "If you keep doing what you're doing now, you'll be president one day. Your brother could be the attorney general and, of course, you'll find something for your sister and your old man?"

"Of course, Dad. You're the reason I'm where I

am today," Steven complimented. As much as he hated to admit it, he knew he was just like his father. Ambitious, hardworking and determined not to let anyone get in the way of his destiny.

"So now tell me about this Megan Chase. Do we know her family? I haven't had a chance to do an investigation on her yet because you usually recycle your women quite quickly. But I see she's lasted for a few months now, and the media loves her. Is she part of the Chase family that we met a few years ago at Martha's Vincyard?" Mr. Monroe said during dessert.

"She isn't part of the Chase family we met at the vineyard," Steven said as he added way too much sugar to his coffee. His father was making him slightly nervous with his concern for his relationship with Megan.

"I'm glad you've finally settled down with one girl. I was hoping Shawn and Bryce would talk some sense into you. I know you hadn't planned on re-marrying again, but remember it's up to you and Bryce to carry on the Monroe name, with more boys of course. Our family legacy and heritage has been around for generations and it must continue. Could this girl possibly be the one to help make that happen for you?" Mr. Monroe asked, concerned.

"Dad, I hope so. She's perfect in every way, sort of like Mom. She's supportive, independent and doesn't care about playing games."

"Just checking, son. But you mentioned to me that she had her own business. There's nothing wrong with a career woman, but the wife of a U.S. senator needs to be supportive of you. Her main obligation should be you and your family. I'm not trying to sound like a male chauvinist. Your mother taught school, but it wasn't as demanding as having her own business. We don't need any more problems in this family. You already had one divorce, and you know I did everything possible to keep that quiet. And I can't believe that one is flaunting the Monroe name like she's still part of this family," Mr. Monroe said slamming his fist down on the table causing the fork on his dessert plate to fall to the floor.

"We understand, Dad, but I promise you I know what I'm doing with Megan. She's a wonderful person," Steven said taking the bill from the middle of the table.

"It's not Megan I'm worried about," Mr. Monroe said, looking at his cell phone screen and then turning it around to show Steven.

Chapter 12

Megan exhaled as she finished packing the last-minute items that Chelsea suggested, or rather demanded, that she pack. Chelsea had finally left and Megan was exhausted. She'd spent that entire afternoon trying on different outfits. Chelsea had put together a list of clothes for Megan and Jade to wear on the show and had even faxed it to the producers.

Megan took a long refreshing shower, dressed and waited impatiently for Steven to arrive. She had planned a romantic evening for them. The candles were lit in every area of the loft and she had champagne chilling in the freezer. Her Thai take-out order was on the way. Everything was perfect including her new black lace panty-and-bra set under her short black dress she wore the night she met Steven. He told her she looked stunning that night and wanted to see her in the dress again. Megan wanted to make sure he had something to hold him over until her return from Hilton Head.

Megan placed her suitcases by the door so she would be ready in the morning. Steven was taking her to the airport at five in the morning and afterward dropping Percy off at Tiffani's home.

After the Thai food was delivered, she glanced at the clock. Steven would be there soon, and she was ready to eat. She decided she would nibble on an egg roll but her cell phone ringing interrupted her trek to the kitchen.

"What's up Syd?"

"Hey, Megan," she said uneasily. "You're calm."

Megan's heart stopped. The last time Sydney said that, there was a picture of her and Steven all over internet. "More pictures of me and Steven?"

"Steven, yes. You, no. I just emailed you the link."

Megan grabbed her tablet and clicked on the link, her heart stopping again. "I'll call you back."

She paced back and forth with her tablet in her hand in disbelief. In front of her were pictures of Steven from that morning at the Women's Day Program. One of which was with him and Veronica. There were actually several with him and Veronica posing with the students or guests at the event. However, the one that had both Megan and the media in a frenzy was captioned "Is the senator getting cozy with his ex-wife again?" In the picture, Veronica and Steven were walking and holding hands as she stared back at him with a loving smile on her face. Steven was smiling at her, as well.

The article went on to suggest that while the senator was more than likely running for his father's soon to be empty U.S. Senate seat, were he and his ex-wife making amends and getting back together?

At the sound of the doorbell, Megan's anger propelled even higher because she knew who was on the other side of the door. And he was about to feel her wrath.

"Percy, you may want to hide under the bed, sweetie. Mommy's pissed," she said as she stormed toward the door armed with her tablet. Percy followed orders and darted under the bed.

She swung the door open, and the handsome smile Steven wore faded into a questionable stare.

"What the heck is this?" She shoved the tablet in his hand.

He came in and closed the door, tossing his overnight bag on the floor.

"Humph." Megan glanced down at the bag. "You might as well pick that up because you only have two minutes to explain."

"Megan, there's nothing to explain," he stated calmly. "You knew I was speaking this morning at Atlanta Memorial College. You knew Veronica would be there."

"Yes, but what I didn't know was that there was still something going on between you two. I can't believe I actually believed you last night when there she was rubbing on you and flirting with you in front of me. Now there's a picture of you two holding hands and staring all lovey-dovey at each other." She snatched her tablet out of his hand and pointed to the evidence.

"Baby, I know the picture looks suspect, but we weren't really holding hands. She was pulling me along because I arrived late, and I was going on in five minutes. She was rushing me through the crowd and showing me where to go."

"And the lovey-dovey smiles?"

"We were laughing at the crowd of girls whistling and screaming, 'We love you Senator Monroe' and some other choice words about how fine and handsome I am. The event was recorded and it clearly shows just what I told you. You're more than welcome to watch it. It was on the local news station earlier. I have nothing to hide from you."

"You think I'm stupid?"

"No. I think you're making a big deal out of nothing. You remember the first pictures that circled the net with us? How I was leaning over and whispering in your ear and you were supposedly staring at me all mesmerized according to the media. When actually I was screaming in your ear because the music was loud, and you were staring up at me to listen better."

Megan sighed and sat on the couch. She closed her eyes and rested her head on the pillow. She didn't know what to believe anymore. She loved Steven, but she was beginning to grow tired of life in the spotlight especially now with this Veronica thing. Even though it was probably innocent, the media didn't perceive it that way. He had come full circle and cleaned up his reputation during the past few months thanks to her but also thanks to his determination.

His scent whiffed in her nose, and she sensed he was kneeling in front of her. She opened her eyes as tears fell from them, and he reached up and wiped them just as more silent ones began to fall.

"I'm not him, Megan. I would never cheat on you or disrespect you. I love you way too much to do that."

He gathered her in his arms and moved to the couch, positioning her on his lap. She laid her head on his chest as he gently rubbed her hair.

"I love you, too, Steven, and I do believe and trust you. I just don't trust Veronica."

"Megan, Veronica isn't interested in me at all. Believe me, she wants Judge Hill. She only invited me to the event at the last minute because she's a friend of the president at Atlanta Memorial College, and she wanted to make a good impression. It was all for show for her. That's it."

"Well, when I walked in yesterday she was all over you…"

"Before you walked in, she wasn't. She always does that whenever she meets whoever I'm dating. She likes to intimidate people."

"Well, she doesn't intimidate me."

"That's my girl," he said planting delicate kisses on her neck and ears. He ran his hand down her side. "I see you're wearing my favorite dress tonight."

"I wanted tonight to be special since I'm leaving in the morning."

"And it will still be special, I promise." He kissed her lightly on the lips. "I smell Thai food."

"Yes, it was delivered right before you arrived." She tried to scoot out of his embrace, but he pulled her closer.

"How about dessert first," he suggested as his sexy, dark gaze rested on her face, and he pulled the hem of her dress up to her thighs.

"That sounds wonderful…" She was interrupted by Steven's cell phone ringing.

"Sorry, babe, I told Shawn to only call if it was absolutely necessary. I'll put it on speaker so I can continue my tongue journey on your body."

"Shawn, what's going on?" Steven asked as he still held on to Megan and ran his finger alongside her face.

"Man, we have a major problem. A reporter just called asking if you were in a relationship with Megan only to clean up your image. I told him of course not, and you two were very much in love."

"Okay, that's true. So what's the problem?" Steven asked as Megan listened intently.

"He also stated he had a reliable source that could state otherwise. This reliable source claims she overheard Megan getting upset on the phone about having to sleep in the same bed as you in D.C."

Megan sat up when she realized who it was. "Susan. She must've heard me say that on the plane. Oh, no! Steven, I'm so sorry."

"That's bull! Why is Susan doing this to me?" Steven said as Megan slid off of his lap with wide eyes. He got up and walked away from her and into the kitchen with the phone still on speaker in his hand.

"Well, apparently her and Bryce were having an affair, but he broke it off with her recently and then fired her yesterday."

"I had no idea about them, but why punish me?"

"Bryce said she's trying to extort money from him. When he refused to give her what she asked for, she threatened to tell the media about what she overheard Megan say that day on the flight. I told the reporter none of that was true and hung up the phone. But you know women. Some of them never forgive or forget. They hold grudges for a long time. Man, try to have a nice evening with Megan. I just wanted you to know so you wouldn't hear it or read about it first from another source. I'll release a statement as soon as it comes out in the news."

Steven pounded his fist on the island in the kitchen. He knew he shouldn't be worried, but he was announcing his candidacy for the U.S. Senate seat in a few days. He shook his head. Megan rubbed his back to console him.

"Baby, don't worry about this. Like Shawn said, she's a female with a grudge who just wants money. We know the truth and that's what matters. Your constituents are more interested in what you can do for them not who you're dating," Megan said, trying to comfort him.

"I guess you know I don't handle stress well."

"I know you don't. However, you have people around you that care about you and have your best interests in mind, especially me. Shawn said he would take care of it, right?"

"Baby, I don't know what I would do without your love and support. I love you so much," Steven said looking into her eyes.

"I love you, too," Megan responded smiling up at him as he picked her up and carried her to the bedroom.

He placed her down on the floor, and she slowly unzipped the side zipper of her dress, letting it fall off of her feet. His eyes raked over her body and then he pulled her to him. His fingers slid down her back, unhooking her bra on the way to her bottom where he pulled her panties down over her heels.

"Leave them on," he whispered in Megan's ear.

"With pleasure, Senator Monroe."

He kissed her softly, twirling his tongue around hers in an unhurried, loving caress. Picking her up again, he carried her to the bed, their lips still on each other. Once on top of her, his kisses became more intense. He kissed her deeply with all of the passion he had in him to prove to her that he needed only her. He hated the thought of ever losing her over something that wasn't true.

"I love you, Megan. You hear me. You're the only woman I've ever loved." He kissed her forehead, the tip of her nose and her lips, which formed a huge smile.

"I love you, too, Steven and would love to show you as soon as you take off your clothes."

He slid off the bed and starting unbuckling his pants. "You're right. Why am I fully clothed, and you're lying there with your sexy self wearing nothing but heels and perfume?"

She giggled. "Hurry up."

He rejoined her, laying his body on top of hers once more and claiming her lips in a seductive kiss.

Megan could feel his erection in between her legs. She wanted to wiggle her hips so he could slip in, but she also wanted to savor tonight since she was leaving in the morning. Instead, she kissed him ferociously on the lips while his hands roamed her smooth body.

She took in his kisses and touches hungrily. She felt the urgency in him as she forced her tongue deeper into his mouth to mingle with his. She wanted him to know that she was all his. Being in his loving arms again made her feel safe and secure.

Megan let out soft moans while he kissed her neck and shoulders before trailing down to her breasts that ached for his caress. When he finally reached her stomach, Megan knew where he was going next. She arched back and let him kiss her inner thighs and then the sweet spot in between that had missed his savory tongue. Megan moaned his name over and over again as his tongue licked her most sensitive spot. Once she climaxed, Steven looked up into her heat-filled eyes and knew she was ready for him to take her.

Steven reached in her nightstand and put on his protection. He grabbed her close to him and flipped them over so she was on top. He guided her down inch by inch until he was buried all the way inside. She breathed out and began to slowly move up and down as his hands clasped her butt and pulled her all the way down on him. Her cries of passion became louder as their rhythm increased with each stroke.

Waves of pleasure crashed through her body as her orgasm erupted, shaking her to the core. He flipped her over as they were still joined together and began to give slow, tantalizing thrusts that caused more sensations to flow through every cell of her body. She wasn't sure how much more she could take as she held on to his shoulders as each thrust from him summoned an erotic moan from her. She began to meet his thrusts pulling him deeper into her heart and soul. Their eyes never strayed from each other's faces as the glow of the candles settled on them. They climaxed together moments later, still kissing and staring at each other intently. He kissed her eyes that were lightly misted with tears.

She giggled. "That tickles."

"You're ticklish everywhere. You even laugh sometimes when I'm kissing your other set of lovely lips."

"Only when you have a five o'clock shadow."

He kissed the tip of her nose. "You're adorable, you know that?"

"And hungry. You wore me out." She slid from

under him, and he repositioned them so that she could place her head on his chest.

"Hmm…whenever we have Thai food we always have dessert first."

"Then we should have Thai food more often. Um…Steven?"

"Yes, babe?"

"Can I take my heels off now?"

He laughed out loud and patted her butt. "Of course, babe, and then let's go eat. You know, I'm really going to miss you."

She kicked her shoes off and kissed his cheek. "I'm going to miss you, too."

He captured her lips and flipped her over on her back.

Chapter 13

"Girl, I am so glad we have a day of rest," Megan said as she and Jade lay out by the pool of the beach house that they were staying in on Hilton Head while decorating the home next door. It was Sunday morning, and the ladies were finally able to relax. They had spent three long days going over the renovations with the crew. On Monday, they were to shop for furniture while the crew finished putting in the new kitchen cabinets and granite counter tops that Megan and Jade had chosen.

Megan was glad for the busy work, though. She hated to admit it, but she needed a break away from her life in Atlanta. With the Veronica situation and then Susan trying to expose Megan's relationship with Steven, she needed a breather. She felt better after Shawn released a statement stating that while Megan did tell Steven she didn't want to sleep in the same bed with him, it was because they'd just began dating and she would feel uncomfortable sleeping next to him so early in the relationship. The media seemed to believe it and some of the reports stated that Megan had moral values and other young ladies should follow suit.

Megan was disappointed when she couldn't be by Steven's side on Friday as he officially announced he was running for the U.S. Senate seat. She was able to speak with him briefly afterward before having to meet with the producers of the show about the progress thus far.

"What do you feel like doing today?" Megan asked.

"Sip on mimosas and eat lobster tails," Jade answered as her and Megan toasted their champagne glasses. "But seriously, let's go have lunch at the restaurant that is catering the food for the show. Those shrimp and grits…"

"…were to die for."

Thirty minutes later, they were dressed in sundresses and headed toward the front door.

"What's all that noise?" Megan asked, grabbing her purse from the foyer table and putting on her shades. She handed Jade her purse and shades, as well.

"I don't know. Is the crew working on the house? I thought we were all off today." Jade shrugged as they walked toward the front door.

Megan opened it and was immediately bombarded with cameras flashing, microphones and tape recorders in her face. All the people were speaking at once saying her name, Steven's name and Veronica's name, but she couldn't understand what they were asking. Jade stood in front of her and shielded her away from the reporters, pushing them back with her hands.

"Stand back," Jade yelled. "Ms. Chase isn't answering any of your questions. Now leave. You're trespassing on private property."

"But we just want to know how she feels about this," a reporter said, handing Jade an Atlanta Newspaper along with a few loose photos.

Jade glanced down at them and then back at the reporters. "She has no comment, and I suggest you leave before I call the police or I take my mace or something else out of my purse," Jade said, unzipping her purse on her arm as the reporters stepped back. She turned around, pushed Megan back into the house, and slammed the door and locked it.

"Oh, my goodness!" Megan screamed. "This is ridiculous. Why are they here asking about those pictures taken at the Women's Day Program? It wasn't that big of a deal." Megan plopped on the couch and raised her knees up to her chin. "If they watch the video, they'll clearly see they weren't holding hands. She was pulling him."

Jade glanced back at the newspaper and then the photos in her hand. She sat next to her best friend and spoke softly. "Megan, this is today's newspaper, and the pictures are from last night." She sighed as she handed Megan the paper.

Megan looked at the picture, and her heart immediately sank. In the picture, Steven and Veronica's arms were wrapped around one another as they spoke to another couple at the banquet that Steven had said he wasn't taking Veronica to.

"That lying bastard!" Megan threw the paper across the room.

"You took the words right out of my mouth."

"He said he wasn't taking her to the banquet. When I spoke to him last night, he said Shawn suggested that he go because he'd just announced his candidacy for the Senate ticket. He said Bryce was picking him up." Megan paced back and forth with tears running down her face. "I'm just so tired of this. Is this what my life has become? Now I have reporters hounding me down out of town looking for a statement!"

"Girl, I'm so sorry. Maybe…he…" Jade comforted, handing Megan a tissue and sitting her back on the couch.

Megan shook her head and dried her eyes but more tears came rushing down. "No…this is too much. Apparently, something is still going on with them. The first time…I let it slide, but this is different. He said he wasn't taking her. Heck, he wasn't even going and now that I'm out of town, he decided to take her!"

Megan's phone began to ring from inside of her purse. She knew it was Steven because of the ringtone.

Megan answered it as calm as possible. "What?"

"Baby, it's not what you think, I promise."

"You sound like a broken record, and I'm going to turn it off right now." Megan pressed the end button on the screen and then turned off her cell phone. She handed Jade the photos from the couch and the newspaper off the floor. "Can you burn these? But I guess it doesn't matter. They're all over the internet."

"Of course. Anything else? A glass a wine? A shoulder to cry on?"

"Both," Megan stammered as the tears began to fall uncontrollably.

Steven rang the doorbell at the beach house and then banged on the door. He'd been calling Megan and even Jade but neither would answer their cell phones. He found out from his cousin Justine exactly where Megan was staying and flew out on his private plane to see her face-to-face.

He rang the doorbell again, and Jade opened the door with a scowl and her hands on her hips.

"What?" she asked with an attitude.

"I need to see Megan."

"Humph. Not today you won't. Now back up so the door won't hit you when I slam it."

Steven was already frustrated, and he didn't need Megan's best friend to instigate.

"I just want to speak to Megan," he said calmly.

"She doesn't want to see you ever again. Now I suggest you…"

"It's okay," Megan said walking into the foyer

and standing next Jade. "I know I told you make him go away, but I need to tell him exactly how I feel."

Jade stepped back and let Steven inside. "Okay, I'll be in the kitchen if you need me." She cut her eyes at Steven before walking out of the room.

Megan walked to the living room and Steven followed her. He hated the situation they were in, but he planned on making it right. He wanted nothing more than to pull her into his arms and comfort her. He hated that her eyes were red and her tear-stained face was swollen from crying. He hated that she'd been crying over something that wasn't even true.

She stood by the window that overlooked the ocean with her back to him. She breathed in deeply before turning around with a glare of anger and a fed-up expression in her eyes. But when she spoke her voice was calm and steady.

"Steven, I've had some time to think this afternoon about our relationship. How we met, how we started to date and why we dated in the first place. I knew you were a playboy. I knew about your exwife and your past escapades, but I still fell in love with you despite the mixed reservations that I had. But I can't do this anymore."

Tears started to well in her eyes, and she turned away. He then grabbed her and pulled her toward him to face him.

"What are you saying?" He screamed out, surprised at the hatred in her eyes.

"This is a life I don't want. I'm tired of the reporters, your past women, the time away from you.

I want my life back the way it was. I went to work, I came home, worked on projects, went to lunch, on shopping sprees, the spa with my girlfriends and lousy blind dates. Today just made me realize even more that this is not the lifestyle I want to be a part of."

"Megan, I completely understand, but what you think happened didn't. I wasn't with Veronica last night at the banquet."

"Did you not see the paper today?" she asked, the calm in her voice was now replaced with anger.

"I mean, we weren't at the banquet together. She was there with Judge Hill."

"Humph, well you two looked real close with your arms wrapped around each other laughing and having a great time with some other couple, and I looked at the all of the pictures. I never saw Judge Hill."

"Those were her parents. I was just making polite conversation with them, that's all. Judge Hill arrived late so that's probably why there aren't any pictures of him. I've done nothing wrong except be in the right place at the wrong time."

"Steven, even if what you say is true, I simply can't do this anymore." She turned away from him, facing the window once more.

A lump formed in his throat, and he couldn't breathe. He hesitated to ask his next question in fear of already knowing her answer.

"You don't want to be with me?" he quietly asked standing behind her with his hands positioned to touch her shoulders to turn her to him once more.

But the hurt he was beginning to feel prevented him from stepping closer to her. He'd seen the resentment in her cold stare and heard it even more in her tone.

Steven didn't wait for a verbal answer. Her silence said it all.

Chapter 14

Megan sat on her couch wrapped in her favorite pink throw blanket looking over design boards and paint swatches for a new project. A new builder to the metro Atlanta area was starting five new subdivisions and wanted Megan and Jade to decorate ten model homes. He'd seen their work on *Decorator's Dream* three months prior and knew their style would be perfect for his floor plans.

Lucy was done with her internship and was now officially a member of their decorating staff. Her first assignment was to decorate two of the ten homes for the project with Megan overseeing. Business was better than ever since their official debut on the Fabulous Living Channel. Plus, the fact that Megan was the ex-girlfriend of a famous senator added to the high demand for their business. They were in the process of hiring another decorator as well as looking for a bigger office. Jade and Megan also thought it was time to hire a full-time secretary instead of using an intern to do office work. After many interviews, they settled on a young woman named Corrine, who was the only candidate not starstruck by Megan and Jade.

Megan had thought about Steven during the past few months. It was kind of hard not to, considering wherever she went there were billboards, campaign posters and bumper stickers endorsing his run for the U.S. Senate. She was glad that he'd won the primary and she had watched some of his speeches and debates. He'd called her repeatedly and sent flowers upon her return from Hilton Head, but Megan didn't want to be bothered. At one point, she considered hearing him out and perhaps giving him another chance but changed her mind when saw him hugged up with a model at some event. Apparently, he'd moved on and was back to his previous lifestyle.

When Election Day arrived in November and he'd won the seat, she'd wanted to call him and congratulate him but didn't. However, she was pleasantly surprised that he'd worn the tie she gave to him and couldn't hold back a smile when he looked into the camera, ran his hand down the tie, and winked.

The sound of the doorbell interrupted Megan's thoughts of the type of hardwood floors to select for her next project. She wasn't expecting anyone and the only way to get into her building was by calling her through the intercom system or punching in the code that only a few people knew. At least the reporters wouldn't be at her front door even though some had been waiting for her recently outside of the parking garage and at work to ask questions about her break-up with Steven and his recent win.

Peeking out of the peephole, she was surprised by who was standing on the other side of the door. She reluctantly opened the door halfway as Percy darted into the bedroom.

"How did you get into the building? I changed the code."

Steven cocked his head to the side with an arrogant grin. "I have my resources. May I come in? I promise not to stay long."

Megan inhaled and stepped aside to let him in. She closed the door but didn't take her hand off of the handle. Her heartbeat sped up, and she hoped he couldn't hear it. He looked handsome and refreshed in a burgundy sweater with black slacks perfect for the coolness of Atlanta in November. He smelled divine, and his presence reminded her how much she missed him.

"What can I do for you?" She was amazed at how calm and steady her voice was but she couldn't let it show that she was a nervous wreck inside.

He pulled an envelope out of his pocket and handed it to her. "I'm having my victory party at your brother's restaurant tomorrow evening around eight. I would love for you to come. I know it's last minute. I hadn't planned on having one, but my father insisted so my mother planned it this week."

She glanced at the envelope but didn't open it. She remained silent as he continued.

"I know things didn't end well between us, but you were there for me when I needed you and winning the election kind of sucked when I didn't have the woman I love by my side to celebrate."

"Yes, I saw that you won. Congrats. I guess in the end we both got what we wanted. You're now a U.S. senator, or will be officially once you're sworn in at the beginning of the year. And I have a slew of new clients because I dated you." She turned the handle on the door. "Anything else? I have a lot of work to get back to," she lied. She really needed him to hurry up and leave before she found herself wrapped in his warm embrace. She wasn't sure how much longer she could remain composed.

"I sincerely hope you'll be able to make it to the party. It's just an intimate affair with close family and friends…and it would be nice to see your beautiful face among the crowd. Despite everything, I was always faithful to you, Megan. I love you very much and miss the hell out of you. I know my life isn't the simple, normal, drama-free life that you're used to. I honestly hope one day you'll forgive me for what you think I did. If we never get back together, just know you're the love of my life, and I'll love you until I take my last breath."

He closed the gap between them, and Megan found herself against the door. She wanted to move.

Needed to move. But her feet were glued to the floor and his intoxicating scent and his inviting mouth, prevented her from doing so. He lowered his head and kissed her gently on the lips as an exhaling moan escaped her mouth. Her tongue joined in the seductive dance he bestowed on her. He yanked off the pink blanket she was wrapped in and he placed her hands around his neck as his hands found their way around her waist meshing her body into his. He kissed her fervently as if he couldn't get enough and as if it he was hungry and only she could satisfy his appetite. And then he stopped, and she let out a moan, wondering why on earth he halted their passion.

"I want you to think about everything I said especially the kiss we just shared that told me everything I needed to know."

He kissed her lightly on the forehead and left without another word, closing the door behind him.

Megan somehow made it back to the couch on wobbly legs as tears burned her eyes. She could still feel the warmth of Steven's mouth on hers and smell his woodsy cologne on her clothes. She dropped to the couch, grabbed her cell phone and told Sydney everything that had just happened.

"So, are you going to the party? I can pick you up on the way."

"I don't know and…wait a minute. On the way? Were you invited?"

"Um…" Sydney paused. "Yes, I was invited, but I wasn't sure if I was actually going to go."

"You and Braxton are traitors. Not only is it at his restaurant, you're the one that gave Steven the new access code, aren't you?"

"Yes, but I did it because you've been moping around for the last three months, burying yourself in work. When you broke up with what's-his-name, you didn't mope and while you buried yourself in your work, you didn't become a hermit. Bryce said Steven's been moody and didn't even care if he won the election or not. He didn't even want a celebration party."

Megan replayed her sister's words in her head. "Bryce said? I thought you couldn't stand Bryce. Called him an ass if I remember correctly."

"He is an ass, but I ran into him at the federal building, and he told me how much Steven missed you and that he hated how things ended. I never believed anything was going on with him and Veronica. Besides, she's engaged to Judge Hill now."

"Sydney, it's not that easy. I…"

"Do you still love him? That's the question you need to ask yourself. Can you go on with your life without him in it?"

The next evening, Megan sat on her couch changing channels and flipping through a home magazine. She finally settled on the evening news to see what the weather would be like next week since one of her projects included an outdoor living and dining area.

Megan waited for the weather segment to come on by putting the television on mute. She continued perusing through the magazine placing stickies on the items she liked. Percy jumped on the couch causing the remote to fall to the floor and the volume went back up. She heard a very familiar deep voice on the television. It belonged to Senator Steven Monroe. He was touring an after-school program with the news anchor. He looked debonair in one of the tailored suits that Chelsea had most likely suggested for him. He was also wearing the tie that Megan had given him again. The news anchor even commented on the tie stating that it looked like the one he wore on Election Day. With a sincere smile, Steven replied, "This tie is very special to me because of who it's from, and I'll cherish it always."

His statement reminded her of the first time she saw his worn wallet that had belonged to his grandfather, and Steven carried it all the time. She flipped the television off, kissed Percy on the head and ran to her closet taking the rollers out of her hair and throwing her nightgown off in the process.

Less than an hour later, she pulled up to Café Love Jones. She took a deep breath and walked inside of the restaurant. An unfamiliar hostess approached her. Megan knew the entire staff at her brother's restaurant.

"Excuse me miss? Are you here for dinner or the private party on the mezzanine?"

Megan glanced at the staircase that was roped off and had a huge bodyguard standing next to it. One of Steven's campaign posters was on an easel.

"The private party for Steven Monroe."

"May I see your invitation please?" the young hostess said with her hand held out.

"Oh...I don't have it but..."

"Then you can't get in."

Megan had to stop herself from laughing. "I'm the owner's sister."

"Sweetie, three ladies just left here saying the same exact thing. I get it. Senator Monroe is once again Atlanta's most eligible bachelor, but it's a private party for family and friends only. So unless you have an invitation, you aren't getting in."

"Look, I can go anywhere I want to in this restaurant and right now I need to get upstairs. So I suggest you tell big bad wolf over there to move so I can get by." Megan was not about to let anything or anyone stand in the way of her mission.

"What's going on?" Braxton asked coming from the hallway that led to another private room and looking at Megan and then at the hostess.

"Mr. Chase, this woman is trying to get into Senator Monroe's private party. She's the tenth person I've had to turn away. She lied and said she was your sister."

"She *is* my sister Megan, who was definitely invited to the party." Braxton turned toward the bodyguard. "Rick, please let my sister upstairs."

Rick removed the velvet rope, and Megan gave her big brother a kiss on the cheek before running up the stairs in her four-inch heels.

When she made it to the top, she scanned the room for Steven. She spotted him talking to Bryce at the bar. Steven's back was to her. She glanced around the room and saw Syd, Jade and Tiffani all wearing wide smiles and motioning for her to keep walking. Sydney even mouthed, "Go get your man."

Megan took a deep breath and made her way across the room. Bryce, who was leaning on the bar, saw her first but didn't make eye contact. Instead he kept listening and nodding his head. As she moved closer, Steven stopped talking and chuckled.

"Amarige?" he asked.

She smiled. "Yes, it's the only perfume I wear."

Bryce patted Steven on the back, gave Megan an encouraging smile and left. She moved to where Bryce had stood and stared up at Steven.

"You came."

Megan ran her hand down his familiar tie. "Of course, where else would I be? It's your big night."

"Would you like to dance?" He held out his hand.

She placed her hand in his as he walked her out to the empty dance floor. "I'd love to but didn't we agree not to dance together again because of where it always seems to lead?"

He nodded his head and glided his hands around her waist as he drew her toward him. "Hmm...well, if I remember correctly, we had our very first dance in this same spot followed by a very sensual kiss."

He lowered his head and kissed her gently on the lips. She heard cheers and claps from their family and friends. They both stopped kissing and laughed. But then his facial expression turned serious.

"I've missed you, Megan. I can't spend another

second without you. I've been miserable these past few months."

"Me, too, Steven. I'm sorry I ever doubted you."

He kissed her forehead and lowered to one knee as tears welled in her eyes. The room became silent except for a few "oohs and aahs" from the women.

He took both of her hands and placed them over his heart as she began to tremble with anticipation. "Megan Rochelle Chase, will you please do me the honor of being my wife?"

"Oh, Steven. Yes! Yes, I'll marry you."

He stood and captured her in his arms twirling her around in the air as their friends and family ran out to the dance floor to hug and congratulate them.

Later on that evening after a few rounds of love making, they cuddled in front of her fireplace facing each other. Steven ran his hands through her unruly curls and kissed her softly on the lips.

"I've never been happier in my life than I am right now, babe," Steven said in between tender kisses. "I knew when I met you that you would change my life forever."

"And I knew when I met you, that you would be my perfect candidate for love."

Epilogue

One year later

"What?" Megan asked sarcastically as she sat on the bed in her hotel suite at the Four Seasons Hotel flipping the channels on the television.

Jade, trying not to wrinkle her lavender dress, sat carefully on the bed next to Megan.

"You're getting married in less than an hour, and you're trying to watch TV?"

"Jade, relax," Megan patted her best friend's hand with a smile.

"Relax? My best friend is getting married, and I'm supposed to relax? Tiffani, Sydney! Are you going to help me out?"

Sydney came over, also in a lavender dress, and

sat next to Megan who was still wearing her slip. Her princess wedding gown hung on the door.

"Jade, leave Megan alone even though I'm surprised at her coolness. Tiffani, I remember you were a nervous wreck on your wedding day," Sydney reminded. Tiffani nodded her head as she finished her makeup.

"Yes, I remember my wedding day. I was a nervous wreck because of the rain."

Megan then got up and walked toward her wedding gown.

"Ladies, help me with the gown please. My dad will be in here soon. And for your information, I'm not nervous because I'm marrying the man of my dreams. I've waited a whole year to marry him, and the day has finally arrived. You know so many good things have happened this year and getting married on New Year's Eve makes it all the better," Megan said as Sydney buttoned up her wedding gown. Jade nodded her head in agreement.

"I agree girl. I'm still in shock that we have our own television show now on the Fabulous Living Channel! The first season was awesome!" Jade exclaimed.

"Yeah, it was cool traveling to different cities with you in a motor mansion looking for the best decorated homes and planning my wedding all at the same time."

"Well, season two of *The Best Decorated Homes* starts filming in a few months so don't go get pregnant anytime soon!"

"You're so silly. I do want children, but I want to enjoy my husband first. That sounds so unreal to say. *My husband!* Ladies! I'm getting married!"

Five hours later, Megan and Steven sat at their table at Café Love Jones, kissing each other softly. Braxton was having his annual New Year's Eve party and the newlyweds and their friends went over to the restaurant after the reception.

Megan had never been more ecstatic than she was at that very moment. She had won the heart of the man she'd dreamed of since she was a little girl. Being with him made her realize that she'd never even been in love until she met Steven Monroe almost a year and half ago thanks to her SUV's flat tire.

Megan glanced around the room, and her eyes landed on Sydney and Bryce in a heated debate as usual.

"All our siblings seem to do is get into heated discussions about the law," Megan said, nodding her head in their direction.

Steven turned to glance at them and then back at Megan with a snicker. "Yes, they clearly don't get along, but we're all family now. Speaking of family, we haven't discussed when we want to plan for ours."

"How about we spend the next few years practicing, starting tonight?"

"Perfect. I was thinking the exact same thoughts."

* * * * *

MILLS & BOON

Desire

Indulge in secrets and scandal, intense drama and plenty of sizzling hot action with powerful and passionate heroes who have it all: wealth, status, good looks… everything but the right woman.

MILLS & BOON
MODERN
Power and Passion

Prepare to be swept off your feet by sophisticated, sexy and seductive heroes, in some of the world's most glamourous and romantic locations, where power and passion collide.

Eight Modern stories published every month, find them

millsandboon.co.uk/Modern

LET'S TALK
Romance

For exclusive extracts, competitions
and special offers, find us online:

f facebook.com/millsandboon

🐦 @MillsandBoon

📷 @MillsandBoonUK

Get in touch on 01413 063232

For all the latest titles coming soon, visit
millsandboon.co.uk/nextmonth

MILLS & BOON

THE HEART OF ROMANCE

A ROMANCE FOR EVERY READER

MODERN

Prepare to be swept off your feet by sophisticated, sexy and seductive heroes, in some of the world's most glamourous and romantic locations, where power and passion collide.

HISTORICAL

Escape with historical heroes from time gone by. Whether your passion is for wicked Regency Rakes, muscled Vikings or rugged Highlanders, await the romance of the past.

MEDICAL

Set your pulse racing with dedicated, delectable doctors in the high-pressure world of medicine, where emotions run high and passion, comfort love are the best medicine.

True Love

Celebrate true love with tender stories of heartfelt romance, from the rush of falling in love to the joy a new baby can bring, and a focus on emotional heart of a relationship.

Desire

Indulge in secrets and scandal, intense drama and plenty of sizzling hot action with powerful and passionate heroes who have it all: wealth, status good looks…everything but the right woman.

HEROES

Experience all the excitement of a gripping thriller, with an intense romance at its heart. Resourceful, true-to-life women and strong, fearless face danger and desire - a killer combination!

To see which titles are coming soon, please visit

millsandboon.co.uk/nextmonth